MW01713203

SANTA, CEO

We've changed with the times, and that's why you see the constant churn, the lines automated, new materials, new processes, doing things faster, cheaper. So that we can support the world's need now, the people constantly pressed for time and overstressed and content to just shovel gifts at each other, mindlessly picked from images on a flat panel display somewhere, tapped into during a flight between business meetings even. Who's really picking those gifts, anyway, Id? Who's wrapping them, who's sending them? Where are the people *in all of this?*

So I'm going to a hotter-than-hell city in the middle of summer to talk to a bunch of new santas, and what do I say that keeps the flames going? How do I keep Christmas going when it's changed so much I barely know it anymore? How do I do that, Id? Without my wife, without my sense of rhythm, without my connection to the legends? What's magic without a purpose, Id? If you can answer me these things, then maybe you're worth the silly image of Santa talking to a shrink. So answer, damn you! Answer!

ISBN 1-59113-434-X

Printed in the United States of America.

The characters and events in this book are fictitious. Any similarity to real persons, living or dead, is coincidental and not intended by the author. However, the Posen Potato Festival is, to the best of the author's knowledge, still held annually in the autumn in Posen, Michigan.

Jacket design by Jeff Skevington

Printed by Booklocker.com, Inc.
2003

Contact the author at dsoubly@soubly.net, or visit www.soubly.net for additional information.

SANTA, CEO

David Soubly

He knows when you've been
bad or good
so be good
for goodness' sake

For KJ,
Who saw it through

NPI

1.

"Reindeer dung."

The rich voice suggested hot cocoa, magic, and giving—strong warmth overrun by tougher things. But the voice also betrayed a mind bent to commerce and decision, timeslicing and competition, faster and cheaper.

"I don't believe these numbers for a minute."

Large, strong fingers fiddled with a silver pen, turning it end over end. One palm slapped the desk, sending papers skittering over the polished mahogany.

"Hm-hm-hmmm," the big voice rumbled, and the hand moved from desk to face, teasing a curly white beard that flowed under a bulbous red nose, thrusting out like a ship's prow beneath bright blue eyes that should have twinkled but didn't.

Half-glasses perched on the nose, and it was through these that the blue eyes stabbed, as if to change the numbers on the page.

"Bridle," the voice continued. "Do you mean to tell me that the government—the *government*—of Argentina is raising a protest over *reindeer dung*? And they need ten million Santeans to cover the removal? Why don't they just *use* the stuff, spread it on their, what do they call them, pampadoodles?"

"You mean *pampas*, sir," Bridle said. Bridle looked like a small man or a large child shoveled into a navy suit. He surveyed his boss. What sort of rumble was this? Disgusted? Taking it out on the Argentines? Or angry, taking it out on his accountant, questioning the numbers, fingers stabbing, beard wagging? Probably the angry side. It so often was these days.

How had it come to this? Good with numbers seventeen hundred years ago, discovered arranging toy sequences in the old shop, brought before the Chief—even then, most of them had begun to drop the more familiar *Santa*—who looked him over kindly, half-elf surveying elf, and decided then and there that he should be an accountant. An accountant. For seventeen hundred years. Bridle sighed softly. After a while, this job could get tiring.

"Something wrong, Bridle?" Blue eyes skewered him in a way they never used to.

"No, sir," Bridle said. "Just wondering why they think you'll pay that kind of money." He watched for a reaction—perhaps a tremble of the beard, arranged against the dark gray suit, the white curls all but hiding the red and green striped tie.

"That's true. How much is that in today's currency, anyway?"

"Well, in US dollars, it's about twenty million. I could give it to you in Euros."

"Euros? Bah!" Santa said. "Another feeble attempt to unify that little band of nations. Nothing but trouble, I'd say. Tell me something, Bridle." He leaned forward, large elbows straining the gray fabric. "Is Argentina *in* Europe?"

Uh-oh. "No, sir."

"Thought not. Then I'll take the dollar figure as a start. Take this down to Silvertongue. Get him to cut it in half. Find a favorable exchange rate and use that as the basis. Twenty million! I want it down to eight and a half, tops."

Bridle winced. Maybe he should see Miracle for this one. Or Angelus for prayer, just to be safe.

"Don't cower, it won't be that difficult." A corner of Santa's mouth snapped up and down. "Now off you go, and get me an answer by the end of the day."

"Isn't that—a bit soon?" Bridle said. "Because of the negotiations, I mean."

"I like giving Silvertongue a deadline. Cuts through a lot of his meandering. Gives him a challenge. A stretch goal. Just like I'm giving you. Now go on, I need to get ready for the Board meeting. See if Roxy's been able to get Oiler, I need the latest status."

Bridle took the paper from Santa's outstretched hand and hopped off the chair, wincing when pain shot through his bad knee. *Doesn't he know that replacing our chairs with these big half-elf ones makes us all feel puny? Probably costs.* Bridle headed to the door. *And probably one of my own cost analyses that did it.*

He sped up as he neared the door, throwing his shoulder into it. On the other side, Oiler chatted with Roxy, as always stunning, her medium-length black hair arranged above dark eyes and around sculpted cheekbones and ruby-red lips. Oiler was quite taken by her—but then, everyone was. As if Oiler had a chance, elf that he was. Bridle scowled. Oiler was the worst kind of elf, the kind that's forgotten the elf side and wants to be a half-elf, human-sized, big and important. Even if it was impossible. What was the old saying? "Talking beyond your size." That was Oiler.

Oiler spotted him. "Hey, Mr. Accountant," he said. "What kind of mood is he in?"

"Not too bad. Kind of disgusted with the Argentines, wants answers now."

"Argentines? How does that figure? What's the problem?"

"Reindeer crap."

"Reindeer crap? You're joking!"

"Nope. The Argentines think there's too much of it. They want him to pay for removing it."

Oiler burst out laughing. "Didn't they figure when they signed the ranch contract that reindeer poop might be part of the deal?"

"Not this much, apparently. You'd better get in there—he asked for you immediately."

Oiler straightened up and arranged his perfectly tailored blue suit ("Imported!" he'd announced, and one of the others—Halter, head of Doll Assembly Operations—had shot back, "Hell, *everything's* imported up here!"). He sauntered to the doors and pushed on them as though their size meant nothing. His grunts and groans gave him away. He slipped through the eventual crack and disappeared.

"Oh, brother." Bridle shook his head.

Roxy looked up from her computer screen, fixing him with her dark, dark eyes. "Aw, c'mon, Bridle, it's just Oiler. He's entertaining."

"I guess."

A buzz. Roxy flipped the Autospeak. "Yes, sir?"

Santa's voice, harsh and metallic, cut through the room. "Roxy, please get in here. I need you to take notes."

"Right." She flipped the switch again and sighed. "That thing always makes him sound madder than he is."

"But he's angrier than he used to be. At least I think so."

"You're not the only one," she said, picking up her laptop. She paused as she passed him, bent over and kissed the top of his head. "Don't let it get to you, sweetie."

It was a nothing gesture for her, but for a seventeen-hundred-year accountant, it was something else. He blushed despite himself, trying not to stare at the beautiful half-elf as she opened the door and stepped inside. Skirts hadn't been that short in the old days.

2.

"OK, Oiler, let's get started. Show me Page Four." Santa peered over his glasses at his Logistics and Operations Director.

"Right."

Oiler presented Santa a slim green-and-red binder, already opened to the Page Four Report. Page Four got its name when someone wise realized it always showed up on page four of the NPI Operations Summary Report. It was actually a facer page of figures (4f), combined with a summary page (4). You could run the whole company from Page Four, making North Pole Industries not much different from other multinationals. Oiler's discovery of this, and his discovery that immense amounts of often conflicting detail existed merely to keep the CEO wannabes busy, had fueled his rapid rise in the organization. He stuck strictly to Page Four, not even bothering to read all that other stuff. If the Chief asked him a question for which he didn't have a ready answer, he simply made one up that sounded reasonable. If it turned out to be wrong, he blamed it on flaws in the detail he hadn't read. In this way, he could set whole departments against each other, initiating turf wars and internecine battles destined to last for centuries.

Roxy opened her laptop.

Santa made the same request he'd made every month for about the last hundred and fifty years. "Take me through the numbers."

"OK." Oiler cleared his throat smoothly. "First, reindeer. Total herds up to three hundred sixty thousand fliers, twenty thousand new calves, ninety thousand trainees, ninety thousand pastured—so we're at five hundred sixty thousand total. Now, new ranches—"

"Can't we do something with all that dung?"

"What?"

"The reindeer dung. The crap everywhere. Didn't Bridle mention the Argentines to you?"

"Why, no," Oiler said; " ...should he have?"

"I always want my people to share information," Santa said. "*You* understand, Oiler. Why can't the others?"

Oiler shook his head.

"Anyway, the dung. Can't we recycle it, make a fertilizer out of it or something? That'd keep the green planet boys off my back!"

"I suppose we could—"

"We'd have to figure out a collection system. Tap into the local labor markets, probably, to keep costs down. And locate some local factories that do that kind of thing. Partner with Cargill, maybe, I don't know, one of the big multinationals," the big half-elf ruminated. "Need a catchy name, too. Something that starts with the same sounds, maybe, I don't know, Santa's—"

"Don't go there, Chief."

"You don't like the idea?"

"No, I don't like the name. Maybe reindeer, reindeer—"

"Why don't you just call it 'Reindeer Magic'?" Roxy said. "Forget about fancy names, people hate that stuff, anyway. Besides, it's what it does that's more important. People will remember the name if the stuff works for them."

"I like that, Roxy. Sounds like something we can work with."

Oiler's withering look dashed on the crossing of her long legs like surf hitting a rock beach. "Well, the marketing people will be able to come up with a name, I'm sure." He waved his pen. "I've got it noted. We can revisit it after the Board meeting."

Roxy smiled. "I've got it noted, too."

"I knew you would. Thanks," Santa said.

For a moment Oiler felt his smallness, pinned between these two half-elves. "OK, back to these numbers, or we'll never get through it. New ranches: New Zealand, Tierra del Fuego, another one in Greenland, a third on Baffin Island. Total new acreage, let's see, six hundred forty thousand. Startup costs, thirty-five point two million Santeans. They're all on their feet now. Patagonians were a little shaky until they stopped eating the trainees. New Zealanders are the best. They just think of reindeer as big sheep with weird horns. It works out well."

"And they thought these ranches weren't going to work," Santa rumbled. "Stupid Board. Though we did have a few problems early on when we were doing the transports, UFO reports, that kind of thing. Press made a lot of money off of that."

"Yes, I remember. Now, santas. Current permanent payroll is forty-two thousand, which is about right. We'll expect some of the fliers to come up lame at the last minute. Rather than bringing in trainees, it's cheaper to stretch the existing teams."

"But we stretched them last year, Oiler, and I heard about it through the Talk It Up program. That and the United Elves Union screaming about casual overtime. Contract talks will be a pain if we keep this up."

"It's what the Board wants. They figure they can bring the union around if they keep telling them the Company's on the ropes."

"What ropes? Those guys on the line can read, they see the numbers same as you and me! I tell you, Oiler, they're starting to see through the nonsense about competition and speed and all that. Who are we competing with? And when did speed matter to a kid on Christmas morning? Except when opening presents." He leaned forward. "And it's getting into the ISO area, too. Our rework numbers are starting to push up, not to mention the misdeliveries. Lingerie to a six-year-old. Tabloids had a field day with that one!"

Oiler raised an eyebrow. "Talk to the Board. They're the ones pushing for it. Helps shareholder value, which helps the permanent santas, and the UEU, when they think about it. Anyway, we're still pushing the hiring program because of attrition and expected growth."

"Make sure they're careful on the Italian hiring. I don't want another Befana incident."

"Nobody knew he was a transvestite."

"Yeah, but it's no excuse. Now what about the temps?"

"The Board scotched your idea about using the homeless."

"Doggone good idea, too."

"I know, but they thought it was going to tarnish the image. Unless you can break the link, keep people from finding out they were homeless."

"Tarnish the image! Oiler, you ever really *look* at some of those department store santas? Homeless ones would bring the image *up* in a lot of cases!"

"Santa!"

"Well, some cases, Roxy. I know they're mostly good people, but when you hire—how many of 'em we got, Oiler?"

"One point two million."

"—one point two million, for three weeks, you get some bad apples. Besides, we'd be helping those people. Sometimes all they need is something to tide them over."

Oiler sighed and nodded his head. "OK, so we'll keep the temp hire at one point two, tighten up the Italian checking thing, and—"

"Oiler, that's it." Santa checked his wristwatch. "I'll just have to pick up the assembly operations and sales numbers on the fly. I assume there's no major issues."

"No, no issues. I don't understand. We still have a few minutes."

"Had. I just remembered something I need to do before the meeting. Sorry." He stood up, towering over Oiler. "We can go over them later." He turned his back and faced the curtained wall behind him.

"OK, then." Oiler snapped the binder shut and jumped down.

Roxy stood up.

"Roxy, stay here. I need you to—I need to get some thoughts down."

He turned and saw Oiler walk, then charge toward the door, opened by a mail courier who'd chosen this moment to peer shyly into the inner office, hoping to sneak the "Confidential" letter inside. She looked a bit puzzled when Oiler hurtled past, arms and legs flailing like a dry land skater, until he crashed into the wall at the end of the receiving area, binder and papers exploding every which way.

Roxy shrugged. "Can I can help you, Spindle?"

The elf struggled against the heavy door and gestured with the envelope. "Something from the Board," she stage-whispered. "They said it's urgent."

"Thanks, Spindle." Roxy took the envelope. The door thumped shut.

"I'll look at it now." He snatched the letter, tore through the Confidential sticker and read greedily before slapping it down. "Bah, urgent! They're just telling me they've brought the new guy onto the Board, the one we approved last month. He'll be in charge of the Finance Subcommittee. An automotive guy."

She regarded him. "You wanted me to stay?"

He sighed again. "Roxy, I'm in trouble with the Board," he said. "No one knows this but you. Unless they've bugged the damn place. I can't put my finger on it. No one's come out and said anything. But you get a feeling."

She blinked and sat back down. "But you're the CEO, the Chairman. How can you tell? If no one's said anything."

"You can tell. Chairman's just a title. It's how these guys play. The higher the stakes, the less is said. But you get signals. Your ideas are resisted. Or brushed aside. Those that stay on the table have their results downplayed.

"Look at the homeless thing. Perfect example. It would be so easy. Bring the homeless through the temp hire program, give them jobs for about a month around the holidays. Sure, you've got to let them go at the end, but it gives them a chance to get back on their feet. If they do a good enough job, they might even get a reference. But the Board started picking it apart from day one. First it was Oswald, talking about image. Then it was Spencer, talking liability. Then Parcell on logistics. Only Donaldson thought the idea might work. They talked it to death and then some. There weren't even any pieces to pick up."

He sighed, running his hands along the curtains behind his desk. Abruptly, angrily, he shot them apart. Dim light filtered into the large office, the dusky almost-twilight of an overcast day late in the north country summer. Outside, mist-shrouded factories and office buildings stretched to the horizon. The thick glass prevented even the tiniest sound from reaching his ears.

He watched the silent movie play before him, small shapes on the move, delivery trucks lined up, goods in, goods out, endless motion both immediate and ancient. He looked at the factories and saw logistics, time motion studies, repetition injuries, scrubbers on the chimney stacks, production rate incentives, quality controls, UEU stewards, depreciation allowances, asset turnover rates, and on and on. Raising his eyes to the horizon, he could not see but could imagine the row upon row of sleek red-and-green-tailed cargo jets, standing ready to transport the NPI Export business to the big players: K-Mart, Kaybee, Target, FAO Schwartz, Steiff, and to the brand new upstarts, the dot-coms, to distribution outlets; his mind ruminating over export revenues, internal operations, international tariffs, hazardous material regulations, packaging calculations, just-in-time deliveries. He winced. He'd *invented* just-in-time delivery, the wild rides through the heavens, the magical distributions. But the job had grown, exploding with the population. Now thousands of delegates did the work, learned the secrets of entrance to impermeable places like penthouse apartments, and he—What did he do?

"Sir. Um, Santa. It's getting close to the meeting."

"I used to like looking out this window." He snapped the curtains shut, turned and walked back to his desk. "I've changed, we've had to change a lot with the times," he went on, sitting down. "Incorporating. Globalizing. Diversifying. Equalizing. Streamlining. Computerizing. Anyone who says a CEO has the freedom to direct things the way he wants has a head full of sand. That gang in there, that Board, and those shareholders egging them on—they've got as much to say about what goes on here as I do. Or you. I trust you. I listen to you. Your ideas work."

"Thank you, sir."

"It's changed the elves, too. Oiler." He waved a hand. "Does he think I've forgotten how to spot when someone's lying? What does he think? 'He knows when you've been bad or good.' What is that, just words? ...I couldn't hear you."

"I just completed it. 'So be good, for *goodness'* sake.'"

"Yes, well. Change. Too much, too fast. Too scattered, too frantic. You look at the people out there, lurching from entertainment to entertainment. Talking Elmos to Furbys to who knows what it'll be this year. Do you have any idea what that does to the production schedule? The screwups? We had four hundred thousand extra Furby eyeballs on hand last year, and then the demand dried up. Four hundred thousand! Can't use them on anything else, because of a design infringement. A design infringement! Whoever would think of protecting a doggoned plastic eyeball?"

"Somebody did."

"I'm venting, I know."

"It's time."

Santa scowled at his watch. "Five more minutes. I need five minutes alone, Roxy."

"I understand." She stood, laptop in hand, and strode to the door.

He watched her leave. The way of the world, right? Wife leaves you, secretary takes her place. He shook his head. Not this CEO. He studied glass cabinets that housed Hummels, Waterford, rare crystals from Africa, a carved jade elephant from India—all presented by emissaries sworn to secrecy, governments asking favors. He glanced at bookcases jammed with business treatises, notebooks summarizing NPI's operations, production statistics, marketing journals, a whole shelf crammed with offal from this consultant and that, addressed to "Mr. Samuel Claussen, CEO, North Pole Industries", each claiming to have the secret he needed to re-vitalize or re-energize or re-make his business, as though it were a bad hairdo in need of a medicated shampoo and a cosmetic perm. (The Board had thought up the Claussen name, too, despite his claim that it made him feel like a fat pickle, telling him that a "street name" (their word) would allow him to tap into, no, "leverage" (their word again) the abilities of highly-paid brainy people who'd tell him how to do what he'd been doing for thousands of years.)

He surveyed thick carpet, huge exotic plants that would freeze instantly in an NPI winter, framed artwork on the walls. Finally, his gaze rested on the smaller-framed, ultimate work of art on his desk, a portrait, a friendly older woman beaming like anyone's grandmother, a smile speaking of comfort, warmth, familiarity, and constancy. By all rights he should take her picture and set it aside, or turn it to face the other way. She'd left *him*, after all.

But he couldn't. He no longer needed to pull the letter from his desk's middle drawer to reread again. "When you are able to find your way back," it said, "then I may be able to find my way back to you. But not until." A lot more stuff besides. She'd been upset for so long. The business did it. There was no stopping it. And no stopping her.

Idiot, his half-elf shrink, had told him a few sessions back that spouses leave for all kinds of reasons—even a spouse as magical as she was. He tried picturing her changing herself to a younger half-elf and hanging out someplace warm, Morocco, maybe, or Rio de Janeiro, but it didn't do much good. Eventually, he'd come to accept what Idiot had told him, that this was a fling with freedom. It made sense. After six thousand years, a person can get a little tired of the cookies and cocoa thing. That's one hell of a lot of hot cocoa. She'd come back. Until then, there was business.

His watch beeped. Late again. Well, tough. He was the CEO. They all needed to remember that occasionally. He stretched, yawned, and riffled the Operations Summary pages before thumping his feet on the floor and getting up. He made a mental note to deal with Oiler later, then promptly forgot it when his hand hit the office door.

3.

Oiler paused in Silvertongue's doorway, facing the back of a talking chair. He was expected, Kelli ("with-a-K-and-an-I") had waved him in.

"Mr. Cooper," the chair was saying, "you need to take this back to the person whom you represent, Mr.—Hernandez? ...Oh, *Fer*nandez, of course, how inconsiderate of me. Take back to Mr. *Fer*nandez the simple statement that NPI feels the Argentine government is covering its naiveté in this matter with a cloud of bluster. NPI is perfectly willing to work out an equitable solution that will benefit both parties. You understand, Mr. Cooper, it's in our mutual interest to keep our business relationship cordial. I know I can trust you as a man of tact and integrity." A pause, a glissando laugh. "Now you're flattering me, sir! But we know the issue is serious, and it taxes our professional relationship." A brief sigh. "So I'm afraid that six million, which you or I might consider reasonable, is simply not workable. Your government needs to understand there are benefits to the situation, which an imaginative mind such as yours would have very little difficulty presenting ... Well, for instance, there's recycling, there's fertilizer. NPI is already exploring the possibility of partnering with intelligent and reliable agencies that recognize the profit potential. *You* understand."

The chair swung round, revealing the rich voice's owner, an elf small even by elfin standards, jet-black hair parted precisely down the middle, small squared rimless glasses fastened above smooth-shaven cheeks, silver pen and pencil winking from a white monogrammed shirt pocket. One tiny hand pressed the green flip phone against an ear, while the other motioned Oiler to a seat. The dark eyes rolled and the mouth grinned. Oiler grinned back.

"Yes, I can understand that four million might seem a little low to Mr. Her, sorry, *Fer*nandez, because of everything he claims you've been through. ...Mr. Cooper, please remind him that adopting an excessively recalcitrant position now would cause NPI to shut down the Argentine operations. ...Yes, shut them down. Which might also exclude you from the preferred delivery routes."

Silvertongue smirked to Oiler's startled expression. "E-business?" He chuckled. "I suppose. But I don't think the Argentine children are ready to forego receiving their gifts the conventional way, do you? ...I'm glad we agree. Now, be sure also to indicate to Mr. *Fer*nandez that the four million also has some stretch. Yes. A little extra that might directly benefit you both. ...I know. ...I always try. I'll wait for your answer. My best to Mrs. Cooper, and the children. Good kids, and so smart, too! I haven't seen them in ages! Call me back today, thanks! Goodbye."

Scowling, Silvertongue lowered the phone. "Jackass. Hang on a minute, Oiler." He pressed a speed dial. "Roxy? Hi love, it's Silvertongue. Take this into the Chief. Tell him the Argentines have accepted four point two five, or eight and a half in dollars, which I believe was his target. Got that? Four point *two* five. Oh, and I'll be faxing their government negotiator the paperwork for signature this evening. Thanks, sweetie, bye."

He switched off the phone and dropped it in his shirt pocket. "I hate green, sometimes," he murmured. "Red, too."

"You don't have their agreement!"

"They'll agree. There's money in it for Fernandez, and his lackey Cooper, who's the only one I ever see. Plus his family. Nice-looking wife, but those snot-nosed kids!"

"Maybe you've been dealing with too many Coopers lately. There are good kids in the world."

"Oh, I know what keeps our sales going. Seen a good kid lately?"

"Nope." They both laughed. "Don't you have to run this past legal?"

"So? That's just Groomer. He'll be late, by the way. An acquisition review thing."

"EI?"

"I would imagine."

"I heard the Chief made a big stink about it at the meeting today."

"Word gets around fast."

Oiler scratched an arm. Silvertongue had that way of pulling small talk out of you. "How could you threaten to shut down the Argentine ops that way? You don't have the authority!"

"What? Oh, you're still on the Argentines. They don't know I can't. It's the suggestion of ruthlessness that can be so effective, more so even than the demonstration. They have more to lose than we do."

"I guess that's true."

"You don't sound convinced."

"No, I believe you. What was that comment about e-business?"

"Oh, *that.*" A dry laugh. "His attempt at threatening me. Said they'd go the e-business route, tap into the dotcoms, get their toys that way. Fine with me, actually. Fits into the overall plan. Of course, I couldn't *say* that, same way I can't say it to the Chief. I just suggested to Cooper they were unprepared to make good on it. They don't have the infrastructure."

"You didn't say it that way."

"Didn't have to. He knows. That's the thing about negotiations. Each sentence has two or three layers to it. You didn't catch the lead-in, so you heard only the first layer in our little discussion. Like skimming the surface. Our friend, though, heard them all. Or should have, if he's any good at it. How'd the cost-cutting meeting go?"

"Not bad. Most everyone showed up. Shepherd's out on assignment, but everyone else—Halter had some emergency and couldn't make it."

"Ah, old head-in-the-clouds. I heard about his outburst at the e-commerce meeting. Talk about making a fool of yourself. Right in the middle of Sprinter's ebusiness presentation on the future of this company, he stands up and lets loose. The 'spirit of Christmas'. If he didn't have such a good production head on his shoulders. I mean, granted, there's the miracles. I'll be the first one to admit that. But it's a business now. A global one, an 'e' one, with mergers and acquisitions to contend with, outsourcing, the whole bit! He's like the Chief that way. He wants a miracle, let him figure out how Santa or any of the half-elves can ever have children!"

"Or how Santa can stay where he is," Oiler said quietly.

Silvertongue looked at him coldly. "You know, the better part of negotiation is to know what to say out loud when. Ah, here's our friend Groomer! Come on in, and shut the door behind you."

Groomer stumped into the office and settled into the nearest chair, still worrying a last bit of hot dog. Oiler would have been surprised otherwise. Groomer loved hot dogs. He took hot dog breaks as frequently as lesser folks had coffee breaks. For a while, his clothes had tried to keep up with his advancing girth, but they gave it up at last. His once-tailored shirts and neckties were now frayed collections of tired fabrics held together by old stains and grease and the occasional new splash.

Whatever Groomer decided to do, he did extremely well. In addition to being a formidable slob, he was also a highly-regarded counsel. He'd presided over the IPO, various product suits, contracts, insurance negotiations, attempted takeovers, labor disputes, international treaties, tariffs, and on and on. In an era which had seen more and more specializing, he remained the ultimate generalist. Drawing on centuries of experience, he could win cases spanning decades, nations and disciplines.

He took a deep breath, wiped his thick lips with a puffy hand, and belched. Odor of pork and ketchup billowed into the room.

Oiler winced, but Silvertongue didn't even twitch. "Glad you could make it. How long do we have until your next hot dog?"

"That's not very nice."

"Just want to keep you happy." Still smiling, Silvertongue snapped the Autospeak. "Kelli, sweetie, no interruptions, no calls, nobody standing around waiting to get in. Have the Commissary send up a few hot dogs and a relish tray."

"Will do," a pert voice answered.

Silvertongue flipped the button.

"Can she be trusted?" Oiler asked.

"Kelli? No problem. She's smart enough to know something's up, but she can't connect the dots. And she's smart enough to know when to leave things be. I treat her pretty well."

"Nobody can be trusted completely," Groomer twanged in a voice that always surprised Oiler, coming from that jiggling frame. "Let's see what you have."

Silvertongue unlocked a drawer and pulled out a manila folder. He distributed a couple of handwritten pages.

"Nice printing job." Groomer squinted.

"What do you expect? We don't want this stuff getting out."

"Who's on board so far?" Oiler asked.

"Sprinter, for one. From an e-business standpoint, nothing else. He thinks he'll save the world with his new business model."

"Well, he's young." Groomer took one of Silvertongue's business cards from its onyx holder and used it to pick his teeth. "What about the operations?"

"Don't need them yet," Oiler said. "They'll line up under the new business model, anyway, and it may be a while before they realize what's hit them. The real impact will be in land holdings and herd management."

"So I gather. Silvertongue, these herd numbers here, how do they connect with Page Four?"

"They're higher here. We keep the RFS units out of Page Four. Keeps us from explaining them. There's an extra forty thousand here. Perfectly good deer, just won't fly."

"Not that they'll need to." Groomer caressed his huge belly and surveyed the room. "Any extra ears in here?"

"What do you think?"

Groomer matched Silvertongue's hard stare. "Let's take the plan from the top. Three big pieces. First, merger and then restructuring the Board. Next, herd restructure and selloff. Then land development and reallocation."

"There's four. You forgot about the santas," Oiler said.

"Hell with the santas," Groomer retorted. "Thirty, forty thousand do-gooders running around bumping into each other. The new recruits never even bother to ditch the red suits, they're so proud. And their support conventions, the SSC's! You know what it's like trying to keep all those guys under wraps, finding motivational speakers who won't blow the lid off the whole operation on some talk show? And that was before we went co-ed. I don't even want to go into some of those problems, the after hours stuff and the guys who get into a little too much of the Christmas cheer. No, I'll be glad to see the whole program go right into the ditch. We ought to be able to shovel half of them out the door, I don't know, give 'em an exit option, Dale Carnegie, the Salvation Army."

"But we need to plan for them," Oiler said. "So it's a fourth point. We'll need ER. Is Gardner in?"

"Partway," Silvertongue said. "I've told her there'll be changes. She knows there's merger talk. But the other stuff, no way. She'd have problems with plenty of it. We need to get her to commit publicly before she figures out the rest of it."

"And now for the rest of it," Groomer said. "No more interruptions. Start with the merger. I've got the essentials of the agreement worked up. The EI guys are hot on this, because they can see its potential, how it'll drive up shareholder value. We've got the usual nits and nats to worry about. We both have underling weasels building their careers on this one. We trample theirs, they trample ours. The whole damn thing is boring. Tinter, their chief counsel, and I have played this game so long we could probably wrap the whole thing up in a couple of hours."

"No doubt," Silvertongue said. "What about the rabbit?"

"Oh, *him*!" Groomer belched again, more pork and ketchup for atmosphere. "He's as bad as the Chief. At odds with the Board, paper-tiger Chairman, trying to put in policies from a couple of thousand years ago. Same old stuff. He'll get booted when the merger and the restructure happens, same as ours. Then we'll combine the Boards, soothe some of the bruised feelings, appoint new Board Chairs, golden parachutes."

"What if he goes public? Screams and yells?"

"Who?"

"Santa!"

"He won't." This from Silvertongue. "C'mon, Oiler. By the time he recovers from the shock, the firm will have moved on. If he goes to the press, what does that do? They'll treat him like every other goofball that pops up at Christmas. You know that's when he'll do it. They'll give him a couple of stories, somewhere between the Grinch and the Rose Bowl, and it'll be over. If he's smart, he'll realize that beforehand and won't even bother. It's not like we're going to cut him off. I mean, this may sound goofy, or even soft, but if I could figure out a way to keep him on, I would. I would. But he's the Chief. And he's either the Chief, or he isn't anything. That's how I see it, and that's how he'll see it. So we'll cut him the best deal you can imagine. I don't know, call it the ultimate golden parachute. All expenses paid, forever. House any size, anywhere he wants. Two, three, whatever. I'd give him a new appearance, a new identity, except he can do it himself." He paused, thinking. "I'd give him his old team, too. If it didn't break his heart."

"Nice sentiment," Groomer drawled. "The Board doesn't run on sentiment. I like the old guy, too, but liking somebody and working off of sentiment doesn't make it in today's world. Never has. If he could see his way to doing things the right way, there might be a chance. Might be. But that's not going to happen, so why bother? He's out, the rabbit's out, we combine the Boards, merge our operations, our assembly lines, our purchasing, supply chain management, and it's a win. Shareholders are happy, we get a good bit of compensation, and it's on to the next stage.

"For the next stage, I'm already exploring that with some of the larger outfits. We can get some of the initial RFS deer pushed into food with very little difficulty. Some of our potential partners tell me they already know what to say to the labeling folks, especially the American FDA. They figure they can start quietly. If we keep a tight eye on PR, there shouldn't be any problem. Plus, it'll help the Sami."

"The who?"

"Lapplanders, Oiler. I'm trying to be politically correct." Groomer chuckled mirthlessly. "We'll take the ones we cull from the traditional herds and drive them into north Sweden. That helps the local economy. We thin the others from all over, gradually. When we go non-RFS, we'll speed up. Then we'll close down whole sites. Silvertongue will have his work cut out for him if we close Argentina."

Oiler picked at his arm. "I thought we were going to try other things before we went into food," he said. "Like theme parks."

"We did." Silvertongue sighed. "It's too expensive. And it only works as a solution for RFS. Since our long-term goal is a fifty percent reduction in herds, you've got another hundred and fifty thousand or so to get rid of. That's a lot of theme parks. Plus you're guaranteed that one of them would take it into his head to fly, and there you'd be—tabloids, press, the whole bit. Especially if the poor kid fell off midway through the flight. The Sami would take them on, but they can't pay for them. We'd end up losing out big time. This is the only way it works."

"I see that now. And eventually, we'll have cut the acreage in half too." Oiler scanned the page. "You know, to do this right, to get the land redeveloped, we need to do it through a subsidiary. Where people can't see the connection between land development and NPI."

"Way ahead of you," Groomer drawled. "I've got the incorporation papers going for GSO Investments. That's our names in the title, so it's a nothing label. The Street will see the connection, unless we separate. But they don't give a hoot as long as the returns are there."

A knock. "Food service."

"Just a minute." Silvertongue nodded to Oiler.

A nondescript, narrow-featured elf entered, pushing a cart laden with hot dogs and condiments. She squeezed between Oiler and Groomer, who irritably moved out of her way. When she picked up the food service order and turned to leave, her foot caught on Oiler's chair. She fell, knocking the paper from Oiler's hand. She struggled to her feet, grabbed the food order and Oiler's paper, and handed the food order to him.

"Not that one!" he snapped. "This is yours, can't you read? The other one!"

"I'm sorry," she mumbled, exchanging papers. She hurried out.

"Illiterate," Oiler grumbled.

Groomer was already three bites into the first dog, relish spattering his embattled shirt front. "So," he said between bites, "who can stop the deal?"

"Traditionalists," Oiler said. "Maybe we should avoid using their lines. At least for starters. Somebody like Halter would be a real pain."

"Not if we set them up for failure," Silvertongue said. "Especially if we need their facilities. We could adjust the targets for impossible quality or quantity, cost reductions. Some combination that sounds plausible enough but really means they kill themselves and still don't make it."

"Then there's the Board." Groomer belched. "Here's how I see them lining up." He swallowed with an effort. "Torvalds is easy. She's solidly behind the EI thing, has had the strategy gang, Hatcher and his guys, working up the what-ifs and the simulations. I hear Beamer's new software package is really something. Shows product fluctuation impacts up and down the value chain, from suppliers to operations to distributors."

"Ah yes, Beamer. We'll need our friends from IT," Silvertongue said. "What about the others?"

"Donaldson will be tough." Groomer reached for the second dog. "He's a good-hearted traditionalist, and he's great with the numbers. But he wants to keep a single focus on the product line. Parcell runs a direct ship company, so he's salivating over the whole thing. And then there's Baylor, the new one. He's Torvalds' pick. Since she heads up the Nominating Committee, it was easy for her to bring him in."

"I thought the shareholders had to approve it."

"That's the *form*, Oiler, not the function. Oh, he's in. Way in. He came from one of the big automotives, and he's got it all—operations experience, global reach, brand management, growth mentality, supply chain expertise, design knowledge. He'll do an excellent job."

"What job?"

"Don't be dense, Oiler. The Chief's being replaced."

"But you can't just take someone from the Board, and—"

"Most companies," Silvertongue said. "Not NPI."

"Bethitdth, idth temprary," Groomer hotdogged.

Silvertongue frowned. "What do you mean?"

Groomer swallowed, a flabby mountain with popping eyes. "We're not stopping there." He returned the half-eaten dog to the tray and leaned forward, an impressive feat. "This company won't be run only by humans," he growled. "I don't care how smart they think they are. It's unthinkable that elves aren't on that Board. Several elves. And one that calls the shots."

In the long silence, Oiler watched Groomer's eyes follow a fruitfly's lazy track and waited for this toad of an elf to whisk out a long tongue and snap the bug in mid flight.

"I agree in principle," Silvertongue murmured at last. "But how?"

"UEU. It won't be easy, but I've got some of it in motion already. There'll be an accident, of the industrial variety. Don't worry Oiler—" Groomer waved a stubby hand "—nobody will get hurt. Not if it goes according to plan. That'll get the union going. They'll strike right at peak production. Then they get a spot on the Board. And that's how we start. Humans. How many years do they have before they retire or die? Ten, twenty? We have hundreds. Hundreds. It'll change."

"I thought you hated the union."

"I do, Oiler. What better way to control them than by giving them the illusion of power? Do you really think we'd let one of their reactionaries onto the Board? Don't worry, it'll be somebody who thinks our way."

"Where will this accident happen? And when?" Silvertongue asked. "I might need to dust off a statement."

"Soon. I can't say exactly when. But first things first. The Board restructuring and the Chief business have to happen ahead of it. As for where, we have a couple of options. We've got a deteriorating situation in one of the furnaces, the metal toy casting area. And we have the new solvent we've put into Halter's area, the flammable one."

"We?"

"Don't ask, Silvertongue. I'll take care of you both. This—" he rubbed his huge belly "—keeps them off guard. The less said, the better. When the time is right, they'll find out who they're dealing with. Then we're in the clear. One of us becomes the Chief. I should say one of you. CEO. The other, COO. I stay Counsel. Nicely done."

Oiler's eyes widened. "COO? What's happening to Racer?"

Groomer gave him an odd look. "With his health problems? He'll retire. Willingly. He's a paper COO, anyway. You think he's calling the shots?"

A slight smile twisted one side of Silvertongue's mouth. "Chief Executive Officer, Chief Operating Officer. You're aiming us high," he said quietly. "Why not you?"

Groomer smiled under hard eyes. "I like where I am." He dusted some crumbs from his shirt. "Is this over?" He struggled mightily to his feet. "Where's your shredder?"

"I'll take them," Silvertongue retrieved the copies. His hand disappeared under the desk, which made a few digesting sounds. "Sounds a little like you, Groomer."

"Words unbecoming a future officer," Groomer drawled, smiling. "We'll meet again in a couple of weeks, after step one."

They headed out, Silvertongue opening the door. "Do I know you?" he asked the pretty young elf sitting at Kelli's desk.

She jumped up. "I'm Peanut," she said. "From down the hall. Kelli had to use the ladies' room, and she told me you didn't want to be disturbed. So I stood guard." She smiled brightly.

Groomer looked her up and down. "A good job. Thank you, Peanut."

Oiler scowled. Must Groomer devour everything? He left Groomer there, for Silvertongue to handle. His head was abuzz. The plans had leapt ahead, far beyond where his initial thoughts had taken him. The restructure and merger, yes. The transformation of the business from direct-ship reindeer-and-human-intensive to e-business, yes. The herd selloffs, yes. The food agreements, no. Industrial accident, no. Succession planning, no. He shook his head. And he was a part of it, too. Groomer. Was he always one step ahead of everyone else?

Deep in thought, he rounded a corner, passing Kelli and the elf from food service. This was exciting, dangerous, interesting, disturbing. He had to get to his office, to calm the swirl.

4.

It had been that kind of Board Meeting. At times like this, incorporation didn't seem like such a good idea. Santa stumped down the carpeted hallway, heavy shoes sinking into the dark green pile. Under the layers of suit, shirt and undershirt he could feel the sweat sliding from armpit to waist, felt it also flowing between shoulder blades down to the small of his back. He didn't sweat this much when he worked out on his bike. Idiot would see him in about fifteen minutes. Fifteen minutes to shake this off and uncover the other Santa.

Elves and half-elves heard his heavy thumping and took cover. He scowled, lower lip thrust out, going over meeting details as he walked. The frown deepened.

He'd been introduced to the new man, the automotive finance guy (Baylor? Taylor?), and they'd instantly disliked each other. How could anyone so weasely-looking, so runty, be Board material?

He barely glanced at Roxy. "No phone calls, no messages, until after Idiot," he said, and gained the sanctuary of his office.

He sank into the big leather chair. Baylor. Weasely wasn't quite right. Reptilian. Yes. Definitely something crocodilian about those pale, hooded eyes that stared back at him as though he were a fat wild pig that needed hypnotizing. Something lizardlike in the handclasp, too, that made him want to wipe his hand on his pantleg. Something ancient, worse than crocodilian—saurian, maybe.

He toyed with his pen, bouncing it on the mahogany. The meeting had begun well enough, discussions on operating statistics showing NPI's basic operations running smoothly, key numbers under control. But then the talk swung toward topics that seemed to be everywhere these days.

First it was improving time-to-market, Oswald saying that the assembly line improvement rates, while admirable, weren't in line with trade figures. Oswald recommended funding a study by the Boston Consulting Group, which figured, since he was an old BCG guy, anyway, and still knew half the partners. The rest of them went along with it, which meant Santa would have to dig out somebody from Strategic Planning to put a program together.

Then Torvalds pitched in, commenting on outmoded delivery strategies, arguing that since no one saw the reindeer or all those delivery santas, anyway, there wasn't any point in keeping the charade going. She argued for relocating key production facilities closer to some of the major distribution outlets. He told her that would set them up for a royal fight with the UEU and pitch the upcoming contract talks right onto the rocks.

"If the issue's jobs," she said, "there'll be plenty of opportunities in the new locations. All the elves have to do is relocate. And I'm sorry, but if they can't see their way to doing that, there's Transition to Outside Work. Beef it up for increased traffic and work out a better exit deal."

"Let me remind you what the elves think about TOW." He glared at them all. "Seven hundred TOW-ROPE cartoons. Remember? With nooses? You think they'll go for this?"

Torvalds shrugged. "Give it to ER to handle."

"Gardner will never go for it," he said. "She's got one of the best business heads of us all, and she can tell this won't work."

"Then convince her. She needs to make a tough call like this. Besides, they might like doing something new, instead of another year at all those bloody toys."

He squinted.

"You didn't think we were going to *build* those additional facilities, did you? We need to achieve growth quickly, we need to tap into new distribution outlets, and we need something with a sales peak other than at the end of the year."

As realization dawned, that damned pipsqueak, the new guy, said, "Why are we all jawing it to death then? Get it in the open! There's a proposal to buy out Easter Industries! I've got the merger deal from your strategy boys. Looks like a win to me."

"EI?" he exploded. "EEE-*III*? —I hate that damned rabbit! Hate him, you hear me? Listen to me! I am not, now or ever, *not* turning eggs out in any of my factories! Never, never, never!"

The new guy smiled. "I wouldn't say 'never', Santa."

"I'll say it again! Never! You forget whose name is associated with Christmas! You forget who decided to incorporate this place! You forget who's Chairman! Well, all of you had better remember that! And I don't want to hear the 'E' word uttered around this table again!"

The silver pen rapped sharply against the desk. There'd been a lot more talk after that, too, on reskilling, reengineering, revamping, re re re re. He'd tuned it out somewhere after the first or second *re.* What was he doing at the head of the horseshoe, anyway? Presiding over a gang of alien, whispering humans and their secret deals? Where had it gone so wrong?

He scowled. This would never do. He was still the head of North Pole Industries, still Santa, still the half-elf birthed out of the union of an elf and a human in a star-crossed romance sixty-plus centuries ago, still the wild rider of the heavens (though he hadn't taken his team out in so many years, now), still the leader of the elves, still the provider of the toys, still the jolly—

That's where it ended. He jammed a thumb into his mouth, grinding the nail. *No. Better stop this now, before I end up in the dumper*. He punched the Autospeak. "Roxy, is Idiot here yet?"

"Yes," she squawked back. "He wanted to give you a little time to yourself."

"Send him in."

He expected Dr. Id to explode into the room, eyes flashing. Instead, the door opened quietly, and Dr. Id smilingly oozed from behind it and slid into the middle chair across from Santa's desk. "Good afternoon, Santa," he said, looking Santa full in the face—something he said was very important. It helped that Id was a half-elf too, one of only a few hundred in NPI. And he was roughly the same age, give or take a few decades: born like so many of them during that brief period long ago, when north-wandering humans had intermingled with the elves for several generations. "Please go to the sofa."

Santa heaved himself onto the sofa. "Let's get started, Id," he growled. Idiot was his second shrink. He'd dismissed the first one, a full elf, because he felt like he was being psychoanalyzed by a little kid. It was weird unburdening yourself of your innermost fears and anguish, only to have some little guy bounce off his oversized chair and trot over to you, head barely coming up to your belly, spouting all kinds of psycho-rubbish. Id was better. The first thing Id had said was, "Always remember: 'The self vanishes upon inspection.' From Freud. So let's get to work, and good luck."

"You're hostile today. You called me Idiot. Why?"

Because you are? "I don't know. Lots of things. I had a crappy meeting with the Board, me against them again. And it helps me remember I'm set apart from others. Like you."

"What does?"

"Calling you Idiot," *idiot.*

"Well." Dr. Id took out a pad. "Why don't we pick up where we left off. You were giving me a history lesson, I believe."

Santa closed his eyes. Where had they been? He took a long, slow breath, feeling the air fill his lungs and his back muscles ache, a good feeling.

"Take your time," Dr. Id murmured.

Santa waited for the dream to overtake him, sliding down familiar paths, year upon year upon year, as mind and memory propelled him into simpler times, the snow whirling about, wolf cries dancing on the wind, magical reindeer of huge proportion and wild wisdom—

—deafening thunder of hooves slamming against iron-hard snow, the cold wind's lash, massive bell-laden backs rippling, thick brown hairs exhaling animal scent, antlered heads tossed against the gale. On and on the hooves rang, their thunder jarring, and he crying above the wind, spurring them on by name, until the hooves pounded nothing, ground giving way in abrupt silence, legs beating air, cabin

and stable vanishing beneath their dancing feet, the sleigh cracking and groaning –

It was so simple then. We slid into the magic almost by accident. We didn't know we were different, half-elves and elves working beside humans so long ago. Then the big ice storms came, and the humans retreated. We sensed their savagery. They became vicious, striking out against themselves and the lands around them. But once each year they would drop their differences and call up the good that was in all of them. They had nothing, really, no toys, nothing beautiful. That's when she and I felt the call, as though our long-practiced crafts tumbled by chance into the great purpose.

We discovered the reindeer, or they us. We trained them, began the midnight rides to the southern lands, dispensing the things we had assembled over the previous year to people who had gone to sleep expecting an empty morning. Their surprised happiness became songs, and songs became legend, and legend and our deeds wove around each other like smoke wreathes from a fire, until we couldn't distinguish where we left off and the legend began, where our efforts ended and the expectancy of delivery began. And over the years and down the centuries, as the humans increased, they took their legends with them, and we became all kinds of apparitions, changeling magic permitting us to express ourselves in ways familiar the world over: Befana. Sinter Klaas. Hagios Nikolaos. Joulupukki.

The sofa creaked. Santa opened his eyes. Dr. Id's pen remained poised over the page. He cleared his throat. "Then what happened?"

"It got out of hand," Santa said. "The human population exploded. Soon we had more than we could handle. Much more. So we started growing the herd, adding other humans who could take on my role, building new factories. Meantime, the humans were busy learning new ways to kill each other, getting better at travel, fouling the planet in all kinds of interesting ways. But they kept their Santa legends going, oh yes. Every damn place they went. They built these big corporations, started the assembly line process, put unions in place. They balanced that with management, got into nuclears and computers and marketing and infrastructure. Whatever infrastructure means."

He shook his head. "I don't know what made me think this was a good idea," he continued, "but I decided it was time for us to incorporate. The elves hated it. They couldn't see why we had to change from our traditional workshops. We did the IPO way back, near the turn of the century. We were global way before it was fashionable, too.

"Back when we started splitting up the santas, we had all kinds of problems, crash landings, UFO reports, duck hunters, American navy planes. One of them even hit a weather balloon. Talk about being off course. Then we ran out of pasturage for the reindeer, and it got too expensive to import supplements. So we got into land, started buying up remote acreage. We had some pretty sharp guys that got into real estate and condos. We lost focus, got caught up in the real estate boom. But we got burned by the bust a few years later. So we sold it off, went back into the land."

"And how had the world changed?" Dr. Id asked. "Technology?"

He nodded. "Computers started showing up everywhere, plus animated films and the rise of the marketeers. The Board decided we needed fresh ideas. So they established a fake identity for me, ditched the red suit, and imported a bunch of business consultants. Pinheads. Every damn slideshow they staged looked the same. They told me I had problems that would take the business right under unless I bought their snake oil. But every time I looked out the window here, I saw the same solid business."

"Meaning what?"

"Their threats were in their heads. They convinced each other of these threats because they all went to the same conferences. They huddled with each other and discussed the same damn things. I kicked them all out, which didn't make the Board happy, but tough.

"After that, we did better, but the pressures still mounted. With humans, Christmas got sliced and sliced until it started to look like something sandwiched between football games and holiday specials. It shattered, Christmas carols replaced by sound bites, humans jumping from one thing to the next and the next after that."

"What about Mrs. Claus? And Christmas, the elves?"

"You know, Id, we saw Christmas as this flame, this bright, steady flame burning through all the years. But now the flame was hitting high winds, you could see it being blown this way and that, almost going out.

"And the elves! I'd lost touch with them. Especially the ones on the lines. So we started the Talk It Up program, trying to find a way that would tap into what they were doing down there. At least, *I* wanted to know what was really going on—I'm not sure the Board ever did. We'd invite some of the line guys in for these really, and I mean *really* uncomfortable lunches, the kind where you spend more calories sweating than you take in eating. Our words would go back and forth, sure, but it was the fifty thousand foot view. And when one of them got up enough courage to say what was really on his mind, it was always the same: the other elves would look down at their food, the Board folks smiled those I-don't-care smiles, and that was it.

"But I knew most of those guys. We spent hundreds of years side by side. There they'd be, sitting across from me, trying to pick their way through this gourmet food, and it was like I was looking at strangers, little guys and girls I'd never seen before. At first I thought it was the Board members sitting there that made them so uncomfortable. But they'd lost touch with me the same way. We had to reintroduce ourselves at those lunches. We didn't need a bunch of strangers watching. The consultants wouldn't hear of that, though."

"I thought you kicked them all out."

"I did. The Board brought them back in, and no matter that I hated 'em all. So we had these strange little lunches, these awkward little dances that didn't tell either side a damn thing. I'd try to ask questions, but I don't think I was very good at it. I'd frown, trying to put into words the question I wanted—I *needed*—to ask. They must have thought I was mad at them, and maybe I was." Softer, momentarily. "Maybe I was. More likely I was just mad at the, I don't know, the whole silly stupid fakery of it all!"

"So they told me not to ask any more questions, which meant I just *sat* there through those things, a big dumb figurehead—just a damned figurehead!"

"And what made me *really* mad—" he was up on one elbow on the couch now, facing Dr. Id, his voice raised almost to a roar "—is the way they all told each other this was a big success! The consultants and the Board, I mean. They'd pull out these reports, funny color charts, the bars going up, numbers going up. Month after month, and the big thing was showing that we increased attendance! The elves must have wanted to come! Never mind that we simply issued more invitations, and they felt they just *had* to come."

He lay back down, sighed, eyes wandering over the ceiling. Dr. Id studied his pen.

"We just got too damn big," Santa rumbled on. "NPI became aware of its success, its size, and so did the rest of the world. So we started getting visits, from suppliers, government agencies. All these guys with one hand out to shake yours and the other hand reaching around your ass to empty your wallet. Parasites.

"Take the Argentine thing. Twenty million Santeans to clean up a bunch of reindeer crap. That's the kind of thing you face, day in and day out. Couldn't they have claimed some kind of local weather disaster, a forage problem? If they'd lied to get extra money to use in social programs, then I could look the other way. But I knew where the money would go, and I'm not about to line some general's pockets with extra Christmas cash!

"And then computers!" He was up on his elbow again. "They hook you into the technology cycle. You don't have a choice. I'm still proud of everything we've done with them. They've helped us improve production times, concept to customer, inventory turn rates, cash flow, market penetration, hiring, reskilling—even flight trajectory analysis, RFS, feed balancing—"

"Sorry." Dr. Id's pen stopped. "What's RFS?"

"Reindeer Fatigue Syndrome." Santa surveyed Dr. Id as though he were spawn from a distant planet. "Another recent development. The bigger the herds get, the more you hear about reindeer just flat out refusing to fly. So we had to send some of them out to pasture and rebalance the teams. Every year it's something. Now it's e-business, virtual partnerships, integrated supply chain management, mass customization. Mass customization! What did they think we were up to, all these years?"

"And then she left."

"I—eh?"

"She left. Mrs. Claus."

"Yeah, but do we have to go there again? *She* left, *she* wrote the letter, *she's* the one who's decided it's time to move on. Glad she's got a choice in the matter! Here I am, right in the middle of mergers and acquisitions! I'm trying to buy High Holly Industries, fending off Kaybee and Toys R Us, I mean what does she expect me to do? What? The whole world's spinning out of control, and Christmas along with it, and I'm trying to keep the flame going, and that's when she decides the cocoa and cookies thing is over? What's that all about?"

"What do you think it's all about?"

"Oh, don't turn the damn question around! It's about—it's about—I don't *know* what it's about!" Santa heaved himself from the couch, circled back behind his desk, all the time pointing a fat finger at Dr. Id while he roared, "Tell me something, doctor! Tell me this! After six thousand years, are we in a menopause problem? Am I going to be nurturing some kind of hot flash thing that's going to last a hundred years? Isn't there enough going on without biology kicking in?"

"...You know the answer to that, I believe."

Santa glared at him before slamming himself into his chair, eyes shut tight. "Stop turning it all around," he muttered. "Not a single damn answer from the one person—who could help."

He looked up, the fire gone. "Yes. I know. You'd tell me they're at the heart of everything we do. The children. The children we could never have. What *are* children, really? What are they? I'm supposed to know. Six thousand years, and I'm asking *this* question. Go on, get out of here."

"But we have—"

"No time left. I'm sorry, my good doctor, but this didn't do a thing for me."

"It takes time." Dr. Id closed his notebook and stood. "You can't expect all these experiences to come pouring out and fit neatly into place. It doesn't work that way. We made progress."

Santa sighed. "Yes, doctor, we did make progress, the same way the damn Board makes progress in the Talk It Up lunches. It's like a teaser for your next session. Maybe there won't be another session."

"...You can make that choice."

"I know I can make that choice, dammit! ...I'm sorry, Id. I am. A shouting Santa isn't exactly the image of Christmas. Just go. Maybe we'll have another—no. Go now. I'll have Roxy set something up, sometime." He swiveled his chair around, so that the back of it faced the retreating doctor. "And I'll use this time to look out over this place. Maybe I'll even open the curtain."

5.

Moonlight gleamed on polished traces. Animal breath steamed silvery in the dark. Giant hooves rang against the frozen ground, sending tiny snowsparks swirling into the cold breeze. Two of the impatient team snorted, and one of the lead pair lifted its massive, antlered head and bellowed, the sound rising and vanishing into the windy night. Gold harness bells jingled ancient songs unique to each reindeer.

All about them, preparations continued. A stream of elves loaded the sleigh, pushing packages of every shape and size into its cavernous and magically insatiable interior. Other elves polished the red-and-green painted wood of the sleigh's exterior, soft cloths caressing rich, polished surfaces. He watched their timeless actions, holding his breath, anticipating the moment when the huge green door would open and the majestic, red-suited creature, half-elf and half human, would raise large hands to lips wreathed in a magnificent curly white beard and call out,

> *"Come Dasher, come Dancer,*
> *Come on, come on, hey! Are you coming?*

"—Are you coming?"—the door knocking in the breeze, rat-tap, rat-tap, "Hey—"

"—hey, Halter! You coming?"

Halter shook his head, scattering dream fragments. Spinner, his floor manager, stood in the doorway, waving a coffee mug. "You want some before we chat?"

"That's a thought." He surveyed the clumps of reports and papers on his desk. "You seen my green pen anywhere?"

"Try your pocket. Next to the red one."

"Geez. Spinner, I wish I had your head for just one day."

"Why?"

"Because you don't do things like forget you put your pen in your own pocket."

"Why'd you forget?"

"I was daydreaming, I guess."

"You guess."

"No, I know. I can't help it. Maybe it's because I can only stare at doll production figures for so long. Not like you."

"But you told me daydreaming is healthy. Brings in new ideas."

"Oh, it does. It does."

"But you have to admit, daydreaming doesn't help you with least-cost application of finishes, or transponder analysis."

He laughed. "Did they have transponders in the mills?"

"Look, I left wool operations a long time ago."

"And you were the best, there, too. Feet planted firmly on the ground. Which is why I have you here." *And why you're in Assembly A, specialty dolls, complex and high profit. No time for daydreaming there.*

"OK, so I'm the practical one," she said. "But there's one thing you have over me, cold."

He raised his eyebrows.

"You can name everybody on the line. Plus their families, their kids, their hobbies. They'd go through fire for you, Halter."

"Even if I'm a daydreamer?" He smiled.

"Maybe because." She wiggled the cup again. So you coming?"

He hefted one of the reports. "I'll pass. I want to at least get started wading through this. Have you started using the new stuff?"

"WonderFinish? Lines one and three, the Happy Henrietta line. Afternoons only. Seems to be working out all right—goes on fast, dries clear and quick."

"I'm still not sure I trust it." He flipped the pages. "Industry notes say it's pretty flammable. Fumes problem, too. Any more complaints?"

"There's a report in your inbox. They need to get used to handling it. Spills are a problem, because you aren't supposed to get it on your skin. Couple elves got dizzy, couple more had a minor rash problem. Everybody was treated at the infirmary. Since then, no complaints."

"I don't like the dizziness part at all. Get the ventilation folks in there, have them check how much fresh air we've got moving over those lines. If it was up to me, I'd pull that stuff in a heartbeat."

"You'd be up against the Council."

"I know, that's what stops me. I don't have enough data to challenge their cost figures. But if I get it, look out."

"If." She snatched the cup from his desk. "I'll get you a cup. But you read that line report."

"Thanks." Halter leaned back, eyes shut. The Elves' Executive Council was NPI's senior operating board. Its authority extended over all assembly and manufacturing operations, as well as suppliers, operations logistics, transportation, and safety. Only the Board of Directors, and the Chief himself, had more clout. It would be tough to challenge the EEC on WonderFinish. He'd need plenty of proof to convince them to pull it out. If they'd do it even then. There were rumors that the solvents issue was near and dear to somebody at the top.

He opened his eyes and reached for the line report, sliding it from his inbox stack and opening it. July 6, day shift—two elves to the infirmary, complaining of dizziness, observed and released after an hour. July 8, afternoons—solvent spill in the materials transfer area, auxiliary venting systems activated, three handling personnel develop skin irritations on hands and forearms, self-treat with industrial skin cleanser, followed by warm soapy water. Symptoms disappear after twenty-four hours. July 11, similar. July 12, midnights, dizziness, treatment the same.

He green-circled a couple of spots, tapped his pen, then laid it down and sat back. His eyes drifted to the stack of journals he'd ordered from Corporate Research: *Industrial Materials and Solvents*

Quarterly, *Operations Research Review*, *Manufacturing Techniques Journal*, *Industrial Medicine*. Each publication contained at least one reference to WonderFinish, trade name for product HA-44, marketed by the huge multinational, Universal Industrial Products, chemical name *dioxyethylpara* something or other. Each reference seemed almost schizophrenic in its discussion of the stuff, tempering high praise for the product's low cost, easy application, and rapid drying time with a caution that it required careful handling, in particular keeping it away from heat and open flame. Only *Industrial Medicine* had been single-mindedly dour, stating that in addition to short-term symptoms, long-term effects were likely but not yet evident.

He rubbed his eyes. This was just trend data, not good enough for EEC. Spinner would agree. Plus, September was coming on hard, starting the three-month sprint to Christmas. It would be harder than ever to change things in mid-stream with everybody going full bore. Why even try?

A tap on his office door. He looked up and smiled at Jenny, his admin.

She smiled back. "You have a phone call."

"Who is it?" He stretched.

"Winnow. Says it's urgent."

"Urgent?"

"He says."

"Thanks." His hand paused over the receiver. Winnow headed toy and model train operations. They had hardly anything in common. What could he possibly want? He picked it up.

"Halter! How are things your way?"

Winnow had one of those sharp phone voices that made you hold the receiver away from your ear. "Same old story: too much to do, not enough time. You?"

"The same." The sharp voice laughed. "It doesn't get any easier, does it?"

"Not really. Your nickel."

"Yes. Well, here's the situation, Halter. I've had something come up, a visit from our Auditing friends. They're doing a spot check on metal finishing today, which means clear the calendar, hustle down there, spruce things up a bit but not too much—*you* know the drill."

Halter saw Winnow's train leaving the station and chuffing towards him. Was it toy or big-time freight, and could he sidestep it? "Sure do. But this affects me how?"

"Well, I hope this isn't too big a favor, but you tell me. I need to spend all my time on the lines with these audit guys, but I've also got a JEDI kickoff going. It's the two-hour intro and tour package—and I was wondering if—"

"Oh, a JEDI?" A toy train after all—orientation for the Junior Elf Development Initiative. "Let me look. What time are you slotted? Ten to noon, and then lunch?"

"Same as always."

"OK. I was going to talk with Spinner in a couple of minutes, but I can cut it short. She can cover a call I was making to UIP."

"The materials guys? What do they want?"

"It's me. I'm worried about the new finish we're using, WonderFinish. Heard of it?"

"No. Problem?"

Spinner appeared in the doorway, and he motioned her to a seat. "Could be. It's got some safety issues, mostly fire and ventilation."

"Sounds like it might be trouble. Can you go for a substitute? How's it for quality and performance?"

"That's just it. It beats everything else hands down. Costs less, is easy to apply, dries like a dream, and looks terrific. And the EEC likes it."

"The *EEC*? So why bother?" Winnow exclaimed. "Throw some extra ventilation at it, some work rules, and move on. You've had haz-mats before, you know what to do."

"Yeah, well, still."

"Halter. You've got a reputation of tilting at windmills already. You don't need to add to it. And this one would definitely be an add."

"I suppose."

"Besides, if the EEC is chasing it, you know they'll win. They will. They'll work incentive angles, awards, discretionary days, all kinds of stuff." A pause. "Anyway, think about it. I like it when you shake things up. But this one, whew," Winnow whistled softly, a weird breathy sound in Halter's ear.

"All right," he said at last. "I'll think about it. And I'll do your JEDI thing for you, too, so don't worry. Go chase your auditors."

"Thanks, I will. And you think about it."

"I said I would."

"I mean it. Ops guys have to stick together. I don't want to see you stuck all alone fighting something you can't change. Now I better run. I'll call down and let 'em know you're covering for me. I owe you one."

"All right. Good luck." He hung up.

"Trouble?" Spinner asked.

"No. That was Winnow. Great guy. Practical to a fault sometimes, but I don't know anyone more honest. He was giving me some advice on WonderFinish."

"And?"

He sighed. "Maybe I *am* crazy. No good data, nothing in the journals to speak of. You and Winnow telling me to pack it in." He took a long sip of coffee.

"Did I say that?" She leaned forward. "You've got me thinking. Look in the report. Problems every other day."

"Yeah, but it's minor stuff. No lasting effects, nothing a little extra precaution wouldn't solve. No way can I go to the EEC on this. You'd almost have to kill somebody down there before they'd pay attention. If even then."

"Was it always like that?"

"Nah." Halter leaned back, eyes finding no pattern in the ceiling. "I take it back. It's gone up and down. A thousand years ago, no question—we did things the way we'd always done. We had the crafts then, the apprenticeship programs. Then we went into a bad period, about a hundred and fifty years ago, where certain areas had to work like dogs. We did crazy hours, turning out toys at an insane rate. We started them younger, too, way younger than the JEDI program. Kids. They didn't know enough to complain about what was going on. Until their families complained for them. So we scaled back from that, restructuring the workforce."

"Did it help?"

"Didn't make a damn bit of difference. We still turned out the toys, we still had the quality, we still lit up the faces of children at Christmas. You wonder.

"Then we brought in steam. And then electricity. And then the moving lines. So we went from a process where an elf would put together a doll from beginning to end, you know, start with the form, then sculpt the arms and legs, then mold the face, then apply the eyes and nose and mouth, then put the clothes on, the shoes, the jewelry—even jewelry! I tell you, those dolls, they—each one had a personality. We matched them up. We literally matched the doll to the kid who asked for it, figured out what would work and what didn't. There weren't two dolls that went out of here that were the same. Because there weren't two kids who were the same, not even twins.

"But now, shucks!" he waved a hand. "Hundred thousand Barbies, two hundred forty two thousand three hundred nineteen Elmos, all the same! And it's like the kids don't care, either. As long as they get their Elmo." Another pull on the coffee mug.

"And the guys on the line, what a struggle! When we first went to mass production, geez! We had dolls coming out of here with two left hands, three eyes, you name it! And the union problems! That's when they formed the United Elves Union. So they could keep something of what they used to be, the craft elves."

"I know." Spinner nodded.

"That's right, you were part of this, too. But you were in the big looming ops."

"Same thing," she said. "The knitting needles we threw out."

"No doubt. We had scrap machines everywhere. We tried all kinds of tricks to keep the workers from going nuts—looking at what the Swedes had done, the Japanese. You name the country, we went after it. Job enrichment, job enlargement, job this, job that. Some of it worked, but most of it—we threw it out. None of it helped.

"But now, I don't know. I think we're in one of those periods where we watch numbers instead of elves. So when it comes to WonderFinish, I figure there's a balance sheet, and on one side there's this number called safety, but on the other there's a whole set of numbers, and they're called cost, finish, dry time, all those things. Those numbers will make all the difference."

"Maybe. But you can still try."

"Yeah. Give me the lance, I'll go after the windmill. You watch." Halter smiled wryly. "Aw, hell, what'll they do to me, anyway? It'll make things exciting."

She studied his face. "What's this about JEDI?"

"Oh, yeah." He grinned. "Our meeting's over." He stood up and headed toward the door.

"It's over?"

"I have to go cover for Winnow on the JEDI program. But I need you to talk to the UIP guys about our findings. Stay here. They'll be calling in about fifteen, twenty minutes."

"All right. Anything you want me to say?"

"Use your judgment. I trust you. I shouldn't, but I do." He laughed, and so did she.

He headed down the hallway, past the drinking fountains and the copier, through the exit and into the cool late summer air. The compound unfolded around him, elves scurrying to and fro, the occasional delivery truck crossing from building to building. The campus was good for exercise, and for thinking while you walked.

JEDIs. What can I tell them? They know more than we do, these days. He glanced at his watch. *Nine fifty-five. Geez, thanks, Winnow.*

By the time he reached the Train Operations Building, several hundred feet away, and hustled to the JEDI Briefing Room, he was thoroughly out of breath. They were already waiting for him when he gained the podium and paused, scanning the fresh upturned faces. They all looked so fresh. Thirty scrubbed kernels, still in the cob. Except for the half-elf towering over them in the back.

He began by telling them how important the JEDI program was—how important they were —because as NPI continued to grow, more and more elves were needed to keep up with the pace. At a mere few hundred years old, they had the promise and energy of youth going for them.

Then he asked for questions, and the half-elf in the back thrust his hand high. "Will we be able to see Santa's original team?"

Some of them actually giggled. "I'm afraid not. The chief's team can only be seen by special appointment. What's your name?"

"Tracer."

Comb that black hair, Tracer. How tall are you, anyway? But those eyes. "Tracer. We'll see. Perhaps something can be arranged."

Now came the fun part. "OK, let's go on tour," he announced, and the expectant silence broke into low rumbles, the JEDIs queuing at the door. Halter swung round in front, leading the group down a narrow hall toward a green door.

Relentless production machinery sounds increased as they walked. They were supposed to see Train Line One, but Winnow had shifted it to Line Two because of the audit. Either way, Halter was in unfamiliar territory, but the kids wouldn't figure it out. After Train Line Two, they'd cross the rail yards and look in on the Recycling Building before concluding with a visit to Assembly Building B, Doll Operations, Line One. Happy Henriettas. Then he'd send them to lunch, and he could get back to work.

They clumped at the door. On a nearby table, bright red and green hard hats jumbled beside a bucket of plastic VISITOR badges on string loops. Halter grabbed a hat and a badge, slipping the string loop over his neck before slapping the hat on his head.

"OK, everybody gets one of *these* and one of *these.*" He tapped the hard hat and held up the badge. The JEDIs rushed the table. He raised his voice. "Make sure they can *see* the badge! The guys on the floor don't like it when they see those badges turned around. Tracer! Don't hang around in the back, I need to give you a special hat."

He watched the tall one stumble forward. One angular elbow landed a solid whack on the side of another JEDI's head. "Hey! Ouch! Willya watch it?" several JEDIs said.

"Sorry. Thanks," Tracer said, taking the upstretched hat.

"How did you end up in the JEDI program, anyway? By the way, it's backwards."

"Oh." Tracer turned the hat around. "I'm the only half-elf, so they figured why have a special program just for me?"

"Makes sense. You know, you should put the badge on *before* you put on the hat, so the string doesn't—" (POP!) "—here, here's another one," Halter continued patiently, exchanging badges. "Turn it around, you don't need to tell yourself who you are. Tracer, we might not always take your size into account. Sometimes we take shortcuts that—Just watch your head, OK?"

Halter turned to the others. He saw excitement and anticipation in their eyes, and he smiled. "Let's go!" He ushered them through the door.

They stood on a catwalk high above the operations. Beneath their feet, the bright metal cars of Train Line Two snaked from station to station. Above certain stations hung panels with many squares of light blinking on and off in mysterious sequences. The smell of ozone charged the air. Tiny spark showers burst from the welding stations. Colors flashed as the cars moved from point to point—red caboose, gray coal car, brown and green pullman. Beyond the crashes and clatters, the ping and hum of the stations, he heard the hiss and snap of compressed air, the plant's lifeline.

Line elves tended machinery and peered at PC's. Halter's voice rose above the production music. "This is a highly automated line. Those of you with training in ops management can see we've got a self-regulated station-to-station setup here. If you haven't seen one before, that big lighted panel up there is an Andon Board —" (dozens of pairs of eyes followed the sweep of Halter's arm to the nearest large, suspended panel) "—which is tied to control data at each of the stations. You read the panel lights and can tell right away what the status is on the floor, what machine might have trouble, what might require quick maintenance, rebalancing the lines.

"Now, what you *can't* see—" Halter pointed to one end of the line, where the various train car shells began their journey "—is behind that wall, where part traffic management begins. That's where the ACPU, the Automatic Car Picking Unit is. The ACPU is tied to the production scheduling system and selects the right car body at the right time, sending the body down the line in a sequence matched to the parts and accessories that go on it. This is more complex than some of the other train lines, because the models that come out of here go to the upper classes of highly-developed countries. These are probably going to western Europe, Japan, and North America."

"Are we still involved in wooden trains?" one of the JEDIs called out.

"Yes. Deeply involved. There's a whole wing here devoted to woodens, everything from top-of-the-line stuff down to simple things, just wheels and a box, that go out on the sleighs to our third world markets. Yes." He pointed to an upraised hand.

"How is this related to NPI's e-business strategy? Will we be doing real time build to order?"

Huh? "E-business is still evolving," he dodged. "The plan is to set up a build-to-order strategy across our lines as soon as we can. But we can't just slap it on top, we'll have to look at our underlying processes first. It could take a while."

"What about a customer portal?" the same voice asked. "Will they be able to look in and see the status of their order?"

What the hell is a customer portal? "If you mean online order status checking, we have some of that in place already. But that's on the business-to-business side. We're not going to do it in sleigh ops. We have a different image there. In sleigh ops, a child makes a request, then waits until Christmas, when the request is magically granted. What would happen if kids could track their orders? Where would the mystery be? You might has well not have Santa anymore, just turn everything over to operations and distribution."

Why are some of them smirking?

A sharp clang!, and all JEDI heads turned. Halter tilted his chin and sighed lightly. "Tracer? You all right?"

"Yeah, sorry." Tracer repositioned his hard hat. "I was trying to get a better look at the paint operations—"

"—and caught the steam pipe, by the sound of it. OK, the rest of you." Halter raised his voice. "Just remember that's why you have hard hats, so don't take 'em off for any reason. Let's continue."

They clanked along the metal catwalk, then down narrow stairs to the assembly floor. They moved through the guts of Train Assembly Operations, line upon line of toy traincars of every variety, engines and cars stop-actioning to the pickup points, O-Scales, HO's, woodens, miniatures, collections to match with tracks, singles to nest in special packages—a blizzard of wheels, windows, numbers, doors, rails, lights, couplers. Throughout the tour, Halter answered the general questions and deferred the train-specific ones, despite the usual distraction of JEDIs wandering where they shouldn't, and of Tracer forgetting how tall he was.

After Train Operations, the group crossed the open compound toward Central Recycling Services. Halter enjoyed taking JEDIs through the CRS Building, watching them discover just how much material moved through here, destined for reuse in the southern world: chipboard mountains, cardboard and foam packing pulled from inbound ops; thousands of glass bottles from commissary; huge hills of office waste paper. He stared at the pile, seeing memos, letters, meeting notes, schedules, analyses, draft copies, consultant reports, time studies, personal observations, misdirected copies, extra copies, spoiled copies, menus, mailings, proposals, computer listings, office humor, old timesheets, benchmarking recommendations—on and on, right down to the papers that subtly assassinated character, the notes that shaped lives by suggesting a high-profile project for this elf, a backwater for that elf; notes and memos that, if pulled from the pile, would describe the long line of internal battles, interdepartmental politics, starts and restarts and false starts, shadings and shapings of the operations, the stuff of the hive that lived beneath the NPI Annual Report. Whole lives were caught up here, elves who worked to live and those who lived to work, the ambitious, the groomed, the ignored and the discarded, jumbled alongside each other and jostled by the forklift tines. And behind all those mountains, somewhere, the high jingle of harness bells, the breath steaming white into the gloom, the keen on the wind—where were they?

"Excuse me!" He shook his head. More questions. He fielded these, then escorted the group from CRS to his comfort zone, the Doll Operations Buildings, their squat redbricked hulks contrasting the sleek recycling building.

Inside, Halter plunged them into the hum and hiss, sticking their noses into line upon line of dolls, straw to stuffed to plastic to porcelain, miniatures to full-sized, mass-produced to hand-finished. He gushed data of all kinds, operational controls, history, marketing facts, tradeoffs, line balancing decisions, risks, costs, returns, anecdotes. He pushed their flagging legs from station to station, punctuating his steady word-stream with returned waves to workers raising clips, tools, and paintbrushes. At times, he'd pause, letting the JEDIs soak up the feel of the place. He ignored any glazed eye, any stifled yawn.

Their last stop was Line One, Spinner's line, impressive in the way it integrated automation and fine tooling to produce mass-customized dolls that looked hand-done but weren't. Halter turned them loose to graze. He'd spotted Drover, his line super, and waved him over.

"How we doing?"

"Not too bad, boss. The usual stuff, nothing we can't handle."

They exchanged glances. "We *have* seen it all, haven't we?"

"Just about. This a JEDI gang?"

Halter nodded.

"How many you think will end up on the floor? After initial rotation, I mean."

"Hard to say. This is Winnow's bunch."

"Uh-oh. A favor?"

"Yeah. I'll get him back."

"Who's the tall one?"

Halter sighed. "That's Tracer. Drover, nothing livens up a JEDI tour like a half-elf."

"True. A youngster." Drover scratched his head. "I didn't know we had any left. Somebody must've snuck off."

Halter chuckled. "Well, there's the southern outposts, Umea, Archangel, and so on. We've got a few in the *kolkhozes*, too, part of the Russian Outreach Program."

"I heard they're going to start moving elves out all over the place. Part of the whole herd management thing. If that happens, we might see more Tracers."

"In about a hundred years. If they do that herd thing, would you go?"

"Sounds like a great opportunity. You first."

They both laughed. "You start using the new stuff, the WonderFinish?"

"Three days ago."

"How's it working out?"

"Too early to tell. You guys know that. I told Spinner yesterday." Drover drew his pager, checked the number, reholstered. "The really big kids must be interested in it."

"So am I. What's your impression so far? Even if it's too early.

"It's a real time saver. Once we get used to it, the guys won't want to go back."

"I've heard good things about it. What about handling?"

Drover hesitated. "Nothing that isn't in the docs already," he said. "We had one of the guys get a little too close to it, he got a little lightheaded, but that's it." He smiled, one side only. "We're being careful. But when the Christmas rush gets here, you won't be able to pry it out of their hands."

"So you'd keep it?"

"With the rush coming? Yes. Well, probably."

"Full bore?"

"I think so. Why? What's the fuss?"

"What if it was your family? Would you do it then?"

"Halter! Stop the inquisition already! It's a haz mat, that's all! Just like a bunch of others we use out here! What makes this one any different?"

He watched the dolls. "I don't know," he said at last. "There's a feeling with this one. Some of them, the lubricants and things, you know straight up what you're dealing with. And they're not mainline. You're not using them on every doll. And usually we get some report, some field stuff even, that says it's OK. This time, nothing. We had to fight to get hazards docs. The higher ups are pushing, but I think they're doing what they're told."

"Higher-ups? You're the head of the whole operation here. How much higher does this go?"

"EEC."

"Ah."

"I don't care. If it's not right, I'll pull it."

"And go up against *them*?" Drover shook his head. "You'd better do it quickly, before the guys get used to it."

"I know."

"Otherwise, you'll be all alone."

"I know that, too." Halter watched the elves busy at their stations. "But that's what they pay me for, to make the tough call. Keep a close eye on it, whatever you do."

"I will. Don't worry, I'll—" Drover's eyes darted to one end of the line. "And *you'd* better keep an eye on that big—Hey! Look out! *Hey*!"

Bang! A couple of heavy steel storage drums crashed to the floor and rolled down the line. Several elves scampered out of the way, and shouts erupted like popcorn. Belts, pulleys, stations and machinery screeched and clanked to a halt. The shouts filled the sudden silence. A repeating buzz told everyone in the plant that someone had thrown the Autostop.

Halter groaned, watching the commotion, JEDIs skittering toward him *en masse*. Then he saw the confused form towering over the tumult like a giraffe stuck in a bus station. "Tracer!" he shouted. "Get out of there!" The form lurched toward him.

"Who's the big dumb one?" one of the elves shouted.

Who, indeed? He hurried toward Tracer. *Where from, and why, and why me?* "What the hell happened this time?"

Tracer looked like a border collie that had lost its herd. "I didn't mean to do it. Some of the barrels looked as though they were going to fall down, so I—"

"So you made them fall down. Very helpful. Listen, Tracer, from now on, you—could you just—not touch anything? Or wander off? Or go places where there's overhanging—anything? Can you do that for me? And for right now, could you just—stand—right here? I've got the rest of the JEDIs around you, so if you could just stand in the middle, alright?"

"I'm sorry! I really am sorry!"

"I understand that. I know you're sorry. Some of us have a harder time than others with—with things. That's why we have to protect them." He was backing away now, trying to regroup with Drover. The buzzer stopped, and the line whirred and clanked to life.

"But I—" Tracer raised one hand to apologize and smacked a JEDI on the way up. "Sorry."

"No, that's—it's all right." He stiffarmed in midair. "Just—stay where you are, all right?" Tracer made yet another move. *I said!* "Stay!" Halter bellowed, then turned to find Drover. He heard one of the JEDI quietly say, "Woof, woof!" quickly followed by snickers and then a chorus of howls.

Drover emerged from the line, shaking his head. "Boy, he's a special one, isn't he?"

Halter shut his eyes briefly, trying to get the giraffe image out of his head. "Thank God the tour's over, and I can send them all to lunch."

"Don't you have to stay with them?"

"They're Winnow's, remember?"

"Winnow's! That's right! Boy, does he ever owe you!" Drover gestured toward Tracer. "Any idea where he'll be assigned?"

Halter winced. "With my luck, I'll get him."

"Couldn't he get an office job?"

"Not before initial rotation, which includes plant duty. You know the rules."

"Yeah, well one thing. If he ends up over here, it's any line but mine! Any line but mine!"

6.

Do I just walk in? Kelli paused outside Gardner's office. *No admin today.* She could hear Gardner on the phone, although she couldn't make out the words and didn't want to. Even though Gardner was a family friend, she still headed Employee Relations, an Executive Vice President.

I hope she'll understand. I wasn't prying. How do I present this? She remembered the hurried conversation with Runner, the food service elf. *And then Oiler bumped into us. Had he seen anything?* She averted her eyes from the admin's desk. *What if she thinks I'm just a snoop?*

A shadow. Gardner had come to the door, the cell phone still placed against her cheek. She looked Kelli over, very briefly, before waving her in.

Kelli sat down. Gardner eased into her richly-leathered chair. Those brilliant black eyes drilled into Kelli.

"I *told* him. Three times. He's got all these programs he wants to run, visions about how he's going to translate, sorry transform, our up-and-comers into the new leadership. Which is fine. But somebody's got to pay for it all, and that means a *real* vision, with objectives and goals and benefits and costs. Yeesh. Plus he's got a direct pipe into the board, with that consultant friend of his, who is it? Tweeki? Twacky? ...Well, whatever. And the programs! He's got all the new santas running around like they're going to save the world! They're launching ideas, projects, all kinds of stuff, with money from who knows where, and meanwhile I've got systems that can't tell me how many santas we have, who's been promoted, who's got what area.

"...I think they're doing a leadership program this month in Phoenix. Yeah, Phoenix! In August! Go figure. Maybe it's a weight loss thing, all that heat." She laughed. "So what university did he come from, anyway?" She sighed, frowning as she pushed a stray lock of dark, silver-highlighted hair back in line with its neatly-waved partners. "Well, didn't they have to do budgets *there*? Anyway, I'll talk to him. Do this. Have a chat with him, tell him you talked to me about all this. Tell him I'd like to have a detailed conversation with him about funding. F-u-n-d-i-n-g. Spell it if you have to." She chuckled. "Thanks. Bye."

She set the phone down in front of her and stared at it, shaking her head. Looking up, she smiled at Kelli, smoothed the long sleeves of her tailored dark blue dress.

"Problems?" Kelli asked.

"Operations. Loose cannon in one of my development areas. It's trivial, we'll solve it, but it burns up my time. Now. What's wrong?"

"Well—I—" The whole rehearsal, the whole here's-exactly-what-I-should-say-and-how-to-say-it package pitched forward and crashed into irretrievable pieces.

"Kelli. I know your family, your parents. I know *you*. You don't need to present to me. Something's wrong. Just tell me what it is."

"I don't know how to start this," she said, "because I don't want you to think that I—that what I was trying to do was—"

"Kelli. Just start. Take a deep breath and go."

"I—OK. I work for Silvertongue, and there's a lot of things he's involved in that I don't understand. He's always cutting deals, making calls. He works very hard, harder than just about anyone, but he always makes sure I go home on time, or nearly on time. So he's good to me. It makes this hard. But lately—" Gardner's narrowed stare didn't help. Where had her words gone? She shut her eyes. "He's had these closed door meetings, with Oiler and Groomer."

"Groomer. Go on."

She opened her eyes at that. "I know it's not unusual to have meetings like that, but you get a feeling of what's right and what might not be. And he was different with this. With other meetings, when they were over, he'd come out, ask for coffee. I don't know, he'd behave differently. So I had a feeling about this. When others came up and asked me things, the feeling got stronger."

"What others, Kelli?" Gardner's eyes stayed sharp.

"Well, I think they were from the union. They didn't say, but—"

"UEU. Figures. And they wanted what?"

"They wanted to know what was going on. I said I didn't know. They said they didn't believe me. I got mad, I said What do you expect me to do? If he doesn't give me any, doesn't tell me what's going on, am I supposed to just come out and ask? So I got to thinking who's using who, and for what? But then they said, Just let us know when he has another meeting, and we'll work with you. And I said Yes." Her voice caught.

"It's all right. They don't teach this stuff in school. Then what?"

"A while passed, and I noticed he had another meeting. I guessed it, because he put them on his calendar himself. I handle everything else, but not these. So I called them, and they said they'd take care of it. They'd send somebody up with the food order."

"Because of Groomer?"

She nodded.

"Pig. He'll kill himself. Everybody's told him. Maybe it's what he wants. So keep going. Did you set it up?"

She nodded, head bowed.

"It's all right."

"So this elf I didn't know, Runner, came up with the food cart. And when she came out, she told me to walk with her. And she told me that they were putting together something big. It was ugly. They were talking about some merger. They had these numbers, they were going to sell off the herds. And some other stuff, too. I don't—I can't remember it all. Because right when she was talking to me, Oiler came around the corner and almost ran us over. I don't know if he saw us, I don't think so. But I got scared. And I can't remember anything else Runner said. Running into Oiler knocked it out of my head." The worst of it was out in the open. "...So was I wrong?" she said, trying to keep the tremble out of her voice.

For the first time, Gardner hinted a smile. "Oh, I don't know," she said. "A merger, a selloff. Pretty standard stuff, these days. What do you think? Should you have done what you did?"

Kelli didn't answer.

"It's hard to figure out what's right," Gardner continued. "Take the long view. In the end, what works for the business?"

Kelli shook her head. "Maybe I didn't think it through. Maybe this is the right thing, and they have to meet like this to make it work. But shouldn't it feel right?"

"It should." Gardner crossed her office to her bookshelf. She caressed the spines, fingers bumping titles describing organization behavior, employee rights, motivation, hiring and firing, legal themes, industrial relations, personality studies, how-to's on recruiting, interviewing, persuasion, negotiation, dealing with difficult people, consensus building, icon establishment, cultural overthrow, change management. She extracted a small red book and placed it on the desk. "This is what you've landed in." She sat down.

Kelli read the title aloud. "*Stupid Stew: A Primer on Politics and Peregrinations Inside Large Corporations.*" Her eyes met Gardner's.

"Exactly. Stupid stew. It's a mess. At the top, we think we've got a handle on things. Meanwhile, the workforce is demoralized, there's politics and intrigue everywhere, hidden agendas, political executions. It's a wonder we get any product out the door at all. And now you're in it. Take the book, it's good reading. It'll give you practical advice. Survival training. Things to keep you from getting killed here. Things up to now you haven't had to learn." She picked up the phone, her eyes still on Kelli, and punched a single speed-dial number.

Kelli riffled the book's pages. She opened to a page, letting the words take her where they would. She barely heard Gardner's voice in the background.

"Hi, who's this? Ah, Peanut, OK. This is Gardner. Is he in? Thanks. ...Silvertongue?"

Kelli's head jerked up.

"It's Gardner. Anyone in the office? OK, close the door. ...Thanks. I've got some bad news for you. It's your admin. Kelli, right. We received a report that she'd been, well, looking into things

I'm afraid. No, I'm quite certain, we followed it up carefully, just as we always do."

Gardner studied Kelli, who had begun shaking. "...I verified the report, and I took immediate action. Yes. Yes, as of today, terminated. Sorry. ...What? No, it didn't specify what she saw, or copied, or where she sent the information. We'll keep looking. You'll have to make do with Peanut for now. ...I *know* it's a shock, you'd think with the screenings we do, I—Yes. Yes, you can be certain we'll be reviewing that policy." With her free hand, Gardner took the box of tissues near her PC and offered it to Kelli. "As of today. I'm calling a meeting on it. ...No, you needn't be present. ...She's already gone. Sorry, but I had to, given the situation. Of course we interrogated, what do you think? That never gets you anywhere, not with the smart ones. ...We'll keep an eye on her. OK. OK, good luck." She put down the phone. "We don't have much time."

On her third tissue by now, she didn't grasp what Gardner was saying. "I—I—why?" she choked out. "I came to you!"

Gardner regarded her a moment, black eyes narrowed. "Yes." She leaned forward. "Keep the book. Now, listen. I'm sorry about your job. But this is about trust. Me trusting you, especially, but you trusting me, too. Hold on." The phone went to the ear again, free hand to the Rolodex. She stabbed the buttons. "Hello, this is Gardner. ...Yes, *the* Gardner." The barest hint of a smile. "I'm sending someone down to you, who's authorized to pick up a laptop and a cell. ...No, there's no order. I'm sure you have some extras. Or I'm sure your boss is sure. I want the best. Communications package, network access, the whole bit. They should go on my personal department charge. That's correct. Emergency requisition. Reason? Confidential. ...All right, but don't write it down. Procurement is for someone who will be responsible for keeping tabs on a very high security risk individual that I personally terminated today. Personally and high security. Write whatever you need to on the order, except for that. Good. And they will be ready when? Immediately? Good."

She put the phone down again. "Congratulations," she said, "you're now in charge of tracking yourself."

Kelli struggled to understand. "I—what are you doing?"

"One more call. This one'll be interesting." Again the Rolodex, again stabbing buttons. "Distribution? Is Router in? This is Gardner. ...Yes, I'll wait, but I need him quickly." To Kelli, she said, "I'll explain in a minute," during the pause. "Router! How are you doing? ...Of course, aren't we all!" She laughed. "Listen, Router, I need to call in a favor. ...Yeah, I know, how many is it this month! I need you to find me a spot on a plane heading to our Gothenburg operations. Yes. Not for me. This is highly sensitive. No, I don't want the jet. That's too visible. What can you tell me about commercials? Or do we have a shipment? ...No, I need it right away. Yeah, it's a special assignment. A monitor. ...I can't go into it, Router, you just have to trust me. ...I'd prefer some comfort, I'm not shipping a pet!" A chuckle. "How soon? Half an hour? OK. Will it be one of ours? Perfect! Call me back!"

She set the phone down again, smiling. "OK. Explanation. Here's the drill. I don't trust those three schemers for a lot of reasons. Especially Groomer. So Oiler bumping into you and that Food Service elf, the UEU plant, has me worried. You're in a dangerous position, and I need to get you out of it. Best way is to fire you. While I'm at it, plant a seed in Silvertongue's mind that his little information empire isn't quite as secure as he thinks. Now you need to go. You're fired, but you're actually on assignment. That's what the laptop and the phone are for. I know, this has got to sound confusing, and you must be thinking what about your character and reputation. Leave those to me. That's the trust part."

"But you believe me."

"I believe *in* you. And I'll make that stick, against any rumor mill. But you have to trust me, and go to Gothenburg, with your laptop and your phone. Yes, *your* laptop, *your* phone. Who did you think they were for? You can't be connected to NPI, but you can work through our Swedish supply base. I know some people in Gothenburg. I'll set it up."

"But what'll I do in Gothenburg, with a laptop and phone? I'm just an admin."

"I don't want to hear that. You had enough guts to come to me, and enough savvy to deal with the UEU and a pretty dangerous boss. They don't teach that anywhere. When I do find it, it's not usually connected with good character. So do more of what you did. Keep your eyes and ears open, and stay connected with the laptop and the phone. We've got a lot of traffic that goes through Sweden, especially herd traffic, and I'll need to know if anything changes. Changes numbers, changes frequency, changes direction. I'll put you in touch with the right people."

"So I work with these people, and I, and I call you back?"

"No. Don't use the phone to call here. Work through the people I connect you with. If the situation calls for it, we'll set up a meeting. It might not be me, it might be somebody in ops or strategy. I'll be working that out." The phone leapt to life. "Gardner. ...That was quick, Router! When does the flight leave? Two hours! Great! Now, do me a favor. Get a room at the main hotel downtown, the one by the Poseidon fountain. That's the one. Extended stay. Start with a month, we'll play it by ear after that. I owe you." The black eyes drilled into Kelli once again.

"Two hours!" Kelli exclaimed. "How will I—"

"Here's what you do. Don't worry about clothes or anything else. I'll get some things shipped out. You pick up your laptop, your phone, and you get on that plane. When you get to Gothenburg, someone will meet you at the airport and get you to the hotel. Because of your size, you'll need to be this person's kid until you get in the room. After that, it'll be all right. We'll handle any problems with the hotel management ahead of time. They're Swedes, they keep to themselves."

Kelli shook her head.

"I know. You're stunned. But we need to move quickly. Just get your things and go. First stop is network support. You know where that is? OK. Get your equipment, and go to the travel door, the one where you send Silvertongue on business. Trust me. Once you get to Gothenburg, you'll be with people you can count on."

Kelli stood up on wobbly legs. "What about my things, my desk?"

"I'll send somebody around. If Silvertongue hasn't trashed it already. Hope you didn't have anything personal there. I'm sorry about that." Gardner rose and, circling around from behind her desk, held out her hand.

Kelli shook Gardner's hand, feeling strength passing from those long fingers to hers. "I'll do my best," she said.

"All I ask," Gardner said. "And more than enough, I hope. Good luck."

Kelli turned, stepping from Gardner's office into a changed world. Her head swam. Fired but not fired. Accused but trusted. Her mother had once told her that a ten-minute meeting with an executive could change your life. Now she knew.

7.

One big hand thumped the desk; sharp blue eyes peered over half-glasses. The curly white beard trembled.

Bridle wilted. Those weren't good signs. That was the problem with accounting: you never knew which number these guys would discover next.

"Bridle."

How could hearing your own name make you jump? "Yes sir."

"This Training number here, does it include SDP?"

"Santa Diversity Program? No, that's under Special Programs, lower down. It's combined with Outreach, Herd Motivation Initiative, those things. If you need a split out, it's on—"

"How do I know how much of this is SDP?"

"—page two," Bridle finished weakly, then started up again. "It's on page two, halfway down."

Santa flipped the page. "Three and a half million. Three and a half *million* Santeans to recruit santas of color, santas of race, santas of gender, santas of age, santas of creed. You know what I just found out, Bridle?"

Now what?

"We're managing workflow fluctuations with agency. Agency santas! A budget maneuver, and it just skyrocketed! Do you know what agency santas are like, Bridle? Do you?"

How the hell should I know? "No sir."

"They're all Asians! Indians and Chinese! So while we're spending all this money trying to bring the 'right' santas through the *front* door, we're letting in whole busloads of them through the *back*!"

Bridle winced. This might get ugly.

Instead, Santa put the report down, folded his arms and hunched over the desk, lowering his voice. "You know, I really should stop doing this MBWA, this Management By Walking Around. I barged in on one of the meetings this morning, new santa training, you know, Phase One Graduation, where they get the red suits for the first time. And you know what? It was an agency group! A bunch of Indians! They're all so damn skinny! Suits hanging off of 'em loose, little brown hands dangling out of the sleeves. Then one of them, I swear to God, this guy says—" Santa straightened up, imitating "—*'Scoose me, Santa. Meddy Cdismus!*" He stood up. "Meddy Cdismus!" he roared. "I'm spending three and a half million at the *front* door, and I'm getting 'Meddy Cdismus' out the *back*!" He broke into a low chuckle. "'Meddy Cdismus,' sheesh!" The chuckle swelled into a long, rolling laugh.

Bridle smiled tightly.

"Ah, me!" Santa gasped, sitting down again. "I know that wasn't 'politically correct,' but what the hell." A final chuckle rumbled out. "I'm going to have to shut that agency loophole down. Send 'em all packing. Go on, Bridle, get out of here." He waved his hand. "But get Roxy, would you? I need to go over the New Orleans trip with her."

Bridle jumped down, took his usual running start for the door, slammed through a bit too hard, and held fast to the handle. He clutched his binder with his free hand, but his pen shot out and hit the far wall, adding its mark to several others'.

Roxy whistled, long and low. "That was pretty good," she murmured. "Was that planned? ...Oh, Bridle, I'm sorry!" she exclaimed.

He straightened up and arranged his suit. "He wants to see you in there," he said, looking for his pen. "It's about the trip."

She hurried around her desk. "Sometimes I can say such wrong things," she said. "...Are you all right?"

"Of course." Bridle smiled, thin-lipped. "I've never figured out how to manage that door."

"Oh, Bridle," Roxy repeated. "I'd talk to him about it, but it won't do any good." She hugged him, momentarily nestling his face against her chest, then brushed imaginary dust from him. "You're such a sweet little guy," she said, bending over her desk to fetch a steno pad and a fat envelope. "See you later." She opened the door easily and swished in, leaving Bridle breathless.

She stood at his desk, waiting for him to finish reading. *There's that frown again.*

He glanced up. "You've got the itinerary?"

"Right here."

"An SSC." He sliced open the trip packet. "I always forget what that stands for."

"Santa Support Convention," she said. "I've heard it called the Santa Supper Club."

"Hah." He scanned the itinerary. An eyebrow went up. "Nonstop commercial! What happened to the company plane?"

"They said it needed emergency repairs."

"What emergency?"

"I don't know. It came up right while I was making the arrangements. Somebody must have found something. They knew you had the trip coming up, so they got a high-level authorization. Oiler signed it, I think. It must have been serious."

"Well, I'll look into it when I get back," he said. "So a cargo with a few first-class seats, probably." He peered at the page. "Yeah. Seats in the front." He slapped the paper down and stretched. "Boy, that's going to be a long flight." His eyes wandered over the desk, taking in pen holder, water carafe, crystal glasses, Mrs. Claus, papers, and finally, a slim red notebook. He picked it up. "Let's see…" The pages snapped under his wide hands. "Ah, good, nobody from Carnegie this time. The last one, all those santas blubbering about their past experiences, yeesh. I'm on at the end?"

Roxy nodded again. "Same speech?"

"Why not? There's only so many ways to motivate."

"Won't they know?"

"They would if they're repeats, but they're not. This convention is for the Phase Two grads, the santas that have completed sleigh management and flight training. They're heading into their first Christmas runs this winter. So they're pretty pumped-up, but they're pretty nervous, too. They've heard the weather balloon story, and they don't want to go down in history like that. I give them a speech on how important their job is, but I also tell them I realize they're green." He stifled a yawn. "Sorry. You're coming on this trip, right?"

She nearly dropped her pen. "What?"

"You don't want to? I realize it's New Orleans, and August, and hot as hell."

"...I—I don't know, I guess I'm just surprised."

"Roxy. Don't you remember the last convention? Above and beyond the Carnegie blubberfest."

A half smile lifted one ruby-lipped side of her mouth. "I remember you were on the phone a lot when you got back. Firing folks, if I recall."

Santa chuckled. "I didn't *fire* them, I *reassigned* them. They may have decided to fire themselves after that, for all I know. Serves 'em right. All that confusion, and I'm up there in the wrong place in the program, and the teleprompter's messed up, the room is too hot, too small, they couldn't find extra chairs. They couldn't find the manager for the longest time, and when they finally found him, he was speaking a language nobody understood, not even him. Some little Greek-Italian guy, curly hair, glasses, mustache, going on and on about stuff, all talk, no action. Babbling. Just babbling."

Despite herself, she started giggling.

"Then they took us to another room for the evening reception, and that room was hot, too, even hotter than the first one. They had this big ice sculpture centerpiece, you know, the type that keeps the shrimp cool. It was carved like a big sleigh, and it was on those skinny ice runners, and they melted through, and the whole doggone thing came crashing down on the shrimp trays and sent shrimp and cocktail sauce flying everywhere. I had santas that looked like they'd been in a war zone, and these other santas that ended up wearing the damn shrimp like they were hair ornaments or lapel pins. And the stink! I mean, when the shrimp got hot, and everybody stepping on them and sliding all over the place and—You find this amusing, don't you?"

She gave way completely then, setting her laptop on a corner of Santa's desk and fumbling for a tissue to dab her eyes and avert a mascara disaster.

Santa waited a moment, smiling. "I guess it *is* pretty funny, when you think about it," he went on, "but at the time it was miserable. So if you ask me whether I'd want to go through *that* again, I'd have to say, no thanks."

She composed herself.

"That's why I need your level head there," Santa continued. "Stuff goes wrong all the time. It's the way you handle it that makes the difference. That's why you've been in charge this time. Didn't you wonder?"

"I thought I was filling in for the ones you reassigned." She shifted position. "What if I mess up?"

"How could you possibly mess up worse than they did? C'mon, Roxy, I've gone through an admin or two in the last few hundred years. You have it over the rest of them, far and away, when it comes to keeping me organized. I really doubt I'm going to have to worry about a melting sleigh with you. I can trust you to keep things on track." The blue eyes steeled just a bit. "And if something goes wrong, I can count on you to do whatever it takes to get it fixed."

"But still—it might not—"

"What?"

She shifted again, pulling down her skirt. His eyes followed the motion absently.

"It might not work?" he finished. "It might not get fixed? I've got plenty of confidence in you, Roxy. If a way can be found to make it work, you'll find it. Enough about the trip." He waved his hand. "There's more."

"Such as?"

"The Argentine government. They're pushing back on Silvertongue's offer. I'll have to talk to him about it." He stood, stretched, and faced the curtained wall behind him. "And there's the new operations statistics, volume projections for the Christmas rampup. We need to increase capacity and somehow not let quality go to hell. I need to meet with the ops heads. I need to get their input on how things are going, before it starts getting crazy."

"Operations? Doesn't the EEC handle that?"

"I don't want 'em, I want to go direct. Talk It Up isn't working. The EEC Report isn't the way to get at it, either. So I want a meeting with the ops guys, then a Page Four review with Oiler, 'cause there's a Board Meeting right after we get back from New Orleans. Oh, and a Central Team Readiness Review."

"CT Readiness Review?"

"Right."

"Isn't it early?"

"Not if they're off their feed or having any other kinds of problems. It takes time to build their strength back up, especially if they get some kind of illness that runs through the stalls, knocks them all down. They had a stomach bloat problem of some sort last year, damn near grounded them all. Bad forage of some kind, we think, but we never did figure it out. I don't want that sneaking up. So if I have to do two reviews, one now and another later on, that's what I'm going to do."

"Um."

"Yeah?"

"Do you think you'll be flying this year? ...It's been a while."

He stared at the curtains, and she glimpsed it: black cold starred night, breath on the wind, toys, ribbons, sleigh creaking and groaning under the weight, crack of runners releasing, lift and glide, ice mists whirling past, his team one beast harnessed to his will, hooves eating air, sky, ground and trees backdropping his shouts.

He sighed. "Not this year." He turned around and plunked down. "Too much going on. Besides—" his eyes twinkled "—it's a big class this year. I don't want to bump into anybody. *That* would start a new legend, for sure."

She smiled, stood up. "OK. But some of the folks would sure like to see you fly again. I know I would."

"One of these years. That's the thing about being several thousand years old, Roxy, you've got time on your side. A few years here or there won't matter."

“I suppose.” She picked up the laptop. “I’ll get going on the schedule.”

“Thanks.” She turned and left the office. “Besides,” she heard him mutter before she shut the door, “there’s nothing to come home to, anyway.”

8.

Halter stared at his computer screen for a moment before shutting his eyes and rubbing them. *E-mail sucks. It's slow, it gives me eyestrain, I delete things and the system doesn't believe me, it stores them someplace else, I run out of space—* eyes opened and returned to his inbox *—junk shows up on my calendar, and I have no idea what it is or how it got there—* (click-click-click)*—meeting notices disappear, and I miss meetings, look at all this crap...here's a notice on benefits, file it...new website on web-based training, come back to that one...one from GALE Association, wonder what—* (click) *—whoops! Gay And Lesbian Elves Association, how did they get away with* that *picture—*(click)*—notice on upcoming ops management seminar—forward to Spinner...uh, oh, here's a joke on GALE winds blowing, somebody's not being politically correct, but it's funny, better shred and...new piece here... hmm. Operations Review Meeting.* (Click.) *Must be from the EEC and—No, from the Chief. Add—to—calendar. There.*

His desk phone rang softly. He had a cell phone, but he'd let the batteries run down again. "Operations, Halter."

"Thanks a bunch, buddy!" Winnow's voice bellowed.

"What for?" He flinched and held the receiver several inches from his ear.

"That new JEDI you sent me!" the receiver barked. "What a charmer!"

This will be fun. "Let's see...not the little guy, not Brandon—these new names, where do they get them—so it must be, hmm..."

"You know damn well who it is! Tracer! Tracer the Terrorist! That's what my guys call him."

Halter smiled. " I didn't send him to you, the JEDI schedulers do that."

"So? They have another name for him, TTT."

"TTT? Who calls him that?"

"My guys. Tracer the Towering Turd. They can get pretty nasty. And he's a tall one, too, even for a half-elf! What's he on, growth hormones?"

Halter started laughing. "Maybe you're not used to seeing one in your shop, Winnow. I'm still stuck on TTT. What'd he do to deserve that?"

"Boy, you name it!" (If a telephone receiver could roll its eyes, this one did.) "From Day One. I'll give you some credit, Halter, you warned me to keep an eye on him. I put him on the snap-train line. I figure, that's fairly safe, some automation, some manual, not a whole lot going on, what could possibly go wrong? But nooo, first thing he does, maybe an hour into the shift, he tips a boxload of snaps onto the conveyer belt, they get into the machinery, and it's AutoStop time! Those snaps can go everywhere! So we put a couple of elves to work pulling them out of all the nooks and crannies, and by the time we're done, we've lost half a shift! So I figure, I better get him out of there for his own good, 'cause I can see the look on some of my guys' faces.

"So I call the line supers over, and we talk a minute, and I can see how enthused they are about this whole thing, so I end up having them draw straws. That sends him to the metal line, the O scale stuff, and things go okay for a couple of days, with my guys keeping close tabs on him. Then I don't know, somebody fell asleep for a split second, and he's wandered off to the paint area, looking at the Automix controls. Well, we're running primaries that day, so there's no need to mix, just pure red, blue, yellow. Naturally his big fat elbow catches the Automix lever, before anybody can stop him, and bingo! We have a couple of nice purplish-brown train sets! Plus the paint feeds and nozzles are all screwed up, so we have to shut down the paint area while we clean up the mess! And that backs up the line, which sends my guys over the edge, because the new piece-rate incentives have them losing money whenever the line shuts down. So they're ready to kill him, and I have to get him out of there in a hurry!"

Halter tried not to laugh. "Sounds like a repeat of what happened with me when I had him last week. I put him on the plastic doll line, nothing special, and he hit a box with one of those elbows of his and sent a few thousand plastic eyeballs everywhere. You know what it's going to be like going up before the Union Safety Board with reports of elves slipping on plastic eyeballs?"

"He's a killer on stilts, I tell you," the receiver squawked.

"So what did you do?"

"I haven't had to do this for a long time. I told the JEDI schedulers to get him the hell out of there. You know what it's like when you raise a JEDI protest, you're seen as intolerant, not mentoring, the whole damn bit. But when I shared the production loss figures with them, and the fact that he was likely to be killed if he stayed where he was, they agreed to move him."

"To where?"

"They sent him to the Central Stables. Fine with me. Let him lug feed around for a while, crack his head on a couple of stall doors. Maybe it'll knock some sense into him."

"Sounds like banishment."

"He wanted to go. At lunch, that's all he'd talk about. He was gung-ho on the deer. So maybe it'll work out in a way. Either that, or they'll have to get him a job changing ceiling lights or something."

Halter chuckled. "Well, our mutual cross is gone. Hey, different topic. Did you get a notice for an Ops Review Meeting?"

"Sure did. Seems a little early this year. I wonder if the EEC has something new."

"It's not the EEC this time, it's the Chief."

"What?"

"Check your email. The chief sent the notice, and none of the EEC are invited, not even Oiler, who usually sets it up."

"...You're right. Huh. Maybe it's a special meeting. It's—what? Three days out? I'll have to juggle my calendar! Maybe it's about the new efficiency numbers. I got a six percent target. You?"

Halter frowned. "I must be special, I got twelve."

"*Twelve*? You're joking!"

"And a five percent output increase."

"No way! Cut twelve percent in ops costs, *and* increase output by five? You sure?"

"I got the usual letter. Oiler signed it, same as always."

"Did you talk to him?"

"Not yet. I left a couple of voice mails."

"Put it in writing. I would. Otherwise, they'll figure you just accepted it."

"I'd rather talk it out with him."

"Well, you have your style, I have mine. But I wouldn't let it go. Sounds like a mistake to me."

"...I wonder. Oiler's on the EEC. Maybe this has to do with WonderFinish."

"With what?"

"You remember, the finish I talked about last time. The stuff I don't trust."

"You mean the windmill. Be careful. Oiler may have started that windmill up on you."

"Maybe. More likely, they're forcing me to use WonderFinish to make the numbers. Among other things." He stared at his email, seeing instead a stream of operations figures that wouldn't slow down. Something was wrong. "I'll have Spinner help out."

"...The rumor mill's been pretty busy lately. What have you heard about merger talks? There's a buzz going up and down the line."

"There's always a buzz. But I agree it's louder than usual. There's the High Holly thing, but that's an acquisition, not a merger, and the Chief's been pretty public about it. That shouldn't have started any rumors."

"Right. This is different. It's bigger, and it's real quiet. Things are happening on other lines. Experimentation. There's work going on in Candy and Confections, from what I hear."

"That's Tinker's area, a new line. They haven't done much in the past. Are they ramping up?"

"Don't really know. The guys'll find out. Something's going on there. And something's going on with the herds, too. There's a bunch of them on the move."

"But that happens this time every year. The usual repositioning and rebalancing, pairing them up with the new grads. What's so unusual about that?"

"The volume. Direction, too. Way too many of them are heading back here. That's the word on the line, anyway."

"Heading back here," Halter murmured. "I wonder where we'll put 'em all."

"Let the stable guys figure it out. Let Tracer. If they don't trample him to death, or he doesn't pull a bunch of feed bags down on himself."

Halter chuckled, his eyes straying to the phone, where the red Call Waiting light had begun flashing. "Winnow, hang on a minute, I've got a call coming in, let me just—" He had already cut over to the incoming call, because the display told him it was Spinner, calling from the line. "Halter here. What?"

Above her taut voice he could hear shouts and voices that made his skin tingle. "You'd better get down here, boss," she said. "There's been a spill."

"What is it?"

"WonderFinish. One of the elves involved in transport—he had a bunch of it on a forklift, and there was a near-miss, he had to stop—"

"How much of it fell off the lift?"

"Three barrels. Two held, but the third—" Her voice caught. "I—we've got a couple of elves down, a couple more shaky, they're locking down the area and—"

"Stay on it, I'm on my way." He switched to Winnow. "I've got to go," he said, "there's been an accident. That damned WonderFinish. I'm pulling it, Winnow."

"Accident! How bad?"

"Bad enough. It knocked down a couple of my guys, a couple more are wobbly, and —It's coming off right now. I don't care. I should have pulled that crap long ago!"

"Halter! Take it easy! Handle the accident first, then figure it out. You want help?"

"Winnow, you don't need this. I'll call if I need you."

"But—"

"I'll *call* you. I'm going in front of them, next meeting. I don't care. They can't shove this down my throat this way, I'll, I'll shut things down, I'll—" He slammed down the phone, chest and gut pumping. He paced back and forth, twice, stiffly, arms rigid at his sides, then rushed toward the door. *It'll be the UEU and everything, too.*

He flew past Jenny, whose shocked "What's the matter?" landed behind him, other elves diving out of his way. He lurched along, eyes locked in a fierce stare, heels pounding the soft carpet, and he wishing each pound would drive home into their smiles and their casual, cultured calculations that this was real, this was what costing and recosting and shareholder valuing and all the rest did, two elves down, the families, the union, all of it swirling as he burst through the exit and into the open yard, sprinting toward Doll Assembly A, his heart thudding *Pull it all. Pull it all. Pull it all.*

9.

Beyond the end of the line there was still farther to go. Tracer groaned, tried yet again to stretch his legs. All during the train ride, he'd been counting signposts marking the long northward journey, figuring that Marker 0 would be it. Instead, the narrow track snaked ahead into the woods. This toy train had certainly been sized for elves. How did the Chief ever make the trip, curled up like this?

The industrial complex had long ago melted into a succession of fields crisscrossed with mysterious roads, and the fields had yielded to woods and wilder pastures. The farther north the train puffed, the brighter the northern sun lit this emerald north-summer world. His gut twitched. *What if I'm not up to this, either?*

The JEDI graduate assigned to him paid him no mind. This task must have irritated her: take the big klutz to the stables, make sure he doesn't trash the train, hand him off to the stable foreman, anyone, just don't leave him alone.

"You'll always feel out of place," his mother had predicted, and even in his sourest adolescent moods he hadn't asked her "Then whatever possessed you to carry on with a human dad who stayed south so I wouldn't know who he was?" He was outsized and sterile in an elfin world without a dad with whom to commiserate on size problems, a standout with a foot each in elf and human societies. *The Chief at least has his magic. What do I have?*

Not to mention the fact that it was weird to have a mom who barely came up to your chest when she was trying to get you to see eye to eye.

The train creaked, clanked and hissed as the brakes were thrown and the cars ground to a halt. The JEDI grad with him returned from wherever she had been and said, "OK. Here we are, end of the line." She bounced off her seat.

Tracer struggled to unbend. "Who picks me up from here?"

"It'll either be the stable foreman or one of the senior hands," she said, following him to the car door. "It depends on how busy they are, but I'm not really familiar with their—Here, watch your head on the—door— " She winced. "You think you're going to need a bandage? Maybe there's a first aid kit in here somewhere."

Tracer righted himself and put a hand to his forehead, brought it down and examined the tiny spot of blood. He dropped his suitcase, yanked a handkerchief from his back pocket and jammed it under his hairline.

She jumped out after him. "You're all red," she said. "How bad is it?"

"I'm all right."

She looked closely at him. "Don't be upset. It's a small train, especially for you. You can't help it. Squat down and let me see it."

He did a deep knee-bend and pulled away the handkerchief. "I've been told that for so long," he said. " 'You can't help it.' I'm starting to believe it."

She examined his scalp. "Mostly an abrasion," she said, and her eyes met his. "It's—it should be all right, and they—should be able to help. At the stables."

He stood up and absently placed the handkerchief against the scrape. "They're not here yet. Isn't there supposed to be a wagon or something?" He looked around, the train hissing behind him. This was the end, after all. The track looped through the woods, so the train could make the return journey. The platform thrust into stony fields extending to hard, blue-hilled horizons. A narrow road paralleled the tracks a short distance before it plunged into the forest.

He took a deep breath, and with the infusion of cool air he sensed pine forest, high hills, snow, animals, clouds. "It's wonderful out here."

She took a sip of air herself. "It's pretty nice," she said. "I haven't really been able to get out, because the program keeps me busy. ...By the way, my name's April."

"Yes," he said distantly. "You told me when we first got on the train. But I'm glad you told me again," he added. "I'm terrible with names." He looked down at her, noted the golden shine of her hair. "What'll you be doing when you get back? What department are you in?"

"IT. I'm in Manufacturing Systems."

"Do you like it?"

"It's pretty interesting, there's a lot to do and a lot to learn."

"But do you like it?"

She hesitated. "Yes. On balance." She peered up the road, seeking the source of a rumbly-jingly sound. "I think the wagon's coming."

He watched the road. The rumbly-jingly sound sharpened into the crunch of wagon wheels over stone and packed earth and the tinkle of harness bells. Presently, rounding the bend in the road, an antlered creature swung into view, pulling a dark, shabby box on wheels. Though he'd seen reindeer before, in pictures and parades, the sight of this tired but determined beast, pulling a wagon sent just for him, filled him with a deep, unexplainable sensation. He sensed the coming days, images and flashes that rooted him and created in his core a foundation where none had existed. The antlered head bobbed with each step, and he stopped only when he realized he was nodding too. He jumbled the handkerchief into a back pocket.

The wagon approached steadily, an older elf perched in the driver's box. He drew the rickety thing alongside the platform and fixed Tracer with an up-and-down steel-gray look. "You must be Tracer," he grunted. "God even to you, Miss," he said to April.

"God also to you, Sir."

"Your mother teach you that, then," he said. "Good. Well, kid, shall we get going? Yes, you." White eyebrows gathered a bit. "Pick up your suitcase and swing it into the back and—Mind you don't take off the young lady's head with it!"

"Sorry." Tracer colored deeply again. "Thanks for taking me out here, April," he said. "Maybe I'll see you when I'm done here."

"You might," she said. "Take care of yourself and—You'll do fine here. Just fine," she finished. "Remember, I'm in IT, Manufacturing Systems. Stop by if you can."

He climbed onto the wagon, which listed to one side. "Trotter's going to have fun with this," the old elf muttered. He made a clucking sound and tapped the reins.

They bumped up the road toward the bend. "My name's Saddler," the old elf said.

Tracer turned for a last glimpse of the railroad platform, and was surprised to see April still standing there, watching them. He waved as they rounded the bend, and the tiny form waved back.

"Nice young elf," Saddler said. "Most have no clue what the old greetings are. Her mother must have taken the time with her. You made quite an impression on her."

"Me?"

"Sure. She was watching you watch me, come up the road."

"She probably couldn't get over my size," he groused. "Or the fact that I whacked my head getting off the train. The simplest things—"

"Is that how you got that brand mark up there?" Saddler flicked the reins, chuckling. "We all take our lumps around here. Especially at the stables, there's so many opportunities. Still, it's always worse when we're clumsy around the females, isn't it?"

"I'm clumsy everywhere."

"You'll get over it. You have to. Otherwise, the reindeer'll kick you to bits."

They bumped along. "How far away from NPI is this?"

"Far enough." Saddler looked sidelong at him. "You think it's exile, don't you?"

Tracer gazed at sun dappling the undergrowth. "Actually, I've been looking forward to it," he said. "Although I don't think I'm going to be very useful here."

"Every JEDI says that," Saddler said. "There's always useful work. Even if your back aches by the end of the day. I'm not saying you'll work the teams—still, you might apprentice, if you're so inclined. If you do well. Don't worry, you'll be busy. As a half-elf, you'll be in demand." His eyes twinkled. "But we can't let you play on our soccer teams."

"What?"

"You think all we do is muck stables? There's still time for fun. Even if this is the most important thing the Chief has."

"So what *will* I be doing?"

"You'll start off hauling feed, turning out forage, and—For the stabled teams, there's a mucking element, too, no getting around it."

"You think I might manage a team?"

"Not so fast! Although, in time..." Saddler studied the road. "You know, most JEDIs want to jump right into something important. What they say, anyway. Every job's important out here, because every job has to get done."

"I didn't say—"

" 'So where's the career path?' they complain. I tell them, 'No deer, no career!' "

"I didn't think—"

"Some JEDIs who come through here go quite far. We had a fat one once, what a troublemaker! Took a team out on his own, thought he could do everything, ended up bouncing right out of the sky. We thought he was a goner. He never tried that again. But he's made quite a name for himself in the organization. So I hear." Saddler snickered. "Were we glad to get rid of him. Always eating!"

"How long have you been working out here, Saddler?"

"Since the beginning. Most of us have. Call us crazy, but we all think this is the real operation, not those toy deals down there." Trotter snorted. "Yes, I know, girl, we're getting close, aren't we?"

"You never go down to the main offices?"

"Oh, sure. Seen a whole lot of operations, too—part of the enrichment programs over the years. Plus, we go down a few times a year for meetings. There's an important one coming up shortly, a Central Team Readiness Review. That's when we go over plans for the Christmas operations. And we get fairly busy this time of year, getting teams set up and balanced for the santas, especially the new ones." The road in front of them began to widen. "Ah, here we are, then."

The wagon swung round a last bend in the road. The woods melted away. Tracer stared. How far had they come?

They stopped at the edge of an immense expanse of pastures, tree-dotted hills, various clustered wooden buildings, and reindeer, herd upon herd—all lit by the long rays of the southering sun. The cool wind whispered under the hair by Tracer's ears, suggesting northern nights that would grow longer and longer as the year wheeled toward winter. Tiny antlered forms, singly and in pairs and teams, arced through deep, distant skies. Smoke curled from brown work buildings and disappeared into the high blue vault. Elves, dressed against the insistent breeze, carried buckets, tools, and paraphernalia as they moved about the clearing, going about a business ancient and important. A few of them caught sight of the wagon and waved.

Saddler waved back, and Tracer closed his mouth and waved shyly in turn.

"Welcome to the Old World, kid," Saddler said.

10.

Sometimes the food was all right, more often it wasn't. Today was a surprise, though: Louisiana crab cakes. Someone in the kitchen was experimenting. Gardner plunged a fork into one of the two plump cakes on her plate. All around her, the clinky sounds of elves eating, the hum of quiet conversations formed a calm counterpoint to her hectic day. At her elbow, the agenda for the upcoming EEC meeting stared up at her.

She enjoyed eating in the regular cafeteria, preferring the steady stream of elves and half-elves here to the muffled and political Executive Dining Room. You had to work much too hard to enjoy your food up there. Here, you could watch, go over the afternoon schedule, make eye contact with employees who didn't know who you were and what you did.

On crowded days, she shared her table with others, discovering through talk what was going on in the operations. If they ever figured out who she really was, would they think she was spying on them? That was the problem with being a VP: your motives belonged to the rumor mill.

She scanned the agenda. *WonderFinish. What's that about?* She reached for her iced tea.

"Hey, look who's into the crab cakes!"

She looked up. Tinker, head of Candy and Confections, grinned at her. "Mind if I sit down?"

"Not at all," she replied. "I didn't know you ate here."

"About once a week. When I'm not grabbing a sandwich or skipping." Tinker pulled up a chair. "How's the top lady in the company?"

She colored. They'd known each other forever, and had once worked side by side. But she'd moved on to leadership positions in manufacturing, marketing, product development. Then the Chief partnered her with Hammer in the critical early union negotiations, putting together the UEU. And now, the VP of ER. Tinker was an irrepressible flirt, and long ago she had appreciated it, but over the years she'd learned how Tinker prided himself on how he aligned to top execs, working himself into the middle of the quiet deals that turned the levers here. He enjoyed using his hoarded knowledge to advantage.

"Busy," she said. "Succession planning is coming up, along with incentive reviews. The Board's calling for transformational learning. Again."

"You sound cynical." Tinker attended to his cakes.

"I don't mean to. The idea's right. New web technologies give us a chance to transform how our folks learn. But I don't think the Board's interested."

"What about the Chief?"

"Lukewarm. He knows in his head what this means to the business, but he doesn't have it in his heart."

Tinker dabbed his mouth. "Sounds like he needs to see it working before he buys in."

"Probably." Her eyes strayed to the paper.

"What's up? You need to concentrate?"

"It's the EEC Agenda."

"Oh, *that*. Do what you need to do."

"You make it sound like the EEC doesn't matter."

"Not intended. But some of the ops guys would say so." Tinker lifted another forkful to his mouth and chewed, watching.

You little weasel. "Why do you say that? What's your opinion?"

Tinker swallowed, took a swish of ice water. "I'm neutral. But even though you didn't ask for a name, I'm going to give you one. Because he's mad enough that he doesn't care." He took another bite.

"Don't play, Tinker. What are you telling me?"

Tinker teased his lunch. "It's the guy in Casting, what's his name—"

"Stoker. You know. Cut it out. Stoker's a good guy. What made him so mad?"

"You refused to hear his case."

"What case?"

"He sent a case up for review, got it in front of you in time for your meeting. He's got a casting furnace that's on its last legs. He's afraid if it doesn't get some attention pretty soon, there'll be hell to pay."

"A furnace in Casting? I don't remember that." Gardner stabbed her second crab cake. "What kind of hell?"

"C'mon, Gardner, this is hot metal ops, fire, pressure, the whole bit. That thing goes, and it will literally be hell."

"Sounds like he should just take action on his own. Why's he coming to us?"

Tinker sighed. "Because the EEC just issued the efficiency figures, that's why. This unit's right in the middle of critical production for a number of the operations, Winnow's in Trains, Bender's in Small Toys, wherever the metal's needed. If we were slow, he could shift production, take the furnace down for a week or so, get the critical parts overhauled, put it back on line, and limp his way to the spring slowdown. But because of the efficiency targets and the rampup, there's no way he can do that right now without putting a dip in the other guys' production figures."

"So he came to us with a deviation request."

"Right."

"I didn't see any deviation request." Gardner put down her fork and reached into her blazer pocket. Out came the green cell phone. She punched a speed dial number. "Gardner. Is he in? Thanks."

"Who you calling?"

"Spokes," she mouthed.

"Finance? Why not Oiler?"

She glared at him. Spokes came on the line.

"Spokes, Gardner here. Listen, I just got some odd information. What do you remember about a deviation request for a furnace in Casting?

"Casting?" Spokes's raspy, no-nonsense voice buzzed in her ear. "Stoker's area?"

"Right. Anything?"

"...Nothing."

Her eyes searched Tinker's. "I didn't get anything either. And I'll bet Crafter didn't get anything. Or Router."

"You want me to go to them?"

"No. I know where this came from."

"Then I'll go to Oiler," Spokes said.

"No, I'll get it on the agenda. We'll see what happens. Do me a favor and get a hold of Stoker."

"OK, but the agenda's packed."

She took a sip of her iced tea, her frown deepening. "I don't give a *damn* what it does to the agenda, they can defer something, make an adjustment...No. *I'll* talk to Oiler. It's on the agenda. Period. The rest of it can wait."

"OK," Spokes said. "I'll get Stoker and make sure we have what we need."

"Thanks, Spokes, glad I can count on you. See you." She put the cell phone on the table, glanced at Tinker. "It's on. Spokes will talk to Stoker."

He whistled. "Just like that."

"Just like that. Hang on a minute." The phone went back to her ear. Another speed dial, this time to Oiler's office. "This is Gardner, is Oiler there?"

A bright admin voice answered. "He's in a meeting, can I have him call you?"

"No. Give him this message. On the EEC agenda, he is to put a deviation request review. For the casting furnace."

"Casting?"

"That's right. Tell him it's mandatory, agreed to by the EEC." She watched Tinker tease a morsel on his plate. "If he has to take something else off, that's his business. He can reach me if he needs to. I'll expect the agenda to be reissued today."

"Today."

"I know it makes a mess of things, but by close of business."

"Will do." The brightness had left the admin's voice.

"Thanks. Bye." She put the phone back in her pocket. "That ought to generate a little steam." She smiled grimly at Tinker.

"I don't ever want to be on your *bad* side," he said.

"Just be honest, and you won't." She pushed her plate aside and leaned forward, elbows on the table. "Now. What can you tell me about WonderFinish?"

His eyes widened. "Why the interest?"

"It's on the agenda." She rubbed her nose, rested her chin on one hand. "Why do we have a pre-agenda discussion at all? On one hand, we have a casting furnace that doesn't make it, and we know nothing about it. Then we have an oddball item that does get on the agenda, and we know nothing about that, either."

"*You* might not. Not yet. But the ops guys know all about it. It's Halter's area, and he brought it up at the Ops Review meeting we had a couple of days ago."

"Operations Review Meeting? The EEC holds those!"

"Not this one. The Chief called it. Oiler didn't even know, and he's madder than hell. But, *c'est la guerre.*" Tinker paused. "You don't look too happy, either."

"I guess I'm just surprised. Maybe I shouldn't be. Hard to know these days what's going to happen next. Anyway, you had this meeting."

"Right. The Chief kicked it off, asking how things were going. There was some talk about the usual stuff. Then Halter started up. He's got that dreamer reputation, and that's a strike against him. Personally, I think that's a bad rap—I think he just has a different style."

"I agree. But it does cause problems. WonderFinish is his?"

"Yeah. It is." Tinker looked at her quizzically. "I thought the EEC knew all about it, and the recommendation to use it came from you."

It did? She smiled. "You're right. I'm sure it did. What did he say?"

"Well. You know—" Tinker grimaced. "I think he had a case this time, I really do. But when he told his story, he was so mad he couldn't get his point across. He had an accident with this stuff, one of the drums split open, and it's got a nasty rep for F and F."

"Fumes and Flammability?"

"Uh-huh. A couple of his guys were overcome, and they had to close down an area while they cleaned up and aired it out. Turns out there were no fires, and the two elves that got hit were fine by the end of the day. But it wasn't enough for him. He pulled that stuff from all his lines—he kept saying that at the meeting. I guess he's under pressure to use it everywhere, it helps him meet his targets. Anyway, he ended up shaking his finger at the Chief and saying he was going to keep it off the lines."

She shook her head. "Sounds bad enough. What does the UEU think? Are they screaming?"

"Nope. They're low-key on the whole thing. Drover, the foreman over there, he's good friends with one of my guys, and he told my guy they understand it's a haz mat, and things like this happen. I think it's the incentive bonus. They're willing to take the risk to get the pay."

"Did that come out at the meeting?"

"Yeah. The Chief asked Halter point-blank, and you knew the truth would torpedo his case. But Halter didn't have the presence of mind to lie in a way that would come out as a misunderstanding, just in case the Chief got a hold of Hammer directly."

And you would have that presence of mind. "But the Chief isn't known for keeping something going if he thinks there's a serious safety issue. What did he decide?"

Tinker looked away. "You know, something's going on," he said softly. "I thought he'd side with Halter, despite the UEU. He knows Halter's head for the business. He knows his heart for the guys. But it's like he wasn't paying attention. He told Halter doll production was critical this year, and the answer wasn't pulling WonderFinish. He should revisit the safety procedures with the UEU. If the UEU made an official statement to pull it, then it would be pulled, but not until."

"That doesn't even sound like him," she murmured. "Poor Halter."

"You should have seen him. I think he turned gray. He just sat back down. He didn't say another word for the rest of the meeting."

"Wow. What about Stoker and his furnace?"

"He didn't even show up. Maybe there was a crisis, you know how it goes."

"I do. So why is WonderFinish still on our agenda?"

"Halter won't let it go. He wants to state his case on record."

"Even with the Chief's decision?"

"Even with the Chief's decision."

"How did you find that out?"

"Winnow. He and I talked yesterday. Winnow's becoming an unlikely bedfellow for Halter. I don't know why. But he's bothered by all this. He's a real practical guy, lots of innovation, down to earth, not political at all. This has him thinking."

"And you?" *And Hammer, for that matter. Where's he got the UEU on this?*

"...Me? Some. But I've got my own problems." He raised a challenging eyebrow. "I've got my own efficiency figures." He pushed back his chair and picked up his tray. "I enjoyed this, we should do it more often."

"Yes, perhaps," she said distantly, before her eyes refocused on him and she continued, "Next time I'd like to hear about your operation."

The plate wobbled. "Sure. Why?"

"I've got a sweet tooth." She chuckled, looking from the plate to his face. "I've got a special interest in candy."

"Next time, then." He smiled. "I'll bring you a box of something."

"Zero-cal," she said firmly.

He laughed and strolled off.

She watched him wander among the tables, pausing here and there to chat, a bird skimming the waters. What a sly one he was, playing his secret little alignment games. She picked up the agenda. *There'll be answers soon enough.*

11.

"Commissary." Groomer stuffed a fat pinky into one nostril. He turned and scraped, waiting. "Groomer here. The usual, six with everything. And an extra jar of mustard, that's a good kid, eh? ...Ten minutes? Great, thanks."

He stared at his smeared computer screen, not reading his email. He examined his pinky before idly sucking on it. Fat fingers drumming the desk, he stared at the phone and jumped when his wristwatch beeped.

He dropped his pen when the phone rang. It rolled off his desk and onto the floor, joining two others he couldn't reach. He swore softly, rummaged a replacement from his desk, and picked up on the third ring.

"Where were you?" a voice wheezed. "Didn't you want to take my call?"

"I dropped my pen."

"Or swallowed that hot dog. Whole." Coughing sounds.

"There's no hot dogs."

"Good. What's the status?"

"Changed. It's changed a bit. There was an accident in Doll Assembly."

"I heard. Isn't that what we wanted?"

"This wasn't planned. We don't have Hammer yet, so the Union's downplayed it. For the incentive pay, I think. That helps. But the Chief's involved."

At length, the receiver buzzed to life. "That *is* a complication, but not fatal. You must have thought this would be bad news. But you had no control over this one. Which happens in this business, more often than not." A dry cough. "As I see it, *Coun*sel, our options remain unchanged. It's actually easier this way. I don't see how you can engineer anything during the chaos, once we send the Chief on his extended trip. So you're better off delaying. Both your Casting and Assembly options remain open."

"I suppose so."

"Of course it's so. And if these options disappear, there will be others. Patience is as important as action."

"There's the Silvertongue problem."

"The admin? So she disappeared, somewhere south I imagine. We'll find her. I don't think she's the player you think she is. But we'll make sure. What have you been doing about it?"

"Besides trying to find her? Checking email logs, finding out what she might know. Which doesn't appear to be anything." He waited. "So that helps."

"She doesn't know. Or she's very good," the voice wheezed. "Or she's being coached. Hmm. On to business. How is RFS?"

"Most of the units have been tagged, and some are already in transit."

"Good. Don't worry about not moving fast enough. Somebody outside may be watching the traffic. We don't need additional attention. I've got the agreements lined up with the right people. All they need to see now is a demonstration of good faith from us. I assume you're using commercial cargo?"

"Yes."

"And they're heading where?"

"The safest post, the operations north of Umea."

"You're not flying them *in* to Umea, surely!"

"Just a few. Most are going through Stockholm and Gothenburg and being trucked up. This would be a hell of a lot easier if the damn things flew."

"And riskier. And more public. Eyes will be on us with the Chief out of the picture." The receiver wheezed and coughed again. "We can't afford to tamper with delivery yet. Remember, all in good time.

The master plan. Merge, restructure, temporary Board appointment, RFS selloff, UEU on the Board, ebusiness shift. That's plenty for starters. Then we can go after the original team. And my promotion."

"I thought we weren't hitting his team."

"We aren't. We're just moving them. We simply need to get them out of the way and get at what's under their feet."

"How much is down there?"

"Enough. It'll make the North Sea look like a fishing expedition. Other than building the pipelines, the operation will be a snap, compared to others. We'll have a low lift rate, which means if we care to, we can flood the world with our reserves. Not that we would. Our best card is to stay low-key and play the world market. We stand to gain very nicely, even with crude prices holding. Stupid humans."

"We haven't played on this playground before."

"I know. It'll be tricky. But we've got experts. The Americans fingered the location. They need all the oil they can get to keep those monster trucks going. Idiots."

"They say those stables are on consecrated ground."

A cough. "I know that. I worked them, well before your time. But things change. We're training herds to fly all over the world. Santas, too. None of those areas are 'consecrated.' When we're done, we can move his team back. If they're not too comfortable in their new home." Another cough. "But that's well into the future. After my promotion, which is after the UEU move, which is after the accident. What have you told Tweedledee and Tweedledum?"

Groomer grunted a chuckle. "One of them's CEO, the other, COO."

"I like that. You're only half lying, not bad for Counsel. Which one replaces me?"

"Silvertongue."

"Oiler's got the better operations head. And Silvertongue, I wonder." A spitting sound. "He's not been particularly effective with the Argentines. That's a small problem, a blip. Beneath a COO's consideration, except to crush."

"It's been a surprise, true. But Silvertongue has the depth. To say nothing of eloquence with the media. He'll solve the Argentine thing soon. When you're CEO, we can use Silvertongue to head things up and rely on Oiler to manage the day to day stuff."

"He won't be too disappointed?"

"I'll make sure he isn't. Or you will."

"Either way," the voice said easily. "Counsel, consider assigning Oiler one of our little diversions. In Assembly or Casting. A good character test. Now. Do either of them know about the last turn of the screw? The original team?"

"No way. Silvertongue said something about giving the old man his team back. And Oiler's worse. He could barely swallow the RFS business."

"Don't be too hard on them. We all have our soft spots. And it isn't such a bad idea to take care of the Chief. Some of us go back with him a long ways. We might momentarily wish he would keep up with the times and do the right things for his investors. But he won't. So I deal with the investors, and with people who will bring this company up to date. Despite our global reach, Counsel, we're a provincial multinational whose single focus our investors find increasingly inappropriate. You never want to hear the word 'inappropriate' tagged to your business strategy, Groomer. Does terrible things with your stock. Your personal portfolio, too. That's never good." The receiver wheezed laughter. "I don't need to tell you that. You're first-rate, Counsel. As I suppose you know. Let me know if anything else requires my attention. Especially the RFS situation. 'Bye now."

The receiver clicked, and Groomer almost dropped it. He took a tissue and wiped the sweat from forehead and phone.

A knock. *Food. That I could use.* "Come in!"

The door opened, and a Commissary elf wheeled in the packed cart.

"There you are, my beauties," he chortled. "Thanks."

The Commissary elf nodded, turned, and almost collided with Oiler, who sailed through the open door, a deep frown on his face.

"Now what?" Groomer muttered, lifting one of the messy dogs.

Oiler shut the door firmly behind the Commissary elf. "Trouble."

"What kind of trouble?"

"The casting furnace is back on the agenda."

The hot dog paused halfway. "I just finished telling —How the hell did that happen?"

"Gardner put it on." Oiler gave him an odd look.

"Oh, hell." Groomer took a savage bite. "Da only elf dat c'd pudiddere and ged away widid." A chili bean leapt onto his shirt.

"I know. She called me about the deviation request denial. She made it clear she didn't like it, and she insisted it go on. What could I do?"

Groomer swallowed. "You did the right thing. Beg your professional pardon, but she has more say with the ops guys than you do. I need to keep her away from the union, too. We have to get her commitment carefully. She's too damn honest." He took another bite. "I wudder whad she dowes," he burbled to himself.

"I don't know," Oiler said. "Anyway, now we've got the furnace and WonderFinish to contend with."

"I heard about the Ops Review. You're empire's crumbling."

"That was the Chief's idea! I can't control that!"

"You'd think he was running the place."

Oiler chuckled, then picked up a plastic knife.

Groomer's eyes widened, and his face contorted like a stricken parent. "What are you doing?"

"I just want half of one!" Oiler protested. "That would leave you with five and a half! Jeez!" He dropped the knife as Groomer, scowling, scooped up a second dog.

"I understand the Chief told Halter to put WonderFinish back on." Groomer prepared the dog for slaughter. "So it's easy."

"What is?"

"Dake WudderFiddish offa jedda!" Groomer hotdogged before performing his eye-popping swallow. "Why leave it on? You've got every political reason to get rid of it. Or defer it. Then let it come up again when the Chief's been removed. If anyone's still thinking about it." He paused. "We may lose the furnace."

"You figured the votes?"

Groomer nodded.

"Maybe we could talk to some of the others ahead of time."

"No deal. That's way too obvious. No, we just have to play it completely aboveboard, and if we lose, we lose. We have the other option."

"Even with the accident?"

"Uh-huh. Halter's sawing the limb he's out on. This time we control it, which means we'll get the UEU going. If Halter gets his hearing down the road, so be it. We can still make it happen later."

"I guess you're right."

"You know I'm right." Groomer belched, then gestured towards the tray. "Go ahead, help yourself. I'm watching my weight."

It took a second before they both burst out laughing.

12.

Kelli cranked open her hotel room window and leaned into the cool Scandinavian air. It was after eight, but the sun still hung low on the horizon. It would be some time before the sun set for a few hours. She peered down the seven stories to the street below. She'd been in the room a week before she'd first clambered onto the windowsill and opened the window. At times like this, she felt acutely her other-sizedness, her smallness.

Not to mention the events swirling around her. Gardner had taken care of her, of course; but Gardner was somewhere in the north. She was here.

First, there had been the discharge at the Gothenberg airport, a huge empty place, bruising her opinion based on televised images of Heathrow, O'Hare, and LAI. She'd wandered a bit, clutching her laptop case, until a sandy-haired man, taller than most, had stepped forward from the Fourex money exchange station and introduced himself: "Kelli? Anders. Please, you come with me."

How trusting she'd been. Anders could have been anyone, not just the tall Swede connected to Sverige Feed Supply, one of NPI's preferred suppliers.

When the hotel door closed that first day, she'd felt truly alone. Anders had provided her with some background materials in a binder. But it had all been a jumble of numbers, and she'd chosen sleep after less than an hour. That sharp knock late the first evening jolted her, but it was merely a clothes delivery, casual and business attire not her own but nicely tailored and fitting impeccably. Gardner didn't let details slip.

Over the next few days, she settled in, and the binder contents made more and more sense. She became an employee of Sverige Feed Supply, and she filed her expenses through them. She learned that Sverige was NPI's sole supplier of reindeer feed and special pharmaceuticals. Officially, she was Distribution Agent C, little more than a trainee, but as she became more familiar with the laptop, she discovered she had privileges well beyond any trainee's. She learned to tunnel into NPI via the Business to Business portal, using her laptop's analytical tools to construct detailed reports of NPI herd activities. The actual herd movements were difficult to trace, but she discovered she could construct a reasonably accurate picture by comparing Sverige's current sales patterns and shipping addresses to prior seasons.

Her information reinforced Gardner's suspicion: the herds were moving. Her heart jumped, but Anders cautioned her to strengthen her analysis: "You need to make sure these movements are different from what is normal this time of year," he told her over a secured cell call. "You see, there are movements among the herds in preparation for the holidays. Herd movements alone don't tell the whole story. Are they concentrating anywhere, you know, are they heading to one place only?"

So she'd fired up the laptop late last night, cutting the data yet again. The graphs didn't lie.

A light breeze played through her hair. She studied the Gothenburg skyline, watched people walk singly and in twos and little groups up the Kungsportsaveyn, the blue electric trains humming back and forth. She'd called Anders last night: "I've gone as far as I can. It points one way."

She checked her watch. Twenty past eight. Any minute now. She swung down from the window ledge, turned and struggled to refasten the windows. On the nearby worktable, the laptop screen glowed.

She used the bathroom, finished, and smoothed her clothes in the mirror, sweeping a couple of renegade auburn strands from her forehead. She filled a glass with water, took a couple of sips and pitched the rest. Back in the room , she sat at the worktable, rocking back and forth until she caught herself.

She jumped when her cell phone buzzed. "Hello."

"We're on the lift. Are we too early?"

"I'm fine," she said, forcing that damned tremble out of her voice.

Endless seconds later, a soft rap punched the silence. Them. Even so, she checked first. Standing on tiptoe and spying Anders through the peephole, she released the lock and opened the door.

He smiled shyly as he entered, the others trailing. "I know this must seem very unusual to you," he said. "We're sorry to intrude like this, but it's the best way."

Two of them arranged themselves around the table; the third, who was blonder than Anders, sat a bit sheepishly on the bed.

"Perhaps, introductions are in order." Anders rubbed his cheek.

The man on the bed spoke first. "Hi, I'm Bill Harris. Hardly a Swedish name, I know. I'm the shipping director for Sverige. An import from America." He smiled over bright blue eyes and extended his hand. She grasped it. So cold! Perhaps he wasn't used to Scandinavia.

The third man, a burly, friendly-looking sort with disheveled black hair going gray at the temples, smiled briefly, white teeth flashing under a massive duster of a moustache. "And I'm Mats Larsson," he rumbled amiably in a voice deeper than any she had ever heard. "Your CEO." He bowed but did not offer his hand.

Kelli bowed back, and in the brief silence that followed she felt keenly her otherness, even her vulnerability. These past several days, she'd been cast adrift in this sea of humans, with only the laptop as a friend. This meeting with three men unsettled her.

"What—what do you know about NPI operations?" she asked.

Anders and Mats glanced at each other. Bill broke the ice. "More than you might think. Let me try to make you a bit more comfortable. Sverige is considered an Inner Circle supplier to NPI. That means that, unlike the great majority of firms out there, Sverige and NPI have a nondisclosure agreement. We've signed an agreement swearing us to utter secrecy when dealing with NPI. We're all officers of Sverige, even if Anders forgot to tell you he's the COO. So we're the few who know. Not even Sverige employees know. They think NPI is just another major customer."

She nodded. More terms! More deals!

"Kelli." It was Mats this time, drawing her eyes to his oddly familiar face. "You must have learned, somewhere in your upbringing, that over the years there have been opportunities for humans and those from your culture to interact. We know you are an elf. So you must not worry about that. We also know that the head of your organization is one of the most marvelous creatures ever to breathe the air of this world. His life and the lives of so many of you extend back thousands of years, over the whole recorded history of humans. You see, the Swedes, maybe more than anybody else, have been in contact with you over these many years. Our northern peoples, the Sami, have tended the reindeer for centuries. They knew of you earliest of all. And in some happy cases, cultural barriers have been overthrown, and—well." He cleared his throat. "You see before you, then, three humans, Kelli, is that right?"

She nodded. "Right," she said. "Yes."

"No." Mats's dark eyes twinkled. "Two humans. One of us is a lot older."

"You are!"

"Not me. Anders!"

"He's lying, Kelli!"

"I wanted her to take longer to guess!" Mats said, grinning now.

"Well, *I'm* not," Bill said. "Notre Dame."

"What?" Kelli shook her head.

"Try to make sense, Bill," Mats rumbled. "So, Kelli. Two humans—and one old half-elf. All in—what's your word, Bill? The hoots?"

"*Ca*hoots. You'd think after a hundred years, Mats, you'd get the language down."

"*Ca*hoots. What you tell us here, we take to Gardner. She's asked us to take care of you. To make sure you stay safe. You will go home to NPI soon, you can be sure of it."

She struggled to hold her lips steady.

He looked at her kindly. "Never be ashamed of how you feel. Especially with what you've been through. If you need a minute, we will all understand."

She shook her head. "No, I'll—It's all right. Just a whirlwind."

"Yes. ...Do you want to go on then, and show us what you have?"

Kelli flicked away a stubborn tear. "Yes. Let's start." She touched the laptop—her old friend. The device whirred to life, and the image redrew itself on the screen.

"What you see," she began, "is a summary of the current herd positions worldwide. The mix has changed over the past couple of years, because of new operations. Most of these are in the southern hemisphere." She paused. "If this is too much detail, or it's stuff you know already, please tell me," she said. "I'm not used to this. I put it together based on things I used to do for..."

"Silvertongue. We know. You're doing fine." Bill got up off the bed and strolled up behind her. "Keep going."

"OK. Usually about this time of year, there are some herd movements, mostly heading to the northern areas. The fliers are going through a balancing program, where they're paired with the new santa recruits. I'm not sure how that works. There's also a group of reindeer I had a hard time getting information on, the nonflyers, R- R- "

"RFS. Reindeer Fatigue Syndrome," Anders said. "What did you find out?"

"They're not listed on the reports that show overall population. But then I looked at this year's figures, and here's what I found." She switched from one program to another, and a colorful graph presented itself. "There are several advanced training grounds up north," she said. "Three are on the north coast of Greenland. A couple more are around the Hudson Bay. One is starting up in the Aleutians, now that the Russian - American situation is better. There's the main operations in northern Sweden and Finland. In the last couple of years, the herds would be carefully sent to these locations. They'd go under their own power, and there was a pretty good balance between them."

She moved the cursor along a blue line. "For this year, that's this line," she said. "It's pretty much the same. But this line—" she pointed to a dotted blue line "—shows traffic heading back to NPI. This figure's double what it was last year."

"Back to the Central Stables," Mats murmured. "This is from our shipment figures?"

"Yes, it's hard to get at the actual herd traffic, so I have to—"

"I understand. You back up to it. This is good work." Mats reflected a moment. "They can't handle that traffic up there, not at Central. I wonder what they're up to."

"Maybe a diversion," Bill said. "Something to keep the stable guys busy so they won't notice something else."

"I don't understand," Anders said. "Why would they deceive each other? It makes no sense."

"Anders," Bill said. "I have the greatest respect for you in the world. But you're Swedish. You trust me. I trust you. You tell your people to get things done, and you don't ask again. They get it done. You trust them. Your problem is, you trust everybody. And the problem here is, there are people–there are *elves* in NPI who can't be trusted. That's how Kelli ended up here."

"Actually, it's worse," Kelli said. "This is why I called you last night, Anders."

"I see it," Mats said. "The yellow line. How did you figure it out?"

"The yellow line is the R—FS deer. I started with population statistics. Most of these don't show the RFS deer. But one report did. And there was a report for last quarter, and a projected report for next quarter—the fourth quarter of this year. A six month span. The RFS number was slashed for every population. No explanation.

"I figured they were the nonflyers, so if they were going anywhere, they'd have to be shipped. I started checking to see if there was a lot of feed going anywhere in particular. There was. North of Umea. I asked myself where would there be any flights or shipments? I started here, in Gothenburg. I did a search on the NPI site for Gothenburg shipments, and I found a report showing some live transports heading from Gothenburg to Umea. I checked Stockholm. Same thing. I couldn't get any more information. I couldn't get any reports on any cargo flights in, but I thought—I thought I had enough?"

"More than enough," Mats growled, his anger directed at the screen. "How long have you been here? Two, three weeks? I've had people who couldn't do this if they spent a whole *year* at it."

She smiled. "Well, all I had was a hotel room, a laptop, and Swedish TV," she said.

Mats roared with sudden laughter. "Swedish subtitles for German films! You don't like it?" But the mirth dropped quickly. "Anders, what's going on around Umea?"

Anders shut his eyes. "There's an old steel bearing factory up there, a leftover from the big war. It's been closed a number of years. It may have been bought by someone."

"Do we know who?"

"No. Maybe a group."

"And for what?"

"I don't know."

"We need to find out," Mats said. "Kelli. Can you put this on a diskette?"

"Of course, I—You'll be sending this to Gardner?"

"No. I'll be carrying it to her. Bill, there's an Inner Circle Meeting coming up in a few days, isn't there?"

"Yes. You'll see Gardner?"

"I'll make a point to."

"What about Oiler?"

"I'll have to. But I won't like it. I hope he won't notice. I've got nothing to say to him." Mats accepted the diskette. He straightened up, looked seriously at her, and then bowed, a gesture at once quaint and highly respectful. "Kelli. You've done magnificent work here. Both our organizations have a debt to pay to you." He lowered his eyes, muttering, "If we can stop things."

"Kelli, it's been a pleasure," Bill said. "Take my advice and stay out of sight. I don't know what's going to happen next, but you may have another part to play. Keep your ear to the ground. Either Anders or I will be in touch with you."

They prepared to leave. "Anders," Mats said. "Try to line up something to do, if only to cross the street to see Järvi and the orchestra. She'll go stirring cracked here."

"Stir-crazy," Bill murmured.

"I'll try. Kelli, if you do go out, please check your laptop into the safe downstairs."

These last words were exchanged at the door. They shook her hand and were off, down the hall and around the corner to the elevators.

She closed the door and leaned against it. She had done it, achieved more than she would have thought herself capable only a few weeks ago. But these uncontrollable tears suddenly flowing down her cheeks, what were they?

13.

Because I'm tired, Id, that's why. This kind of tired I haven't felt before. If it was just the responsibilities, that would be one thing. But it's the other stuff, too. Running at the Board. Keeping the UEU happy. Fending off the dotcoms. Figuring out what to do with the press. Somewhere in all of this I should be remembering what time of year it is, summer tailing off into fall, when the pulse quickens and the step gets lighter. Then you feel like you're part of Christmas.

We consumed every part of these months, day and night. Getting the herds in order. Making sure requests from around the world got to the assembly areas, planning the routes, repairing the sleighs, polishing the bells, tapping into the deep magic of this place. You could feel it in all the operations, sense it in the bones of the earth. It overtook the elves. They'd get a certain look about them, they'd greet each other differently.

We connected to the legends, rewriting them year after year. There was always something that made us change and grow. People would stop working in fields and cities and remind themselves that Christmas was coming. That it was time to suspend the small and mean stuff and replace it with the light and the good. Especially for the children. The older people would remember days when they themselves were young, and because those weren't always good days, they'd try extra hard to capture a magic they never thought they had.

The world, Id, has its problems everywhere, and the magic I have provides very little relief against that. But that doesn't stop me from placing that drop of magic into the world. It's like a drop of water that hits the surface of a pond, creating a wave that reaches to the farthest edges. Some years it's so tough you wonder why you go on. Suffering everywhere. Wars reaching to the edges of the earth. Kids being put to work, people losing arms and legs to railroads, mines and factories. Malnutrition, poverty everywhere, diseases old and new, starvation, genocide, hatred. Why bother? But we have, because we know we make a difference.

But now, nuts. Whole weeks go by without the word "Christmas" coming to my lips. I'm dealing with profit margins, market demographics, growth opportunities, branding, product mix, nominations to sit on some board, university invitations, gifts, strategy pitches, snake oil salesmen. I hate it all, and it's all necessary, they tell me, to run a global multinimble shareholder something or other in today's world. It's money chasing money chasing money chasing money, and I keep waiting for the turntable to spin so quickly that we'll all fall off into the muck somewhere. Will it happen? Who knows?

So now I'm trying new stuff that's really old stuff when you get down to it. Central Team Readiness Review. I'm told it's early. Operations Review Meeting. I'm told the EEC does that, and when I hold it anyway, hoo boy! the noise I hear. Getting back to the heart of the operations isn't going to happen by me going to an SSC next week and pitching another go get 'em speech to the recruits. All those red suits! When's the last time I wore one? I don't even know if mine fits any more. And the team! All I do now is call Central Stables and ask Strapper how they're doing. It's at least a day out and a day back, and that's time I just don't have.

The team, Id. What a wonderful group of beasts! They have a grace, a way of anticipating what you need to do! When I was in that sleigh, no matter how tough the night, I could rely on them finding the right path. Invisible to anyone who didn't know what to look for. But they could see those magic roads tracing the skies, glittering avenues they could follow, that climbed invisible mountains and pitched into unseen valleys and skirted unknown disasters. The air! Cold, clean and wild, scented of snows and ice, smokehouses and winterberry. A lungful of that would cure you for a century!

You know how we spend Christmas now? Sitting on our duffs in front of the fireplace, like we're both retired! She made the cocoa, said she was happy I didn't have to go out anymore. But something was wrong, Id. Something was wrong. I traded the one night I used to go out and worry her half to death for hundreds of nights on the road, hiphopping the world, this meeting or that, the company officer. But I didn't want things between us to change. If anything, I needed her more than ever, to help me when the days and weeks got to be too much. Instead, whee-bang! Out the door this spring, with one note and a "Don't call me, I'll call you!" So it's me and the fireplace this year, and the hell with her and wherever she's going to spend it. I'll be damned if I go out.

What the hell am I doing in New Orleans, Id? Tell me that! Santa Claus in the French Quarter. What's that all about? Old half-elf bumbling around the world because his wife left him and he can't have children, ever, so he's off finding himself in the business? Dynamic CEO, the ambassador of NPI, Mr. Samuel Claussen the Fat Pickle, talking up innovation at the Economic Club or discussing marketing strategies at the Canberra Merchants' Association. Dinners, speeches, product announcements, ribbon-cuttings, my God. Where's the Santa in all that?

Don't tell me it's just me being morose before I go on another trip. I run around dozens of times a year. Me, the king of fliers, traveling the world in airplanes! Go figure.

It's becoming alien to me. The world is lurching from this to that and this that this that this that faster and faster, grabbing on to something for an instant before dropping it in favor of something else, Christmas a sound bite, giving presents electronically, Santa-dot-com, point and click and presto! There's the new spirit of Christmas!

My God, Id, we used to make *things for each other, learn each other's preferences, choose the materials and the colors, design the item, and* present *it. That was the whole idea. Before NPI, we'd take requests, give them to the craft elves, and work the materials, shaping just the right gift.*

But we've changed with the times, and that's why you see the constant churn, the lines automated, new materials, new processes, doing things faster, cheaper. So that we can support the world's need now, the people constantly pressed for time and overstressed and content to just shovel gifts at each other, mindlessly picked from images on a flat panel display somewhere, tapped into during a flight between business meetings even. Who's really picking those gifts, anyway, Id? Who's wrapping them, who's sending them? Where are the people *in all of this? They talk about the New Economy replacing the Old Economy, but I've seen pictures of their roads and their bridges and their courtrooms and their slums, and I don't see how the New Economy is doing anything to take care of that. It just looks like old greed in a new skin, like putting new paint over rotten wood and saying everything's fine.*

So I'm going to a hotter-than-hell city in the middle of summer to talk to a bunch of new santas, and what do I say that keeps the flames going? How do I keep Christmas going when it's changed so much I barely know it anymore? How do I do that, Id? Without my wife, without my sense of rhythm, without my connection to the legends? What's magic without a purpose, Id? If you can answer me these things, then maybe you're worth the silly image of Santa talking to a shrink. So answer, damn you! Answer!

14.

The long ride south gave a half-elf plenty of time to reflect. Tracer yawned and stared out the train window, watching the sun slide beneath the darkening horizon. How would he ever stay alert for the Central Team Readiness Review? Saddler dozed in the seat facing him; Strapper, overseer of all Central Stables operations, occupied the next car forward.

No doubt Strapper had reports and briefings spread out and laptop lit. He had an incredible capacity for detail. Day after day, he garrisoned himself in his office behind stacks and stacks of paper, not even emerging for coffee. Shortly after Tracer's arrival, Saddler introduced him both to Strapper and to Strapper's doorframe. Even that sharp whack! hadn't fazed Strapper. He pulled tired eyes from his report, extended a limp hand, and said, "Glad to meet you. Door's always open." Saddler said that Strapper was really a kind soul, once you got past the paperwork.

The train chugged through a lightly forested area, the sun flickering behind trees' black boles. Tracer leaned back and shut his eyes.

He'd begun as he imagined all JEDIs did, lugging feed and cleaning out stables. The Central Stable elves had been friendly enough, though a bit guarded. Two things set him apart: his size and his JEDI trainee-tourist status.

But there were the deer. Everyone here called them that. And they were magical. Simply to touch them, to feel the warm muzzles, the rough tongues quick to accept an apple, gave him a thrill unique in his brief few hundred years. Their eyes had such an intelligent, penetrating light. They accepted his attention with simple trust, and he found when he was with them that his motions were sure and true, nothing out of place, no pails kicked over, no feed bags dropped. From the first stable he'd entered, encountering shadowy forms and warm familiar darkness, pungent feed and hay and dung and urine and bodies—he'd felt his heart lift and settle, as though the tumblers of his life had snicked into place.

Main-office activities interested him less and less. Sure, there were plenty of reports and email and closed-circuit telecasts, but his days were so full that he couldn't bring himself to sit in front of a machine and learn the latest gossip. He preferred watching the soccer matches the elves held in the center grounds, a wide, grassy expanse that provided plenty of space for these free-for-alls that seemed to occur about every other day. He'd even refereed a couple of the games, and suffered some good-natured swearing when one of his calls didn't go someone's way.

The train bit into a curve. Saddler stirred and snorted. "A-a-ah," he groaned, stretching his legs. He blinked a couple of times, yawned, and squinted out the window. "How far have we come? Or did you nod off, too?"

"I think we've got about an hour to go."

"Looks like it. I think the station's after this batch of woods." Saddler looked Tracer up and down. "How've you been finding your little exercise with us?"

"I'm learning a lot. And I'm sore, too, but that seems to be getting better."

"You'll never completely get rid of the aches and pains," the old elf said. "But you may get used to them. And you may get used to the place, too. ...Some of my folks say you're doing a halfway decent job. For an office guy."

Tracer smiled. "I don't feel as clumsy around them."

"They're no different up here. Elves are the same size the world over."

"I meant the reindeer."

Saddler burst out laughing. "I should have known! They said you had a soft spot for the deer!"

"Who?"

"The JEDI coordinators. They report on you. You *did* know they were doing that."

"Yeah, I know. And you're reporting on me, too."

"Of course. But up here, the reports are a little more direct. You mess up with feed or handling, the deer'll let you know. Or one of my guys will. We're not shy."

"They weren't too shy in the plants, either."

"That's because you kept doing things you weren't supposed to. How would you feel if you're a plant elf, and your daily bonus is tied to the number of whatevers you produce every day, and then this big tall clumsy thing barges in and knocks your rate back for the whole week? Face it, kid, from what you told me you were out of place, you knew you were out of place, but you didn't have the sense to keep your hands to yourself!"

Tracer colored. "I get it now."

"Don't let it get to you, and don't let what I said get to you, either. Just learn from it. I like what I'm seeing. If you were a loser, I wouldn't have invited you to the Review."

Tracer's pulse quickened. "Will the Chief be there?"

"He hasn't missed one yet. Plus he called this one special, a little early. Maybe he's getting back on his team."

"Why do you think he hasn't been flying?"

"Who knows? Things happen, you get busy, you're the CEO, you forget the world you came from. Happens with JEDIs, too. Not too many of them come up here anymore. Those that do, they're ready to get out the first day they can."

"I asked to see his team."

"You did."

"I should have told you about it earlier," Tracer said, "but I didn't think it was such a big deal. You were busy with the fliers in the north pasture and were out late. At the end of the day, I asked Strapper about it."

"And? Not that I don't know the answer."

"It wasn't as bad as you might think. He said no, but it was more of a 'not yet'."

"Do you know why?"

"He said I needed special clearance. Then he went back to his reports."

"He takes care of the team himself."

"So? It's not like I was going to take that over. I just wanted to, you know—"

"Yeah, I know. But he's very protective of them. Nobody sees them. And the rest of us are just too busy. We've got upwards of five hundred teams, plus spares and flight trainees, which when you do the math is about fifty-five hundred deer. And we're considered a small operation. We'll be bringing in the santas in another couple of months, which means about five hundred full-size guys and gals packing this little train, and you ought to hear the complaining *they* do, when they finally get a chance to stretch. We bring in extra food, extra cooks and support staff, and it's hell time. Stuff breaks, falls apart, some of the deer always get sick, you name it. Who's got time to look in on eight special ones? Let Strapper take care of them! That's about the only time he gets any fresh air, anyway!"

"Because of all those reports. Are they all related to the operations?"

"Mostly. But he's got personnel reports, regulations, herd inspections, financial audits, the kind of fun stuff someone like him gets to do. He used to get out a lot more. Now, it's purely office time."

"That has to get old."

"I imagine it does." Saddler hesitated. "He *has* changed. I've seen it. His face especially." He watched the trees flicking by. "Sometimes I think elves were never meant to be in offices," he said softly. "The folks from down at NPI, they all look so pale. Offices are where secrets happen. No, that's not always true. We have them here, too. But we used to be creatures of the earth, knowing its rhythms and— If we had secrets, they were part of this rhythm. Do you get what I'm trying to say?" His eyes searched Tracer's.

"I'm not sure. I was born down there."

For the longest moment, their eyes connected before Saddler broke, scanning the fields marching past. "So. So we're out of place after all."

Tracer followed the old elf's gaze, sailed with a hawk gliding over the steely land. "Maybe it's not such a bad thing."

15.

Roxy glanced from the laptop to her traveling suitcase and shook her head. *How many times have I packed that thing. "Business casual." Sure, it works for the guys: chinos and polo shirts when it's warm, chinos and sweaters when it's not. Then they take the damn chinos off and put on jeans and they're done!* Her gaze drifted to Santa's closed door. Even he'd said packing was easy this time. For her, it meant appropriate tops, matching slacks, "casual" scarf, "casual" brooch, "casual" earrings, hairstyle, shoes, handbag—even the "casual but professional" assortment of business-related tools: laptop case, cell, emergency stuff to throw into the carryon.

And shoes! Guys just had flat-heeled wonders, those stupid-looking boat shoes to go with all their tan and tan-green and green-tan and gray-tan and tan-gray pants; or several variations of elf- and half-elf-sized sneakers, walking shoes, what have you, the white wonders to go underneath the jeans (or, too often, the stupid wrinkled chinos). But for her, it was high-heels, flats, low-heels, open toe, closed toe, tan, maroon, black, navy, on and on. *Some of it's my own damn fault. If only I didn't enjoy driving them nuts once in a while.*

Somehow it had all fit. She'd probably overpacked, but then, this was her first major business trip with him. He hadn't noticed the risk, either. People would link them. Maybe he knew and chose to ignore it. There would be talk. She'd have to bring it up with him somehow.

I can't do it face to face. Her fingers tapped the handle. How hard his wife's departure had been. You could see the hurt flash from under that tough hide. It made you want to take care of him. But there was a big difference between comforting someone and taking the relationship into more private areas.

And it was wrong. He'd been with his wife for so long, and they were still joined far beyond a simple ceremony or a simple piece of paper. They'd spent centuries together. Now that partnership was being tested. Maybe it would ultimately fail. But if it did, a new relationship wouldn't be the reason. Not with her, no matter what others thought.

She sighed. This was so far beyond simple chemistry. He was the magic that made it all work. That magic and its inner workings belonged to one only other than him. How that magic had been bent over the years to the will of the business, and how it was being bent and tortured now, because the one who knew him best had left him, who knew? If he had been far younger, the magic still forming inside him, perhaps things might have been different. *So in spite of it all, in spite of what they think, he's lonely, and I'm lonely, too. That's how it stays. Is there someone magical for Roxy? Well?*

The door remained closed. What were they up to this time? She checked the calendar: Silvertongue again, but no topic. Most likely, they were going over the SSC speeches, or maybe trying to figure out their next moves with the Argentines. That was another thing. The more far-flung NPI's operations seemed to get, the more the problems circled home.

The door edged open, and Silvertongue forced his way out. The Chief said something that caused him to stop and answer, and the big door came to rest against his back. Trouble. If it had been Bridle, she would have jumped to help him.

Silvertongue's arm looked especially funny, flailing away like that. Muffled grunts and groans escaped him. She stayed very interested in her PC. Eventually, he squeezed his way out, shaking his pinched arm. He glanced at her to see if she'd noticed, and she glimpsed the relief on his face. If he only knew.

He approached. *Damn, why couldn't he just slither off?*

"Hi, sweetie. Ready for your big trip?"

"Sure am." She forced a smile. "My bags are packed."

He whistled. "Looks like you'll have enough."

"You're a guy, what do you know? Besides, all those midget clothes you pack, you can fit things in the overheads every time."

He chuckled. "You'll be in first class."

"Yeah. On a commercial cargo. What happened to the corporate jet?"

"Oiler grounded it. Stabilizer problem, I heard, but I'm no expert. You can't tell the difference, anyway. Even our cargoes support business travel. It's all first class." He checked his watch. "Oops, another meeting. Good luck! I'll want to hear all about it when you get back!"

"I bet you will. Give the Argentines hell while we're gone."

"I didn't know that was common knowledge."

Oh, you're pretty common, little guy. "It isn't. Just me and him. And whoever you've told." A buzz. "Gotta go. Keep the fort while we're gone!" She whisked around him to Santa's door, smiling as she opened it easily.

There he was, surveying his kingdom. He twisted back and forth, stretching, before closing the curtains and turning around. "Maybe we can stand on the flight. I get so tired of sitting."

"We could try. You squared away with Silvertongue?"

"Pretty much. But he's not squared away with the Argentines. Funny, something so easy should give him so much trouble. Maybe he's got other things going, I don't know. You ready?"

"My bags are at my desk."

"You should have sent them down with mine."

"I know, I didn't think of it. I'm not used to this."

"Good. It'll be exciting then. It doesn't take long to get used to it, and then it's no fun at all." He snatched his burgundy briefcase, swept around his desk and around her, pushing through the door and holding it open.

She reached for her bags. "Here, let me help you with those," he said.

"I feel kind of funny."

"Why? You forget who used to set the harness on the sleigh. Muck out the stables at one time, too." He checked his watch and whistled. "We need to get moving. I don't need to delay the flight and have us stacked up at New Orleans."

They hustled for the elevator. She wondered what to say to him when the doors closed, but he already had his cell phone out. "...Yeah, this is the Chief. Is he in? ...Oh, right, I forgot. Have him give me a call when the meeting's over. Thanks. Yeah, tell him it's about our performance numbers. PE. Right. Thanks, bye."

He stuffed the phone in his pocket. "Spokes. I forgot there's an EEC Meeting today. I'll get a briefing on it when we get back."

"How'd your CT Readiness Review go?"

"Not bad. A couple of the guys wondered why we were holding it so early this year. Teams seem to be in good shape overall, so that's good news." He watched the elevator buttons flash. "Couple things I should look into. Sounds like we're bringing in extra deer from the field. Saddler was asking about it, but he didn't have the numbers to back it up. Strapper didn't have anything either. Maybe it's rumor. I don't remember Oiler saying anything at the last Page Four. Then again," he rumbled on, "Oiler is Oiler. So I should get closure on that. Ah, here we go."

They had reached the ground floor. He strode toward the executive garage, and she hustled to keep up. *Thank goodness for flat heels.* "What was the other thing?"

"Hmm? Oh! Strapper's got one of the new recruits, another JEDI this season. A half-elf. Makes it interesting. They introduced him, but I forget his name. He asked me if I'd visited my team lately, and would I mind if he visited them. I told him it didn't matter to me, he should just clear it with Strapper. Strapper was glaring at him, so that might be a problem. For the new guy. You know, Roxy, it *has* been a long time since I visited them, hasn't it?

"I've been telling you."

"Well, when I get back, going to see them will be the first thing I do. Even ahead of the EEC. It's time I connected with them again. High time."

They'd reached the car, a dark green stretch limo with facing rear seats. A youngish half-elf stood by the passenger door, and another stepped forward and took her bags. Santa kept his briefcase. He made an "after you" motion with his free hand, and they clambered in, facing each other. Before the short silence could get out of hand he opened his briefcase and extracted a sheaf of reports.

The car glided from the garage. Building after building rolled by, modern offices with glittering windows and polished steel frames yielding to production complexes, long and low brick blocks, smoke curling from the stacks, elf- and half-elf-sized trucks, lifts, construction machinery rolling on the narrow roads linking it all. Then railyards, acres of cars, some filled with coal, others with who knew what, a documentary of supply and distribution, raw materials in and finished product out, supplier-to-manufacturer relationships, end-stage integration processes, partnerships forged and dissolved, times lean and fat.

"You won't find Christmas on any map," her mother had told her when she was a kid, before NPI had either name or shareholder base. "We're a one-way mirror," her mother said, describing special southbound tunnels. "We present a shadow face to the world. We have touchpoints where our wagons deliver the toys. But they see only a few of us. They don't know the real story."

How things had changed. Wagons replaced by trains. Trains complemented first by propeller and then by jet planes. And now, herds everywhere, a new elf outreach program, landholdings, countless human santas, layer upon layer of operations.

She studied his face, features once so disposed to laughter but now frowning, speed-reading something either disturbing or simply too detailed, given the stacks of information requiring instant absorption—and action: how he had had to grow into a job both massive and delicate, obvious while intricate and hidden. How had he contained all of this, convincing children and hoodwinking adults, all the while hiding these wide-ranging operations?

She looked back outside. Still more buildings. Trucks, lifts, elves, barrels, pallets, machinery, power stations, smokestacks, wires.

"Impressive, isn't it?"

Startled, her dark eyes met his bright blue ones. "Yes, it is. It's amazing how much it's grown."

"And the growth isn't all here, either. There's the electronic piece, the partnerships, the herds, all the outside stuff. Sometimes even I'm amazed by it all. You know, the thing is, the people in the southern lands talk about the Old Economy and the New Economy, e-this and e-that. Trouble is, I look out this window and ask myself

Who are we all kidding, anyway? Those aren't just electrons we're buying and selling out there. Somebody still has to make the toys. You can't convince me that some slick batch of billionaire-by-the-time-we're-thirty web boys have it right, where all you have to do is e-trade or e-partner or e-whatever. Because they're still getting into a car and driving someplace, even if it's only to the golf course. And that car still had to be cast and stamped and assembled.

"And me, running around the world. One minute I'm the Chief, the next minute I'm Samuel Claussen, CEO of North Pole Industries, thanks for the intro, let me tell you all about NPI. I'm putting on and taking off a personality a hundred times a week! Every time I get in a plane to head to a conference, I become what the world thinks I am. But when the hotel door closes and they're on the outside at last and I'm, oh, in the shower, I change back to who I am but who most of the rest of the world believes doesn't exist!"

"But not everybody."

"No. Not everybody. There's Inner Circle. And others. And there's been contact over the years," he added, a hint of a twinkle in his eye. He looked out the window again, his smile fading. "Trouble is," he murmured, "we're forgetting the magic that knits it all together. Those santas—how did they learn to fly? Skills, yes—but it's really the deer. Ever see a santa fly without his sleigh? Doesn't happen.

"But we forget that. We forget the legend is bound up in the magic the same way it's bound up in what's going on down there, down in the southern lands." He ran a large finger absently through his beard. "I wonder how many of them down there are using their trucks and their emails and their funding plans and their portfolios, because they don't have anything else standing between them and their mortality? When you live for six thousand years, you don't know what it means to fear death.

"But legends can die. Worse yet, they can be twisted. That's what happens to us here, you know. The whole growth of NPI, the merger, the IPO—it's all because those people down there have reshaped us."

She shook her head. "How do you mean? I don't follow."

"The way they've changed Christmas. Everything going to money. They've reinvented Christmas and me and all the rest, and that shapes and reshapes the legend. It's what's underneath—" The finger moved from beard to between large teeth. "Underneath it all is the magic, the consecration of the grounds here. ...You knew the grounds were consecrated."

She nodded.

"That's what keeps it going. That, and children. As long as the children continue to believe, we'll continue to operate. But you watch. You watch. The world will turn and turn, and the day will hit when there won't be a kid anywhere that we'll connect to, and then..." He looked out the window again. "Maybe it doesn't matter. Our spirits will be trapped in the iron by then, in PPE, in shareholder value. Christmas will be a well-structured transaction."

"Does it have to go that way?"

Finally, he sighed. "Yes. I think so. I can wish it otherwise; but when I look at all the things I have to do, it seems like the original calling is gone."

His cell phone jingled. "Like I said." He grimaced, reaching into his pocket. "Claus. ...Well, thank you. I'm sure we'll have a good time. Back before you know it. Give you time to work out the Argentine thing. Thanks, I ..." A chuckle. "Thanks, I will! You have a good few days as well! 'Bye." He put the phone back. "Silvertongue. Wishing me a good trip, and hoping I'll get some rest. You, too. That was kind of surprising—I wouldn't have picked him to make that call. Considerate."

"He's a sly one."

"They all are. That's the first rule. But sometimes the fox can have a heart, too."

The car eased to a stop. "After you," he said, as the driver held the door.

They left the big bags for others to handle. Clutching her overnighter, she trailed him up the gangway, his feet clanking as though he wore those big boots, after all. She smiled at the pilot (half-elf? human?), passed down the aisle, and settled herself in a window seat. She heard a big sigh from across the aisle as he flopped into his own seat. She glanced his way. A sheaf of papers already dressed his lap. His eyes narrowed at something—numbers, invariably.

She was still absorbing what he'd said to her in the company car. Few had seen that side of him.

She noted the cherry-red cheeks, the famous bulbous nose, and a recent single-vertical-line frown. Something bothered him on that page. In a moment, one large hand would start drumming the seat arm. What drove him these days? He'd invented some of it, just as some of it had recreated him. Was it that? How insistent was the drive? Was that the only reason his wife had left him? Or was it worse than anyone knew?

He looked up, straight ahead, and she began fumbling in her carryon for her mystery novel. She was still rummaging when his cell phone beeped.

"Spokes, please. ...Spokes, hi, I'm on the plane. Let's go over the High Holly numbers before we get cut off here, I—No, whatever you have just has to *wait*, understand, until we get through these numbers, I—Look, Spokes, I'm not going to tell you again, we talk High Holly and your stuff waits, because this is critical, and we need immediate action. I'm clear when I say *immediate*, right? Because you know what these markets are like out there right now? Look what happened to Transcom yesterday, when they reported second quarter earnings below expectations. A twenty percent shot in one day. Took all the other transportations right into the toilet, and the money going into the NASDAQ to chase some more of what-does-Beamer-call-them, vaporware companies. I'm tired of little college boys in suits running our company, Spokes, but there it is, what can we do except try to figure out ways to manage that herd. Why can't they all come down with RFS and let us get back to the stuff we do? So tell me about High Holly. I can hold it up as a lightning rod and keep 'em all from stampeding."

He chuckled, but the clouds regathered instantly. "Tell them it's too damn much, and I don't care if you put it in diplomatic language or not, Spokes, I'm getting tired of it! The fact that their specialty PPE is more advanced in the silk plant area doesn't give them reason to hold us by the short hairs! ...Yeah ...Yeah, only *remind* them that the reason they're hanging out there on the block is that their asset turnover numbers are in the tank, and their production processes are nowhere near where they need to be! If you need help delivering that message, get Crafter. Right, because he can be a real s.o.b. in these things. I'd put Gardner in there, too, but not to deliver any specific message. ...No. The whole thing should get turned over to her when this is all done. The best mind we have in the whole business, Spokes, we both know that. Knows the production side, the Union, Marketing, PD, you name it. Been there and done it all. Outclasses everyone around her without even trying, and more than a match for anyone who'd dare to go up against her... Yep. ...No, not Groomer, that fat little turd. ...Sorry, I know how good he is, but still. Bring him in to take care of the legal things, and then get him the hell out of there. And you know what, Spokes? Keep an eye on him, too. He's at the bottom of this EI stuff, you can believe it. ...Yeah, my feeling too. A lot more than we know. Makes me wonder who the hell's paying him. OK, now, what was it you had that was so—"

The intercom razzed, the plane taxiing, steward now standing before him and Roxy and advising on oxygen mask deployment and flotation options, actions out of place on a plane with only two passengers.

Santa raised his voice over the background noise: "I couldn't hear it, Spokes, they've started takeoff here. It'll just have to wait a few minutes, I can't even hear you, they're telling us to shut off the phones. I'll call after we're airborne. 'Bye."

He switched off the phone, leaned back and shut his eyes. Some papers slid from his lap and drifted to the floor. He tossed the rest on the empty seat beside him.

She spoke up. "Anything I can help you with?"

He glanced her way through eyeslits. "Not unless you can fire some of the elves around me." He shut his eyes and sighed deeply, burrowing into the plane seat. After a moment, she heard his voice blend with the hum of the warming engines. "Roxy, one thing to learn if you ever get as busy as I am, is how to get some sleep on an airplane. Every time folks travel with me, they miss no opportunity to review stuff. They ask me to make decisions they should be making. Only they're too busy coming to the CEO position, not to me. So I'm constantly talking to them. That kind of flattery I could do without. ...This time, I don't have to worry. So I'm going to sleep. Finally." He sighed again. "Wake me up in New Orleans."

"But that's hours away!"

"I know. I'll be awake long before then, I'm sure. But don't wake me first."

"What about Spokes? You want me to call him?"

He yawned. "I want you to follow my example. The phone—stays—right—here." He patted his pocket. "I've switched it completely off. I'll apologize to Spokes later. No phone, no laptop, nothing. Let's pretend for a few hours that NPI never existed."

He rubbed his head against the cushion, looking somehow both sleepy and defiant. Moments later, his big head drooped. How many others had actually seen him asleep, the Chief, old half-elf at last, worn out by demands. How many voices swirled around him, day after day after day? How welcome, sleep!

And how vulnerable he looked. Despite the magic, despite the size and range of the operations, despite his stubborn endurance, he was only one creature after all. Where was your power when you slept?

"Flight attendants prepare for departure." The same words. How routine became ritual if followed long enough. She checked her seatbelt. New Orleans. Hot and steamy this time of year, according to the brochures. *And I prefer it cool. A whirlwind, too. What'll we do for excitement after this?*

A profound urge to sleep washed over her, even though she hated takeoff. Drowsily, she glanced across the aisle. Was he so powerful he could impose sleep upon her this way? *That's foolishness.* She smiled in secret, irrational humor. *Foolish, foolish Roxy.*

The plane accelerated into takeoff. The usual airport buildings and weird motor vehicles flashed past, ground giving way and tilting oddly as the plane banked and headed south. Now she could discern the long dark slice of road down which they'd come, the factories, office buildings—smaller and smaller they became, tiny images to be pressed into storybook pages, the book now closing, gilded covers hiding the magic from the real world of humans in the southern lands. Her eyes closed at last, the tiny images changing to the merest points of light, sketches against the dark canvas. Real and notreal, her mind sighed slowly, passing into sleep. *Notreal. Real. Real. Not.*

16.

Black eyes scanned the office, resting on bookshelves, not seeing titles. Fingers drummed on the desktop, while the mind raced, a collage of events, conversations, encounters, reports, elves and half-elves, meetings, email. Connections formed, broke and reformed, slipping into possibilities, options, consequences. In the eye, a single image revolved slowly, the hub, an elf in a wheelchair. *Damn that Racer! What's he up to? And Groomer, others! Where does it end? Tinker?*

She punched Spokes's speed-dial. Busy. *Damn, damn!*

She pressed her palms against her eyes to drive out that spinning chair. When she brought her hands down, Router framed the doorway, brown eyes regarding her with friendly concern. He passed a hand through his always unruly iron-gray hair.

"Tired?"

She nodded.

He came in and sat down. "Something more."

"Yes."

"Look, Gardner, there's always machinery in those EEC meetings."

"Yes." She clipped the words, even though it didn't help. "What was that grounding order you mentioned at the meeting?"

He bit his lip. "That was an odd piece of work, wasn't it? I'm the one who signs grounding orders, normally."

"Right. So what happened?"

"Damnedest thing. I got an email from Oiler, a heads-up to keep me out of trouble. A maintenance audit exposed a possible problem with one of the tail stabilizers on the Chief's plane. No violation of procedures, no negligence, anything like that, but the SSC was coming up, so Oiler took it upon himself to put through a grounding order. The note was apologetic. Oiler invited me to look through the records if I needed to."

"And?"

"He was right. You had to connect the records over a period of time. A latent fatigue problem might have been building."

"And you're repairing it?"

"We're tearing it down tomorrow, see what we can find."

"I don't trust him."

"What?"

"I don't trust Oiler, not as far as I can throw his damn stabilizer."

"Why? The note said—"

"I don't give a damn what his note said! It's Oiler! Close the door!" She leaned forward. "You were at that EEC meeting, you know what the hell it's like. You, me, Crafter, Spokes, Wheeler on one side, and that damned—*spider*—that damned Racer and his trio on the other!"

"But Gardner, come on! Crafter's Manufacturing, Wheeler's Marketing, PD never shows up! And Spokes is Finance! The big guns belong to us! Look at how the vote went."

"I know how the vote went! Five to four, and we got the furnace repair pushed through! The whole point is, Router, I had to force the damn thing into the agenda! They'd taken it off, or somehow it never got there, a deviation request none of us saw, Oiler with his on-again, off-again games! So there's Stoker, head of Casting, presenting his case, and you could see he couldn't figure out why we were so dense—so dense, that something as dangerous as a casting furnace going up needed any debate at all! But there's those bozos, whittling down his case, forcing him to admit the risk is small! If the shutdown sequences work! If they work! And him arguing with them about budget cuts that put enough bandages on those sequences, on that furnace, I—Router, if you hadn't stepped in with what you said about the stabilizer on the Chief's plane, and how much risk we could tolerate. That was brilliant, brilliant."

"Well, thanks, I—"

"But you know what, Router?" She chewed a finger. "You know what? I think they knew—I think we *all* knew—which way that vote was going to go. Because—because there may have been another vote behind the first one. A vote we don't get a chance to cast." Her eyes roved the office, settled back on his. "Maybe more than one, who knows? Ever hear of WonderFinish?"

"Wonder what?"

"Exactly. Supposedly we approved its use in operations. Hazardous, but effective. And they're putting all kinds of pressure on Halter to use it, and he's going crazy trying to get it on the agenda, somebody to listen to him. He's already had an accident with it, and he's worried sick about it. But instead, when it comes time to figure out where to step up production, who do our friends pick on? Halter! I had to fight to swing it around to Tinker's area! Why all this pressure to use WonderFinish? *You* know nothing, *I* know nothing, I bet Spokes doesn't either, God knows who else, but we're supposed to have approved it! You see the pattern, Router?"

"They're using the EEC's name."

"Exactly. And they know they can only do it for a little while, before we figure things out. So what are they doing, putting us in a box? We'll break out of it before long." *Unless*— She took a deep breath, tried to keep her swirling thoughts from racing too far ahead. "Router, there's a special Board meeting tonight."

"You're kidding."

"Nope. Spokes just told me. He only found out because he'd bumped into a Board member in the hall and asked him what he was even doing at NPI. It's a special session. Spokes figures it has to do with herd management, there's extra deer coming into the Central Stables, but I told him that's bullshit and he knew it."

"OK, so what do you think it is?"

"I think—I think—" Kelli flashed in front of her: *"—they were putting together something big. It was ugly. They were talking about some merger. They had these numbers, they were going to sell off the herds. And some other stuff, too."*

She saw it hit him, too. "Coup?" he mouthed incredulously.

She held out her hands helplessly and shook her head.

"C'mon, Gardner, how could they even think it? The magic comes from him, the control, the direction—everything! They couldn't possibly pull it off!" He tapped her phone. "Call the Chief if you think it's happening."

"He's already on his way to New Orleans. Spokes is trying him right now." She punched his speed dial. "Line's busy—Damn!"

Router leaned forward. "Gardner. Calm down. It's too crazy. They can't make it work. I know you think you figured out something, but there could be a hundred other reasons. The Chief will be back in a couple of days, and business will go on. You've got lots of other things to worry about."

She smiled. *OK, maybe I'm crazy. Maybe I've assembled the puzzle the wrong way. Deep breath.* "And *you've* got herd rebalancing."

He winced. "It gets goofier every year. You had to remind me the volume's up. I talked it over with Oiler, and he says it beats him. He thinks it has to do with strengthening PR this year. We need to offer another glimpse into life at the North Pole."

Her eyes widened. "Not another North Pole Newsday."

He shrugged. "It's possible."

"Oh, Lord, those things are disasters every time. Remember three years ago, when they tried it? Extra booze for the reporters, disclaimers, production reports, view the herds. What an effort. And then in the middle of it, the Australian reporter slaps a reindeer's butt. What a mess, blood everywhere."

"Well, the deer told him what's what," Router said.

Her desk phone jingled softly. She stabbed the handsfree button. "Gardner."

"Hi, it's Spokes. Who's there with you?"

"Router. Did you get him?"

"Yeah, but he rode right over me on the High Holly thing. He kept apologizing, but by the time I could get in a word, he had to hang up."

"Because of takeoff. Damn! Well, he's on his way."

"He could turn back. He said he'd call right back. Fifteen minutes, tops."

"How did he seem?"

"The usual. I tell you, Gardner, even with what went on in the EEC, I don't see the whole applecart tipping over. I'll give him a call, see what's what. …Gardner? You there?"

"…Yes. …Spokes, I think you're right," Gardner said. "Maybe it's nothing."

Router studied her. "There's an Inner Circle meeting tomorrow," he offered. "Could the Board Meeting be connected to that?"

She took a deep breath. "I'd forgotten."

"They'd have good reason to meet," Spokes squawked over the handsfree. "The herds have been especially sensitive this year, RFS is a big issue, and there's tons of swirl around the supply chain and e-business. Tons."

Her eyes narrowed. "Operations stuff."

"Yeah, but it's tied in with rethinking the business model. Plus Sprinter's e-commerce vision, rebranding, the electronic marketplace, all kinds of stuff," Spokes said. "So it's strategic and operational. It makes sense the Board would meet."

"But the Chief's struggling with the whole rebranding issue himself. He should be there, to get his views across."

"Well," Router said, "he can't be everyplace at once. The SSC this year is crucial, because the agency mix is up, and RFS has made rebalancing the teams tougher than ever. So those new santas have to be ready. He might have given his views to somebody ahead of time. Or he could tie in to the meeting from the plane."

"That's easy enough. I'll ask him that, too, when I get a hold of him," Spokes said. "…Gardner?"

"…All right." The connections were dissolving again, changing first into a web, then into a mosaic, then finally into no pattern at all. She'd clutched an ugly, intact crystalline nightmare that melted irretrievably behind their words. "All right. Just let me know what he says. I'm beginning to feel like—never mind. Thanks, Spokes."

"OK. Talk to you in a bit."

She disconnected the line and stared at her phone, chin resting on folded hands. *Spokes, Router. What do they know? What do I do?*

Involve everyone in a chase, for what? Mats. How could I forget? What's he found out that he needs to see me?

"You were saying," Router murmured.

Her cheeks warmed, and she quickly ran one hand front-to-back through her hair. "What?"

He tilted his head. "You said, 'I'm beginning to feel like…'"

"Oh, that." She looked away momentarily, then looked back, her trademark half-smile returning. "Just that I'm beginning to feel a little foolish about certain things."

He leaned forward. "That's the last thing you are, and you know it," he said earnestly. "Care to share what's on your mind?"

Her eyes softened just a bit as the barest something passed between them, a comforting wisp. "…Maybe. Maybe soon. But not now. Now, I just have to resort some things. I need to think about—oh, transformational learning, incentive planning, other stuff. Inner Circle. I'll be seeing Mats tomorrow."

"Larsson? What for?"

"He wants to see me. You should be there, too. He has some information you'd be interested in. Herd-related."

"Herd-related! Mats?"

"Special assignment. Remember Silvertongue's admin?"

"Oh! What was her name?" He shut his eyes momentarily. "The one that got fired, because she was snooping around or something?"

The half-smile froze. *That rumor mill is quick.* "It's Kelli. *I* fired her."

"*What*?"

"Because she was honest. There's quite a story in it, and it involves our three friends—Groomer, Silvertongue and Oiler. And probably Racer, too. No. Not probably."

"Wow. But you *fired* her. For being honest?"

"Yes. Had to. Be careful, maybe I'll have to fire you!" She laughed, and so did he. "Actually, I did it to protect her. And it's worked out. For her, and for us."

"She's the one you had me ship out of here, when you made that special call!"

"Right. And now I can tell you why. You know what?" she continued, the half-smile giving way to a full one. "I changed my mind. Let's have that conversation. Call it prep for our get-together with Mats. But let's send for some coffee," she said, shaking her head. "This is going to take quite a while."

He rubbed his chin, returned her smile. "I've got the time," he said.

17.

Gray light pierced a slit in the dark curtains. Tracer groaned and turned over, and the elf-sized bed groaned back. Morning had again arrived too soon, and with it frozen feet. "Damn elfin beds." He scowled at his bare shins and toes. "They'd better make that bed they promised me." He closed his eyes against the puny stuff around him, and his mind produced delicious images of full-sized beds, full-sized tables, door headers higher than his Adam's-apple, chairs, tools—even food. Then he conjured up a full-sized naked female half-elf. That would never do, because the full-sized something else was especially dangerous in cramped quarters. He opened his eyes and sat up before remembering that the oil lamp dangled too low. Fortunately, it stayed on its hook.

He reached up and arrested it before swinging his feet around and slapping them on the stone floor. "Numb again, dammit. How cold is it?" He cast about for his socks. Maybe he should shower before the elves commented again about enthusiasm for the deer versus smelling like them.

That was another thing. Showers. They were in another building, which meant trekking across the residential grounds. And of course they were all elf-sized, with waist-high handles. The water temperature was capricious, too, and the extra seconds he spent fumbling for the handles felt like ages under a suddenly scalding or freezing stream. He couldn't jump out of the way, either: the stall was way too small. Crouching was damn near impossible, and crouching was what he had to do if he wanted water to reach above his chest. As for dropping the soap, well.

He sighed, refocusing. Eventually, he fumbled in the bedside drawer for matches, lit the oil lamp, then eased himself up. He shuffled to the window, drew the curtains, and peered outside.

Elves moved through a clearing ringed by similar cabins. His enthusiasm for the deer had yet to match the unhurried determination and level of work these small folk could sustain. At first, his muscles had screamed against this physical labor, until after a week or so Saddler had introduced him to the elves' secret salve—terrible smelling stuff whose slow but relentless heat kept aches and pains mostly at bay. His hands had blistered from the rough work, and he'd run through more than his fair share of bandages and wraps (the damn stuff was elfin-sized as well, requiring twice as much off the roll).

He stretched again, joints popping and crunching. He hadn't been to the activity center to pick up email or get on the NPI net for some time. It all seemed like a distant hysteria, anyway.

He thought about the trip, details surfacing like rocks in a stream. Strapper had certainly been angry with him. All because he'd asked Santa whether he could visit the team. Santa hadn't minded, but Strapper, wow. He'd hauled him into that paperbound office of his, kicking up a big fuss about how if as a JEDI he thought he had special privileges, he'd better get that out of his head right away, and what was the idea of asking the Chief point-blank for a clearance that should have come through him, Strapper? He'd tried to defend himself, hand flailing and sending a particularly large stack of papers flying. He could still see it: an information column that blasted into a million bits in one grand splat!—a sound almost as satisfying as seeing the weird color Strapper's forehead had turned. Some kind of dusty rose. He'd seen carpeting that color, once, before it had been mercifully replaced.

But Strapper hadn't said no. Of course, he'd hardly said yes, either. Forgiveness or permission? Tracer decided on forgiveness. If only he knew where they were stabled.

A red ray snaked across the clearing and splashed one of the cabins. Then he remembered the special assignment. Saddler would pick him up shortly after dawn. So no shower. No breakfast, either. He'd just have to live with a rumbling gut.

He'd barely pulled on his clothes when the expected knock nonetheless startled him. In his haste, he forgot to crouch before opening the door.

"That must've hurt," Saddler observed, entering the cabin and peering about. "They told me you were into the oil-lamp bit, the old traditions," he said. "Not a bad thing. You don't have to, you know."

"I know."

Saddler wrinkled his nose. "Is that a special aftershave for the deer?"

"Sorry, I—Time got away from me, and by the time I remembered we had a special thing to do, there wasn't time to shower."

"Can't say I blame you totally," the old elf grunted, turning and making for fresher air. "Crossing the grounds to take a shower isn't the most convenient thing you'll do. Of course," he continued as they stepped outside, "it's even less fun in the middle of winter. You'll find out. If you stay here that long."

Tracer finished closing up the cabin and climbed into the waiting wagon. "You ready to send me back?"

Saddler glanced at him, hi-ed the team into motion. "I wouldn't say that," he said. "...But you might be ready for a different rotation. Your choice."

"I'd rather stay here."

"Hmm. We'll see."

The wagon rumbled out of the clearing. Tracer yawned and stretched. Eventually, Saddler said, "Your smell shouldn't spook the deer, once we wrap you up a bit."

"Wrap me up?" Tracer puzzled. "I don't get it. How far out are we going?"

"It's not a matter of how far out, it's how far up."

"Up?" His heart jumped. "You mean—"

Saddler nodded, watching the wagon track. "About time you learned how." One eye stabbed Tracer's way. "You all right with it?"

"I? Yes, I—it's fine. It's just a little—unexpected."

"Well, Strapper wasn't completely comfortable, because of that stunt you pulled at the Review, asking the Chief about his team. But we managed to convince him."

"All I did was ask if I could see them!"

"Yeah. And what do you mean, 'all you did?' I told you how Strapper is with them!" Then he smiled. "But I like it. Shows you're not afraid to ask for what you want. Strapper liked it, too, though he won't admit it." After a moment, he continued, "Plus, you've been doing way more than the usual half-assed job we get out of a JEDI. Way more. So we thought we'd give you a shot at flight training, see if you could fly around without killing yourself."

"Thanks for the vote of confidence," Tracer said wryly. "And the compliment, too. Though I don't think my work rate comes close to anybody else's."

"You can't expect to be a deer elf right out of school," Saddler said. "It takes hard work for years to tune your body. We didn't invent that salve I gave you because we were all sitting around feeling good. Don't worry about how much you're doing. Nobody else is." They bumped along in silence for a couple of minutes. "We've got our work cut out for us this year."

"How so?"

"Two things. It looks like we're going to have a whole lot of extra deer. Strapper's having fits over the numbers. There's at least twice as many deer as usual, hundreds and hundreds of extras, and we're just not equipped."

"How is it we're not equipped? These are the Central Stables!"

"Don't get caught up in the elitist talk from some of these folks, kid. Sure, we're the Central Stables, the jewel in the crown. If you believe the management talk. But that doesn't mean we're the biggest operation. The really big ones are south of here, still north by human standards, but quite a ways away. So we've got these deer coming in, and now we've got to figure out where to put 'em all. Plus, there's extra flight training, the works. I know what the guys will say about it."

He snapped the reins absently. "Then there's RFS. It's a bigger problem than ever this year. So that means we're busy trying to work in substitutes and at the same time trying to get a handle on what the problem really is."

"Is anything working?"

"We've tried lots of things. We've adjusted schedules, looked at feed mix, even sexual opportunities, thinking maybe they're just damn lonely. We've looked at handlers, trying to find a pattern. That's the problem. There isn't one. And none of the things we try seems to work."

"Maybe it's too much tinkering."

"Yeah, we thought so, too. So we backed it all off, to see what would happen. Nothing. No change. But I'll tell you. Once RFS gets started, it can spread like anything. That's why we have to be so careful, make sure the RFS ones get singled out and repastured. Unfair to them, maybe, but you have to look at the whole herd."

Tracer frowned momentarily. "You know, maybe they're just sick of things."

Saddler stiffened. "What do you mean?"

"Nothing we're doing up here," Tracer added hastily. "And probably nothing we're doing anywhere else. It's the nonsense down there."

"Nonsense?"

"Down at NPI. All the craziness. Politics, mergers, programs, the whole bit. You only visit there, right? So you haven't really felt it, even though you hear elves talking about it. It's different when you're in it."

"I'll bet. But what does that have to do with the deer? They're up here with us."

"I know, it's—" He searched for the right words. "It's like how animals can sense an earthquake before it happens. Or they can sense when the wind changes and there's a storm coming. You've seen it a thousand times."

"I have. We have a saying up here: 'The deer know.' "

"Right. When did RFS start showing up?"

"A few years ago, why?"

"A few years ago." Tracer shut his eyes. "Maybe something started happening down there…and they sensed NPI was heading in the wrong direction."

"But they're just deer!"

"Deer that can fly," Tracer looked hard at Saddler. "Try that on folks and get their reaction. No, that's the reason. I can feel it. It's right. And if you're a magical deer, a deer that can fly, the only way—the only *vote* you have is whether or not you fly." His eyes ranged over the fir-studded fields. "Imagine having all that magic in you. But you're so discouraged, you decide not to use it. And that's your vote." He turned back. "That's why we'll never fix it here, Saddler. Because the problem isn't here at all."

Saddler was silent a long moment. "You may be right," he said finally. "But it doesn't help a whole lot up here. Here, we just have to fix things the best we can."

Tracer sighed and stared over fields coloring in the rising light. The wagon bumped and creaked along. He closed his eyes and saw thousands of them, wheeling and turning amid the clouds, gigantic flocks of improbable birds, antlers scraping the sky.

A jolt. He opened his eyes.

Saddler had stopped the wagon and was watching him. "You sulking?"

"I wasn't sulking, I was…" The last words trailed from him as he stared, sleep and wakefulness merged, eyes taking in deer aground and deer skyward, elves dressed in thickly padded white suits hitching rough-hewn training wagons, little more than scrap boxes on wheels, to the teams before taking them aloft. He watched as other elves, dressed in more reasonable cold-weather gear, spoke into handheld radios, communicating with the sky teams.

"Close your mouth and get down," Saddler grunted. "Time to wrap you up and get you going."

Legs and arms obeyed the distant call, swinging him out of the wagon. He scarcely noticed Saddler's small hand at his elbow, steering him toward a wooden hut. He almost collided with a white-suited elf who waddled from the hut and then stopped, staring Tracer up and down.

"Where'll you find a suit for *him*?" the elf asked Saddler.

"We'll manage. We had one specially made."

The dream continued, despite a whack to the head stepping through the door.

"This must be the one," said an elf barely visible in the shadows. "I'll get the suit."

They stuffed Tracer into the billowing white garment, a six-foot sausage forced into a padded parachute. When they turned him around, they discovered he was now too big to pop outside, no matter how hard they all pushed. So they had to pull him back inside, take the suit off and do it again outside.

By this time, he'd become Tracer the misfit again, towering over them all like a giant slug. "Glad I can be such a source of amusement," he grumbled.

Saddler steered him across the grounds. "Don't let the smiles bug you. We all feel pretty goofy in these things the first time. Though you *do* look like an approaching weather front," he chuckled.

"Oh, thank you. Thank you very much," Tracer groused.

They stopped in front of a work wagon larger than the rest. Tracer prodded one flimsy side. "This thing is safe?"

"The padded suit helps," Saddler reflected. "These wagons come apart all the time during crash landings, so it doesn't make any sense to build 'em too sturdy."

"Crash…" Tracer had started to sweat.

"Whoa, here comes a new one now!" Saddler shouted, pointing, and Tracer banked about, his eyes picking up an angular blossom wheeling across the morning sky. The bloom sharpened into a pair of reindeer hitched to a work wagon, a white shape bobbing in it. In the landing zone, a couple of elves studied the descent, occasionally speaking into handhelds.

"Uh-oh, too fast," Saddler murmured, and Tracer stared in terrified, sweaty amazement as the flying team landed at too steep an angle, the deer keeping their feet but the wagon pitching into the ground and shattering, the white thing bouncing free and rolling end over end like an irregular puffball before coming to rest at last at the far end of the field. One of the elves with the handhelds steadied the shaky team, while the other ambled to where the puff-ball struggled to its feet.

"That happens a lot," Saddler observed. "The deer get the flying and landing bits down all right. It's when we put a work wagon on them that things get interesting."

Tracer watched the white thing dust itself off and limp toward the team. "You expect me to do *that*?" he asked, sweat dammed at his eyebrows. "Just—bound and roll and—get up like that?"

Saddler gave him an amused look. "Naw!" he said. "Not at first, anyway. That's Hitcher, one of our most experienced fliers. Hasn't broken anything in a long time."

"But he just broke that wagon!"

"I meant an arm, a leg, a collarbone. Collarbone's a pretty common injury, actually."

"...Oh."

"Anyway, we don't do that to somebody just starting out. We'll give you an experienced team and a flier that can keep you in line."

Tracer swatted his forehead with a fat white arm, scattering sweat beads. "Aren't there any ventilation holes in these things?"

"You want comfort or safety?" This from a sharp-featured elf who wobbled up in his white suit and squinted up at Tracer. "Wow," he said. "Talk about contrasts. I should get extra pay for doing this."

Tracer peered down at him. "Who's the nice-mannered kid?"

"This is Bounder, your partner. I need you two to get along," Saddler grumbled. "Where's the spirit of Christmas when you need it?"

"In the sky and in the deer," Bounder said. "You know. Besides, it's August."

"Tell me about it." Tracer still flailed about his head.

"I wouldn't worry too much," Bounder said. "By the time you get up there and get some wind in your face, you'll be happy you have the suit on. This our wagon?"

"Yep," Saddler said. "Good luck, kid. I'll be down here with a handheld. If it helps you out, we haven't lost a JEDI yet."

"I don't know how I could feel much better."

"I'll go get the team," Bounder said.

That left Saddler and Tracer and silence for a bit. "You know, it was even wilder in the old days, before we figured out the padding."

"That helps," Tracer grumbled.

Bounder returned, leading a couple of reindeer who looked as though they'd been through all this too many times. Tracer couldn't help but think they gave him the same look Bounder had.

"This is Mystic, and this is Parsley," Bounder said over his shoulder, hitching the team to the wagon. "Introduce yourself."

"Parsley," Tracer murmured, running a calming hand over one of the animal's shoulders. "Odd name."

"After a few thousand deer, you start running out of flying names," Saddler said. "But you have to wonder: 'On Dasher, on Parsley.'"

Bounder snickered.

Tracer caught the deer's sharp smell, felt the rough warmth of their hides. Catching gold beams deep in their dark eyes, he murmured to Parsley about her blue harness, to Mystic about her copper bells. He discovered a special rubbing spot between Mystic's antlers.

"Told you, Bounder," Saddler said. "I think you'll have fun up there."

"Hope so," Bounder said. "C'mon, Tracer, it's time to break you in."

Tracer separated himself from the team and climbed in the wagon, which complained no small amount under his weight.

Bounder glanced at the rickety wooden frame. "Hm."

They rattled into the middle of the field. Tracer's heart raced. This was it. He gazed skyward, seeing teams circling and maneuvering like strangely shaped birds. Soon he'd be up there. Dream and reality crashed like seawater on sharp rocks.

Bounder followed his gaze. "First flight—there's nothing like it. The big thing you have to realize," he said quietly, "is that it's real. Once you get that figured out, really figured out, the rest is easy. Here we go."

To Tracer, accustomed to plane flights, the liftoff was a surprise in itself. They simply took a few steps forward and left the earth, the ground falling away gracefully as though they were riding a balloon of air. Was this the way teams took off from rooftops? He struggled to reorient himself, gripping the side of the wagon.

Bounder was saying something into his handheld, but Tracer didn't care. He was a sky animal now, or rather an awkward padded monster stuffed into a wagon and granted the grace of uplift by the magic of the deer. Tracer the klutz and Tracer the bird.

The team banked lazily to the right. Amazement yielded to excitement, then exhilaration, then a boundless joy, as they sliced through the air, the reindeer beating their hooves against nothing as though galloping on hard ground. The wind cut his face, drying his sweat and making him grateful for his suit's cocooning warmth. He found himself leaning into turns, anticipating climbs, relishing sudden dives. He smiled and waved at other teams sharing the same wide spaces, where before they had been wonderful but improbable images pinned to the blue. The sun flashed behind serrated clouds. When they banked earthward, trees and buildings swam up and flitted past like green and brown feathers. Tracer the bird was winning.

Only a few seconds later, it seemed, they descended. Landings were much more challenging, the team locating and falling toward tiny targets without losing the wagon. But Mystic and Parsley had done this far too often to get it wrong. The team adjusted to Tracer's extra weight, balancing speed and pitch to land squarely on target, the wagon barely thumping as it hit the surprisingly solid earth.

"Whoo!" he exclaimed, leaning back.

"So you liked it," Bounder said. "Good. We'll start training you in flight instructions a little later. Just take a minute and realize what you've been part of." He handed Tracer the reins and jumped from the wagon.

Tracer leaned forward, still amazed by it all, then heard but didn't understand at first the sounds of splintering wood, only felt the world give way under his butt as the wagon seat collapsed. His legs flipped and his backside plunged, the reins he clutched snapping the deer's backs, and suddenly he felt motion wild and ominous, wagon, team, and scissored half-elf shooting skyward, shouts from the field rapidly yielding to the screeching wind. He had no time to be terrified, seeing his toes pointed against the sky and struggling to raise his head above the wagon's frame. Desperately, he clung to the reins with his left hand as his right beat air for a moment before finally grabbing on to something solid. He had to brace himself against the bucking frame, heaving himself upward. At last, he surfaced and looked around.

They were high, far higher than the first ride. The world had fallen far away. The wind pushed at them—or was it pulling them?

He spied guide elves, scurrying dots on the ground, saw sky teams ceasing maneuvers and chasing, only to peel away and break formation. He shut his eyes and strained to keep his body from plunging through the frame.

When he opened them again, the practice field had disappeared, and they had spun over wild lands, forested landscapes, boulder-studded fields. The wagon bounced behind the team, jarring them, interfering with their flying. He cast about frantically. How would he ever gain control of the team in the position he was in? And even if he could work himself onto some kind of seat, what were the commands?

Another crash, and this time the whole side of the wagon shattered, falling towards the distant earth. He plummeted through the opening, his weight wrenching back on the reins, and then they were all falling, wheeling and tumbling, trees and sky and ground and sun and dark flashing and flashing and flashing and then suddenly and sharply branches, needles, hard things that tore them, punished them, destroying the wagon, wood and animals and reins and padded suit all tossed together, crashing at last to the hard, hard earth, and he in his last moments feeling dream and notdream shock into one, the bird grounded, white suit blossoming red at points, so beautiful, so beautiful.

MAGIC

I

1.

"Spinner, I'm all alone."

"I know."

"Winnow told me it would happen."

"He did."

"Yes." Halter stood, paced behind his desk a couple of times, then sat back down. He snatched the first available piece of paper and read, "All hands announcement today, ten o'clock. What the hell is it this time." He slapped it down.

Spinner's eyes never left him. "You're not totally alone," she said.

"What do you mean?"

"There's me. And Winnow."

"But both of you are saying WonderFinish goes back on the lines!"

"Halter. Don't be unfair." She folded her arms. "Winnow's a very practical elf. He's seen a lot of things. He's got a good relationship with his guys. He puts in new things, knows when to push and when to back off. But he's in no position to help. He knows the stuff's questionable, but he's looking at the balance sheet in a way that maybe you can't. And he's seeing your own guys, and the pressure from the EEC—"

"They didn't even put it on the damned agenda! It wasn't important enough for them! Instead—" his eyes searched the desk, his hand darting out to crumple a one-page email "—they hand me *this*!"

The paper trembled in his hand as he scowled at it. " 'Due to an unforeseen emergency requiring the shutdown of Casting Furnace Number 3, operations areas not affected by disruptions in internal supplies will be required to step up production over the next few weeks. This action is intended to provide a buffer of non-metal units in anticipation of a shift of personnel from these areas to metal toys later this month, to achieve production targets across all lines. Affected areas initially include Doll Operations and Candy and Confections.' "

He threw the sheet down. "What bureaucratic gobbledy-gook! Why can't they just say we've had a problem, and everyone needs to pitch in?"

She scanned the page. "When did this come out?"

"Last night. Sometime after the EEC Meeting whose agenda I got cut from," he said bitterly. "Why couldn't somebody have called me?"

Her eyes darted from the page to study his face a moment. "Would that have changed things?" she asked gently.

"Yes. No!" He pressed a hand hard against his forehead, eyes shut tight. "No, it wouldn't. I'd still be in the corner I'm in, with Drover and all the others seeing the production stepup and knowing WonderFinish is the only way they're going to make it."

"It's only for a few weeks. Maybe we can pull it after that."

"With what cause? By that time, the guys'll be wedded to it!"

"It's still dangerous."

"Yes, and the argument is, half the stuff in the plant is, so what's the big deal?" He shook his head. "No, there's nowhere to go on this one. They've put me where they want me." He looked away, she hearing the rapid pulse of his foot banging the floor. "Whatever happened to us, Spinner?" he said. "Don't you remember? Can't you? The smell in the air, the frost on the fields. Hard work, sure. Long hours. Fires to be tended, oil lamps to be filled. Parts all over the benches. Smells of glues made from pine resins, finishes made from nut oils. Craft brushes and crafters. Can't you see it anymore? Didn't you have the same things? The looms? And before that?"

She nodded.

"Instead, it's all machinery now," he went on. "But it's not just the machines on the lines. We can handle those." He pointed upward. "It's the machines in here. Acres and acres of machines, whole departments of them. And they crash into each other like waves, with consultants and shareholders egging them on. Where's the sense in all of it? And every so often, along comes a push for cutting out the politics, reorganizing to flatten things, improve accountability, and all you ever get are new departments and more paperwork! What the hell does paperwork have to do with what we're doing here?"

"But we need it, Halter, come on! If you didn't have it, you wouldn't have had anything to go on with WonderFinish."

"Yeah, and what did that do? They twist the paperwork into what they want. I can tell the truth a hundred times over, support it with every report and article I can lay my hands on, and it'll just be old Halter the Daydreamer again. I'm discounted, because I have the audacity, the *stupidity*, really, to connect back to the Christmas I remember, the Christmas we used to shape and—and *give* to the people, Spinner! *Give* it to them! Not—" His voice tightened. "Not—shove at them."

"Come on, Halter." She leaned forward. "It isn't the way you see it. Not all of it. It isn't worth getting yourself all—"

"It is." His jaw worked. He leaned forward too, their faces close over the crumpled page. "I know the damn names they call me. I know them. I run—*we* run—one hell of a good operation here. But when I want to connect it to tradition, I'm called old, and outmoded, and a daydreamer. I'm not—*practical* the way you are. ...So tell me, Spinner—" his voice almost a whisper "—how do *you* ...help *me*?"

Her eyes welled despite all her efforts. "...I give you balance," she whispered, the words pushing out in irregular puffs. "...I bring you back. Just because somebody doesn't dream, it doesn't mean—they don't—appreciate—"

He shut his eyes and leaned back. "Sorry. I'm so sorry. You do bring me back. You do. Better than anyone else could. And I need it." He opened his eyes and smiled, and she could see in his expression that for him the storm had passed.

He stretched, stood. "Ah, nuts!" He barked a laugh. "We've got a damn business to run, and production figures to manage! I had a windmill fall on me along the way, but what the hell! Let's push that aside and go out there and get it done!" He flopped into his chair. "Besides, there'll be another windmill soon enough, and I'll be obliged to go after it, right? Spinner? ...Spinner?"

"...I don't think you should stop."

"What, with WonderFinish? I already have," he exclaimed. "It's over!"

"Not WonderFinish, either. Not any of it." She kept her voice under control. "You're the dreamer. Just—don't stop."

He studied her sadly. "I won't do that to you again." His mouth twisted upward in a quirky smile. "And I *can't* stop dreaming. I can't. So if I can't stop it, no one else is going to be able to stop it, no matter what they do. I won't stop dreaming until the day I die." He swiveled in his chair, staring at nothing. "If even then."

2.

When the handhelds finally started working again, he had long since disappeared. Bounder had already rounded up all the elves on the field. They huddled around Saddler, who shook the red device and snapped it on his palm.

"Ouch! Hey!" a voice squawked over background roaring and whistling. "What the heck are you doing down there?"

"Sorry, didn't know we were back on," Saddler shouted. "There's too much static on this thing! I can barely hear you!"

"Yeah, well I can hear you loud and clear, so I tell you what, *I'll* shout and *you* talk!"

"Right. Who's this, Skye? You see him?"

"Yeah. Yeah, I saw him. For a second or two, anyway, before my own team started giving me hell. Went past me like a rocket!"

"Which way?"

"North. You must have seen him!"

"Just making sure. Stand by, I'm going to get the others on." He stabbed a green button, and a chorus of pops and whistles filled the air. He waved the handheld in exasperation. "All right, who do we have here?" he asked. His eyes followed tiny teams crisscrossing the sky.

Two male voices answered. "Shrike," said one. "Skimmer," the other barked.

"All right, who saw what? Skimmer?"

"Same thing," Skimmer said. "I heard what Skye said. Shot past me, I started my team after them, and then it was like I had two mules on my hands. By the time I figured out which end was up, he was gone."

"Yup," Shrike agreed. "I thought mine were heading straight down. Then we lost the radios, and nobody knew what to do."

More whirrs and crackles. Biting his lip, Saddler scanned the sky. "...Well, he can't have gone far," he said. "He should be somewhere around the Near Zone. You don't see anything at all?"

A long pause before the three fliers answered in sequence.

Saddler sighed raggedly. "Then he's gone down."

"Or gone farther out," Skimmer said. "He must have been hitting delivery speed when he went past me."

"That could put him almost anywhere," Bounder muttered.

"Or straight into the ground, the way that wagon was breaking up on him," Saddler growled. "Near Zone's my guess, and that's a lot of territory, even so."

"I could scan the Zone, look for signs," Skye said.

"Not by yourself, you won't! I lost one today, I'm not losing any more! We'll tag-team. I don't want anybody losing sight of anybody up there. The way these teams are behaving, and these radios, I—Just, the three of you stay close, all right? I'll get some other fliers up there, get you some company. We'll do a sweep of the Zone."

The handheld crackled, then a different voice cut through the static, a low, firm female voice. "You won't find him in the Zone."

"Demon! What do you mean?"

"I did a recon on him, way out."

"I should ground you for that!"

"But you won't." Demon coughed gently. "I had to pull my team up for a minute, same as everybody else, but I fought them through it, kept an eye on him. Wasn't much more than a speck, even then. I had to hit delivery speed just to keep him in view. Even then it didn't help much."

"What do you mean?"

"I mean all of a sudden he disappeared. I think he dropped. Like a stone. I could barely see him as it was, and then he was gone."

"How far out?"

A pause before Demon continued in that same low unaffected voice. "I was out at the Edge when I lost him. My guess is somewhere beyond."

One of the other fliers whistled, an eerie squeal over the electronic space. "Jesus, that's all big rocks and trees, ravines and all that out there," Saddler said. "If he went down out there, I don't—Demon, you're *sure*?"

"Yes."

"Because if he *did…*"

Nothing but crackles on the airwaves. Finally, she said, "I don't like it any more than you do, Saddler. But it's what I saw. …I could go back out."

"No, *dammit*, Demon, I don't care *how* good you are, something's wrong, the deer just don't bust apart like that, every team acting like they've never flown before and—It's like there's something in the air, and if we try to push on it, I…! No we've gotta figure this out, set up teams and—God, beyond the Edge! We'll have to get provisions, send pairs out at delivery speed, and even then, those places …" He finished in a bitter groan, "We'd have to land in the safe spots and go in on foot. And what we'll find—" He shook his head. "We'll be lucky to find what's left of him by spring."

Crackles and pops. Then Skye. "Saddler, we can't just leave him."

"I'm not *saying* that, I want him back as much as anybody. It's just that we—if we don't *plan* this thing, if we just run out and chase him, we'll put ourselves at risk, go over the same ground, and—" He stopped a moment, his mind flashing to training schedules, corporate pressures, extra deer coming in for who the hell knew why, press releases, santa matchups—before he shook his head violently. He sighed, a loud, desperate sound. "I need everybody in."

"What?" Skimmer exclaimed.

"Everybody! We gotta plan this. Get our routes figured out and go out there organized. I need real units under everybody, too, not flimsy little wagons that are gonna bust apart as soon as you hit an air bump. In, now!"

"But—"

"*Now*!" Saddler stomped to the edge of the landing field, heels digging into the semifrosted ground. Bounder and the others trailed like so many geese. They watched the teams land, Skye, Shrike, Skimmer, and last of all Demon, diving down as though forcing her team to recognize they could perform beyond their limits. Some of the elves broke from the huddle and tended to the teams, while the four fliers, awkward in their white-padded suits, waddled toward Saddler.

"OK, boss, now what?" Skimmer asked.

"We need real machines under you," Saddler said. "We'll use speed sleds."

"But if we're going out beyond the Edge, sleds won't help," Shrike objected. "You can't take them through that terrain."

"Yeah, but they're better for aerial searches," Saddler said. "Nothing'll work on the ground out there."

"Can we even get him back on a speed sled?" Skimmer said. "He's a pretty big guy."

Demon was busy peeling off the white suit. "We can get him back," she said. "Just extra weight. God, this stupid thing makes me sweat."

"We'll head back to the grounds to get the sleds, organize some of the faster deer," Saddler said. "You all feel like going back up, or should we send others?"

"Naw, we saw him," Skye said. "We'll go. But we'll take any extra help, too."

A shout went up from the landing field. One of Demon's team had stumbled and was kneeling in the tall grass. "Knew I pushed them too hard," she said. "Half a second." She jumped out of the suit and left it lying on the ground.

They watched her dash to the field, slender and agile even by elves' standards, body thin and hard like a knife, straight close-cropped red hair. In an instant, she'd reached the fallen animal, brushing aside the handler, talking closely and earnestly to the beast, eye to eye. Seconds later, the animal managed to regain wobbly footing.

"There's one who knows her own mind," Saddler said. "Knows the deer, too." He raised his voice. "We've got to get going! Come on!"

Demon sprinted back. The other fliers peeled off their suits before jumping into a couple of nearby transport wagons. They bounced and jostled down a road that seemed much too long now.

Saddler, Bounder and Demon had squeezed themselves into the first wagon and bumped along, Saddler snapping the reins unnecessarily. He reached under the seat for a handheld, punched a couple of numbers. "Come on, come on!" he growled. "Strapper?"

"Strapper here."

"It's Saddler! Listen, there's been an accident."

"On the field?"

No, not on the field, we had a flier go down, the JEDI."

"The JEDI? He wasn't alone, was he?"

"*Yes* he was alone, it was a bizarre set of— I'll explain the whole thing later, one of the wagons broke and the team took off."

"Which way?"

"North. A long ways, we think. We *think*, because he didn't have a handheld or anything. Demon followed him out a ways. Listen, Strapper, we need speed sleds and recovery teams, the best deer, provisions, rescue gear, all of it. Wait, what?"

Demon had laid a small hand on his arm. "Have them get my advanced team."

"OK. Strapper, you hear? Get Demon's advanced team ready, plus the others. Get 'em set up on the central field, we'll pick 'em up from there. I'll tell you more when I get in." He snapped the radio off. "Jesus, he probably thinks he needs paperwork to release the sleds!"

Bounder stared ahead. "I should never have gotten out of that wagon first."

"How the hell would you know it was going to break apart under his butt?" Saddler said. "Don't kick yourself for nothing."

"What really happened out there?" Demon murmured.

"Well, it's pretty easy, I think," Bounder said. "We had his first flight, we landed, I got off the wagon first, turned to one of the handlers for a split second, and then crunch! bang! There's seat boards on the ground, the team's back in the air, and all I can see are the tops of his feet! I never saw a wagon move like that!" He scowled at the surrounding countryside. "I should never have left him alone!"

Demon studied the sky, interpreting cloud patterns. "That sky's roughening up," she said. "We'll have some pretty good cross currents to deal with." She smoothed back already well-behaved hair. "Where did he come from, anyway?"

"He's a JEDI, you know that. And he's been a disaster wherever he's been," Saddler said. "You should have heard what they said in the plants! Everywhere he went, it was something. And now here. Just when we think he's settling down —"

"No, I mean where did he really come from," she cut in. Her eyes never left the sky, despite the bounces. "It's like our whole world parted today to let him through."

"What, so he could kill himself on the rocks?" Bounder snapped.

Saddler glanced at her. "Demon, what is it? You were all but born up there. What are you thinking?"

Her eyes scanned the clouds restlessly, picking up clues. "You ever see teams do what those did out there?" She asked. "…Thought not. So let's think about it. You're a big guy sitting in a wagon, the seat gives way under your ass, you fall backwards, maybe snap the reins, and then the team reacts by doing what? Bounder, Saddler? What?"

Saddler snapped the reins. "They'd jump forward. Then they'd stop."

"Exactly. But that's not what they did, was it? 'The deer know,' Saddler. Unless you think it's just a saying now." She stopped looking at the sky and looked at him.

"Maybe," he grunted at length. "So what do they know? Like Bounder said. They know enough to get out of the way and let a half-elf JEDI go to his death?"

"You think he's dead, then?" she asked.

"*You* said he dropped like a stone beyond the Edge! You think he's alive?"

"Bounder. Bounder. It's not you." She put a wiry arm around him. "Don't do this to yourself. There's nothing you could have done."

He clamped his jaw. "I have to go after him."

"You'll go with me. Don't worry. If he's someplace to be found, we'll find him."

They had reached the main grounds by now. Strapper had already set things in motion. Elves hurried back and forth across the central field, where several speed sled teams stood waiting, four reindeer at each low-slung, dark and slippery device.

Saddler stopped the wagon midway along the field. He waved at Strapper, a tiny figure standing at the far end of the field, just outside the brown administration building. The figure waved back.

Saddler jumped down and joined the others, who had already gathered in a little knot, eager to be going. "All right," he said. "Demon. You've done this before. Who else?"

"I have," Skye said. "Just not out so far."

"OK. Demon, you were the last one to see him. You'll be in charge up there. Get everyone out as fast as you can, but don't stretch them past delivery speed. I asked Strapper for strong deer, but there's pacing even so."

"Agree. We'll do the assignments on the field."

He counted the sleds. "Go in pairs and stay in close contact," he said. "Five sleds, so you'll have a couple of extra teams to bring up to speed. Skye," he continued, eyes snapping back to the group, "go through the checklist, make sure they've given you everything you need, wind gear, provisions, emergency care, flares, radios—everything." He thought a minute. "Folding stretchers, too, if you can fit them… Anything I miss? Anything else?"

The fliers glanced at each other. "I think we're ready," Demon said.

"Take them out. …*And*," he said, stopping them in mid-turn. "Make sure you all come back. With, or without him. All of you."

"If he's there, we'll find him," Demon called over her shoulder, leading the fliers onto the field.

He watched her a moment, small and steely, leading the others. "Right, Demon. …If he's to be found." He spun about, climbed back in his wagon, and flagged down a handler for the other wagon.

Strapper's form grew as Saddler headed his way. Strapper had the perpetually harried look of someone crushed into inadequacy by mountains of process and paperwork. That he had fielded the sleds so quickly was surprising.

When the wagon reached the administration building, Saddler jumped down. “He’s out past the Edge, Strapper.” He hitched the team. “Down in the rocks, somewhere.”

Strapper sighed. “There’s no way, then.” His dark eyes, swimming behind glasses, scanned skies unfamiliar to him these days. “I liked him.”

“I did, too.”

“Everything else going on, and this had to happen.”

“Reminds you of what’s important, Strapper. I mean, what could possibly be worse than this?”

“Yes,” Strapper said vaguely. “It does remind one. Are there enough sleds?”

“I think so.” Saddler shook his head. “What do you tell rescue teams when you know what they’ll find? How do you keep them going without lying to them?”

A shout from the field. The five sleds shot skyward, circled the field once, a high V against charred clouds, then flashed north at delivery speed, disappearing in seconds. Even though he knew it was senseless, Saddler waved them on.

“You don’t have to tell them anything, Saddler,” Strapper said. “They’ll bring him back if there’s nothing but dust.”

“Yes.” Saddler put his arm down. “Even if he only made two flights.”

“I thought it was only one.”

“You have to count the one that—well.” An elf dashed out of the building and up to Strapper. “We’ll have radio contact throughout, so we’ll—Strapper, what?”

Strapper had taken the piece of paper from the elf and was reading it rapidly, his eyes grown even larger and more lost. “My God,” he breathed.

“What?” Saddler said. “What could it possibly be?”

Strapper held out the page. Saddler snatched it and read it, then read it again as though the second time through might change the words, might undo the NPI letterhead and the Board statement, the actions and the call to a mandatory all-hands news briefing. He looked up. Strapper was staring at him. When he found his voice at last, he croaked, "A joke. A joke, Strapper. It has to be. If not, then—what—"

Strapper stared at nothing. "It's not," he said, his voice dull. "What'll happen to us, Saddler? What'll we do?"

3.

This time, there was no ice sleigh. But it was still hot and sticky in the huge convention hall. Roxy pulled a handkerchief from her handbag and dabbed her forehead, hoping she wasn't in for a mascara disaster. From her strategic seat at a table near the back, she watched the harried fake-tuxed staff hustle around hundreds of white-clothed tables, whisking away dinner plates and plunking down desserts and sweaty icewater pitchers. What did they make of two thousand red-suited conventioneers?

She'd hardly touched her chicken kiev. How many chicken ranches did they decimate, and how many herds of cows did they milk to feed this gang? And tubs of jambalaya for the more adventurous. She poked the bird again, then set her fork aside.

She scanned her program card. One of the half-elf senior trainers waxed way overlong on something or other. Many of the santas were shifting position almost continually. *Good thing the Chief's last, or they'd never have stuck it out this long. The steam here is almost visible. Just like the bayou.*

That had certainly been different: a bayou boat tour with the Chief, half-elf CEO decked out in a "Save the Whales" T-shirt, searching for alligators amid the brown stinking water and the half-submerged, rotting houseboats. Grumbling at the fat-bottomed passengers, too. It had been his idea, over her pre-event jitters, to take advantage of the free time between hotel checkin and his closing dinnertime speech. "Doesn't happen often enough. My getting out like this," he'd said.

So they sat, discovering the alligators and more. "When I do get out, I have to be so careful," he said. "I see the glances, hear the whispers, especially from the kids. Even on a boat like this, when we've got a corner to ourselves, you never know. I have to avoid using the 'e' word. Sometimes I even call them 'people.'" He chuckled.

"I hadn't realized how hard it must be."

"It is." He bit a lip, scanned the steaming waters. "People give me that look, you know, the 'could it be?' look, and just as suddenly, I see their rational minds take over. Impossible, they think. So if I did start talking about—certain things—they'd probably see it as some old guy's rant, and they'd leave me alone.

"But the children, well. They're not so easily fooled. I'll be on a trip somewhere, my head full of statistics and schemes and politics and strategies and next steps. Then I'll see some kid giving me one of those looks, and all of a sudden it all falls away, and I'll be wondering how much of me did he really see? Like I've been caught doing something wrong. It happens especially when they're little. Their teen years are when they lose it."

"Lose what?"

"That 'seeing' thing. It goes away as they get older. I think it gets burned out of them, like a fog burning off. Maybe they burn it out of each other. I don't know. But it goes away, gradually. And it's a tough, tough thing to watch."

She studied him a long moment. "How did you figure it out? About teenagers?"

Lush vegetation slid lazily before them. "…Because I *am* children, in a way," he said. "And even though neither you nor I nor any other half—any of us can ever have children, I still think our human part allows us to connect with them. Some. But I *don't* understand them that well." He glanced about before continuing conspiratorially, "You'd think after six thousand years or so…"

She smiled. "You'd think."

His eyes twinkled briefly, but when they looked away it seemed the very blue had left them. "You know, Roxy, you have it just a little easier. I can change my appearance whenever I need to. But you can change something else. You can wake up one day and decide from that day forward you aren't going to work for me, and you can do it. You can. It might be hard, but you can. That's not something I can do. I'm locked into what I do and who I am, and over the years it's grown more and more complex. More buildings, more machinery, more folks with their fingers in the pie. So now there's less and less of me and more and more of the business. The business.

"And we're doing it to everyone who works there now, asking—no, *compelling* them to become the business, to think, breathe and live it wherever and whenever they are. It isn't enough anymore to let them go home, we have to be *in* the home with them, so that they're like animals, almost, with one eye open and on the lookout, no matter what. So all of us are the business, and now that's all we are."

Applause jolted her back into the room. Where were they? The same speaker droned. *Some guys just can't finish. Shut up already! Nobody cares about your bullshit accomplishments!*

She shifted. Spokes. That was one stubborn CEO. He'd never called Spokes back, and she'd given up reminding him. She'd even tried on the boat. But his fatigue had won, and he'd leaned over the waters to say, "You're right, I haven't called him. And I won't. Not until later, or maybe even tomorrow. And something else. I almost wish I didn't have to do the speech. Then it would be a full day without NPI. What a Christmas present that would be!"

"What *do* you get for Christmas?"

"Smiles. Kids' smiles. Or I used to. Hot cocoa, cookies. Used to get that, too. And a hug, and a welcome home." His mouth worked briefly. "Used to get those. Now, hmm." He cleared his throat. "If I'm lucky, the stock'll go up a couple points. Or there'll be a corporate dinner, somebody currying favor with a special event."

And she decided to risk it. "What'll you do Christmas Eve?"

His answer sounded prepared, rehearsed and re-rehearsed. "Tend the fire," he said without expression. "Tend the fire. You never, ever know."

The speaker "in conclusioned" for the final time, waited until the terse applause died before holding up one hand. "Now," he announced, "it gives me great pleasure to introduce the one being who brings it all together, the one for whom we wear the red suits—our symbol, the strength of Christmas—our Chief!"

Two thousand red-suited santas jumped to their feet, applause thundering through the hall. Roxy stood, wincing at the intro sentence. All those meetings between the speech committee and the communications consultant, concepts framed and reframed, "Santa" excised but spirit retained, teasing and tousling and mussing and moussing the words, happily presenting at last a gelded sentence, a boned, content-free version suitable for the weakest tooth in the house.

There he was. She noted a dimple in the roar. He'd refused the suit again. The first time, he said it didn't fit, it was too hot, it had no proper pocket for his reading specs. Now he no longer bothered. Even so, what he represented filled the room, he standing behind the rostrum, certain of his authority, white beard waterfalling over his dark suit.

He waited. The crowd seated themselves, roar quieting to a rumble and then to a buzz and an occasional hoot. He cleared his throat. "Is this thing on?" he boomed into the mike, and dozens of santas jumped. "Thought it wasn't," he rumbled. "Maybe I'd better speak up a bit." Titters from the crowd. "But to get serious for a moment," he continued. "How's everyone feeling tonight?"

"Good!" popped from various points, and he bellowed, "I can't hear you!" sending them over the edge again.

"OK!" The pandemonium receded. "Now the first thing you must be asking is, Where's the red suit? You do this as long as I have, you don't need the red suit. But it's still great to look out and see so many people wearing the red for the first time."

Applause and shouts. Roxy focused on the white beard wagging like a beacon, the rest of the room darkening as though she viewed the brilliant curls through a tunnel. His words washed over her—all the points correctly defined and perfectly delivered, moving from the meaning of Christmas, to the joy of children seeing Santa, to the responsibilities attending the red suit.

Something was missing. It was all the right words. Was it the heat? How he said it? Or had he changed so much that he didn't fit the words anymore? *Or maybe it's me that's changed.*

The crowd roared on. He swept towards his well-prepared conclusion. "So remember," he boomed, "when you wear the red, you're wearing—you *are*—Santa Claus. Everything I've said before this, all that you've been taught, carries that responsibility. Children everywhere will come to you with their simple and sincere requests. Honor those requests, enjoy the children, and stay true to your colors. Now, go out and have some fun. Ho-ho-ho, Me-rry Christmas!"

That sent them all into pandemonium, hohoho's bouncing off every surface and colliding in the high spaces. They had jumped to their feet and now milled around, talking. Some had already left the hall to get an early start on French Quarter fun.

Roxy threaded her way through it, ignoring the usual glances, making her way toward the side door where he had disappeared. She passed the podium. One of the half-elf coordinators shouted over the din, feedback punctuating his sentences, reminding the santas that if they wanted to hit the streets and enjoy the French Quarter, that was all right as long as they changed out of the red suits first.

Time to regroup. She pushed through the door and checked to see if he was heading the way she'd suggested, down the side hallway to the service elevator. One big shin flashed as he turned the corner. She dashed after him and caught him in the hallway.

"Well, what do you think?" he asked.

"Hot," she said. "And long."

"The heat does that." He picked up that terrific pace again. "How many folks we have here? Other than speakers. Event handlers, coordinators."

"Let's see." She trailed off, counting. "Ten or eleven."

"Ten or eleven. Half-elves?"

"To keep suspicions down."

He punched the service elevator's up arrow. "Right. So that's what, a hundred, two hundred santas per coordinator. Wow." He shook his head as the doors opened. Ugly quilted padding surrounded them. The doors slowly rumbled shut. "Sure hope they can keep them all under control."

"Well, most of the time there's no problem," she said. "From what you've told me. They're excited, but most of them are responsible, so they put the suits away and keep things pretty low-key."

"I know. It's the borderline ten percent. That's one of the reasons why we do this in New Orleans. In case they break loose. People will think it's just another oddball event down here." The freight elevator lumbered to a halt, the doors grumbling open. They stepped onto the top floor, where rooms had been blocked for the CEO entourage, which included various speakers and coordinators. No new santas here. "I like 'em, but not that much," he'd explained only once.

He still glanced up and down the hall. "That service elevator was a good idea, Roxy," he said. "Gets 'em all out of the way for a while." He headed for the presidential suite at the end of the long hall. "Tell you what," he continued, "why don't we give it about an hour, and then check out the Quarter. We can meet in the lobby around nine."

"I thought you wanted some peace and quiet. You're hardly going to get that out there. Especially if one of them spots you."

They'd reached her door. She stopped, and after a step or two so did he. "Yes, well," he said, rubbing his nose. "But you haven't seen the French Quarter, and who knows when you'll be this way again, and—believe me, it's an experience. All that heat, all those people. You can be Santa Claus down there, and it won't make a damn bit of difference. You'll see. You game?"

She hesitated, then smiled. "Yes. Yes, I'd like to see it. Around nine?"

"Nine it is," he said, and stumped down the hall to his suite.

She glanced at her watch before sliding the key card into the lock. Just before eight. An hour to unwind. She closed the door behind her, surveyed the unfamiliar large surroundings, a suite almost as large as her apartment. *So this is corporate life among the higher-ups.*

She hadn't been to the bathroom since before dinner. Sitting, reflecting, it occurred to her how long a day it had been—first the landing, checking in, a brief rest, then the bayou tour, the dinner, the speech, and now, a few minutes to herself before the Quarter. She finished and took care of things, stood and looked herself over in the mirror. Her makeup had held, but there were signs of weakness in that bright light. She dabbed at herself. Then she stopped. In an hour, she'd be back in that heat, walking the streets with him, sweating, staining. No. *It's time I took some time off as well.* She reached for the cold cream.

When she was done, she sized things up. No ruby red lips, no shading to accentuate the eyes, no shadowing to sculpt the cheekbones, no mascara to lengthen and thicken the lashes. For an instant, she glimpsed the youngster peekabooing. But the eyes didn't emerge.

There was the real Roxy. Not what he saw, not what the elves saw. Someone might see her one day.

She grabbed tan loose-fitting slacks hanging behind the door and stepped out of the bathroom momentarily, rummaging in the adjacent closet until she found a generous white cotton shirt. She stripped heels, skirt, blouse, replacing them with shirt, tan slacks, and low-heeled shoes. She loosened her hair with her hands, feeling cool air reach the inner places. A couple of steps returned her to the bathroom and the honest mirror.

Even so. She turned sideways, noted curves and shapings impossible to hide. *Even so.*

She walked to the bedroom, picked up the remote, and switched on the TV before kicking off her shoes and plunking on the bed. Some kind of American game show was on, lookalike squinting contestants answering questions only an idiot could get wrong, egged on by a wild crowd and a plastic host. She flipped the remote and landed in a public TV special on the inner lives of some northern tribe, grinning round-faced people who must have smelled awful in those furs, complete with living-color close-ups of a seal gutting. She winced. That took guts, no pun, especially the feasting part afterwards. She flipped again, hit some kind of sitcom, and settled back.

A couple of minutes later, the phone startled her. She stared wildly at it a moment before snatching up the receiver. "Hello," she mumbled.

"You coming?" Santa's voice boomed in her ear. "It's nine-fifteen. I'm worried that a gang of those jokers is going to show up and whisk me away."

"I'm sorry—I just—"

"Take your time," he said. "I understand. You sure you're up to it?"

"I—yes, just give me a few minutes. See you." She shook herself awake, found her shoes, and made her way to the bathroom. *A little cold water is what I need.* She splashed her face and neck. *I can't believe I fell asleep like that.* She examined herself, grabbed her handbag and headed out.

"That's a different you," he said, when they met in the lobby. "Did I wake you up?"

"I guess I didn't realize how tired I was."

"It happens. Especially when you're not used to traveling. You look comfortable."

"Thanks."

"Well, showtime." He led the way, and they spun through the revolving door and onto Canal Street.

They entered the simmering French Quarter, and even though it was the summer season, people clogged the narrow street. She hurried to match his pace. He was right: instead of the tan chinos and green polo shirt, he could have dressed in the suit and had the reindeer in tow, and it wouldn't have raised an eyebrow. Actually, the bald guy in the white suit coming their way didn't seem to have any eyebrows.

They turned from Canal to Bourbon, passing the steel posts thrust into the Quarter streets to prevent cars from mowing down the celebrants. A solitary sax man belted out a jazz riff, open case speckled with coins and bills. They pushed into a thickening throng of sweat, colors, arms, legs, textures, skins of all shades, music overtaking and surrounding them, a collision of sounds bold, raucous, lively, mapped to the signs hanging over the storefronts, advertising food, oversized cheap mugs of beer, nude dancing, hot music, weird shows starring the locals, massage and other dark and smoky delights somewhere upstairs. Spilled beer and Cajun spices assaulted their noses. They could barely see the kaleidoscope storefronts, Caribbean pastels hidden by clustered behinds, and some stumblers already so full of beer they'd be early targets. Strangers hawked free tickets for oddball events, or tried to convert them to various religions.

One such, a wild-eyed young lady whose blond hair exploded every way, thrust a strange amulet into Santa's hand, while her partner, whose hair was neat, short, and multihued, watched them the way those bayou birds had cased the gators.

Santa turned the brass thing over—a curious combination of a grizzled sea captain and a naked wench entwined about a ship's wheel. "Leave the tangles of your life," the inscription on the wheel said. "Join the one true way."

"No, thanks." He tried to give it back.

"But you must take it," the exploding hair said. "You must. If you don't, you will have bad luck until the end of your days!"

"Ah-hah, and just how long do you think that would be?"

"It will be long enough," she intoned. "The stars in the sky will change their positions, and the poles will shift from place to place, before your luck will change."

"…Roxy, do you think she knows who I am?"

"I doubt it."

"You are a *god*!" exploding hair cried, while her multihued partner voted *alligator* with her eyes.

A fat guy in his thirties wandered up, all stomach and insufficient tie-dyed shirt and docker shorts and spindly legs and white socks and clunky shoes, a 32-ounce beer sloshing in one puffy hand. "Hey, do what she says, man!" he said. "Lemme see that omelet!"

"That's amulet," Santa handed it over. "You can have it, for all I care."

"He cannot!" The blonde reached for it. "He has not gifted the gods!"

"How *do* you do that to your hair?" Roxy wondered softly.

The fat guy turned the bright thing over in his free hand, waving the priestess off with his sloshy one. Another guy, normal sized but appearing thin because of the fat one, slouched up, the 32-ouncer overlarge in his hand. "Hey, Frank! You ready? What're you doing?"

"Getting religion from this nun, here. Wow, look at this! There's a naked lady on this thing! What kind of gift do I have to make, anyway? This looks like—OW!"

The multihued one had dug her nails into his free arm. "Give it back, you creep," she growled in a masculine voice.

"Can we go now?" Roxy whispered to Santa. "I'm not sure what that thing is. ...I mean the one with all the colors. ...Either one, actually." She tugged his arm. "C'mon!"

"Just a minute." Santa dug into a pocket, smiling at the frizzed one. "Here, will this do?" he said, offering a gold Santean.

She grabbed it. "Oh, wow!" she silly-puttyed. "That's really cool!"

"Let go of my goddamn arm you, whatever you are!" Frank bellowed. "Billie, get this thing off me!"

Billie stepped up. "Let go of him, before I—Shit." He stumbled on the curb and fell on his ass, pulling the other two on top of him in an explosion of beer and swearing. Several people watching applauded politely.

The blond one's eyes never left the gold Santean. "Let him go, Oswald. The Old One has given the special gift."

From somewhere under that pile of tie-dyed beer, Oswald grunted, "So get off me, already, lardass! You heard the lady!"

"*Now* can we?" Roxy tugged harder.

"Merry Christmas!" Santa allowed himself to be led away.

"Do *not* talk to these people anymore!" she said. "Who knows what could happen?"

"The trouble with you, Roxy, is you have no sense of adventure." He chuckled. "Things could have been a lot worse. That beer missed us completely."

"What were you doing giving away a Santean? Your own policy says don't do it!"

"I *am* the CEO. If I give away one lousy Santean, what's the big deal?"

"You know, you may be a CEO up there, but when you get out, you're just like a kid! A big kid, too," she added under her breath.

"That's flattering," he said. "You take good care of me, Roxy."

"Can't we just go listen to some jazz?"

They dodged up Bourbon. Confusing sounds assaulted them, but beneath the cacophony a steady, disciplined beat thrummed, pulling them along. The other sounds faded behind the crisp riff coming from a corner stage bar. Lights, colors and smells melted and merged, chaos changing to purpose. The music shaped and coiled, a fractal sound mass that swept people in, enveloping them in rapid-fire sound, string bass and drummer holding the heartbeat while tenor sax and trumpet fought it out on top. They pushed their way inside, where the close heat and smoke added to the atmosphere, and they made a lucky find of a just-freeing-up table near one of the many doors on the place, somewhat near the action. They pulled up tall chairs, and Santa paid the higher-than-street prices for a couple of chilled mugs of beer.

She'd never been in a place with this many people before, conversing, sweating, laughing, some struggling to stay attentive to the music, some aspiring to replace the bowler-hatted black bass player, or the old white drummer, or the black trumpet player, or the beige sax man. She watched Santa take a pull from his mug, give a satisfied sigh, and sit back. She took a polite sip. How tempting it would be to pour anything cold down your throat, and what better than this when you had nothing but watching to do? She set the mug down and pushed it a few inches away, watching faces, expressions. "What causes people to end up like that?" She raised her voice above the din.

"Like what?"

"Like that blonde—frizzy thing. Selling weird religious art! Where does she get it, anyway?"

Santa took another pull. "You never know. Maybe she got herself a Mercedes selling that stuff."

"Be serious!"

"I am. She hasn't ended up like that, by the way. She's just there right now. She's found herself up to this point, and in a few years, she may find her way into being a stockbroker. Happens all the time."

"Not with that hair, it doesn't!"

He laughed. "No. But you can change hair. People do. You changed too, today."

"That was a practical decision you wouldn't understand. Try keeping makeup in place in this heat!"

"Looks good, though," he said. "Try it when we get back to NPI, see what happens."

She let it go. "And those other two, that just—walked up," she muttered.

"Who, pork and beans?" he said, and she laughed. "People don't stop being kids just because they get big, Roxy. That's what makes our job so much fun."

The band fired up an intense stride song, and they lost themselves in the smoky growl of the sax defining the line. Santa ordered another beer, while she nursed hers. She had no idea how long they'd spent in that place, cooked by music and heat. When the band took a break, she and Santa tumbled outside and into an even more densely packed crowd.

By now the Quarter had hit its stride, a raucous burn. They decided to cross Bourbon and take in the other side on their way back to the hotel. The usual cast lunged up, and they began sidestepping.

A frizzy disaster loomed in the near distance. "Here comes your future stockbroker," she said. "Maybe we should cross the street."

"Nah! She's probably forgotten all about me." He made right for them.

Roxy winced, expecting the worst. But when they drew up almost face to face, she could see the blonde's eyes were elsewhere. "Oswald, look! I can't believe they're all dressed like that, in this heat! What a bunch of morons!"

"Targets, you mean," Oswald growled. Oswald's makeup had begun to run, an alarming sight. "Let's hit 'em."

From behind, Roxy heard an unusual commotion, a collection of loud male voices, followed by something she wanted so badly to misinterpret, ho-ho-ho's rising unmistakably into the steam. The hair on her neck stood up, and she spun around, catching Santa by the arm and twisting him about. "Oh, my *God*," she exclaimed. "Of all the *stupid*—"

She stared at the red and black wall lurching up the street behind them, big boots thumping and stumbling, fat belt buckles glinting in the party lights, and beards, beards, beards, bobbing and wagging like a collection of evil little clouds, some tugged and stretched thin, some beer-stained, some falling off grinning and fatlipped faces.

Santa's eyes widened a bit, then narrowed into that stabbing blue known to terrorize NPI execs. "I thought we told those idiots to lose the suits before they hit the streets!" He stumped toward the advancing wave.

"What are you going to do with them?" she exclaimed, struggling to keep up with him. "You can't just talk them out of this!"

But he was already in their midst, arms outstretched, palms down. "What are you doing out here, dressed like this?" he shouted. "You know the rules! Get back to your hotels!"

The wave broke, or rather, various wavelets crashed into each other. One of the santas stood forward and looked Santa up and down. "Hey, it's the boss!" he said loudly. "Or ex-boss! Whaddaya think, fellas, should we do what he says?"

Shouts followed this. A few santas wavered sheepishly, and one of them said, "Maybe we oughtta go back and get out of these stupid things. They're too damn hot!"

"Look at what you've done to them!" Santa shouted. "Beards half-cocked, beer stains everywhere! You're a disgrace! Is this what we trained you for?"

The exploding hair lady stepped up then. "Leave all this behind!" she shouted. "Repent, and follow the ways of true faith."

That quieted them long enough for Santa to glance at her and mutter "I don't need your help right now, you know," before one of the santas called out, "Hey, is that Mrs. Claus? 'Cause if it's Mrs. Claus, she sure has changed!"

"Listen you guys," Santa thundered, "will you *please*, just, get out of the damn suits. I don't *care* if you have a good time out here, even too good a time. I don't. But not in the suits!"

"Listen to the Old One!" the blond called out. "He has much wisdom! And he has sacred gold!" She held the Santean aloft for both the santas and the gathering crowd. In the small befuddled silence, she *sotto-voce'd*, "You know, we could make a pretty good team. Oswald used to be a great partner, but lately, the makeup thing–"

The lead santa cut her short. "Hey, why should we listen to *him*, anyway? He's history! He doesn't call the shots any more!"

For just an instant Roxy saw the big shoulders sag.

"What are you talking about?" Santa bellowed. "I don't care if this *is* the French Quarter! I'm still the one you report to, and I'm telling you to get out of the damn suits!"

"You tell him, dude!" somebody from Santa's side of the street yelled.

The lead santa just grinned. "That's pretty good!" he said, nodding. "You just keep on going, don't you! Just like you did during the speech, like you were still running things, even though the Board was making its announcement about you! That was pretty cool, playing like you didn't know a thing, even though the game was over!"

Roxy dashed up and took his arm.

"Hey *hey*, who's the babe?" a santa shouted, and someone from their side of the crowd followed with a "C'mere, mama!"

"Shut *up*, you *total* morons!" she spat, and they did for a minute. She watched the blue leave his eyes again, glanced at the lead santa and saw some hint of an exchange, human to half-elf, the challenge wavering in the human's eyes as well.

"Hey, he *doesn't* know!" another santa shouted, and she watched the lead santa, seeing the game played a turn too far, seeing the terrible way a face can crumble when purpose leaves it, step back and say, "Hey, maybe it was just a joke, you know, a really, really bad joke! And we didn't know any better, so we—Hey, I'm *sorry*, man!"

He'd already spun and stalked away from them, Roxy feeling the arm first tremble and then stiffen and then the legs start churning, her own forced to keep pace, pulling her arm back for balance, santas falling away behind them like a red nightmare, sounds dwindling—"Repent! Or you will have bad luck!" and "Hey, does anybody want to buy a red suit? I can be reasonable!"—striding and striding, she looking at him, not daring to break in, he shoveling partiers and stumblers aside, charging block on block back to the hotel.

Finally, she ventured, "Maybe it *is* some kind of a joke. A really stupid, stupid horrible joke."

"That would be nice," he growled. "Except it's not. That damned Board, I should—" He set his jaw and pushed on.

When they reached the cool hotel lobby, he stopped. Sweat rivered from his white brow down the sides of his face and into his beard. The curls shook as he scanned the place, not seeing the surrounding people, baggage from late arrivals, short queues at the reservation desk, a couple of businessmen discussing something in overstuffed lounge chairs. He saw and did not see her. "Let's go up on the mezzanine. There's a bar, we should be able to learn something."

They took the sweeping red-carpeted stairs to the mezzanine, to Charley's Cajun Corner. Amid stylish, we-don't-really-live-here alligator and houseboat décor, they grabbed two scaly barstools. Fortunately, it was all but empty, the television switched to ESPN. Wiping his face, Santa ordered a beer for himself and a coke for Roxy. When the bartender brought change, Santa asked him to switch on CNN.

They had to wait ten incredibly long minutes before the financials came on and even then, stock performance was the top story, a one-day plunge tailgating yesterday's Transcom fiasco.

There it was. "In other financial news today, in a surprise move, the Board of Directors of North Pole Industries announced that Samuel Claussen, CEO since the inception of the Company, will no longer serve in that capacity. In the interim, the Board has named Jerome Baylor, a relative newcomer from the automotive sector, as acting CEO. Wall Street reacted favorably, feeling that Baylor's focus on cost-cutting and restructuring for the new economy will bring new discipline to NPI, whose recent financial performance had not been in line with analyst expectations. NPI stock closed today at 79 5/8, up 2 and an eighth. When we come back—"

"My God, Baylor," Santa groaned. "Of all the nasty moves. You hear those words, Roxy? 'Not in keeping with analyst expectations.' *That's* how a CEO lives or dies in this world." He sighed. "Baylor. He'll kill them. How could they?" He frowned. "But they didn't say I was out, did they? They said I would no longer serve in that capacity. So maybe that means I'd be taking the day-to-day stuff over, something like that. I bet something happened to Racer, he finally got too ill to go on. They knew I didn't like the CEO thing. But COO, that's different. I'd have all the fun but not the PR work. That must be it. Why didn't they tell me?"

She felt like a bayou bird. "Maybe Spokes was trying. You never did call him back."

"Spokes, yeah. I can count on him. He'd give me a straight answer, not all this financial crap." He patted his shirt pocket. "Where's my phone?"

"It's probably up in your—suite." She fished in her handbag. "Here, use mine."

"Thanks." He grabbed it and punched in some numbers, held it to his ear for a moment. Then he frowned.

"Something wrong?"

"I probably just punched it wrong. He's on speed dial?"

"Yeah, seven-eight."

He tried again. "I'm getting a weird message. The phone number isn't valid. It's not your phone, is it?"

"I don't *think* so. Let me try my voice mail." She took the phone back, hit her preset. "I'm getting the same thing," she puzzled. "That's very odd."

"Maybe there's a glitch." His voice tightened just a bit. "I've got to get a hold of somebody. Who's here again?"

"Event handlers and speakers. That's the policy, so we don't draw attention."

"Damn! Well, it's working against me now, isn't it?" he growled. "Event handler's better than nothing. Who's the best we have?"

"Parker's the senior."

"Bartender! Can we get the front desk from here?"

"Certainly, sir. There's a phone at the end of the bar."

Santa walked the length of the bar and was about to pick up the receiver when Roxy said, "Wait. Look." She pointed to the television, where the NPI logo flashed.

"Concluding our financial news today, we recap the NPI ouster of Samuel Claussen. The former CEO's whereabouts are unknown, so we do not have his comment on his abrupt departure from the Company, nor what his future plans will be, now that he is no longer involved with NPI. We will continue to update this developing story."

She stared at him openmouthed before dashing toward him, he shouting "Idiots! Fools! I'll shut the whole damn thing down on them!"—the bartender's head jerking his way. "Where do they think the magic comes from? Where? Where? When I get back there, I'll shut it down so fast, they'll—" she and the bartender converging on him, she telling the bartender "It's all right, it's just some bad news, I can take care of him," with a free hand pushing Santa, feeling his hard resistance, until the words truly took hold, muscles relaxing just a bit, he sinking into the nearest chair, eyes circling until they fastened on her, intense, blue blue, the mind underneath racing, unsettled. The eyes wandered again.

"Look at me, look at me!" she exclaimed.

The blue eyes returned. "Maybe they want me to make some kind of statement," he said, "come back and say something about how the business needs to change, and then they can give me a different..." She was shaking her head. "Oh but they can't be *serious*," he gasped. "Who's going to take care of the reindeer, oversee the production figures, make the deals?"

She was still shaking her head. "But the past few years you've delegated it. Except maybe the deals. The rest is being handled by others."

"So they don't want me at *all*?" His voice faltered, eyes pleading.

She couldn't. "I don't think that's it," she said carefully. "I think it's more like what you said just now, about the analysts. Maybe this is just a move to, you know, boost the analyst ratings."

He nodded, but plainly his mind had already moved on. "I know what you're trying to say, Roxy. I don't think so. Something else is going on here. They think they can run it themselves. Maybe, maybe I should let them. For a while. See if they can do as well as they think they can. But—" He shut his eyes hard a moment. "No, I'd better get back there. As fast as I can, and–"

Her phone chirped. She stared at it on the counter, like it was a strange bug. She started to pick it up, but his big hand closed over it first. Startled, she drew back, watching the hard eyes watch her as he put the receiver to his ear. "Hello, it's the Chief, who's this? Silvertongue! Silvertongue, what the hell is going *on* up there? There's stories all over the news about this, I'm supposed to be packing my bags and—Were you part of this? Were you? ...Well then, who? The *Board*? Idiots, why couldn't we have worked something out? ...Why did they think *that*, for crying out loud? Is this some kind of stupid Wall Street thing? ...All right, so they figured out they can improve the little-boy analyst numbers, did they figure out *how* they're going to do it if I come back up there and shut down the magic? Are they going to do it without it? And what's Christmas going to look like, anyway? When I get back—...What do you *mean*, they've closed it down? ...So they think I can't—what about the phones, too? What's to stop me from calling in, stirring up—...Yeah. ...Yeah, I know. ...Well then, give me the God-damned new codes, for crying out loud! ...You *can't*? Who the hell pays—" He bit his lip, held his breath a moment. "...All right. Yeah, I understand you're in a tough spot, are they listening in or something? ...OK. Who can I talk to besides you? Not an insult, but there's some folks I need information from. I want to know who—...Oh, so it's only you. So the official negotiator talks to his ex-Chief." His voice dripped bitterness. "So I'm on the receiving end of your special blend of, of dung-hole magic. ...Yeah, dung-hole. Don't think I don't know. So what—"

He waited a long time, eyes on Roxy. "*Very* generous. I suppose I ought to thank you for the little things. ...Well, what do you expect, you think *money's* going to matter right now? ...Yeah, all right. And thanks. Well, is there a special code at least for getting through to *you*, so I can talk to one snake in the den? ...Sorry, yeah, uncalled for." He motioned to Roxy, who had already pulled pen and pad from her handbag. "Go ahead." He jotted down a combination. "Thanks. I'll give it to Roxy, too. Can she get back there? ...Not for a while, I understand." His voice had gone flat, businesslike, distant. "OK. OK, Silvertongue, and thanks for having the decency to call, I—oh, they did. To keep the other elves from—" He nodded his head. "Yeah. Well, can you at least tell them—" his voice broke, and he tried again "—at least let them know I..." He looked away from Roxy, head bowed, and cleared his throat a couple of times. "OK. ...Thanks, Silvertongue, at least get *that* message to them. Maybe a little later, when I've had a chance to—think this over, I'll be able to give you something to tell them all. OK, OK. You, too. Understand. 'Bye."

He switched the phone off and stood, shoulders still hunched. The bartender watched them both. Santa pulled the hankie from his pocket and wiped his face and eyes. Roxy edged toward him, put a hand on his shoulder, but he moved away. Abruptly, he threw back his head, shaking it, the massed white-on-white curls glinting in the dim bar light. He took a deep breath, sighed sharply, took another one, his shoulders heaving.

When he tried his voice again, it sounded stronger. "Well, Roxy, it looks like you're out of a job." He attempted to laugh.

"What do you mean?"

He turned around then, and she tried not to react. "Well, *I'm* out of a job, so it stands to reason that you are, too."

She put a hand on her hip. "I'm not working for *them*," she said spiritedly. "What's our next move?"

A touch of the old blue returned. He chuckled, stiffly, handed her the phone. "Roxy, they've given me any money I need, which means you won't go hungry, either, as long as you stick with me. Two-edged sword. Let's get out of here."

She scrambled to pick up her things and follow. "What do you mean, two-edged sword?" She hustled alongside him toward the service elevator.

"Silvertongue's my only pipe into that place, now." He punched the up button. "He's a master of the game. There's an obvious card he could play if he needed to, with you and me out here by ourselves."

Her eyes widened. "Oh, he *wouldn't*."

"Oh, he could. Or he could be made to. With el—with folks like Silvertongue, you never know. He could do it on his own, or simply be speaking for others. Afterwards, he could apologize profusely and say it was all business. Which, in essence, it would be. Lovely game we play. Besides, Roxy, you're just too damned attractive, with or without makeup. And stop blushing!" he grumped. "I'm only stating facts."

"A blush is a fact," she murmured.

The elevator doors opened, and they got on, she hesitating. But he was all business, CEO without a firm to run. "We'll need to pack our things and get the hell out of here," he said, "and the sooner we do that, the better. Get your stuff from your room, leave the key, and meet me in my suite. We can set up our plans from there." He fell silent a moment. "I wonder if any of the coordinators are still here, or did they jump ship. Wish the damn santas had." The doors opened and they stepped out.

"We'll have to do things quietly," he continued, as they headed down the hall. "Especially together like this. They've figured this beautifully. I can't send you away, you've got no place to go, and as long as you're close by—"

"I'm a big girl, I can go out on my own. I could set up with one of the suppliers. Not what I'd want to do."

He looked sidelong at her. "Not a bad idea. Why wouldn't you? Hang out for a while, see what develops, work your way back."

She stopped him with a bold hand on his arm. "Because then *you'd* be alone," she declared. "Unless you feel like getting all your conversation from Silvertongue."

He smiled. "All right. We're in it together. Can you see who else is around here?"

"I'll call the front desk. Let me pack my stuff, and I'll meet you in fifteen minutes."

"Good." He stumped down the hall.

She watched his back a moment before continuing the few steps to her own room. What *would* they do? She fished the keycard out of her handbag, opened the door. Whatever they did, they were partners now. She closed the door behind her. Partners. Unless the tabloids got a hold of it, gave it the wrong spin. But was it really the wrong spin? She shook her head sharply, to clear it. She knew herself, and she knew him. Of course it was. Of course.

4.

"So how bad was it?"

"It wasn't *fun*, Groomer. He was shocked and angry. And he was hurt. God only knows what that combination will do."

Groomer belched, reached for another hot dog. "There's the Roxy card," he twanged.

Silvertongue sighed. "I'm not playing that one. I already told you."

"Mm." Half a hot dog disappeared into Groomer's fat face. "We godda boove agaidst da udders," he mashed.

"Who do you have in mind?" Oiler asked.

"Jussa midit." The eyes popped. "Peanut out there?"

"Oiler, take a look."

Oiler stepped out of Silvertongue's office and back in. "Nope."

"Well, Gardner, Spokes and Router," Groomer said. "For starters."

"We can't do that now," Silvertongue protested. "It's too soon. Baylor needs time to consolidate his position."

"We can at least plan it now," Groomer said. "I know it's too soon to do anything. We get something going like that, all the elves will go crazy. Besides, Gardner's way too solid. She's strong with the union and her people, too. It's going to take a lot of work."

"Tell me more about the Chief," Oiler said. "How did it sound? Should we worry?"

"I don't think so. I played it carefully. Even wavered my voice a few times."

"Careful you don't play the part too well," Groomer said.

Silvertongue glared at him. "He thinks it's the Board's idea the airspace was shut down and the comm codes were changed. He knows he can't just call in to anyone. He's tried by now. He can call in to me on the special line. So the single point of entry is established. And I can call him or Roxy that way. Anyone else tries, it's blocked. All they get is a busy signal, no message."

"You think Router will figure it out?"

"Possibly, Oiler. We need to be ready if he does. That's where my message comes in. The Chief—I wonder what we should call him now? Maybe the Ex, that works."

Groomer grinned, his mouth a mass of chili and ketchup.

"The Ex asked me if I could pass anything along to the elves." Silvertongue's eyes grew distant momentarily. "He couldn't bring himself to it," he murmured at last. "So I said, Sure, and I read him part of what I'd prepared. He seemed satisfied with it."

"All Mom and apple pie, I bet," Groomer drawled, watching him.

"What I read him. I left out the part about wanting some time to himself, to think things over, far away from any association with NPI. I've got that framed as something that would come off as a reasonable reaction to a surprise move like this."

"So he basically says farewell," Oiler said, nodding, "tells everybody thanks for the six thousand years…"

"Yep. And then we wait, and when and if Router puts it all together, we've hidden all the actions under the normal bureaucratic pile. The airspace and comm codes are normal security measures following the exit of a key employee."

"Won't Router see through that?"

"He might. But he won't be able to prove it. I've already taken steps to ensure the codes aren't just disabled, they're reassigned. That makes a big mess to try to undo. It might even be impossible." Silvertongue smiled.

Groomer scooped a chili bean from his shirt to his mouth. "A good day's work," he observed. "Now comes the rest of the job—" he lowered his voice "—the part the Board doesn't know." The other two hunched forward. "RFS operations have started."

Silvertongue whistled. "That was fast."

"I know. Greed makes speed. Hey, that should be a slogan." Groomer snickered. "We've got an initial plant going north of Umea. We're using a mix of elves and some of the local Sami, so we're actually being good corporate citizens, helping the local economy. I was surprised how quickly the deal came together, but give some humans the opportunity to make a pile of money, and just look out.

"Baylor will start to consolidate. It'll be a while before he moves against any of the execs. The Wall Street boys didn't really tie poor performance to anything other than the Chief. So getting at the others won't make much sense to them. Our job is to plant some seeds, figure out ways to link the Street's low opinions to problems in managing employee resources, finances, and distribution and herds."

"Gardner, Spokes and Router."

"Precisely, Oiler. Now, Baylor's going to disrupt things anyway, because that's his nature. Even though he says he won't make any rash moves, he will. He'll slash the budgets, restructure things, buy and sell whole business units, bust up historical relationships, bruise and batter the employees, double and triple the workload, put morale right into the toilet, and generally drive fear so deep into the organization you might never be able to get it out. All in the name of achieving a vision, which is to say, a brighter reflection of the light he thinks he shines by."

"And this is good?"

"I didn't choose the bastard, Silvertongue, the Board did. Or maybe the Street did. The Street'll love all this, because it looks like change and lean operations and maximizing profits. Never mind what it does to the schleps who have to make it all work. You watch. This is an American model. We'll go from speed to frenzy and never even notice the difference.

"But this is off point. This churn provides us with natural cover. So while Baylor's creating this dog's breakfast he calls a vision, we'll be doing the RFS stuff and getting things ready for the industrial accident. And it'll all come together."

"What do you mean?" Oiler asked. "What will come together?"

"You don't think Gardner's going to sit by and watch while Baylor puts all this in place? While he tears apart her precious little 'employee first' programs and replaces them with his own? Not her.

She'll take him on. That'll help. It'll undermine her position and create an even better atmosphere for the accident."

"You're going through with it, then."

"This isn't a Page Four exercise." Groomer scowled at Oiler. "The situation's better than it was before. Of course we're going through with it. It's helped by the EEC action on Stoker. That creates increased workload in Halter's area, and it brings in elves who are unfamiliar with the operations. A natural opportunity for a WonderFinish problem. Which will fire up the UEU and give us the opportunity to get our foot in the door on the Board." He sat back, satisfied.

Silvertongue's brow furrowed under his neat hair. "It's awfully close to the fire, this game," he said. "And the EEC had a hand in WonderFinish. We could get burned."

"We won't," Groomer replied. "It'll come close. But we'll come through it all right. And then, of course, there will be some 'executive appointments.'"

Oiler chuckled, but Silvertongue said, "Let's not run things too far ahead. This is if nothing comes up in the meantime."

"What could come up?" Groomer swept the crumbs from the empty tray.

Silvertongue stared at the tray. "There's thousands of elves and half-elves out there," he said. "Hundreds of suppliers, representatives from various countries, competition, the press, the action groups. There's the merger, and how folks inside and on the Street will react to it. Everybody's a question mark, Groomer. We *think* we know how they'll react. But they could all move in a direction we don't anticipate. Or they could move in a hundred different directions at once. It's all possible."

"Bah." Groomer waved a fat hand. "You're too wrapped up in your negotiation games. We're into action mode now, my friend. We've planned a bit, but now we put on our racing gear and go. We handle things as they come to us. Your job is to keep an eye on your fat friend and his mistress—"

"I *said*," Silvertongue spat.

"Traveling companion, then. Keep an eye on them, continue to be his lifeline into what he thinks is still the old NPI. Even as it's changing under our feet. And Oiler." Groomer looked at him. "You're in charge of WonderFinish. Can you manage?"

"Shouldn't be a problem."

"What?"

"I said, it shouldn't be a problem. I know how to make it happen."

"Then make it happen. And make it convincing. Just not too convincing. Nobody gets hurt in this, Oiler. I can't have the inconvenience of an investigation, with everything else going on—you understand."

"I do."

"Then we're finished, for now," Groomer said, struggling to his feet. He extended a fat hand to each of them. "Always a pleasure doing business with the best," he said.

5.

"I should have listened to you."

Gardner straightened some papers on her desk. "You *did* listen to me, Spokes. You just couldn't believe it. Neither could I. Or Router. When I told him, all the bits I'd tried to connect, neither one of us thought they'd actually go through with it."

"Is he coming?"

"Yeah. He's bringing Mats."

"Larsson? I haven't seen him in ages. What's up?"

"Inner Circle."

"That should be a lively meeting. I wonder how the suppliers are taking all this." Spokes frowned. "I don't get it. How does the Board expect to keep this place going? It just doesn't make sense. You go six thousand years with the Chief, and then all of a sudden you think you can do it without him? What's Christmas without Santa?"

"It's not about Christmas, Spokes, c'mon. It's about money, investments, deals. Has been for quite a while. This just makes it public. Christmas will still happen, children will still get their toys. If the back end looks completely different, who cares? Everybody's happy, so there you are."

"There I'm not. He may have been wrapped up in all the politics lately, but he was still the Chief. What was his reaction?"

"There's his statement, telling us he believes in the new leadership and the new direction. Telling us it was time for him to—"

"Aw, bullshit." Spokes scowled. "Look where it came from."

"I know. Our favorite trickster. But we're in no position to do anything about it. Look what just happened, that business with the union, new incentives for Christmas. New incentives! The guys are eating it up, and they're loving the new management for doing it! Even if they don't like the fact that the Chief's out. Spokes, just where do you think new incentives are supposed to be approved?"

"Labor Relations. You."

"Exactly. Because the way they're paying for these, pulling it out of next year's anticipated profits, a shell game with the Street—it never works! Unless they do some kind of elaborate hide-the-weenie in accounting, and if they do, heaven help us if it ever comes to light! The Chief and I never went at incentives this way! We knew better!"

Spokes hesitated. "So how'd they get around you?"

She stood up and turned her back on him. "Two possibilities. One, they just went over the top and made the announcement, gave it an ER blessing it never had. Which would put me in a box with Hammer and Hammer in a box with his guys. Two—" her shoulders drew together "—it's someone in my organization. Someone who's switched." She turned around and sat down. "I'd rather it be one, not two. And my money's on Racer, the little spider. So that's what I'll believe. But I'm keeping my eyes open."

"You know, I could fight the incentives. I was as surprised as you are. I don't know whether it's one or two in my organization, either."

"You fight those incentives, the Union will eat you up. You're stuck, Spokes. Me, too. And there's no telling where Hammer is now. He could be in a box, or he could be following a trail of glory. Or so he might think. I need to talk to him. Even if it's a flat-out violation of the bylaws and the contract."

She sighed. "Face it, Spokes. Suppose you and I figured all this out, and Router too, and maybe a few others. How could we have stopped it? Other than warn the Chief, and you tried to do that when you called him on the plane. Now they've pulled it off, and it's a different world, and we need to know who's involved, who's getting rewarded, and—" she swiveled her chair to face her bookcase "—what's going to happen to us."

"More change," he said. "We could come out swinging."

"Not this time, it's what they want." She kept scanning the titles. "Thoughtful change is one thing. It's when businesses get caught up in—in change frenzy. That's what hurts. Because it's like a, I don't know, a bomb blast, and it takes down everyone in its way. Whether they should go down or not." She swiveled back. "I talked to Halter."

"Doll production? Why? WonderFinish?"

"Actually, no." She studied the desk a moment. "He's given up. You can read it in his face, what he's gone through with it. What he's going through now. The guys like it too much, it helps them meet their targets. So the union doesn't say anything. But he talked about it being like a knife, a really sharp knife. It almost cut him once, he said. He thinks it'll cut again."

"Has he talked to Hammer?"

"I don't know." She looked up. "Actually, I do. Hammer won't act against the wishes of his guys. And there's lots of good news about the stuff that keeps the line happy. In spite of how they feel about the Chief. Lots of incentives and extra pay have been baked into this one. Above and beyond the general incentives just announced." She sighed. "Besides, you know Halter. If he thinks it's his problem, he'll try to solve it on his own before he goes for any help."

"But he came to you."

"Because he can talk to me. I'm out of the line of fire. Or at least that fire. And it wasn't WonderFinish, it was—they stepped the rates up on him. Again."

"Again? What were they?"

"Twelve percent costs and five percent output."

"That's already too high!"

"I know. But it's fifteen and ten, now."

"Fifteen and— ! What about other areas?"

"Halter only told me his."

"What are you going to do?"

She folded her arms on the desk. "I didn't promise him anything," she said. "Not right then. Look at what's happened. WonderFinish approved, but you and I don't know anything about it. He states his case to the Chief and gets it knocked down. He tries to get it on the EEC agenda, and it doesn't stick. So if I tell him straight up that there's something wrong about all of this, what'll that make him do?"

"Go nuts. And come out again, screaming and yelling."

"Right, and who'll pay attention? Halter the dreamer has a problem, can't handle it, imagines a plot against him! Even if it's real. And you know what, Spokes? You and I can smell it, but we can't prove it. Production stepups are normal this time of year. Especially when your area has to cover for another, like Halter is for Stoker. Haz mats are everywhere in a plant. WonderFinish is just another one."

"And if we said something, that's the answer we'd get."

"Right. And worse yet, we'd look like we put our noses where they don't belong. The plant guys are—well, you know. You've been there. They work this stuff out on their own. What do we know about why those decisions were made? That's the damnable thing, Spokes. We need more before we can do anything about it. And we need more of the plant folks, too. I don't think Hammer can put it together yet. It's like a boil. You can see it, but you can't lance it yet. And with everything else going on—"

"So what did you tell him?"

"I hated the answer. I told him we'd look into it and see what we could do. I told him to lodge a complaint with the EEC. I bought time, Spokes. I bought time. No matter how I rationalize it, with everything else happening. He knew it, and I knew it. Oh, he was very polite." One hand worried the other's fingers. "He thanked me for my time. Thanked me. For nothing."

"It's never nothing where you're concerned."

"No? No, I suppose not. But where do we put this one? Ahead of other things? Who'll suffer if we do that? And if we don't?"

Spokes didn't answer.

"Well." She looked up. "Ah, here's Router. And Mats, my old friend! How have you been?"

"I'm well, of course!"

Gardner smiled, standing with Spokes and extending her hand. "It's so good to see you again, Mats. There's a bigger chair for you over there."

"Thank you." Mats sat down heavily, and Router closed the door. Eyes connected in silence. Mats cleared his throat. "Odd," he said.

"You go to an Inner Circle meeting, and it's as though nothing has happened. Everybody talking business. But then it's over, you stand up, and oh, boy! Nobody's talking about anything else."

"Mats, what's the reaction on the outside?" Gardner asked.

"Kind of early to tell. I left before the news really broke."

"How's Kelli doing?"

Mats smiled. "She's a good youngster. Works hard in a tight space, and smart, too."

"I know." Gardner smiled, but her eyes still questioned. "I'll pass that along to her family. She's well?"

"Yes. She's going a little stirring—*stir*-crazed in the hotel day on day, but I have a couple of my top people looking after her."

"That's good." Gardner allowed herself a small, relieved sigh. "I sent her into a tough spot to get her out of a tougher one. At least she's on the outside now, looking in. Though I suppose the same could be said of us. I'm hoping, with everything that's happened here, that the big danger is past, and they won't try anything."

"We think so. But we're watching," Mats said. "She's going to be on an assignment that may put her in some danger." He tapped his shirt pocket.

"What do you mean?" Router asked.

Mats pulled the diskette from his shirt. "Gardner, turn your computer screen so we can all see it. Now, can you put this diskette in there? Thank you."

Kelli's work lit up the monitor. Mats summarized Kelli's analysis of the RFS situation, feed shipments and herd traffic patterns pointing toward Umea. Spokes whistled. "This is all her work, Mats?"

"Even as you see it. I've added nothing."

"You're keeping her. Because if you're not, I want her."

Mats chuckled, a low rumble. "What, so she can draw financial charts for you? She's far too outdoorsy for that!"

Router was still staring at the screen. "I could use her in distribution," he murmured. "With a head like hers—"

"She's *mine*," Gardner said. "Mats is just taking care of her for now. Right, Mats?"

"Right," Mats said, and a good-natured eye-to-eye exchange flashed between them.

"Good. So what's this new assignment?"

Mats's eyes returned to the screen. "She's going on a trip up to Umea," he said. "We've learned a few things since she put this together. Once we figured out that all these deer were going up north, we started looking for the herds. There's a factory near Umea, one that was abandoned shortly after the big war, about fifty years ago. An old steel bearing place. The grounds and most of the surrounding area were overgrown. That's where we think these RFS deer are going."

"You think, but you don't know." Router rubbed his eyes. "Why?"

"Because we aren't in close enough to prove anything, yet. All we've been able to figure out so far is that the herd shipments end there. We think they're gathered in some of the wild areas round about, but we haven't found them. There's too many deer coming in for the land to sustain them all."

Spokes frowned. "Who owns the factory?"

"I had Anders Bjöörn, my COO, look into that. It was purchased a little while ago by a different company. GSO Investments."

"Never heard of them," Spokes said. "I don't like it."

"We don't either. We're going in closer. Something about the way these deer come to the factory grounds, spend some time, and then disappear. The numbers prove they are disappearing."

Gardner's eye's widened. "So they're gathered, shunted into the factory…"

"…And they don't come out," Mats finished.

"We have to stop them," Router said finally.

"Except we can't," Mats rumbled. "Not yet. Figure this out, my friend. I'm heading up a supplier, and you're all, well, kind of in a hard place. And we can't prove anything. Yet. So we have to let whatever it is continue. I don't like it either, Router. Those deer did nothing wrong except they don't fly.

"But we have a few options. I spoke quietly with some of the Inner Circle people, suppliers I think I can trust. We'll hold a meeting, somewhere, that nobody will know about. And we'll talk about production supply. This will be tricky. Our own people are expecting a good year, and for us to slow down will be very surprising. But if we do it right, it will choke off the inbound parts supplies, just when NPI needs them. And that will make a, what is it, royalty mess, because the goons running this place want to step up production. And the union wants it too, because of the incentives. We heard about those at the meeting. The incentives you approved."

"Bullshit!"

"Yes, I could smell that in the room, no matter how well ventilated it was." Mats leaned forward. "But they have taken a tooth or two away from you, and our friend Spokes here, by making you look like heroes to the union. If you reverse things, you will look the villain. If you announce the incentives to Wall Street, they will think you're playing loose with their money. So what we engineer will have to be something that looks and smells normal to all the noses that might be sniffing. And in the meantime, we build evidence we can use to destroy their credibility and restore order. If we don't run out of time first. To build evidence. That's where Kelli's assignment comes in, Gardner. I'm going to send her up to Umea to have a look around."

"Not by herself!" Spokes exclaimed.

"No no. Bill Harris, my head of shipping, will go, too. Others as I need them. It has to be a small team. We'll work out the details. We need to see what's happening to know what we have to do."

"But why send her?" Spokes said. "She's had enough excitement already, from what you tell me. Why not leave her in Gothenburg, where she can continue to watch the traffic? Why put her in more danger?"

"Because you don't know what she's been through," Gardner said. "She was in the middle of all this before it broke. She's seen the secret meetings, or at least been outside the door when things were set up. She ended up working with a union plant that exposed some of this, and she came to me with what she had. I had to send her away, to protect her. I don't even think she found out half of it."

Mats rubbed his chin. "The UEU? They know?"

"They know something, Mats."

"Why have they been so quiet then? They use a plant to figure out what's going on, and what do they do? They do nothing? Why?"

Gardner sighed. “There could be factions in the Union as well. Or ambitions. Who can tell? Maybe they were truly surprised, and they haven’t yet reacted.” She swiveled away from them, exposing her thinking in soft tones. “Or maybe there’s something being hatched with the merger, the EI thing, some kind of negotiation. Oh, the merger’s on. That much is certain. More than ever, with the Chief out of the way. Racer was lying through his teeth at the end of the EEC. Just a little flourish to keep us off balance.

“You’d think I’d know all this, but I don’t. This company has become a beast, something fearful, where no matter what you think you know, you push against these giant boundaries that stand between you and all sorts of unknown things. So you move ahead into that strange gray space, hoping you’re not walking off a cliff.” She turned back. “Stop me before I get too crazy. Where do you think the Chief is?”

A long pause. “Far away,” Mats said at last. “Wasn’t he in New Orleans?”

“Yesterday,” Gardner said. “I tried to reach him.”

“I tried, too,” Router said. “Nothing.”

“And I’ve *been* trying,” Spokes groused. “All along.”

Gardner shook her head. “He’s cut off,” she said wearily. “So now, we have to think. If we were him, cut off from our reason for being for thousands of years, what’s our move?”

A long silence. Mats cleared his throat. “Perhaps…” he said softly. Gardner looked at him quizzically. “I have a hunch,” he said at last.

6.

Long, red sunrays didn't take the chill from the evening air. Kelli shivered, pulling her sweater close. Such a short summer here, and already over. There'd be frost soon. Still, she preferred street sounds over silence. Then a chillier and harder blast than the rest stung her cheeks, and she sighed and fastened the hotel window. Silence it would be, same as last night.

She returned to the bed and looked at whatever was on the TV for a while. She walked to the small table, staring down at "Stupid Stew," open to page 83 all week. The maids had been good about leaving it untouched. Thankfully, Anders had pulled through with symphony tickets a few nights back. That had been a welcome diversion, even with the hassle of checking her laptop at the front desk.

They must have had the Inner Circle meeting by now. And Gardner's meeting with Mats. Her eyes misted momentarily, thinking of her own meeting with Gardner that had launched her so far from everything familiar.

Familiar no longer. How could they have pushed him out? And putting in some human. Baylor? Who was that? What did he know about running the place? Had this been part of the discussion she'd uncovered? Had she missed it? Maybe Silvertongue hadn't known.

Maybe Mats had been delayed. Maybe he couldn't meet with Gardner. A chill ran through her. Maybe Gardner was in trouble now. So many maybes! And she was on the outside. Was it safer?

Waiting was just awful. Her cell phone had rung once in the past three days, and she had nearly jumped across the room, but it had only been Bill, checking. "I'm bored silly," she'd said, and he clucked sympathetically before reminding her how important her work was, and that things were likely to get much more exciting soon. She couldn't tell over the phone whether he was genuinely concerned or just saying the right business things. Dealing with humans was still so new. She'd heard Americans were masters at appearing interested. But his voice recalled his blond hair, his blue eyes, and the way he first sat so awkwardly on the bed.

He'd asked if there were any significant changes to the numbers, and she reported that the Umea pace hadn't changed. "Hmm. Kelli, thanks again. I'll be in touch the next couple of days, to let you know what happens next."

That had been before the announcement. Had all their plans changed?

She surveyed the darkening cityscape. There was always Nordstan, down at the far end of the Kungsportsavenyn, past the canal and the statues. The walk was good, even if you could do just so much shopping. She buttoned her sweater, slipped the laptop into its special case and tucked it under her arm. On her way out, she grabbed a light jacket from the closet and paused at the bathroom mirror. *I'm a small creature in a big Swedish world.*

The lady at the business services desk looked her over without comment, checking her laptop into the safe once again. The special key stretched her pocket. She pushed through the revolving doors and into the evening air.

The Kungsportsavenyn always invigorated her, even as she had to pick her way around so many tall Swedes. She passed the park on her right and crossed over the Rosenlunds canal, noting familiar shops and buildings lining the water on the far side, the gently sloping lawn on the near. She began to cross the bridge. When she reached the middle, pausing to look over the canal, just the inkling of a feeling teased her. Somewhere in all the clusters of people walking the Kungsportsavenyn, eyes watched her. A tickle raised the fine hairs on the back of her neck. She sped up. When she reached the canal's opposite bank, instead of continuing down the Avenue she turned right and headed down the street that hugged the canal, passing shops close by the water, then turned left and left again, a quick circle around the short block.

On the approach to the Kungsportsavenyn, she wheeled about. No one. She hurried to rejoin the Avenue traffic. Maybe she should take the trolley back to the hotel. No. Nordstan would be crowded and safe.

At Nordstan, she scuttled into the first large department store she saw. Crowd echoes faded behind her. Idly, she scanned the first merchandise at hand, stationery and writing sets, hoping she would feel alone, protected in a side aisle. She didn't. *Am I going "stirring cracked?" Me so small, and everyone else big, watching? I can't let this happen!* She concentrated on a flower-patterned stationery set lifted at random. *I can't let this get to me. There's nobody around. A couple of deep breaths, come on, come on.*

A hand on her arm sent the stationery clattering to the floor.

"Kelli, Kelli," a familiar voice whispered. "Sorry. I knew I'd startle you. I couldn't figure out how not to. It's all right."

She looked up. Bill. She took a deep, trembling breath. Improbably, there he was, setting down his briefcase to retrieve the stationery and replace it.

"I—How did you—How long have you been following me?" she sputtered.

He reddened. "Sorry," he said. "Since just outside the hotel. I was coming to get you, actually, when I saw you leaving."

"To get me! Why?"

He picked up the briefcase. "Your laptop's in here," he said. "We had fun getting it. You should have seen the look the old lady at the hotel gave Anders. I didn't know Swedish could be spoken so quickly."

"Give it to me." She reached for the briefcase.

"You can trust us, Kelli," Bill said. "Don't invent danger. There's too much already. We're meeting Mats and Anders at the airport. Let's get a taxi. I'll explain on the way, but I'll caution you now against referring to you-know-who by name."

"I know that! They teach us that and remind us constantly!"

"Sorry. I don't know—a lot about—things. Let me know when I—you know—make a mistake or something. Now please, come with me."

Do I have a choice, if he has my laptop? She followed Bill outside. He flagged a black Mercedes taxi and all but pushed her into the back seat before tucking himself in next to her. "Airport, please," he said to the white-haired driver, and the car noiselessly eased from the curb.

He half-turned toward Kelli, who had curled herself onto the seat, her left side pressed against the door. "Sorry about that," he said, "but it was important to get you off the street."

"How did you get my laptop? I thought the hotel had rules!"

"They do. But we had an agreement with them, in case of an emergency. Like this."

"Why?"

Bill glanced at the driver, kept his voice low and matter-of-fact. "You were being watched. They'd managed to figure out where you were."

The little space in the cab sharpened and closed in.

"I very much doubt they would have done anything," he continued. "This is business, not war. But they'd have tried for that laptop. We didn't want to take any chances."

"What about my stuff in the hotel? I left my phone and everything there!"

"Any printouts?"

"No."

Bill sighed. "That makes it a little easier. We'll handle checkout. Your stuff should be all right. You won't really need your phone, where we're going."

There went that heart skip again, and she knew she must have given him an at-sea look, because he continued gently, "We're taking a small trip to Umea."

"But that's—"

He put a finger to his lips. "It won't take very long—a week or two at the most. Mats has gone as far as to have some of his people pick out clothes for you while you're up there—it'll be quite a bit cooler." A corner of his mouth turned up. "Just be grateful Mats had the sense to delegate that little assignment."

She relaxed a bit and smiled, seeing big amiable Mats fumbling through petites. She closed her eyes. *Here we go again. Off to Umea. Right into the heart of things.* Eyes still closed, she chuckled.

"OK," Bill said. "What?"

"I was just thinking, how only a few weeks ago I was sitting in front of Sil—in front of a desk, scheduling meetings and screening calls. That seems so polite, so dull, and so long ago. I wonder." She opened her eyes and watched stubby pine trees float by the window. "How many of those dull and polite tasks covered up—? I wonder what's going on now, up there?"

He shrugged. "Hard to say. None of it very good. Here we are. We'll meet Mats and Anders inside."

The cab nosed its way curbside at the Gothenburg terminal. Kelli stepped out and stretched a moment, trying to dispel her disorientation. It worked some. Bill touched her elbow, and she let him escort her into the building.

It didn't take long to find the others. They walked to an alcove and hunched into some gaudy, uncomfortable chairs ringing a shin-high table.

"Well, we are back," Mats rumbled. "Does anybody want the lovely coffee they have here? ...I don't either. Let's start. Kelli. We're sorry that you've had to be—shoveled around in this fashion. Perhaps Bill has explained it to you?"

"Somewhat. We were in a cab," she said.

"Ah. This is how it is, then." They leaned close. "We've taken your analysis, Kelli, and learned some things. The closest major town to where the herds are going is Umea. But they are actually going farther up the coast, nearer to Skellefteå. That is mining country up that way. There are lots of people and lots of languages spoken in Umea, but the country gets wild in a hurry. And cold. There are factories up there, mostly mining work. One is being used for a different purpose. It was abandoned for many years, but a new group has purchased it. The herds are going there. But the numbers of deer in the area stay the same."

Kelli frowned. "I think I know what you mean."

"Something is happening to them," Anders said. "They don't just melt into the countryside. It's the factory. We just can't prove it. So we would like you and Bill to go up there and have a look around. Then report what you find."

"Why me?"

"We need someone small, an elf," Bill said. "If we have to go in—if we're seen, an elf gives us credibility. And you've proven what you can do."

She gripped her chair. "I'm already being watched. How will I escape notice?"

"There's a little time," Mats said. "They think you are still at the hotel. We have not checked you out from there. So as long as Bill was careful, here—"

"I was."

"—then there is time. We get you on a plane to Malmö and then to Umea. We have an office there. There is a family that will take you in. You will become one of their children. Then you will go for a ride in the countryside. You will meet Bill. And from there—" Mats paused, took a handkerchief from his pocket and wiped sweat from his lined brow "—you will find things out."

"And when I, when we do, what then?"

Mats stared sadly at the table. "We don't know," Anders said. "With things the way they are at NPI, we don't know if the information will have an effect. It will depend on a number of things. One of which is where *he* is. This nobody knows."

Mats looked up. "I've been thinking and thinking," he said. "Where would I go if I were him? Kelli, I am closer to him than these two are. He was in New Orleans, at the Convention there. They keep those things quiet, so there will be nothing in the press. Even now he may realize that to go to the press would be wrong. But he will leave New Orleans. And he will try to get back."

She shrugged. "Why can't he just get on a plane and head back?"

"Because they've closed things. This I did not realize until I left, after the Inner Circle. I should have guessed and said something to Gardner. But it has only been a day, not a year since this happened." He sighed. "Only a day."

"And so we meet here, because at least we must try to do something," Anders said. "So we have chosen clothing for you and packed bags. These are already checked and ready to go."

"What if you didn't find me? What if I'd gone downtown?"

"No." Bill shook his head. "We knew. It was tough, Kelli. We wanted to give you privacy, but we had to know where you were, when we had to make a move."

She glared at him a moment, but the look in his eyes calmed her.

"There's another reason," Mats rumbled. "A long shoot."

"Long shot," Bill sighed, and she smiled.

"There are ways back to up there. One is through here. He may come this way. So I have been waiting. And I'll wait another day. And another, if I need to. Then go back to work. I still have things to ship to that place, which I will eventually be able to do. There is business still."

Bill stood, scanning the concourse. "I'll be—I don't—Mats, you won't have to wait! Isn't that him?" He pointed.

"Don't do that!" Mats said. "Fingers down! Let me—" His face broke into a smile. "Ah, old friend! My thinking pays off," he said. "And Roxy, too. You folks wait here."

Bill sat back down. Kelli watched Mats move casually into the crowd. She strained her eyes but saw nothing. What had they seen? Mats approached a dark-haired couple and placed his hand on the man's shoulder. The man turned and flashed the barest smile. Mats led the couple to their table. Who were these people? Then she recognized Roxy.

"You can blink," Bill said. "He's changed himself."

"I—" She closed her mouth and stood.

"So, I have a welcoming committee," the dark-haired man rumbled. The Chief. But the hair, the smooth face!

"This is Anders, my chief of operations, and Bill, who heads up shipping," Mats said.

Santa shook both their hands, and Roxy followed. "Who's the staring one?" he said.

"This is Kelli," Mats said. "She's one of yours."

"No longer, Mats. What the hell is she doing here?"

That stung, but Roxy clasped her hand.

"It is an interesting story, old friend," Mats said. "Kelli was in the thicket of things and saw some things. She went to Gardner with what she knew, which wasn't quite enough and wasn't quite soon enough. But it was a good try."

"Well, then." The blue eyes drilled her. "You haven't answered. She's here. Why?"

"She had to go somewhere after Gardner fired her."

"Fired her! So *Gardner's* in—"

"No no. Gardner fired her to get her away from Silvertongue. Kelli was in danger, her position was badly composed by her efforts."

"Compromised," Bill offered. "And she's here now, trying to help from the outside, doing what she can."

"Which is what?"

Kelli started to speak, but Mats cut her short. "She's in my organization, studying herd traffic, and so on."

"And?"

"Nothing significant yet. But she has done good work."

Why is Mats lying? What if the Chief asks me? He was still looking at her.

Eventually, he relented. "You can let me know what you find out, Kelli, when I get back. It may not seem like it, but I *do* appreciate that some folks are still on my side." The eyes shifted to Mats. "Mats, I'm going back. That's why I'm here."

Mats's eyes softened. "Sit down, old friend," he said quietly. "We must talk this through."

"What's to talk through?"

"You can't get back there. Not this way. They've shut it down."

Santa stared at him a long moment before plunking into the nearest seat. They took seats around him. "OK, so you say I can't go back there. Then no more riddles. I can understand them shutting the airspace down and cutting the comm codes. But you're here, your people are here, Kelli's here. There's business, things to move back and forth, people need to travel. They can't just shut the whole space down."

"But they have. From what I can see. I don't know for how long, that's true. Anders?"

"We've been advised that travel is suspended," Anders said. "Indefinitely."

"That explains why I couldn't call you. They've cut me out of Inner Circle, too. But what about goods? Surely there's—"

Mats laid a restraining hand on Santa's arm. "Think for a minute. Think what happens if you go back. What do they do? What do you do? You can make no moves there. Unless you tear the place up from bottom to top. What would that do?"

"It may be happening already!"

"May be. But you will not make it any better by going back."

"Why not?"

Roxy leaned forward. "We talked about this on the plane. Mats has a point. I know you want to go back, which is why we ended up here. But it won't undo anything. And making a public statement just makes it all worse. Remember? Not because of what it would do to NPI. Because of what it would do to you. You'd be seen as an angry old man, nothing more. The press would make you lash out, and the angrier you got, the less credibility you'd have. In the end, it won't help at all." She looked at Mats. "I couldn't stop him."

"Whoever could? Before. But they have now. At least for a while."

"But I can't just—" He scowled and looked away, his chest rising and falling.

They waited. "This time you must," Mats said at last, his voice the gentlest Kelli had heard it. "They are in trouble there. I was there for an Inner Circle meeting, and I only just got in before it happened. I talked to Gardner. She has very few options right now, but she is a fighter. Others also. I got out only yesterday, and now I find I can't go back, either. So this is hard on me, too, knowing those who are struggling there." He cleared his throat. "This is very difficult for you. But you must be patient and trust us."

"Bah! Trust! How do I know who's who anymore! Tell me that! How do I know you all didn't decide—" he stood up abruptly "—that you'd had enough of me."

Mats stood as well. "You cannot mean that."

"But I do." The voice was level, flat, dead. Kelli could hear no warmth or timbre suggesting Christmas. "I do. Mats, I'm sick of it, all of it. Have been for a long time. Maybe part of me knew that. Maybe *she* knew it, too, or figured it out first, and that's why she left. And don't think that doesn't hurt every day. I'm sick of the machinery, the politics, the selfishness, the greed, the shortsightedness, the churn, the flail, the—whatever. And now with this latest—Now I need to make myself sick of the whole place. I need to go away. I need not—to hear Silvertongue treat me as though I'm special, when I'm so much baggage in his schemes. I need to be through with it. If they think this is how Christmas should be, a shell covering lies and maneuvers—well." He looked at Roxy. "Why don't you stay here? I'm sure Mats'll find something for you to do."

To Kelli's surprise, Roxy glared at him before jumping to her feet. "I already *told* you! If you want to hurt people, and elves, and everyone, that's your damn business. I'm not in that equation. I'm staying with you. I don't care what Silvertongue or anyone else has to say about it. If you haven't figured that out, Mr. CEO, then figure it out now!"

"You can see who the boss is, Mats," he growled, and into the uncomfortable silence he dropped a sheepish sigh. "I'm sorry. Sorry to all of you. It's just that this is hard. Hard. So I'll make it easier. I'm going."

"Going! Where?"

"Mats, I have no idea. Just—away from here, away from where I have my nose rubbed in it. No, don't follow!" he said, moving off. "I have money, I have freedom, I have it all! Can't you see?" He took a couple of steps toward the crowd. "I'll be free as a bird, just like they say! Nothing to worry about! No Christmas, no personnel, no shipments, no cost pressures, no toys, no children, no anything! For the first time in God knows how long! Vacation! So let me go, Mats!" His hoarse voice trembled. "Don't you stop me, too. Everyone has stopped me for so long."

Mats looked long at him. "All right, old friend. Do we call you the minute something changes?"

"Call Roxy. But not for a while." He stepped back toward the group, and when he spoke, Kelli heard cold kindness, as though he were unable to find the right tones. "Don't worry. It'll be fun. Business without the Chief. Try it. It should work just fine. But,

Mats—" and his eyes gave off just the barest hint of the old twinkle "—don't be surprised if I show up at the strangest time and place. Don't be. With me, you never know."

A corner of Mats's mouth twisted upward. "That much is true," he said. "So you don't know where you will go?"

"Yes." Santa rubbed his nose, a motion so familiar it brought sudden tears to Kelli's eyes. "I know I'm going to the ticket counter. I know I'm going on the first flight on the list. I know I'm going to land in whatever airport it takes me to. And I know I'm going to get on the first flight I can from there. And I'll do that and do that and do that until I feel as though I'm done." He took Roxy's arm. "And this youngster is going with me, because *she* can't be stopped. Not by all the Silvertongues in the world. Let them try. They'll have to find us first." He shook Mats's hand. "So, Mats, if you see the rest, if you see Gardner, tell them—tell her—wish her well, wish her luck. Maybe someday, we'll all sit down together again, and we'll know—we'll *know*—what to do. And how to be. But until then." He dropped his hand. "C'mon, Roxy, let's have some fun."

He released Roxy's arm, spun on his heel, and strode off, a dark-haired man melting into the scattering crowd.

Roxy grabbed Mats's hand. "I'll stay with him. I don't know what'll happen next."

"Roxy, he is up and down and all over right now. It will be that way for a while."

"I know. Thank you, Mats—and you others, and you, Kelli. He knows. Thank Gardner and the others, too. He knows what they're up against. Thoughts go through that old mind that none of us can see. We can't even imagine." She dropped her hand. "I have to go, before he gets away."

Mats smiled. "Go then."

Roxy hustled to catch up with the Chief. They blended into the crowd, turned a corner, and disappeared.

"And we'll see them again," Mats murmured. "But when, and how, who can tell?" He sat down heavily, the others with him.

Eventually, Kelli broke the silence. "How did you recognize him? After he dyed his hair and shaved off his beard. He looks so young!"

"He didn't dye his hair and shave his beard. He changed," Mats said. "He can do that. And has, over the years, when he needs to. He, and she. Not Roxy. His wife. When she left, last year, we thought she might change and not be seen for a while."

Kelli absorbed this for a moment. "You didn't tell him about the factory. Why?"

"I couldn't. He'd know exactly what it means. It would have torn him to bits. He would have gone there, and then—" he studied the table "—an outcome that might have destroyed it all."

"All?"

"All. Business, Christmas, Santa. No. Not business. Business we have. We always will. It is the great survivor. Almost an animal that can chew off an arm and grow a new one. Business." He continued staring at the plastic surface. "An animal that consumes us all."

7.

"Mom, can I see the reindeer again?"

"So soon, honey? You just saw them last week."

"But it's so much fun to watch them fly!"

"You can't do that if you're just lazing around in bed like that!"

"I can't help it, Mom. My arms hurt and my neck feels funny around in front."

"Let me help it feel better. Maybe I can help you get out of bed."

"Mom, what are you doing? Why are you licking my arms like that? It hurts! Mom, stop licking my face! Mom! Mom!"

Hot breath. Darkness lifted slightly. The world swam up, gray-veiled, swathed in pain. Tracer fought to open his eyes despite the pain. A rough tongue slapped his face again. He opened his eyes, and a huge blurry shape slowly became a reindeer head.

He inhaled a couple of times, very shallowly. Pain stabbed him on each intake. Finally, he croaked, "Parsley?"

Parsley grunted. The huge head withdrew. Now he could discern her shape, standing beside him. One of her legs was red.

He tried to turn his head. This world seemed studded with boulders, brown and black humps rising near and far. One of the lumps had antlers. He took as deep a breath as he could. "Mystic!" he called. The lump didn't move.

He lapsed into the dreamworld again.

The pain forced his eyes open. He tried to raise himself on his left elbow, but pain spiked his arm. He tried his right with more success. He needed to breathe heavily but couldn't and guessed he had a couple of broken ribs. Fire slashed his upper chest, and he remembered Saddler's comment a hundred years ago, about collarbones.

He stared at the antlered lump. Mystic still hadn't moved. Parsley stood off to his left. "Hey, girl," he croaked, and she hobbled up, her head bobbing sharply downward whenever she put weight on her right foreleg.

"I'm going to die out here," he muttered. "You, too. And both of us in a lot of pain. At least Mystic's out of her misery."

Parsley grunted, nuzzling his hair. Despite his pain, he smiled. "Well, if you have to die, might as well die with a deer."

Parsley jerked her head up. She snorted, then hobbled off. She stopped and bellowed, facing a wooded area to their right.

Crackling sounds. "Oh, great," Tracer grumbled. "Probably a pack of wolves or something. So I get to be eaten alive, too." He set his teeth, watching.

A huge shadow pushed into the clearing. Tracer's eyes widened. He'd never seen a reindeer like this, high sweep of antlers, huge head with wise regarding eyes. "What—what," he breathed, then fell back as pain shot through him. He stared at the iron sky, fighting for breath.

Parsley's face filled his vision. He could feel more warm breath, the strange deer nuzzling his broken body, inspecting. The warmth charged him. He winced when the nose touched his left arm.

When the nose moved on, he cautiously raised his arm, scarcely daring to believe it. Was this just another dream? The pain had faded to a shadow.

Now the nose brushed his collarbone, ranging up and down his chest as well, and with each nuzzle, Tracer felt pain yield to an overwhelming fatigue. He didn't know he could be this tired. He forced his eyes open. A huge long reindeer face greeted him. Deep-set, black eyes shot with gold gazed into his for a moment, before the deer continued its methodical work. Everywhere that marvelous breath reached, the pain melted before it like ice before a warm breeze. He closed his eyes again, reveling in the magic of it, magic deeper even than that which allowed these deer to fly. It washed over him, transforming his body from a collection of broken sticks into something that bled no more, a structure that could support him again.

Presently, the breath withdrew. Tracer lay immobile, eyes fastened, fighting the urge to fall asleep for hours. He tested limbs, chest and breathing, discovering that although his arms and legs felt heavy and pain-edged, he could move them fairly well.

Nearby, Parsley snorted and shook her head. He could make out a faint tinkle of bells. He struggled to sit up and open his eyes.

Bits of wagon wood lay scattered over a field of deeply tufted grass and lichens studded with sentry boulders, irregular shapes in a darkening world. Night approached—but whether it was the night after the crash or some later night, he didn't know. Somehow he'd managed to land on a grassy area amid all those rocks. His suit had many tears, some ringed dark red. How much blood had he lost?

Then he spied Parsley and the strange deer standing over Mystic. He assembled his footing underneath himself and stood a moment, breathing deeply, before wobbling over to them. He looked down. There were some things magic just couldn't fix.

He rubbed his hands over his face and eyes. It wouldn't do to leave Mystic's body unprotected in that wild country. But was he strong enough to do anything about it?

He started to waddle toward a stand of fir trees, but it was too hard. He'd have to remove what was left of the flight suit. That ordeal left him badly out of breath and exposed to the sharp, cold wind. Moving more freely now, he searched the grove for anything useful. He found a large, dead branch whose butt end had been stripped from the tree, forming a strong, flat shape. It would do. He dragged himself back to the deer.

Mystic's body, impossibly twisted, lay next to a mossy area nestled between two tall boulders. Using the dead branch as a crude shovel, he scooped aside the moss. The soil beneath, a sandy loam, crumbled easily. Even so, the job seemed unending, the dusked silence broken only by his digging, the ragged sounds his breath made as he worked, and an occasional snort from Parsley or the other deer.

When he had dug a shallow, deer-sized pit, he sat down to regain his remaining strength. The next part would be the hardest.

Although Mystic's body was lighter than he'd expected, he still struggled, alternately pushing and pulling it, inching toward the pit. At last, Mystic's body reached the edge, and with a final shove,

Tracer positioned it in the shallow grave. After another long rest, he took the mossy sod he had laid aside and covered the body as thoroughly as he could. He laid the dead branch atop the mound, then made several trips to the fir grove to bring back the heaviest branches he could manage. These he also laid on the mound, hoping to deter inquisitive visitors. When he had finished, only the tips of Mystic's antlers protruded. He could do no more.

He peered at the deer, their antlers silhouetted against the darkness. "Well," he rasped, "where do we go from here?" He shivered against the cold wind. "My suit," he muttered. He picked up the white blob from the ground and struggled back into it.

The strange deer stepped forward until it almost touched him, then curled its forelegs underneath itself, kneeling. He stared, mind empty. The deer stood, snorted, kneeled again. Then he knew. He flopped over the back of the deer like a large white sack. The world heaved and jounced when the deer stood. He buried his face against the deer's neck, smelling the coarse, hollow-shafted guard hairs and feeling the warmth from the beast's back spread into his belly.

He swayed and bobbed, the deer walking, splay hooves clicking with each step. Parsley trailed, a dim unlimping shade. The strange deer must have healed her as well. The rocking lulled him, and the warmth comforted him. Dark reality and darker dreams mingled, shapes that seemed to threaten, ends of old thoughts played and replayed. Sometimes he awakened from what he guessed was real sleep, sensing they had moved much farther on, but the dark landscape hadn't changed. Occasionally, he thought he heard falling water, wondering drowsily when the freeze would still its voice.

The deer carried him until the southeastern sky paled and the landscape around them sharpened. They had left the largest rocks behind. Now they plodded across fields that might have served as ancient pastures, dressed with lichen and an unknown cold-weather grass. Dark firs accented the fields, the odd boulder anchoring them.

They picked their way down the side of a ravine, at the bottom of which a small stream tumbled and laughed amid the shadows. They crossed the stream on a jumble of rocks—or was it the remnants of an old bridge? He flickered between dream and day.

They climbed the far side, and the deer stopped and snorted. Tracer raised his head. The sun crested the distant horizon, lighting a gentle slope and a small green valley. In the middle of this clearing stood two buildings: a small stone cabin that looked abandoned, its faded green door unhinged; and a long, low wooden structure nearby that might have been red once, but that now leaned into an uncertain brown future.

They made for the second structure.

On the far side, a weathered door sagged into the grass. The deer pushed inside, and instantly Tracer's nostrils stung with the strong smells of animals kept close. He could hear other deer grunting and blowing, the knocking sounds of hooves against old wood. The place was warm, close, and acrid, but so comforting.

A straw mass hunched at one end of the building. The deer carried Tracer to the straw and knelt. He tumbled off. He needed to investigate those sounds, but he was just too tired. He peeled off the suit, pushed it aside, and with reindeer sounds and smells all around him, he burrowed into the straw and fell at once into a deep, dreamless sleep.

8.

The big plane circled Heathrow. Roxy glanced at Santa, whose massive head still drooped. She turned back to the window, watching airport lights twinkling past. She moved her head all about, trying to pull the tension out of her neck and shoulders.

What would they do here? "London's as good as any," he'd growled, scanning the Gothenburg departures board. "I can launch in a hundred different directions from there." So London it was, an ancient, jammed knot where you could lose yourself for as long as you wanted. Maybe the diversion would do them good.

She studied his dark head. *That* had taken some getting used to. "Stop staring," he'd snapped, answering her knock on his hotel door in New Orleans so long ago. "It's one of my tricks. *She* can do it, too. She probably made herself into Madonna, hanging out on a southern California beach. Rollerblading, possibly. We should try that someday." He'd smiled, then frowned, an emotional ride she still hadn't mastered. "We're going to Gothenburg," he'd announced, and her "Why?" went unanswered.

This was tough. Anger followed by laughter, warmth followed by cynicism, understanding followed by prejudgment, statements like "Gothenburg" followed by silence, then by sudden explanation hours later, the brooding erupting into words, raging uncontainable thoughts spraying like hot gases venting from a lava bed. He spewed lengthy, rambling diatribes on Christmas, the business, elves, production restructuring, deals, suppliers, consultants, just-in-time supply, recycling, herd management, product, market position, children, share growth, fools, demands, media, contrived meetings, on and on and on, invective targeting those elves he considered ringleaders in this sorry mess; or worse, the bitter, almost vicious references to *her*, never needing a name, only a pronoun conjuring a year of suffering buried under business pressure.

Sometimes Dr. Id would be there, Idiot paraded, an example of let's-skirt-the-truth thinking, typical lackey whose drain on your wealth was sustained by orbiting the answer, because reaching the answer would eliminate the support need "and we can't have that, can we?" he'd burst out during that long flight to Sweden. "No, Mr. Consultant, never give us your answer, because then we might send you packing, and off you'd have to go to invent a new business crisis that only you can solve. They're weasels, Roxy, weasels. The whole lot of them. Or what's that ugly eel, the lamprey. They fasten on you and never let go, with their schools on client management and engagement and schmooze and inking the deal and never letting you know what they really think. Never letting on. They do work about work, never the work itself. They infect your thinking with their vision of what's right for a business you've spent centuries working at, *bleeding* at! As though being on the outside is the badge of honor that makes their mystical thinking better than yours!

"Who's better at thinking about Christmas than you? Or me? Nobody! But tell that to those elves and half-elves! Their hidden agendas and their ambitions to run the operation. They'd be the darling of the marketplace. They think it's their terms, but it's really the terms of the weasels, the lampreys, the ones whose only purpose is to make money and more money and more money off the backs of the folks who are left doing the hard work. And off the misdirected thinking of the ambitious wheelers and dealers, too. No, we're better off staying away!" And this followed moments later by, "When I get back there, I'm going to clean house! No more humans and internal intrigue! I'll make up a list and—"

That was the worst, the rage uncontrolled, a messy overflowing pot of hot words that scalded guilty and innocent. It took all her efforts to interrupt the stream from that brilliant, injured mind, reminding him he didn't have the option to clean house, risking a turn of the deadly arrow.

So why the hell she was staying with a has-been executive on the outside of a company he no longer understood? "What's in it for you, Roxy? Spying? A book deal?" She'd raised her hand to slap him, hard, never mind who or what he was, her expression yanking out his clumsy apology. "I under*stand* how this hurts you!" she'd snarled. "Come out of yourself long enough to realize how others are hurt as well!" And she'd snapped her book open, willing herself to read under his stare, page after page of words forgotten, her eyes moving by rote left to right, left to right to get through it.

She unclenched her jaw. It wouldn't do to rehash the pain. They were stumbling through this together.

The airport lights swam up fast now, and the plane buzzed into prelanding, stews stalking the aisles, passengers hurrying to their seats. She turned at the sigh.

He blinked a few times and glanced at her. "Almost there," he grunted. "Figure out where we're going to stay?"

"I didn't know that was my job," she said.

He laughed. "It used to be." He yawned, covering his mouth. "I've got a place that'll probably do, out of the way on the north end. It usually isn't busy, so we shouldn't have trouble getting rooms. I'm not going to stay in London very long, anyway. Too crowded, and way too noisy. A few days will be enough."

He fell silent, and they concentrated on landing, followed by the usual crush, wait, move, and wait again as they deplaned and wandered through Heathrow for their luggage. They found one of the many "not for Americans" lines, each of which terminated in a thorough British civil servant. The air was indoor New Orleans, languages gabbling in every direction.

"You know, if birds traveled, this is what it would sound like," he observed.

She chuckled, her eyes hopping punk outfits to saris to evening wear, to jeans to weird shirts someone had had to approve. "Probably as colorful, too," she said.

He turned to say something else, and one big hand whacked the head of a small child hanging from the spangled arm of a red-sari'd woman. That set the kid off, which set the mother into an explosion of foreign words, the kid crying for effect now.

Santa reeled and almost crunched Roxy's foot. The Indian woman pressed her point, whatever it was, and he raised his hands in a supplicating gesture against the flood, his cheeks turning a shade of red Roxy had never seen, not even in the cheapest greeting cards. She stepped to his side, and the Indian woman launched on her, too, locking them both in a verbal pindown.

A small brown hand and skinny arm pierced the scene. "'Scoose me, Santa," a quiet male Indian voice said. "'Scoose me." Roxy followed the voice to a thin, dark-complexioned man, shock of black hair perched like a surprise on his head and wiry arm extended toward the woman, the other arm dragging a rolling carryon. The Indian man began answering gently in the same language. This went on for a while, as the Indian man smothered the fire, despite hostile glares from the kid.

With a final, unilingual "Harrumph!" woman and kid dismissed them and moved forward a few steps. That left Santa and Roxy appraising their wiry savior.

"Hello," he said shyly. "I am Ravi. I thought I could help."

"I'm Roxy. And thanks. What language was that?"

"Hindi." He rubbed his nose. "And some pretty good words she used, too." His singsong voice rolled r's and clipped words. He glanced at Santa.

"You said 'Santa.'"

"I did."

"How did you know?"

"I'm not sure. You are different looking. I just knew. I was in one of your programs."

"One of my programs?"

"Yes. Agency santa. I was hired because you didn't have enough of the regular guys. So a whole bunch of us applied and went through the training. But then someone killed the program."

He sighed. "Ravi, that was me. I had a problem with agency folks coming through the back door, when I needed more new hires for diversity. I cut the agency funds to improve our diversity numbers."

"We are not numbers, Santa, we are people."

Santa's face darkened a moment before he smiled. "I like that. But stop calling me that." His eyes darted about, as they inched forward.

"All right." Ravi didn't move.

"Are you in line?" Roxy said eventually.

"Yes. Do you mind if I share the line with you?"

"No," Santa said. "Not at all. You kept us from getting chewed limb from limb."

"She would have tired one day," Ravi said. "But she was going pretty good."

"You travel lightly," Roxy said.

"I sent most of my stuff ahead. I won't be staying long here." He looked away for a moment. "I'm sorry about what happened," he said (pronouncing it "soddy"). "With NPI."

"Thanks, it's appreciated," Santa said gruffly. "But you're not a market watcher. Because if you were, you'd have a different opinion."

"Well I am sorry. What will you do?"

"Roxy tells me there's very little I *can* do, and when I stop and think I know she's right. But I'm going to do something soon, I just don't know what. Like go to the press."

"No."

Uh-oh. Be careful, little guy.

"Why not? Why does everyone say that?"

"I'm sorry. I'm not in your company. So I don't have their point of view. But from my point of view, if you went to the press, you'd make one of those statements that bitter guys make from the outside. And the more you try to show your side, the more they'll isolate you. I'm sorry, but that's how I see it."

"...Roxy, if everybody gives me the same advice, either I follow it, or I declare everybody wrong and go my own way. Which is it?"

"Ravi, it's your turn." She pointed.

Ravi introduced himself to the tired little civil servant, who ciphered him before motioning to Roxy and Santa. "Identification, please."

Is this an elf who's gone bad and been kicked out? The little man glanced up from her ID, a bureaucratic lizard stirring. "Do you find something amusing in this, Miss—" he squinted at the card "—Roxy Smith. How convenient. How long has *Smith* been your last name, Miss *Smith*?"

"My—my whole life."

He lifted an eyebrow. "And how long might *that* be, Miss *Smith*?" His voice sketched a lifetime of petty miseries, freely shared.

"Well, I—"

"Is all this really necessary?" Santa cut in. "We're on a business trip."

"Did I speak to you, Mr.—Claussen? I did not. But what sort of business brings you from Sweden to England?"

"The toy business."

"I see. And no doubt Miss *Smith* is your consultant in these matters?"

Her face burned, and she started to answer, but the little man said, "and your suitcases no doubt might contain a toy or two, samples perhaps, that you've not declared on your duty card?"

"What kind of lie—" Santa growled.

"I *could* request they be opened," the little man went on.

She stared at him. *Does he even see us? Or is he reciting some civil servant handbook?*

Again the brown hand intervened. "They are traveling with me. He is my employer, and we have business in London. We'll be staying at the King's Cross on the north end, if Her Majesty's servant needs to find us. We could open our suitcases if you care to hold up this line, but—Have you heard of NPI?"

The little man surveyed him coolly. "Of course."

"He used to be a top executive there. He has his own business now. At the moment, he has free time, so he could surely write to the Heathrow authorities on—certain things." Ravi smiled. "Shall I open my suitcase?"

The little man appraised him, then peered at her, the lizard deciding Stay on the wall? Strike? Finally, he waved a limp hand. "Go on then, off you go."

"Thank you," Ravi said. Santa and Roxy collected their identification. "You know where you can find us."

But the tired man was waving his next target into position.

They hurried off. “Thank you again,” Roxy said. “It seems you turn up at the right time.”

“Just luck,” Ravi said.

“I wonder,” Santa grunted. “King’s Cross. That’s where I was going to stay.”

“You still can,” she said.

“Right.”

“Well, folks.” Ravi gripped his carryon handle. “I’m off to get a cab. If you stay at the King’s Cross, perhaps we’ll see each other again.” He threaded through the crowd, a mass of dark hair on a slender frame soon lost in teeming Heathrow.

They hailed their own cab at the exchange. Santa had already confirmed two King’s Cross rooms by phone.

The cab veered and plunged. Roxy gripped the seat against the swerve, the lurch, the sudden stop. Cars of all sizes and the occasional lorry darted or lumbered around their pirouetting cab. “Where do they all come from,” she said, when she felt confident enough to exhale evenly.

“Beats me,” he said. “Everybody swears they don’t drive when they’re here. So all these folks must be locals.”

They lapsed into silence. Eventually, he said, “Interesting little man, that Ravi.”

“Yes. He seemed to come out of nowhere.”

“Well, he’s small. What did you expect?” He chuckled. “But you’re right.”

“I wonder if we’ll see him at the hotel.”

“Probably. I wonder where he’s heading. Didn’t he say he wasn’t in London very long?”

“Mmm-whoa!” She caught her breath as a small red roadster squeezed past on the left. The cab doubled back, and she became completely turned around, until they bolted down a narrow sidestreet and screeched curbside, the cabbie saying, “Right, then, here we are,” and the two of them emerging and paying and heading through the sliding doors.

She caught herself looking for Ravi at check-in. She knew she wasn’t rational, looking behind herself as she headed down the hall to her frumpy, dark-paneled room, feeling watched as she freshened herself for the dinner they agreed to take in half an hour (that damned CEO still pushing a schedule). She ran a cool washcloth over her face, smiling. Where was Ravi supposed to be, hanging like a bat on the shower pole? She looked anyway. *Must be lack of sleep. Whatever time it is.*

She synchronized her watch to eight o'clock (five minutes fast, which worked when she didn't adjust it away), and headed down to the lobby.

He was already there, pacing. "Can't you sit still?" she said. *Fair weather or foul?*

"Mmm," he said. "I just can't stop thinking about the business. Even though I'm supposed to." He guided her towards the restaurant, a seventies-looking arrangement in back. "So here I am, walking up and down, inking an imaginary buyout of High Holly Industries. For all I know, it might still be happening, 'cause we set everything up that way, but it isn't me doing the dealing. It's a pretty weird feeling. Two, please." The host seated them in a booth next to a couple of businessmen scanning the outsized menus.

"What should I get?"

"Anything but beef," he said. "I think British cattle are made of wood."

She studied the list, a few traditional dishes tucked among the hotel's special teriyaki and Hawaiian offerings. Evidently the management here was proud they'd rented an overseas cook. She found a teriyaki chicken, imagined wooden birds, and ordered, adding a Chablis. Santa ordered Kauai Ham ("I have *no* idea", he muttered), plus the house red.

"Well," he sighed. "London. Maybe I'll stay here a while after all, stretch out for a little bit see what's what. Take in some sights. If they're not thick with tourists."

The waiter returned with their drinks. "Cheers," Santa said, touching her glass. "Isn't that him over there?"

And my skin didn't even tingle. She turned. Ravi sat a few tables over, immersed in his entrée. He didn't see them. She turned back. "Want to invite him over?"

He shook his head. "He'll probably stop by when he's done."

They sipped their drinks, reflecting. "Is this the first time we've sat down to a dinner since New Orleans?" Santa said at last.

"I think you're right."

"Well, let's not let it take so long next time." He took another sip as she put her own glass down. "I think I need time to just—stop for a while. You, too. Roxy, we've been running and running in this crazy world for so long that—well, it might just be the right thing right now to take a breath. Take a breath. Then go back."

"Go back."

"Yeah. It doesn't end here. It can't." He swirled his wine. "It can't. But *they* think it can. That's where they're wrong. I've got a couple of choices here." He rubbed his nose the old way. "I can go into some bizarre kind of retirement. The magic dies, and I die, too. Or… Or. I go back. Set things right. The problem is, with how they've shut everything down, there's no way back. No way they know of. Not without me hooking up with my team, and I can't see that happening.

"There are some very old ways back. Some in Europe, some in north Asia, even North America. Over the years, I've done just about every route."

"But not lately."

"No, not lately." He sighed. "And there's no way of knowing whether, if I found one I could … Not without the team. Still." He assisted his thinking with another sip. "If it's a land route, coming in the old way when they'd be going after the air lanes…North America is best for that…"

She watched him, a faint sense of alarm rising, wondering whether she was losing him yet again in a maze of options known only to him.

He scowled suddenly. "Baylor! God Almighty!" He leaned forward. "Did you see that miserable little man who tried to hold us up at the airport? I mean, did you really get a good look at him? What a miserable little excuse for a human! All dried up and bitter. And do you know, Roxy? Do you know, that's *exactly* what Baylor looks like to me! Insignificant little man! Somehow shaping his own personal hurts into an ambition, a drive that shovels us out of the way and installs him on top of a corporation. If you go by essence he should be nowhere near the top, but if you go by pure greed, pure out-and-out Wall-Street happiness, he belongs! Belongs so! Oh, how idiotic! And how they'll suffer because of it! But not the Wall Streeters, not the college boys whose idea of work is to manage money from a distance, the greedy little snots."

The waiter brought their entrees. "Think about it, Roxy," he continued, she fiddling with her dish, trying to find the *teriyaki* there (Hawaiian grill marks?). "Think about a twist of fate that would have landed Baylor in that—that ticket counting position. Whatever it was that was so important to that little turd. Sorry." He finished his wine, signaled for another. "So instead of Mr. Whatshisname, you'd have had Baylor standing there. I guarantee you, *guarantee* you, there'd be no difference. None. Instead of inflicting grand designs on a global enterprise, Baylor would be inflicting small miseries on travelers unlucky enough to be in his line. Because it's the motivation that's the same. Maybe that's too harsh, I don't know—but the only difference between Mr. Tickettaker and Mr. Baylor is that one is running a ticket stand and one is running a corporation. Or he thinks he is. Because—What's the problem?"

She stopped sawing. "I just wondered whether the wooden thing extended to chickens."

He laughed. "Lord knows what they've done *here*." He separated chunks of charmarked ham from rigatoni noodles and pineapple rings. "*Bon appetit*!"

The waiter brought the wine. They were silent now, busy with dinner. Roxy hadn't realized how famished she was, wooden chicken or not. At length, Santa remarked, "I don't think I want to visit the part of Hawaii *this* guy came from… Maybe inside the volcano."

She nodded and smiled.

"Here he comes," Santa continued. He didn't mean the waiter. "Ah, Ravi," he said warmly, "good to see you again!"

"Yes, and for me as well." Ravi's smile faded when he saw Santa's plate. "Oh, dear. The Kauai Ham."

"You had it too?"

"Whatever it was."

Santa chuckled. "Grab a seat."

"No, please no, I am done, you both should enjoy your dinner in peace."

"Dessert, then. On me. Do me a favor. You order something, and if it comes here with a pineapple ring or a grass skirt on it, I'll know to skip dessert."

Ravi hesitated, then smiled broadly. "Done, then." He pulled up a chair. The waiter whisked about to take the order and bring coffee.

"So, Ravi," Santa said between bites, "I've kicked you out of the company I no longer run. What are you going to do?"

"Well, I don't know. I'm really good at taking things as they come."

"What made you decide to become a santa?" Roxy asked.

"Actually, I wasn't suited for what my parents wanted me to be. And all my friends as well expected me to be following a specific path. Lots of people from India are either mathematicians or doctors or computer specialists. Or they're running hotels in America. So my father and I sat down some years ago and talked about things. He asked me to consider where my heart was. Was it in business, or was it in science, or was it in something else? He himself was a well-known surgeon at that time in Madras. I was a skinny kid, I liked chasing girls and carrying on. So my heart had less to say about things than—than certain parts of my physiology. But I thought about it, and I could feel the whole weight of family history, my grandfather and uncles and great uncles. So I came back to him and said it was science, and he was relieved. We decided I should go to U of M and get started on my formal education."

"U of M… University of Madras?" Roxy ventured.

"No, University of Michigan. We talked about that too. India's future is kind of, well, tangled. We are still I think in some ways coming to grips with what our nation must do with the British things, what's left anyway. Common-language newspapers, the rail system. These things brought the nation together years ago. But now there are problems, not only with these things, but with population control and Pakistan."

"Seems a long way from an answer to what she asked." Santa pushed his plate away and signaled for another glass.

"I am sorry, but that's the way it is with people and their big decisions. There is always a story. Anyway, I went to U of M. I would be a thoracic surgeon. Those guys were the hot shots, you know, running around saving lives and when they had time getting women. That's what I thought. I lasted about a year, learning all about tachycardias and arrhythmias and all kinds of big labels that mean your heart's trying to kill you."

"Only a year. Why?"

"I couldn't stand the sight of blood. It was pretty embarrassing. We were invited to the gallery at St. Joe's to watch a bypass procedure. That's pretty standard stuff if you're going to do thoracic surgery. I don't think I lasted past the initial incision. Fainted dead away." Ravi smiled shyly. "It's kind of funny now. But it wasn't at the time." He leaned away as his dessert was set in front of him, an ice cream concoction happily devoid of Polynesia. "They tried, though. They revived me in a corner, said nice things like this kind of thing happens all the time, and then propped me up for another go. Same thing. I think the surgeon had resected the ribcage by that time. No way. If they hadn't caught me, I'd have hit my head on the way down. So I had to quit med school."

"Wow. What did your dad say?" Roxy asked.

"He's a pretty understanding guy, and after he blew up a couple of times and saw it didn't work, he said I should find something else, quickly. He offered to take me back to Madras, but I said I'd tough it out where I was. So I went into computer science, started as an agency programmer for one of the Big Three, gained some experience, and then…" He looked down.

"And then?" Roxy murmured.

"There was a girl. I don't want to talk about it. Sometimes your heart—goes places." He looked away. "Anyway, I needed to make a fresh start." He sighed. "And I wanted to do something I thought would help people. Something that would make them happy. Something simple and direct. So I saw the ad, and a couple of people I knew were thinking about it, too. So we decided, why not? And that's my story."

"What happened to your friends?" Santa asked. "After I pitched the program."

"They took it in stride. They didn't join up for the reasons I did. So they put their heads together and decided their next adventure. They hitched up with some people, relatives I think, in Bahrain, something to do in oil." He looked away again. "But that wasn't for me. I needed to—*need* to—well." He took a bite of ice cream. "The santa program made sense to me. Somewhere deep. And now it's gone, too. So I've decided to head back to Michigan, hang out for a while, try to get my head and heart back in shape. Funny, isn't it, the places a thoracic surgeon can't even touch."

"And we met you in the airport," Roxy said at last. "And you just knew who he was."

"I just knew. Maybe it was luck, maybe something else. I don't know how I knew." Ravi smiled. "And I was able to help."

Santa studied him, and Roxy wondered whether it was generosity or the muddle of a third glass of wine that next inspired him. "Well, you could hitch up with us, at least for a while." She tried not to stare at him as he continued, "You were going to America?"

"Well, yes, in a few days, but—I mean—are you sure you want me tagging along?"

"I wouldn't call it *tagging*," Santa said. "You seem to get us out of trouble a lot."

"Twice," she said.

"Well. Anyway, the offer's on the table. You can think it over."

Ravi studied his ice cream, then looked up and smiled. "What's to think over? It sounds like a wonderful adventure." He raised his coffee. "Cheers, then."

"Cheers," Santa said. "Here's to the three of us, and to adventure, and—" he studied the empty glass morosely "–and to larger wine glasses."

9.

"May I come in, *Coun*sel?"

Groomer nodded, eyes on his email.

Racer creaked into the room. "No hotdogs!"

"For now." Groomer clicked the mouse.

Racer studied him. "I understand Silvertongue continues to struggle with the Argentines."

"Maybe they want to try out the new CEO."

"They won't get anywhere." Racer scratched the back of one hand. "Baylor would show them the door, if it got to him. Which it shouldn't, if Silvertongue does his job."

"He will. Sometimes there's no accounting for how your externals react."

"I wonder at his effectiveness, *Coun*sel. The Argentine matter is a small thing, a second-rate act. It should be disposed of quickly. We can't have our negotiator distracted. Baylor needs to work on EI. I trust *you* are working on that as well?"

"Of course. It's like any other merger. I hardly need Silvertongue for that."

"Perhaps not. But I challenge you, *Coun*sel, on whether this is truly the same. Remember what certain people will see here. There are overtones that affect how this deal is seen by the world. That's where we need our friend with the silver tongue. He's keeping our former CEO happy?"

"Well." Groomer twisted a finger in one ear. "'Happy' may be too strong a word."

"Satisfied, then." Racer made some horrible kind of wheezing sound, perhaps laughter. "Satisfied enough, and thirsty enough, to stay in contact. Useful. Are we watching his paper trail?"

"Yes. Silvertongue has that as well. Credit slips, reservations, manifests. We know where he is at all times. We know that he flew from New Orleans to Gothenburg, and now he's in London. Silvertongue's idea to extend credit pays off. He has no other way to support himself, and all the paper comes back here."

"Expensive."

"But the alternative is a lump sum or cutting him off." Groomer belched and rubbed his belly. "We don't want to push him into a financial corner."

"Understood." Racer rubbed a wheel. "So long as we know what he's thinking. Gothenburg. That's where the admin is, isn't it?"

"Kelli. Was. She left."

"To where?"

"We don't know. We're looking. Maybe Sverige."

"Mats."

"Possible. Still, it's outside NPI, which makes it less of a threat."

"I wonder. A supplier. Well, we have actions we could take, although they would take time. Sverige is currently an important part of our business, but we could go elsewhere. Until we don't need reindeer food any more." Racer's eyes lidded over. "Hm. Nothing good comes to mind. Nothing *deserving*. Let's just watch the traffic into Gothenburg. And see if you can find the girl. Now, about Sweden… How is RFS?"

"Ahead of schedule. There've been more candidates than expected, so the inbound volume's pretty high. We've started a couple of lines, and the production rate right now is about twenty tons a day. There are some disposal issues to work through, quickly, because if we don't figure things out soon, somebody from the Swedish authorities will raise hell."

"If they find out. Part of your job, *Coun*sel, is to make sure that the—less palatable activities not be exposed to those who shouldn't see them."

"I know that! The herd side is more pressing. We could end up overgrazing."

"You'll handle those details. I shouldn't have to remind you that we hide and reveal things as we choose, to set up our opponents, or our media players. For example, EI. I said it was on hold at the EEC. It isn't. You and I are both working very hard on that. As are others we can trust. Soon, we'll be in a position to make the announcement.

"Now. Let's talk about the new order. Baylor will be talking to Gardner again shortly. He'll give her a nice pep talk about joining the new organization. I wonder how she'll take that. With the incentives that we put in place, she should stay confined for a while. The operation will be like a pincer. On the one hand, we've undermined her position with the union by releasing the incentive agreement, which Hammer approved, thinking it had been negotiated by staffers on both sides. On the other hand, Baylor will throttle the salaried programs."

"I think you underestimate her."

"Do you, counsel? Then why do I direct so many actions at her? I think I respect her very well." Racer wheezed and chuckled. "More things will change in the near future. We can move forward with our operations in the north. Baylor is a very practical man, and if there's an opportunity for money to be made there, he'll be happy to see that happen."

"Would you like me to set some things up?"

"I'll handle this one personally, Counsel. You have enough to do. This one can spin more slowly. An unusual mode of operation, these days. There are companies to engage, consultants to deal with, specialists to bring in to ensure that the concept is solid. That will take some time. But we can start surveying now. We should do the rest gradually. Like boiling a frog. You remember the little story I once told you? Put a frog in boiling water, and he leaps out and lives. Put the frog in cool water, and gradually raise the temperature so that he never knows he's in danger until—well. So we need to work this carefully. Let the operation come to grips with the new order, and quietly dismantle the pieces that need dismantling. In the background."

"Some of those pieces should have been dismantled years ago."

"Not really. You sound as though you had bitter experience with them, my friend. Perhaps during your JEDI tour? Too many stables to muck?"

Groomer returned Racer's long, appraising look. "I just think it's an antiquated part of the business, that's all," he said at length. "People have moved on. They don't need the icons. They simply need more, and more convenient, ways of getting presents delivered to their targets. Christmas isn't a holiday, it's an obligation. The faster people can get through it, the more conveniently it can be done, the better. So you map marketing preferences, prestock distribution outlets, line up your just-in-time transit activities, redesign your delivery processes, put a portal on the front to surprise and delight, and you win."

"Today. For a time. Until your competitor ousts you." Racer coughed. "A harsh assessment, Counsel. What about the children? Don't they need to see Christmas?"

"Children can be taught new icons. The marketplace does it to them all the time. Letting the old icons go frees us to operate in the new world. And we can get on with herd disposal, real—the other ventures we have lined up."

Racer studied him. "Real ventures. An interesting term. …One more action."

"Oiler has it. He's working out the details. The accident should happen very soon."

"How does he seem with it?"

"Reluctant."

"I thought so. I would be alarmed if he were too eager. But I'm also—*concerned* with his reluctance, Counsel. Reluctance is not something that works in the position for which he's being prepared. Reluctance, or undue consideration. Thoughtful companies, Groomer, are dead ones. Only speed and ruthlessness prevail. Consider that, and consider Oiler, and, for that matter Silvertongue. And you. And me. While I may seem reflective, Counsel, I always play a game that matches speed to the situation. So that I am always a move ahead. I think you do the same. Let's hope we never end up playing each other. Though the challenge might be interesting."

Groomer smiled, his eyes not in it. "Let's hope not," he said.

MAGIC

II

August
Somewhere North

My name is Tracer. I am a half-elf working for NPI industries in the JEDI program. I've decided to write this journal and leave it in this cabin in case something happens to me.

I think it's still August, but this far north it's hard to tell. The daylight seems strange, side lit, the sun is at a low angle, and snow has already fallen a few times and is starting to stick. So maybe it's really September, or even later.

There are so many things I don't know. I don't know where I landed, or how long ago that was. I don't know how long I lay wounded, or how long it took for me to be carried here, or how long I rested in the stable before coming inside this cabin. I don't know how the deer that rescued me knew where to find me. Maybe it was guided by the same magic that provided its healing powers. Sometimes I even wonder if I dreamed all of it, but I am still very tired, and I still get faint twinges from time to time that remind me of how badly I was hurt.

It's taken me a while to believe those animals in the stable are really Santa's team. I couldn't believe it when I saw their condition and the condition of the stable. They've been neglected for some time. The stable was an indescribable mess and is still in pretty bad shape after this first day's work. Even though this cabin is my size, which is to say Santa-sized, it's hard to believe he ever lived here. He must have abandoned the place many years ago. Even that doesn't make sense, because without some kind of care these deer would surely have starved. Why has he left them like this?

They are very thin. They were too weak to protest when I worked my way into the stalls to feel their ribs. Some of their hooves look infected, but this may clear now that I've had a chance to clean out the stalls and put down fresh straw. Whatever healing magic they possess doesn't seem to extend to themselves. The only bright spot is the water. Fresh water actually flows through troughs in each stall, and it seems to come from a source somewhere behind the building, which I'll investigate when I'm stronger and there's more time.

As I worked today, all I could think of was how this could possibly have happened. Surely Santa wouldn't allow things to get to this state! It shakes my belief in him. His own team!

It started when Parsley nuzzled me awake. She's a wise and patient animal, but she's driven by the same sense as the rest of them, a tapping into something deep and remote that I don't understand. I can feel it everywhere around here but can't put it into words. It's like the rumble of a huge and powerful train, passing at a far distance in the dark. Something is stirring far under the surface here, something that continues to reshape itself despite the fact that on the surface the stall doors are starting to sag, and the hinges on the cabin door have sprung, and the feed is infested with some kind of sluglike vermin.

So the something pushed on Parsley, and Parsley pushed on me. I remember getting up very slowly. Brushing the straw from my arms and legs felt like the work of giants. So I sat down and rested a minute, while Parsley waited. I could see she wondered why I didn't get up and move around, but I just didn't have it in me.

The other deer, the one that rescued me, was nowhere visible, but I could hear the other animals moving about in their stalls. The smell was intense, even after my long exposure to it, and I knew I had to get them fresh air before I did anything else. So I got back on my feet and headed to the stalls.

I won't describe the awful conditions I saw. I can't, I can't: it will make me too damned angry to continue, and in any case I'm not sure I could put into words the kind of long-standing, silent misery that I saw. I don't care if he's CEO. If he doesn't know about this, I'll make him know. And if he does—

They were locked in. I had to find the keys, or find a way to snap the locks, and quickly, before my rage got me and I went beyond my strength trying to tear those damned doors down.

I staggered outside and discovered a large shed behind the stable. This was locked too, with a combination lock, but whoever had locked it last hadn't given the lock a spin, because it opened when I tugged on it. Inside were no keys, but there were tools of all kinds, and one of these looked like a bolt cutter, which I snatched up.

I started back toward the stable. Out of the corner of one eye I saw my rescuer standing on a short rise a small distance from the cabin. She gazed at me, chewing thoughtfully. I decided I would send the rest of the deer her way when I got them free. Fresh forage would do for a start.

Cutting the locks was hard and frustrating work. My own strength was limited, but they had been in there so long I didn't want to leave them inside a single minute longer. Still, I found myself forced to rest after each success, even before I threw the latch to lead them out one by one. I had to be ready in case they stumbled on the way. A few of them were limping, and that's when I noticed their hooves. I also noticed the one stall whose door had been kicked open: a desperate and life-saving move.

At last it was done, and there they all were, standing on the little rise in cold sunshine, four males and four females, plus Parsley standing sleek and small next to their large and angular frames. Their heads drooped, except for my rescuer, who had gained some strength through grazing these past days.

I felt sick. Why were they locked in? Is this some stupid, shortsighted policy invented by the powers that be in our crazy organization? Or Strapper. It has to be him, worried about Santa's team escaping. Worse yet, perhaps they did escape once, and he's petrified they'll get away again and so keeps them locked up whenever he isn't here. When I see him again, I'll have to be restrained.

Four males and four females, and I with no idea who's who. I tried calling their names, but my voice is quite weak, and none of them even bothered to look up. I watched them for a bit, regaining my own strength, encouraged to see them bend their heads and find the lichen they so desperately need. After a while, I made myself get up and go back into that horrible-smelling place. I won't describe it. I'll just say that I turned out the soiled straw, washed out the stalls with a hose I found coiled in a corner (supplied by that same mysterious water source), and put down fresh bedding.

By the time I was done, the sun was low. I realized then that I still had to eat, and I had ahead of me still what I thought would be the major task of getting them back into the stable. But I was wrong. Maybe they sensed what I had done for them this day. I'd like to think so. The more likely reason was the cold night wind and their own fatigue. I hailed them generally, not by name (my voice still a dismal croaking), and they shuffled off the rise toward the stable, to file past me and into their stalls. It was then that I discovered most of the feed shipped up from the Central Stables had gone bad or buggy. I have to hope their foraging will sustain them—the feed problem will need to be resolved another way, on another day.

I didn't lock them in. I installed Parsley in one of the two spare stalls and made my way here. There's a pantry in the back, where I've discovered sufficient food for myself. But today I just opened a can of stew and ate it cold—too tired to do much else. I'm surprised I could stay with the journal this long. The old green couch is beckoning, if I can slap enough dust out of it. Let tomorrow bring what it will.

Next Day
Somewhere North

A new day. Everything that could hurt, hurt today. Oh, well. I fixed myself some cold stew out of a can for breakfast, which would be pretty awful under other circumstances. But stews and soups will be my staples here.

I began by turning them all out of their stalls. We seem to connect on some plane—fatigue, perhaps. The day was crisp and cold, the ground frosted over, and their hooves clicked and crunched as they made their slow way to the rise. I let them graze unattended. I know they were too tired to stray very far this morning, and they in turn seemed to know (or I hoped, wished *they knew) that I was here to help them.*

It was a day of discoveries. I discovered a closet in the cabin that contains some work clothes that actually fit me reasonably well (though their cut and style are a bit odd), which means I'll be able to keep from smelling too much like the deer if I end up staying here a while. There is also a fair-sized utility room, with an old washing machine and wringer, and lines for hanging clothes.

I found the diverted stream that supplies water to the stable and cabin. The stream actually bubbles out of the ground a short distance from the stable, its waters warm at the source. Perhaps there's an underground hot spring. I also noticed some heavily tarnished plates on a workbench in the shed, brass proof from their raised letters that this is indeed the legendary team.

This morning I cleaned out the stalls again, and by noon I was hungry enough to make some soup. This I heated in a hanging kettle over a small fire I built in the fireplace, having also stumbled across a fair supply of dried firewood in a sheltered rack next to the shed. In these cold conditions, it hasn't suffered overmuch from rot. I wish I'd found that wood yesterday—last night on the couch was pretty cold.

Hot soup was a welcome change from cold stew. The soup and stew cans are quite dusty from their long life on the pantry shelf. But their ingredients were heavenly, for I now realized how truly hungry I was.

After lunch, I went outside to see what had become of the team. They had drifted apart, and were grazing singly or in pairs a good deal farther from the cabin. But I knew they wouldn't stray. I turned my attention to the stables again.

I decided to take inventory of the feed, and was heartened to find that some of the newer bags escaped the infestation of bugs that attacked so many of the older bags. I spent some time separating the newer bags, which had been carelessly dumped among the older ones. I used two new bags to fill the feed troughs, knowing how eagerly the team would devour this when I brought them in for the night.

Feed will be a problem. Saddler told me this special feed provides nutrients beyond those that the deer can get from lichen alone. I don't know when or if anyone will visit. I have little faith in a system—or a CEO—so neglectful of something so central to Christmas. But maybe that's the problem, that they and the business have drifted away.

When the feed runs out, I'll have to make a decision. I hope by then I have at least one deer well enough to fly back. As to what I'll ride in, I'll have to figure that out. I've seen nothing to suggest a work wagon anywhere around here. I'll probably have to build one, but out of what?

Back to my day. After sorting the feed, I decided to see what tools I had. I glanced at the team and returned to the shed. The shed was dimly lit from two small windows, and after my eyes adjusted I could see benches and tools, hooks with work lanterns dangling amid harnesses, bells, clamps, wrenches, mallets, and some other tools unfamiliar to me. Tucked against the left wall was a set of shelves sagging under the weight of dozens of jars. I read the labels from several of these, and happily discovered one large jar labeled "Hoof Salve." I resolved to use it this very evening.

As I went through the tools and supplies, I gradually came to realize I was sorting them according to the tasks I'll be doing. Additional heavy brushes will be used to brush the deer's coats, supplementing brushes I'd already found in the stable. I'll use the green paint for the cabin door, once I've properly rehung it. I can use the hammer and nails to repair the sagging stall doors; the screws and screwdrivers for cabinetry; and the polish and polishing cloths for brass nameplates. I found a stool and pulled it up to the bench, sat on it and rested my chin on my hands, daydreaming about all the things I'd be doing.

When I woke up, the light in the shed had changed, and I realized with a jolt that I'd left the team unattended for hours. I snatched up the hoof salve and hurried from the shed. I peered about in the gloom of the quickly-advancing northern twilight, relieved to see the dark clump of bodies on the rise. They had actually moved closer to the stable. I shouted and waved my arms at them, and they responded, making their slow way to the familiar shelter. I saw them to their stalls, and noted with deep satisfaction their delighted grunts as they discovered good feed at last.

I set the jar of hoof salve in the straw pile where I'd spent my first night. Treatment can wait until the morning. I left them busily eating and went to my own dinner.

Next Day
Somewhere North

It snowed again overnight, this time a couple of inches. Early this morning, I heated water over the fire in the cabin and brought the kettle out to the stable. Using the bar of soap I found there, I spent a good part of the morning washing down their legs and hooves, looking for any problems. These I treated with the hoof salve. When I finished, I turned them loose to graze for the day.

I rested for a bit before making a simple lunch of soup and dried fruit snacks. I felt—I feel*—torn between wanting to get it all done, wanting to make it all right for them, and realizing that I have no control over the fatigue that prevents me from getting there. It's the same feeling I have when at the end of an active day I sit here and find the energy to write these words in case this is all that will remain of who I am, and who they are, and what this has been, and what I've tried to do here.*

When I finished lunch, I put my bowl in the sink and headed out. From habit, now, I glanced toward the rise. I was glad to see they'd dispersed again, ranging farther away. A few of them had strayed out of sight, but I knew where they were.

I made my way to the shed. I decided I would spend the few hours I had before darkness polishing the brass plates I'd discovered yesterday. I grabbed polishing cloths and polish and set to work. The plates were heavily tarnished, and my fingers started hurting before I was halfway through the first one. The more I polished, the more detail emerged. Soon I had finished Prancer, *complete with reindeer image and bells surrounding the name. I set it aside, stood up, and walked outside, flexing my now-green fingers. The deer hadn't moved around much, and I sat on a small boulder outside the stable for a while, watching them, before I slipped into the shed to continue my work.*

By the end of the afternoon, I'd finished all the plates. I went outside with a bar of soap and washed my hands downstream from the stable. I returned to the shed and looked at the eight plates gleaming in the soft light, rich in detail. Now the simplest of tasks would be the most challenging. I could fix them on the stall doors, but which was which? The deer still hadn't responded to me calling their names, and so I'd just give them all a shout and a wave, as though they were one many-bodied deer instead of eight separate ones.

I figured I'd better try one more time. So I went to the stable and put more of the good feed in their troughs. I stood at the door a moment, thinking, watching the serene forms. They had moved back closer to the stable, once again in anticipation of being brought in for the night. Instead of calling them in, I walked up to the field where they were grazing.

They hardly noticed me as I moved among them, my feet crunching the lichen. Their ribs still show, but they now have more energy than before. They're becoming familiar to me, large and magical though they are. I wandered in their midst, sure of myself but not sure, knowing this was the thing to do but not knowing why. I put my hands on the warm backs, feeling the roughness of their hides. And then, with my hand just behind the head of the deer who had rescued me, I quietly said, "Vixen."

She turned. I moved away. "Come, Vixen. Follow," I said, and she did. I led her to her stall, and she obediently clomped inside, her nose finding the feed immediately, contented grunts coming from her as I fixed her brass plate on the recess in the frame above her broken door.

It was that way with each of the others. I walked slowly between the large bodies, selecting one, and then running my hand over the deer before pronouncing the name that came to me. I felt as though I were naming them all for the first time, male and female deer suddenly made magical through the utterance of a word charged with purpose, history and action: Prancer. Comet. Blitzen. Cupid. Dancer. Donder. Dasher.

Last of all I brought in Parsley, magical in her own way but comfortably familiar still. I wished I had some brass to put over her stall. Not that it mattered at all to her: she contented herself with her feed like the others. I left them as I did last night and trudged to the cabin, where I scraped open the door and pushed it back into place behind me. Maybe tomorrow I'll get started on those hinges.

Next Day
Somewhere North

This is a day I'd rather forget, but I guess it was inevitable. I think it's a combination of going from confinement to open air, from no food to lichen to rich feed. The entire team, except for Parsley and Vixen, has come down with diarrhea. It frightens me to see it, because in their condition a prolonged bout could be life-threatening. Mercifully, however, the signs point to a brief spell caused by their compromised digestive systems making the adjustment to food.

I didn't let them go to the rise today. I thought I'd better keep them bunched in a small lower clearing near the stable, with the water source nearby. They seem to understand that all my actions are organized around their well-being. Even though no fences contain them, and even though the choicest lichen grew on the rise, the deer made no move to go there. I may be giving myself too much credit, though: perhaps they were simply too tired.

They spent the day in the clearing, and I spent the day puttering around the stable. I did a check of the outside, looking for things that need repairs. Though weathered and brown, and even though the whole building leans, the basics are sound. The glass in all the windows is also intact. In the stable, I examined the stall doors, deciding on what I would need from the shed.

The worst door was of course Vixen's: she had literally kicked it free from its hinges. I decided to start there. I found some spare pieces of wood and an old wooden ruler in the shed. Then I spent a good part of the morning measuring, sawing, and hammering, and by lunchtime I had the door repaired.

I prepared hot soup for lunch, poured it in a narrow-mouthed brown stoneware crock, and headed outside to the same small boulder by the stable, where I'd sat yesterday with my green fingers. I'm beginning to see this gray boulder as my "thinking rock": a flat, smooth seat that somehow seems able to take the least bit of heat from the pale sun and store it as welcome warmth. I sat on it, sipping my broth, dividing my attention between the nine deer and the stable. I had a fleeting thought that he *might have sat on this same stone centuries ago, pondering a day's work done, the magic young, fresh, growing.*

But another part of me said that was damned presumptuous, that I was sitting on a rock outside an old stable way up in the north country, that he *had departed long ago, and that what magic was still here lingered with a neglected team, certainly not with a collection of sticks and stones, bales of straw, a pantry full of soups, and a half-elf a fraction of* his *age accidentally stuck here. As quickly as I had the thought, though, it was pushed aside by that deep and remote something I felt the first day. I still feel it whenever I stop, whenever I get quiet enough inside. I feel it now, writing these words. It's in the team and the stable, the rocks and the grass, the lichen and the trees. It whirls through here on the wind, drives into the boards on the backs of snowflakes, is in the blue of the sky and the shifting shapes of clouds. It flows through this pen and onto this page, so that I string together words I can scarcely believe have been written by me, Tracer and yet not Tracer, half-elf and more, restored by a deer as magical and timeless as anything this earth has brought forth.*

After I finished my soup, I took another hard look at the stable. Something wasn't adding up. I got up, set the soup dish on the thinking rock, and paced slowly about the perimeter, the first time getting the size of the place, and the second time counting windows and matching the count to my mental picture of the inside. I counted twelve windows in all: five on each side for the stalls (Parsley is in one of the unused ones), and one on each end.

That was it. From inside the stable, I've only seen one end window, on the end where the straw pile is. The other end is walled off. I hurried into the stable to prove it to myself. From the door (which opens in the middle on the side of the stable facing the cabin), I looked both ways. I saw a window over the straw pile to my right, and a blank wall to my left. I walked slowly up to the blank wall and studied it closely from top to bottom, chuckling to myself as I realized what a loony I'd look like if any of the deer wandered in and saw me staring at a blank wall. And indeed I found nothing to suggest it was anything other than a simple, smooth surface. I puzzled over this for a moment before heading outside.

I found some old wood and stacked it against the wall, then climbed on it and peered through the window. I couldn't see a damn thing. I couldn't even tell whether the window opened onto an empty, darkened room or was simply boarded up from the inside. I contemplated breaking the glass with a piece of wood or a rock, but I realized I'd have to fix whatever I broke, so I let everything be.

I kicked away the wood and caught the team staring at me. I gave them a shy wave before sneaking into the shed for more wood.

I finished fixing up the rest of the stalls this afternoon. Most of the stall doors were in pretty good shape, needing little more than squaring up using existing turnbuckles and chains, or tightening and resetting the hinge screws. I gathered the tools into a small pile by the door. Then I gave each of the deer (except Parsley and Vixen) only a little of the feed, to see how their systems would take it.

At the close of day, I called them to their stalls, heartened to see that they took to their feed with obvious interest.

At last, I picked up the tools and headed to the shed a final time. As I put the things away, I noticed a large book resting on a shelf high up. I knew I hadn't seen it before. Well, no matter—I was too tired this evening even to raise my arms and pull it down.

And now, back in the sleepy warmth of the cabin, having used the last of my energy to light the fire and cook and eat my supper, I finish this entry, hoping I have it in me to go from this desk to that green sofa. If I'm this tired tonight, how will I ever care for them tomorrow?

A Few Days Later
Somewhere North

Well, it turned out to be my turn, only my problem was fever and an upset stomach. I spent most of the first day tossing on the green sofa, trying to stay warm while I worried about the deer. It had only been one day since their illness. What were they all doing? I dragged myself out there and turned them loose, noting groggily the relative cleanliness of their stalls and realizing that I would have no strength for them that day, other than to paint some hoof salve on the three that still needed it. They could sense I felt like hell.

I wandered through that strange land fever takes you to, while the sun drifted in through the cabin window, first at one angle, then another. Strange images and words played over and over in my mind. I kept walking around and around the outside of that stable, stopping at the mystery window and peering inside at nothing. In my dreams, I called the team by name, and their figures swam up before me. I imagined that they actually answered me, using words, but as I write this account a couple of days later I can't recall what they said nor, for that matter, what I asked them.

At some point in the muddle, the voices seemed to sharpen, coming through the partially-opened cabin door. Perhaps some elves had come from the Central Stables to drop off a load of precious feed. I forced myself up and staggered to the door, peering outside but finding nothing. The team appeared to have been interested in something beyond the rise, but they turned their heads my way when the cabin door scraped. We stared glassily at each other a moment before I closed the door, shuffled back to the couch, and collapsed onto it.

When I finally woke up, the fire had died to a dull glow, and the cabin had cooled considerably. My fever had broken, and I was drenched in sweat. Except for that dull glow, the place was quite dark. Day had worn considerably into night. Panicked, I jumped up, threw on the blanket, and rushed to the door. Were they still outside?

I peered about. My heart sank. I could barely see the lower clearing through the gloom, but there were no shapes there. I heard nothing. Swearing under my breath, I grabbed hold of a work lantern and lit it, the bright flame piercing the darkness. I hurried outside, fearing that they'd wandered to some undiscovered place which in their weakened condition would be dangerous. I called them hoarsely by name, my voice rattling through the darkness. Then I listened, holding the lantern high.

Sometimes your fears just get in the way. Holding the lantern above my head, I heard a snort and shuffling sounds from the stable. "Of course!" I croaked happily. They had done the natural thing, an ancient habit, returning to their stalls on their own. I walked into the stable. Sure enough. I tossed the blanket on the straw and moved happily among them, putting down some feed, talking to them and rubbing their wise heads.

The next morning I awoke more refreshed, but still moving a bit slowly. I decided to wash my fever-soaked clothes and other items, using the old washing machine and hand-wringer and hanging the clothes in the utility room to dry. I tried out some soup for a very late breakfast, and that seemed to work. Then I went outside. They had already let themselves out and stood bunched in the lower clearing. I resolved then that, for all our sakes, today would be a slow day.

And I made it just that. I spent some time mucking out their stalls, but afterwards left them in the clearing while I ranged over the surrounding lands. Though I was dressed for it, the air was quite cool, and the sharp breezes stung my cheeks. My heels crunched lichen buried under a thin snowcrust. The sun angled over the tops of firs, dark tree-shapes against a deep blue sky. The only sounds interrupting the immense silence were wind-borne: the rustle and moan of evergreen branches, or the surprised cry of an arctic bird. One such bird exploded into flight directly in front of me, a flurry of stubby wings propelling a round white mass. Otherwise, nothing interrupted the great gulfs of soundlessness. Against such silence and space, not only does NPI seem to be a dream, but even the ultimate purpose of that grand team seems less real than their immediate animal needs.

The low sun had already slid behind the treetops when I returned, greeting the team now on the rise. I wandered idly among them, my mind still moving along the snowscape, tapping into this fathomless calm. Eventually, I led them down to their stalls and saw to their feed.

I was closing up the shed for the night when I remembered the book. I decided it would make a comfortable, quiet end to a reflective day. I went back in the shed and pulled the book down from its high shelf. A cloud of dust came with it. For all its size, it felt strangely light. I worried that its worn pages would crumble to nothing in my hands.

Even now, as it sits comfortably on the desk next to my empty stew bowl, I look at its faded red and green cover and wonder. I'm strangely reluctant to open it. I'm torn between what I think this book might contain (do I dare read it?) and what it most likely contains, which will probably be disappointing. How I've gone this long without opening it, I'll never know. But now it's time.

Another Day
Somewhere North

The book occupied me well into the night, through numerous cups of hot tea. It turned out to be less than what I'd either hoped or feared. It's not a book on how the magic started or how the team was discovered. Nor is it a log of feed deliveries and other business transactions interesting only to auditors. The best way I can describe it is as a sort of "how-to" book, a book of methods, describing how to take simple materials and combine them to make salves, medicines, soaps, lubricants and polishes; how to balance sleigh runners; what to do for split-hoof, bloat, rockwear, windburn, withersmart, hornrub, and dozens of other exotic-sounding maladies whose ancient names probably describe many of the things we still treat today. In the chapter on harnesses I learned tricks to keep leather supple and strong, specialized knots and tiedowns, and in one amazing section, techniques for tuning harness bells, adjusting tone and brightness and training your ear to recognize a given team, even down to the individual deer, by its bellsong.

I had to force myself not to look at the book during breakfast. Otherwise, I'd have spent the whole morning at it, neglecting the team and my duties. As it was, they were already filing out of the stable by the time I stepped outside, and I chuckled to myself, wondering if I was overvaluing my caretaker role. Then I remembered the thin ribs, the dull eyes, the matted fur, the vermin, the stink, the infections, and I no longer doubted.

The supply of good feed is running low. I'm amazed that in the days I've been here no one has stopped by. I can't believe the Chief wants his team to starve. Or Strapper. He'd be as horrified as me, though maybe for different reasons. After all, this place, these animals are the center of it all. No, something must have gone terribly wrong. But what? I owe it to these marvelous creatures who despite their magic have placed their shy and stubborn trust in me.

At least for now. They are steadily gaining strength, and I wonder whether once recovered they'll set off themselves to their own destination, driven by that deep pulsing magic, snapping the fragile bonds that have begun to form between us. I hope not, but I'm beginning to realize that the magic will carry us all along to a different place in the end, and whether that happens together or separately remains to be seen.

The feed crisis still weighed on me as I finished up in the stalls and sat down on the thinking rock to take a break. I sorted through the details once again.

Either something's gone wrong, or an evil so diabolical I can't bring myself to believe it has been unleashed in that organization, or—and here a strange, sinking feeling came over me when I first thought it up—there's been a bureaucratic slipup, a communications error, a procedural mistake of the highest order. No matter what's happened, though, the Central Stables are still there, and the rest of NPI can't have vanished in the few weeks I've been away. I realize, though, that sitting around waiting for the feed to come to me isn't going to work. I'll have to return to the Central Stables to get it and while I'm there knock some heads together, starting with Strapper's and whoever else I find responsible. I know that probably isn't fair, but starvation isn't interested in fairness.

How will I get back? I watched them moving slowly in the upper pasture. *The only ones strong enough to make the flight are Parsley and possibly Vixen. Even so, Vixen isn't strong enough yet to pull anything. As for the rest of the team, there's no way.*

Then there's the simple problem of what Vixen and Parsley would pull, assuming I can balance them as a team, big and small as they are. I've seen nothing resembling sled, wagon, or (come to think of it) sleigh anywhere on the property, and what pieces of wood I've found I've used to repair the stalls.

My next thought made me laugh out loud, which caused a couple of them to look my way, mouths moving with lichen. If I'm going to get back at all, I'll have to ride one of them. I figure they somehow know how experienced I am as a flier, and this made me laugh even more. But there really is no other way.

I'll have to ride Vixen. Parsley's too small, and I doubt she could find her way back to the Central Stables on her own. Nor will I be able to help her. Two questions came immediately to mind: is Vixen strong enough, and will she tolerate someone riding her?

I wasn't laughing anymore. There really wasn't any other solution. I got up from the thinking rock and fixed myself some soup for lunch. In the afternoon, I sorted through the remaining feed, going through the tedious process of opening the sacks, separating the good from the vermin-infested stuff, pouring it handful by handful into the storage bin and dumping the bad stuff into some old bags. The bugs were everywhere, and I had to stop several times to brush them off my skin and clothes, all the while hoping that neither they nor their eggs will start a new population explosion in the bin.

While I worked, the thought of me flying one of Santa's reindeer bareback to the Central Stables kept flashing through my mind, outrageous, ludicrous, the single solution. I suppose I could walk Vixen overland, but I have no idea how far out I am and how long such a journey will take. There's not enough feed for that.

I remember one of the methods taught to us in the so-long-ago JEDI program, about describing the future state, seeing your goal. I can do that, all right. I can see myself astride her back, the ground falling away, and the rest of the team dwindling to dots. It doesn't help much. What do you do when the future state terrifies you? Of course, I realize the current state has me picking bugs off my arms and eating soup and stew every damn day. One possible future state involves learning to enjoy lichen, and that doesn't seem particularly appealing, either. So I'm back to imagining myself flying.

I smiled, working through the feed. Vixen will be trying to fly for the first time in quite a while, and I'll be learning how to fly for—well, for the first time. This will be interesting.

By the time I finished, the short afternoon had drawn down to dusk. I called them all back in. I followed Vixen to her stall, talking softly to her as she buried her long face in her water trough and took an extended, greedy drink. I said something like, "Well, girl, we have our work cut out for us tomorrow, don't we?" She lifted her head, blew out a little as she turned, and when she looked at me it was with an expression of—well, of understanding, as though she had long known what needed to be done and had merely been waiting for me to come round to the same conclusion. Her black, gold-flecked eyes held mine for a long moment before she casually turned away and began eating. In that glance she pulled forth and transferred just as much of that deep rumbling magic as I'm capable of sustaining, and she seemed to know that I knew it, too.

Sitting at this old and now familiar desk, writing this account, the book of methods at my elbow, I can feel the magic with each account I write, each day building on the last. We—this team and this half-elf and those two brave little deer who brought me to where the contact could be made—have journeyed through accident, near starvation, and abandonment. One has died already. The ones here almost did. While that danger is past for now, still they might never fly again if this abandonment continues, and they are confined to the lichen-bound fields round about, dwindling to ordinary deer because the business has no use for them. Or they could choose not to fly. Imagine that—Santa's RFS team. What would become of them then?

The book beckons. But something about what I've just written strikes me as not quite true. It's this. Those deer will direct themselves, either to fly off on their own, or to stay, or to wander to a wild corner of the world as their instinct tells them. I begin to wonder whether the magic originated with them, long centuries ago, and then he *was drawn to them, compelled to find them; or whether* he *first built this cabin and they followed; or whether the place always existed, and they simply swam out of the mists to occupy it.*

I need to read the book now, to keep connecting and connecting. Tomorrow, the exercises will begin.

Another Day
Somewhere North

I stayed up late again. The book kept me going. The next section discussed brass plates, which I read carefully. After that, I sat and stared a bit, my mind groggy with fatigue but still restless, unable to find sleep, worried about how to approach things today. Absently, I turned the pages of the book, until I reached a page whose simple title I read, reread, and had to read yet again to convince myself it was real. "How to Train the Deer". Written in the same strong hand. Its contents energized me and propelled me farther through the night than a reasoning, recovering being would sensibly go. I won't repeat here the words in that section—the book is here for anyone to see. But those words are enough to make me want to skip breakfast today, and I had to force myself to eat, anticipating the morning's efforts.

It took a bit for Vixen and me to adjust to our roles. After all, she's been flying for thousands of years, pulling various sleighs through all kinds of weather and across countless miles, while I've made just two rather unimpressive flights.

For one thing, I couldn't even find the guidesticks the book mentioned. I figured they'd been thrown away thousands of years ago. Why would Santa's deer ever have to relearn how to fly? So I had to make do with a couple of branches cut from a nearby fir tree and stripped of their needles. I could see she didn't think too much of them.

To make matters worse, I was too impatient. Maybe I was thinking of the feed. Possibly I was just irritable from lack of sleep and an incomplete recovery myself. Either way, by the end of an hour's hard work, she was wheezing and snorting, I was panting, and the snowy field was pockmarked with dozens of hoof- and footprints along a narrow track we'd pounded back and forth. The other deer watched our progress with interest, but with no apparent inclination to join in.

I approached her for the umpteenth time, guidesticks at the ready, and called her name. She jerked her head up, and if ever a deer could glare at someone, this one did. I had the distinct impression that she thought me more a half-wit than a half-elf. I glared back, eye into eye, until at length I couldn't help it, my face breaking into a smile, then a grin, until finally I was laughing out loud, laughing long enough to have to sit down, snow finding its cold way to my butt. My laughter ranged across that open space, bouncing off the tops of the trees, and with her head bobbing up and down I fancied she was laughing too.

After a while, I managed to get up. I left the guidesticks in the snow and reached out to rub her long nose. I left her standing there while I went down to the stable and drew a bucket of water to bring up to her. Then I took the empty bucket back down and spent the rest of the morning cleaning out the stalls.

After lunch, we were both in better spirits. I decided to slow down and watch and listen more, observing how she took to certain actions but not others, how her breathing took on a certain rhythm when she concentrated, how she held her head a certain way when she was tiring, how she pawed at the lichen and arched her head back when she was frustrated or growing impatient.

Instead of having her take a running start this time, I simply held the guidesticks a little ways off the ground just in front of her and encouraged her to step over them. After we had accomplished this little task, I tried holding them farther out. Nothing doing. So I developed a little ruse: I held the guidesticks just in front of her, as before, but as she prepared to step over them I pulled them back just a bit. Surprised, she adjusted her motion, jumping forward a little to clear the sticks. I did it again, pulling back a little more this time. Again she made the adjustment, pawing the ground and bobbing her head afterwards. She knew by now that it was a game, and because I didn't want to spoil the way it was going, I tried to keep things fun. All the while, I was worrying about such things as when to start motioning with the guidesticks to soften her landings and keep her from splitting a shin.

We spent the better part of an hour at this game, and by the time it was over I was the more tired of the two, since I was doing all the jumping back. I decided to move some distance away and hold up the guidesticks as before. She decided to walk up to where I was and step over them. From her head bobs I knew she was laughing at me, so I slapped her across the backside with one of the sticks, letting her know that fun was fun but we had work to do.

I moved off a little farther. At least she'd get more of a walk, I reasoned. I assumed the coaching pose and waited. She did something then that I'll never forget. She bobbed her head once and backed away, putting several more yards between us. Then she took a couple of short steps and simply bounced free of the earth, describing a lazy, floating arc of about thirty feet. I was so surprised I didn't realize that instinct had taken over, that I was moving the guidesticks up and back and then down, matching her motion perfectly as she came to rest some twenty feet beyond where I stood. When I found my voice I shouted, the sound ringing over pasture and trees. She advanced a couple of steps, and I backed away, raising the guidesticks. Again she stepped backward. Then she took those two steps and floated over the pasture once more, landing softly some distance away.

She was proud, and I was jubilant. I don't know how many times she sailed over the field. I'd seen so many reindeer in the air before, at the Central Stables. But this was special. I couldn't get enough of her, and she couldn't get enough of flying.

Suddenly, though, she stopped, lay down, and started gulping what snow she could find. I realized then that neither of us had sense to remember she hadn't been healthy for very long. We were through for the day. Tomorrow will bring more challenges.

Several Days Later
Somewhere North

These last few days have been simply amazing. Two huge discoveries awaited me, starting the day after Vixen made her first flight. That morning, as I was busy mucking out the stalls, a gleam caught my eye. It came from high up, where what I thought was a blank wall joined the dark ceiling. I set down the wheelbarrow of fresh straw and stared.

Actually, there were two gleams up there. My eyes resolved their images, but my poor head didn't want to believe what it saw. Hadn't I been over that wall? I approached it slowly, as though it was somehow more than a collection of boards. When I reached it, I stopped and peered at the gleaming hinges and the long dark line cut between them. I followed the line on the left side, then the right, as it turned to the vertical and ran half hidden along the edge where the stall doors met the wall.

A door. How could I open it? I looked down. Some straw hid the point where the door met the stable floor. I kicked it aside with one foot and looked closely. The line ran smoothly but for two spots about three feet apart, where it raised up a handwidth.

I couldn't believe I was doing what I was doing. I knew I had seen nothing but a smooth wall here several days ago. Yet here I was, putting hands into the handholds and pulling and lifting, the door gliding easily up and back.

There was the mystery room revealed, and I knew exactly what the large shrouded shape crouching in the dim light was, and what it meant, even before I saw the telltale runner peeking out from under the cloth.

I slipped into the room, my feet kicking up little clouds of dust. How long had it been since it had been used? I raised a corner of the cloth, glimpsed red and green scrolled wood panels inlaid with gold leaf. My hands trembled, and I dropped the cloth. His sleigh. I felt like an intruder, penetrating places I wasn't supposed to reach. But I could see that his sleigh would also need some attention before it could be used.

I stepped back into the stable proper. This latest task brought me up short. Why was I doing all this, if he hadn't ridden the damn thing through the skies since who knows when? Of course I'll take care of the deer, Christmas or no Christmas, but the rest of it? To what end?

How was it that the door appeared, where I'd seen no door before? Standing there, I couldn't convince myself that I had simply overlooked it, despite being weak and ill. I reached up and pulled it shut, closing off that mysterious room, feeling the deep rumble once again as it patiently guided steps, motion, action. In that moment, standing at that door, I knew I'd prepare it all, sleigh, team, cabin, stable. I'll restore it to what it had been, to what it's supposed to be. I'll work the team, set the harnesses, tune and polish the bells. I'll work in wood, stone, cloth, leather and brass. I'll set that work against sky, ground, wind, water. I'll make everything right for Christmas, and if Christmas, the true Christmas, isn't to be, then it isn't meant to be.

Late that afternoon, after working with Vixen (who now flies over the entire field at will), I made my second discovery. I had some spare time after practice, and I'd noticed for the first time a narrow, mostly hidden path that led into a fir stand at the far end of the pasture. It would make a pleasant walk at the end of a long, hard day.

I headed down the path, picking my way amid firs and juniper scrub. Snow had drifted into these sheltered areas, slowing my progress a little but certainly not challenging me. Silence shrouded me as soon as I left the clearing. I don't remember thinking anything as I walked along that path. It was more a sense, a feeling, a pushing from behind meeting a pulling from ahead.

I didn't have far to go before the path dumped me into another clearing, one quite different from the lichened pasture I'd left. I stood at the edge and held my breath, staring at the long, low wood and stone building in the middle, surrounded by stone cabins, sheds and other outbuildings.

From this beginning, from this single, small factory, the entire grand operation had grown. How had the elves come to occupy these cabins, build the first crude structures? How many times had these buildings been built, torn down and rebuilt, only to be abandoned at last?

I roamed the small complex. Though shabby, the cabins and sheds are still in reasonable condition. A couple of the cabins stand apart from the others. These are somewhat larger, so half-elves might have lived here. I felt so at home here, as though these grounds have always existed just for me.

I made my way to the factory door and tried it. It was locked. When I went to rub the glass of a nearby multipaned window, to peer inside, I noticed that one of the panes had already been cleaned of grime. The interesting thing was that the chosen pane was at my eye level, suggesting that another half-elf had visited here fairly recently. I looked around for other signs and noticed softened dents, old footprints in the snow. The prints circled the old factory building, and they were too indistinct for me to determine whether they came from or disappeared into the fir trees on the opposite side of the clearing from where I'd entered. Certainly there was no path that way. I'm not much of a sleuth, but I thought I made out two pairs of prints, or perhaps it was just one pair coming and going. I couldn't tell how old the prints were, either, and whether they had been made before or during my occupation. Then I remembered the voices I thought I'd heard through the haze of my fever. Was it them?

I stood deep in thought, feeling some sort of profound disturbance. This was an intrusion. Reason was against me here, but no other explanation worked. Why did they come here? What are they looking for? Who are they? They didn't come to drop off feed or check on the deer. What are they up to?

I peered through the cleaned glass. I could barely make out shapes of what looked like work stations arranged in long rows in the gloom. I walked back to the door and tried it more forcefully this time. I wasn't too surprised when it squawked open. I stepped through the door and back a hundred years.

I walked amid these wooden tables, their worn and roughened surfaces blanketed by dust. Opening drawers, I pulled out old tools, hefting them, feeling the solid heaviness of the old technology. Had any of the elves I'd encountered in my rotations, Halter or Winnow or anyone else, lifted these same tools, day in and day out, so many years ago? I marveled at those elves' strength, for the tools felt heavy to me, lifting them for only a few minutes, not hours on end.

The air had a musty, still quality to it, not dead, but sleepy, as though a few open windows, a few lamps coupled with the sounds of craftwork would awaken it. And indeed it looked as though the work could start right up again. I puzzled over the tools in the drawers, the brushes on the benches. Did everyone here just decide one day that it was over, that these tools and benches had no further use, and so they simply abandoned them? Was there perhaps a strange twist, a switch deep in the Chief's head, leading him to such an abrupt and dismissive decision? And had he, could he possibly have come to the same decision about his deer?

I shook my head violently, put down the tool I'd been holding, and hurried out of the place. I clanged the door behind me and leaned against it, taking in deep lungsful of air. I needed to get back to the Central Stables to sort things out. Mystery upon mystery pile themselves upon me—from starving deer, to a sleigh-room appearing in a smooth wall, to unknown footprints, to a sleepy and abandoned toy factory. Both Christmas and Santa seem to shift and turn on me, presenting first one face and then another, and the further into the exploration I go, the less I understand. I only know I've been too long alone in these far north fields. I need to ride Vixen back to Saddler and Strapper and the rest of them, to do my part straightening out this corner of the world before its hold on my mind grows to the point where I might simply cease to care and elect instead to ignore them all, to isolate myself, and to take my chances with the lichen and the deer.

I hustled back to the pasture then and spent the waning daylight moving among the team, content to rest a hand occasionally on a broad, rough back. If they sensed my fading agitation, they gave no sign, only continued to eat.

In the days between those two discoveries and now, when I'm making this entry, Vixen and I worked hard to ready her for the flight we both knew was imminent. We progress quickly now, each driven by a sense that time dwindles. Certainly the feed does, and my anxiety grows as I begin scraping the bottom of the bin. It will have to be soon, our leaving, or else all the progress we've made will be erased. The sleigh stays tucked away now, and the factory sleeps in its clearing. There's too much else to do.

Vixen's strength has returned rapidly, as though fed by the flying. Now my anxiety has less to do with her abilities than with mine. How on earth will I ever stay on her back? No amount of special feed will make me *fly. But it has to be done, and so a few days after finding the sleigh, there I was in that tattered and padded white suit, ready to take my rides and my spills. When they saw me in the outfit, the team gave me one of those looks that reminds you that animals are smarter than elves or half-elves in the long run, or at least more dignified.*

I thought I would have to work into this gradually, starting out by draping myself on her back, but Vixen knew what was up and didn't want to take any more time at this than needed. Even so, that first ride was a real doozy, what little of it I remember opening my eyes to see. It must have lasted only a few seconds, and after we landed—and I had managed to stay on board throughout—she turned her head and snapped her teeth at me, which I interpreted to mean I'd been holding on just a bit too tightly.

After a few more rides, it got through my thick skull that, because it was in the team's interest that we both survive the flight, there was no way that Vixen was going to let me fall. Even if I tried jumping off, she'd swing around in midair and catch me as I was falling. Probably.

So, with a shrug, I gave up wearing the flight suit. It was stinking pretty badly, anyway.

We began to fly farther and farther afield. I'm amazed at how small this compound looks from the air. The cabin, the stable, the little pasture, the sleepy factory, and the work cabins—tiny buildings draped in snow and bordered with threaded bands of dark firs. From such a beginning, that so much magic could burst forth!

Now, as I write these last words in this exhausting, sprawling entry, I find myself accustomed to how these things reveal themselves—stable, deer names, book, sleigh, factory. I'm comfortable because I realize that I am everywhere underpinned by magic, that deep unknowable something thrumming along according to its own purpose. Over these past several days, I've come to know just the tips of it, expressed as it is in the stones and wood of these places, the words on the book's page, and Vixen's marvelous recovery and flights. I have no doubt that, if it should ever be mine to understand, the magic of the sleigh will be revealed—if I should survive and return. I have no doubts as well that I will be surprised, perhaps even terrified, by the jolts in the path I'm destined to take.

Some Days Later
Somewhere North

This entry is short. The time has come. These last few days, Parsley has joined us in the flights. I've examined the feed one more time, seeing whether there is any more that will help tide them over. There isn't.

The trouble is, I don't have any idea how long I'll be gone. I don't dare risk delivery speed with Vixen, because she'd agree, and then it would kill her. Parsley could do it, but Parsley can't find her way back to the Central Stables, so there's the fix.

I asked Vixen last night if she was ready. She gave me one of those long looks that seemed to ask me the same thing before bobbing her head, snorting and stamping, the sounds filling the stable.

This morning, I've divided up all the remaining feed and filled to the brim their troughs. For the briefest instant I thought of confining them, worrying that they might wander off and injure themselves. Reason returned. These were his *deer. Was I going to be like Strapper and shut them away from light and air in the name of caution and protection? While I could understand the feeling, I still couldn't bring myself to forgive him for having acted on it.*

I'll have my answers as soon as I can get back there. I've cleaned and ordered things as best I can in the cabin, seen to the deer, and left them in the stalls while I made these final preparations. Vixen and Parsley await me in the field.

No, that's not true. Looking through the window from here, I can see that they've all filed out of the stable and are now standing on the rise, looking my way. They have a patience born of purpose. They will be all right.

So I will have quite a crowd to send me off. I must close this book now and set it next to the other one. I only hope I have violated no trust, crossed no boundary improperly. If I should fail, and neither the team nor I survive, let this book be a record that I—that we*—have done all we could in the tradition and spirit of Christmas. It's a spirit reaching back to a time far earlier than I know. It lives here, in this place, in this* now. *It must live on. It must.*

MAGIC

III

1.

She had just finished breakfast when the phone rang, and even before she heard Mr. Folkeson's voice drop half an octave she knew it was time. She rose from the table, wrapped the remaining knäckebröd, and put the milk in the icebox. She moistened a cloth at the sink and wiped down the table. Her heart pounded. She tried not to listen but heard his half of the conversation anyway.

"*Javisst*. So it is up past Kåbdalis, then. It will take a little bit of time to get there, you realize. Where are you? Not the town, but how far from where we are going? ...Then we will meet you. ...Probably, well the roads are pretty good, unless they have been building up that way, so it will probably take us a couple of hours. ...Yes. ...Yes, see you then."

Mr. Folkeson stumped into kitchen and brushed back a stray gray strand as he sat down. A slight smile flickered across his heavy, lined face. "Well, Kelli. We are going on our motor trip today, a somewhat long one. Up into the high regions, into an area we call Norrbotten. The north country. Bill will meet us beyond a small town there called Kåbdalis. We must dress warmly. I'm told there is already snow on the ground in the high areas there. He will have some extra equipment with him. I think you will need to be prepared to go overland."

She forced the trouble out of her voice. "I'm ready, *Pappa*," she said. "I just need to know whether I'll be staying up there."

"That is not the plan." He smiled. "Still, you might pack something small, for changing, just in case. If everything goes the way we've discussed, you will be back here before the day is over. I know Bill." He strode to the kitchen window, gazing over the meadow behind the house. "He does not leave things to chance." Without turning, he boomed, "*Mamma!* It is time for us to make our little trip!"

Thumps rattled the ceiling light. Moments later a tall, dark-haired woman entered the kitchen. She regarded Kelli with pale eyes accustomed to sweeping cold landscapes. "I will get our things," she said calmly, as though this was a trip to the town market. "Kelli, you come with me, please."

Within minutes, they had climbed into Mr. Folkeson's gray Volvo S70, heading out onto the narrow road linking Skellefteå with the more northern towns. Mr. and Mrs. Folkeson sat in front, exchanging an occasional comment in Swedish, while Styrbjörn and Solveig, her "brother" and "sister", fought each other for rights to a handheld space conquest game. She stared at the hilly countryside rolling by.

From Silvertongue to Gardner to Gothenburg to Skellefteå. And now to points north. One dream folding into another, new images overlaying old. With each push something was gained, something else lost. How easily the Folkesons had accepted her into their home these past weeks. The children especially. Solveig had taken her on long walks in the surrounding meadows, while Styrbjörn, the older, had shown her his videogames on the family PC and had invited her to play (and to lose). She was sometimes able to forget her otherness, then, the fact that she was young by elfin standards, yet so much older. She found herself a peer in their world, these children growing swiftly older and so easily able to embrace the things technology pushed their way. Their blond hair contrasted sharply with the dark, graying hair of their parents.

Trees, hills, meadows, sky. On they traveled, the land becoming hillier, the already cool temperatures chilling. First the snow splashed distant hills, but soon she could feel it in the air and see it in the iron sky. The white hills advanced to meet their tiny, crawling car. Occasionally, the family passed through a village, and each time she sat up. Was this the one? Or this? Or this? But they kept on, the children silent now.

At Arvidsjaur they turned again. The road narrowed, slicing into the hills. At length, they passed through another village, and then Mr. Folkeson pulled the Volvo over and waited. Her heart jumped. She peered at the landscape, taking in hummocks, snow, rocky soil, cold meadows and bogs, mists oozing among them. How would they manage this country? Sweat from her hands stained her little overnight bag.

An approaching vehicle growled. Soon, she could make out the growing shape of a three-wheeled ATV appearing and disappearing in the bogs and mists, a tall rider astride it. Mr. Folkeson stepped out of the Volvo, and Kelli climbed out of the back seat. They stood, Mr. Folkeson with a hand on her shoulder.

The ATV roared to a halt beside them. Styrbjörn and Solveig examined it eagerly. She stared at the tall, white-suited man in the ski cap. He dismounted and shook their hands. "Damn thing makes too much noise. But it's the best for getting around out here. How are you all doing?" he asked, his eyes on her.

"We are all right," Mr. Folkeson said. "We are prepared to wait in Kåbdalis this day and the next. "What do you think?"

"It won't take very long. Kelli, are you ready?"

She clutched her bag. "Yes."

Bill looked her up and down, and she felt herself go hot and cold. "There's a couple of outbuildings, looks like an abandoned farm, not far from here," he said. "I've got some things for you there. It's a white suit—standard issue at that place, I'm told. In this weather, you'd better just put it on over everything you're wearing. The wind's a little brisk today, and the mists are pretty cold." He held his hand out to Mr. Folkeson. "Well, sir, we're on our way. You have your phone?"

Mr. Folkeson patted his pocket.

"I'll call you, probably later today. You know what to do if you don't hear from us by dusk tomorrow."

"Yes."

"All right, then. Kelli?"

She shook *Pappa's* hand. He held it for a moment. "Be careful," he said quietly. "Our family wishes you luck."

Her eyes strayed to *Mamma* watching her through the window. She waved, hoping she at least looked brave in this tall world. She followed Bill to the ATV. He unsnapped the seat and flipped it forward, revealing a small storage area. From this he extracted a ski cap. "Here." He handed it to her. "This'll keep your head warm. Hope it fits."

It did, and very well. She tucked her hair under the cap. "How far is it?"

"The old farm isn't far," he said. "But after that, we've got a bit of a ride across open country—about twenty minutes. We cut off a lot of the road to the place that way. I really don't want to be seen going up the road." He straddled the ATV. "Hop on behind me and hold on."

She climbed on, hesitating just an instant before putting her arms around his waist. Even with the suit on, he was slender, and she could easily clasp her hands together. Was it so easy, then, touching a human like this?

"All set back there?"

"All set."

The engine roared. "Here we go!" he shouted, and they sped off, bouncing over the meadow. She glanced at the receding Volvo, Mr. Folkeson's form dwindling. He had an arm upraised, but she didn't dare wave back.

How were they going to sneak up on anybody with the engine roaring like that? Her overnight bag banged against her back, surprise bumps punishing her. She peered around Bill's shoulder, and this helped a little, because she could get some idea of when to expect the next jolt.

After a few long minutes, they reached a couple of buildings that leaned from the mist like broken teeth, their once-bright red paint dulled by years of weathering. The ATV bumped to a stop, and Bill switched off the motor.

She stepped off. "That is one loud machine."

"I know." He shook his head, looking at it. "We're going to have to park this thing a little ways away from the plant and walk in."

She looked at him. "Won't there be security?"

"Yes, but … Well." He gestured to the nearer building. "There's a suit like mine in there. It should fit. You can pull it on over what you're wearing. I'll wait out here."

She hesitated before climbing the slight rise. Was this a storage shed? She pushed the loose-hanging wooden door and eased inside. The door slapped shut, plunging her into musty darkness. She elbowed the door to let in some light. *Get a grip, girl. Nobody's watching you here.* She wedged a foot against the door, found an old piece of wood and used it as a prop.

The white suit fluttered from the doorhook like a huge, impaled moth. She struggled into it, but once she had it on it fit very well. *Bill's done his homework. Pappa was right: he doesn't leave things to chance.* She kicked aside the wood and stepped outside, jumping when the door banged shut. *Hope he didn't see that.*

Bill leaned against the ATV, waiting. He raised his eyebrows.

"Ready," she said. "Now what?"

"There's gloves in your pocket. Put them on. Let's talk a minute. The plan is pretty simple, but it has risks. The main plant is on the other side of these hills." He gestured to the landscape bunched behind the abandoned farm. "It won't take long to get there, but because of this stupid engine, we'll be parking at the edge of the hills. I scoped a spot where we can get pretty close, and the hills will block the sound."

"How long have you been up here?"

He stretched his arms. "Long enough to do this without maps now. I've seen the outside of the place, from a distance. I've managed to take pictures of the herding operations, the deliveries. And the trucks that eventually come out of there. They head north up a two-track. My guess is Jokkmokk, which is pretty close. I got a pretty good idea of what's in those trucks. I think you do, too. But I haven't been inside the plant. There's a couple of contacts on the inside, elves, but they're pretty scared. So information's sketchy. But they've managed to tell me what to wear. And one brave soul even found a way to set up a spot along the perimeter where, with luck, we can slip onto the grounds.

"Now, security. We can't just walk in the front door. But we *can* slip around the side, where there's a small entrance and an old delivery bay. My contact couldn't figure out what it was for, but he knew it would get us into the plant, in an abandoned area. They have cameras, but not on this side, since it's unused. I can't get through that opening, but you can. You can let me in—there's a door there that's locked from the outside.

"Once we're in, we can walk through the place, because we look like we belong. I've got a couple of fake badges. That'll make us look like a human and elf team. Which we are, but not the kind they want." He chuckled tightly. "This isn't my normal line of work, by the way."

"Mine either. What if we get caught?"

"Mats has me in there because he knows I can BS my way out of almost anything. If that doesn't work, well... We'd be detained. There'd be a deal, an exchange—our release for keeping quiet. But Mats could try to push this in front of the public. Even without our evidence. We know NPI wants to keep this very quiet. So he could threaten to go public. That would leave us stuck for a while." He sighed. "Try to focus on a positive outcome, though. That's best. If we go in looking like we belong, we should get through it all right."

"Let's get going, then."

"Kelli." He took her arm. "You could still say no. Out here, whatever. I know this is—I know you're being asked to—"

She looked up at him. "I sat outside Silvertongue's office, while they hatched their little plots. I almost got caught, I almost got fired, and I got thrown on a plane to Gothenburg. I stayed holed up in a hotel for weeks figuring this stuff out. I met the Chief, I saw what they did to him. Now I'm up here. I'm ready to see this through. If I can *fight* those—those creatures trying to change NPI into what it's not, what it shouldn't be, then—I want to do what I can. I'm going." She scanned the hills separating them from what she could only imagine. "But I'm scared."

"Me too," he said. "But look on the bright side. It'll keep us on our toes." He gestured to the ATV. "Shall we?"

She nodded, her throat tightening. They climbed on the little monster and rumbled off, pounding over humps of lichen, splashing through cold fens, skittering over patches of snow. They left the bogs behind, slipping into the hills, Bill taking a long-planned route.

After a few minutes, they began tilting down the far slope. Bill steered the ATV down a narrow grassy track between tall firs, sliding along snow fields whose drifts were deeper on this side. He slowed the ATV, and the motor lost some of its roar as they snaked among the trees.

Now they crawled, the engine a low throb in her ears, until finally Bill swung the ATV into a tiny area amid several firs and switched it off. A low hum replaced the engine. Kelli frowned. The plant.

They stepped off the ATV. "OK," Bill said. "Here's what's next." He took off his gloves, and so did she. He unsnapped the seat and reached into the storage area, grabbing two badges and what looked like a pair of belts. He handed her a badge. "Clip this on your brea—on your pocket, there," he said. "And this little beauty is a work of art." He held up the belt. "See the buckle? It's actually a small camera. All you have to do is face your target and adjust your belt, like so. There's enough room for twenty-seven pictures. Don't ask how they got that number. Probably all that would fit. Here, put it on." He held out the smaller belt.

She slipped it around her waist, the buckle sliding shut with a satisfying snick. It fit extremely well, just as the suit had. She glanced at him. *How much of this is planning?* But he was busy slinging a pack over his shoulder and adjusting his own camera belt. "Ready," she said quietly.

"OK." He held out his hand, and she wasn't sure why until he said, "Shake hands for luck."

She placed her small hand into his larger one, a cool, firm grasp. He held her hand an instant longer before gesturing toward the little cluster of firs. "We go around these trees and down a path around a small hill. You'll see."

He led the way, his feet sinking into the snow. The crunch of their footsteps rattled against the growing hum. They hugged the hill, climbed a slight rise, and slipped into an evergreen bank shielding them from the plant. The hum increased. Bill led her through a narrow path, evergreens close on both sides, before stopping and motioning her to squeeze around him. She pushed forward and separated the last branches, and the complex unfolded beneath her, a high barbed-wire fence ringing it.

It looked so ordinary. The main building, a large, redbricked structure with high windows, stooped over lesser structures like a fat red hen watching her brood. Rumbles and clangs .punctuated the pronounced, steady hum. Her eyes widened. *We're so close.* Even here, some short evergreens hid them from casual eyes. No snow had clung to this lower, sheltered area. *No footprints, then. Good. Only a few hundred feet to go.*

The wind shifted, a breeze billowing from the complex, and she gasped. Bill grasped her arm. "Not the best smell in the world," he said. "But you have to be ready for it. When we go inside, it'll be—it'll be pretty bad. I hate to say it, but take some deep breaths out here, just to prepare yourself."

She forced herself to breathe deeply, taking in lungsful of the stuff, feeling it reach in and pollute her very core. She hated NPI, hated the elves who'd conspired in this, hated even Bill now for forcing the dead-flesh smell to invade her. She jerked her arm away.

"...You all right?"

"Yes, I—Sorry, I should have expected it. We know what they're doing."

"Knowing it and smelling it are two different things. Let me know when—"

"Let's just—get it over with."

"All right," he said. "Stick close."

They took off their ski caps and crept toward the compound, taking advantage of the evergreens. She saw no movement, but the sound continued to grow.

After a couple of agonizingly long dashes across open spaces, they reached the barbed-wire fence. They hid themselves as best they could in the branches of a stunted evergreen that had wrapped its roots around the fencepost. To her surprise, the fence here had deteriorated or been pulled away, but she couldn't tell whether the gap had been created recently. No matter. It was their doorway into that stinking place.

Bill unslung his pack and laid it against the bush. Unzipping it, he pulled out a small lopping tool. He snapped several more links where the fence was still intact. "I don't want to be squeezing through this thing on our way out," he whispered, stashing the cutters. "Let's head in. Once we're inside, we have to walk normally, even if we think somebody's watching us. It's our only chance. Ready?"

"Ready."

He hid the pack under the shrub, then straightened and led the way again. Gravel crunched like gunshot. Heart pounding, she forced a stroll to that awful main building and its abandoned entrance. Beside the doorway, she spied a curious metal chute. Bill gestured to it, and she knelt down and clanged through, fighting panic at the noise and trying not to choke on all the dust.

She popped into a dimly-lit, musty area. Old machinery, some kind of tool and die equipment, squatted like discarded beasts in the gloom. The rotten smell had penetrated this forgotten area, seeping into wood, dust, oil, even metal. She fought it less now, locating Bill's full-sized door. A rusted lock and chain draped the latchbar, and when she pressed the bar they slid to the floor with a terrifying crash.

He was there, but his face and body were turned toward the complex, crouching and listening. He slipped inside. "Anything?" he croaked.

"Nothing but this old machinery," she whispered. "Now what?"

"We're good so far," he whispered back. "Put this on and follow me!"

He gave her a green plastic hairnet, such as a surgeon might wear, and put another on his own head. He led the way through that tangle of old stuff, odd metal shapes, wooden frames, belts and old lights, as though he'd been this way thousands of times. Who had given him his information? He hadn't been on the inside. How could he thread his way so surely through all this?

They reached a door on the far side. "It gets interesting now," Bill murmured, his hand on the handle. "This is it." He opened the door.

She half expected to enter *the* production area, the one that would expose everything. Instead, they encountered a well-lit corridor. Elves and others, half-elves or humans, slouched along this hallway. Bill began a steady, casual walk straight toward them, and she knew she must do the same. Why couldn't they see the blood banging away across her neck? Two, then three, then several turned as she passed. She tried not to glance at them or make eye contact, but their flat and hard faces remained engaged in dull conversations.

The smell sharpened with each step down that long hall. At last, they stood before yet another door. From within throbbed machinery, the hissing of air hoses. Bill glanced meaningfully her way before gripping the handle. They stepped through.

The whiteness of the place attacked her, bright white marred by red and reddish-brown splashes. Then she saw the carcasses, and she would have reeled had Bill not grabbed her arm. Stripped of their hides, pink and headless, the corpses rotated slowly on bright steel hooks. Bill had paused, hand thrust through belt, and after a gasping moment she realized he was already taking pictures. The smell coiled about her and suffocated her. How could elves possibly work here? Yet there they were, small shapes amid the stiffening, shimmering pink-white flesh, guiding the things onto a conveyer belt.

She walked beside the belt, carcasses at eye level, then stopped, steadied herself, and took two pictures of the flesh gliding by. A couple of elves looked up, curious, and one of them strolled over. "Can I help you folks?"

She tried not to stare at him, her mind ablaze with questions, taking in dark eyes, unkempt hair, a red-spattered white suit.

"We're from Central," Bill said. "We're here to see how the startup is going."

"Not bad. We had our moments when things first got going. It takes time to get the hang of an operation like this."

"I would imagine. What have you encountered?"

"It's strange. Once you get over what you're dealing with, it's like any other process—balance the lines, move things along, inspect. The manual operations are more difficult. They're farther up the line. Where from Central did you come?"

"What about the folks, are they adjusting?"

"Most have. A few haven't. The screening operations helped, I think. Did you help put those together?"

"No, we're in logistics." Bill ambled along the line at carcass pace, and the elf kept pace. "My specialty is shipping, and my partner's is process writeups. But we're here to see everything. How are they doing the initial operation?"

"You can see it if you want to, it's back that way." The elf gestured toward a set of doors across the line. "We're using an American model, based on how they process their beef. We herd the animals into a holding area, where their antlers are removed. Then they reach another staging location, where they're funneled into single file. A collar gets slipped over their heads, and then we give them an electric shock strong enough to stun them and render them mostly unconscious. We found, the same way the Americans did, that if you kill them outright there's a change to the meat. It's triggered by a stress hormone. So we do it this way. Then the hoofs are removed and the skinning and gutting begins."

"Aren't they killed before then?" Kelli tried to keep her voice under control.

The elf looked at her uncomfortably. "They're dead by this time, yes." He addressed Bill, who was nodding all too casually. "Lastly, the heads are removed. The carcasses are set on the hooks you see here, and the heads, hooves and antlers are discarded." The elf made a face. "If you want to see a process that's screwed up, you should see disposal ops. I don't think they planned that one at all. They're trying to work something up on the fly, but until they do—"

"OK, we'll look into it," Bill said. "Thanks for the tip."

"No problem at all, Mr.—"

"Tanner. John Tanner. And my associate, Render." Kelli nodded. "We'll get out of your hair, we know you're busy. Besides, I think your friend needs some help over there."

The elf hustled back to the line. "Let's move it," Bill whispered. "It'll only be a minute before he figures out there's no problem."

They continued down the yellow-marked lane. Kelli's heart thudded. So many magical deer now reduced to pale lumps. How could they do it?

They passed through double doors, entering a high-ceilinged room where dozens of elves and humans or half-elves stood beside rows of polished, stainless-steel tables, cleavers flashing, chopping sounds filling the stench-laden air, blood red-bright in the sharp glare of high-up sodium lamps. In seconds, carcasses changed into chops, roasts, steaks, leftovers. They tossed the chunks into color-coded bins. One elf hosed the blood into a central collecting drain. Others carted barrels filled with indescribable items to a special hopper that swallowed them whole.

She could take it no longer. "I need to find a bathroom, quick," she grunted, and Bill stopped taking pictures long enough to point.

"Through those double doors," he said. "I'll meet you on the other side. If you don't see me, just keep going and meet me at the ATV." He steadied her. "Be careful."

She broke loose and lurched off, heedless of anyone who might notice. She barged through the doors, found the bathroom on her right, and stumbled into it, noting with numb relief that no one was inside. She lurched to the nearest sink, leaned over, and released. She coughed a few times, fighting the sting at the back of her throat. Scrabbling for a paper towel, she wet it and sanded her eyes and mouth. She cranked the faucet, pulled down another towel and put it to work, then another and another. She forced her gut down, spasms yielding to a rising panic that she would be discovered.

Eventually, she reached the point where she could first dry herself, then place one foot before the other. What had Bill said about acting naturally? She forced herself to open the door easily, as though she were returning from a teahouse ladies' room to a seat on the veranda.

Bill was nowhere in sight. This part of the factory dealt with packaging, elves and others tossing the cuts into boxes and sealing them up for delivery. Although the activities here were a bit easier to take, she still hurried to the next set of double doors. When would this madhouse tour end?

She thought she saw somebody tall break away from the packing stations and head her way. The dimly-lit area she had stumbled into was still unused. Machinery, tables, files and furniture blocked her way. She threaded the maze, hearing roaring sounds, or was it footsteps on cement, someone large stalking? She began to run, a tiny figure darting among the shadows. She tripped, fell, tore her suit and skinned a knee, picked herself up and ran again. *What's that rumbling? Trucks? Impossible!*

She reached a doorway and leaned on it, panting hard. No one had followed her. The rumbling throbbed in her ears and seemed to be just outside the door. She tried to catch her breath, but her hand slid down and caught the door's exit bar, and she was through and into the cold air outside the plant. She staggered forward.

She saw the frontloaders first, giant yellow machines with heavy steel jaws. They were working at piles of things, transferring heaps of the stuff into waiting dumpster beds aboard trucks. She reeled, seeing but not wanting to see these piles, brown hills, irregular shapes that resolved themselves into antlers, and the shorn heads with the eyes, noses, tongues splashed outside the slackened mouths, and all the while the frontloaders working, working. Her hand strayed to her waist, found the camera, and she snapped picture after picture, hands working where her mind would not, eyes unclosed and burning in the imagery, legs rubbery but holding, and snapping and snapping pictures, wanting it to end but unable to make it do so, as the machinery moved back and forth, shoveling, lifting, dropping, until she heard the clang of a door and she saw the tall image out of the corner of one shocked and staring eye and she felt rather than recognized that it was Bill, Bill who had been to horrid areas himself and who now took her arm gently, then more firmly, and at last shook her and dragged her away, roughly, a couple of workers looking with interest in their direction, around and away from the rumbling and the hills and back around the far side of the plant and through the fence so that it was over, he now straightening, barbed wire between them; and what they had seen, been through still going on, going on down there, the deer, and more and more of them being shoveled through the front, more and more and more, and he carrying her now, staggering back up the slope to the nest of firs and to the ATV, placing her on it, pulling off her hairnet and reaching gently into her pockets, hands close to her, finding gloves and ski cap and putting them on her, and then reaching gently behind her to unhook the belt and remove the camera whose as yet hidden images mirrored the searing inside, then jumping in front of her astride the ATV and having to take her arms and clasp them about him and then roaring off, speed now the thing, and she at last breaking, resting her head on his back, her grip tightening, the tears flying off and trailing into the wind behind.

Somewhere during the ride he must have made the cell call to Mr. Folkeson, because now they had rumbled across the fields and bogs, past the upthrusted teeth of the abandoned farm and so back to the road, and there was the Volvo and there was her family and there was some semblance of safety, some return to what she wished could be normal and happy, if only, if only she hadn't seen.

Bill halted the ATV and pried himself gently from her grasp. *Pappa* had jumped from the car. She leaned forward and braced herself with her hands, hearing their voices distantly. "So it is done, then? It was too much for her!"

"We had to do it."

"But not with her!"

"We needed someone small for the entrance, Gøran. You know that. And we asked her if she wanted out. I feel pretty awful, too, knowing what she saw."

"Is it as bad as we thought?"

"It is. Take care of her. See that there isn't anything else, *anything* else, that happens to her except for what you can do to make her well."

A car door slammed, and scant moments later she felt *Mamma's* strong arms reach around her and pull her from the ATV. She found her feet then, shook herself free, and took the few long steps to where they were standing.

"Bill." Her voice croaked like an old bird. She tried again. "Bill."

He turned and looked at her. His mouth worked, but he said nothing.

"Make sure those pictures get—wherever they need to go. Wherever. Especially those—the last ones—the—"

Mrs. Folkeson's arms encircled her.

"I will. Don't worry. When the time is right, these will see the light of day."

A thumping sound rose from somewhere beyond the hills. Bill cocked his head. "That's not good," he said. "Get her out of here, and get her out of that suit as soon as you can. I've got to hide this thing. Kelli. Kelli!"

She lifted her head.

"I'll see you as soon as I can. I promise. Stay with them, please! Rest. You've done all you can." He started the ATV, its rumble mingling with the thumping. "Now get out of here, all of you, before that chopper clears the hills!"

He roared off and disappeared, heading for some hiding place long planned. She allowed herself to be hustled to the car, stowed inside, and there was Solveig next to her and Styrbjörn beyond, watching her. She bowed her head, hearing two car doors slam shut, the engine roar, and feeling the car jump into motion. Solveig took her hand and held it, and with her other hand shyly tried to brush away the streaming tears, saying "Why are you crying now? You're safe with us!" and Kelli sobbing, the tears unstoppable, washing over her face and spilling onto Solveig's hand but unable to wash away the pictures, the machines, the hills, the eyes, the eyes.

2.

Big hands drummed the table. "Hmm."

Roxy looked over the top of her menu. "You already know what you want?"

"My usual, almond chicken."

She whistled. "That's a lot of starch."

He peered over his half-glasses at her. "At my age, I'm supposed to worry?" He took the glasses off and put them in his shirt pocket.

"I need something a bit spicier," Ravi murmured.

"You guys are made of spice, that's why."

"Will you behave?" Roxy hissed.

The waitress, a dark-haired, thick-lensed blur, appeared at their table. "Wha yu wa?" she asked Roxy.

Santa glanced at Roxy, eyebrows raised.

She ignored him. "I'll have the number seventeen, the ginger chicken, light."

"Yu wah su? We ha chi wi rice, eh drah, hah sour."

"Can I get won ton?"

"Wah tah essra."

"OK."

His eyes never strayed from Roxy.

Ravi ordered General Tso's, hot, and Santa ordered almond chicken. The waitress surveyed the table. "Ehthee dree?"

"Tea, please," Roxy said, filling in the slight silence.

"HahteeOK." She hurried off.

Santa leaned forward. "What the hell *was* that?"

"Be nice," she scolded. "These people work very hard, and English is very difficult for them. I haven't heard you try their language."

"I could."

"Part of the magic?"

"Yes."

"Then you'd know. Besides, waitressing is probably hard work."

"I can imagine."

"I wonder if you can. Any kind of work like that."

"Like being a chauffeur. *I'll* have to drive you both everywhere," Ravi grumbled. "Unless you want to keep taking taxis. Serves me right for having the only driver's license."

Santa frowned. "I've done plenty of work like that in my day!"

Bowls of soup were slapped down in front of them, as well as plates of impossibly tall white rolls. In the background, Chinese music played softly.

Santa winced when the waitress sloshed the soup his way before running off again. "You don't think she's mad at me?"

"Maybe, but I doubt it," Ravi said. "I haven't heard you worry about that before."

He frowned at the little man, but not too seriously. "You know, you really haven't known me long enough to make a statement like that."

Ravi looked up from his hot and sour soup and nodded amiably.

Santa played with his egg drop soup, the hot thick liquid sliding over his spoon. "I don't know how much longer I'm going to stay in this car town. I hate being idle like this."

"Well, maybe you *should* work for a while," she said. "Get some kind of job, take your mind off things."

"I don't know, Roxy." He took a sip. "We agreed I shouldn't do the executive placement thing, and that makes sense. Who needs to get back into that? How long have I been here? Two weeks? Three?"

"...But a job might be a good idea."

"Oh, I'm not objecting to the idea, take my mind off—have me do something different. It just doesn't feel right." He busied himself in his soup.

Ravi tried next. "You're a CEO. And now you'd be just some guy working a regular job someplace. How could that feel right?"

The blue eyes flashed Ravi's way. "I'm pretty good," he said. "You forget, Ravi, I've been around about a hundred times longer than you'll manage to be. So I can be adaptable, if I need to. Oh, I could say this is about a CEO not wanting to do the regular guy's work. But I did that work, before. Time was, I made toys by hand, too. Side by side, with the other el—the other workers. So that's not why it isn't right."

"I didn't mean—"

"I know you didn't *mean*. Don't take it the wrong way. But there's something more here. There's something hollow about business today. I don't know if it's an American thing, or what. I read it in the paper here. I don't know, they—the executives see it one way and the workers see it the way it really is." He took another spoonful. "Damn, that's got to sound stupid."

"So what's so wrong about a job here?"

"Roxy, nothing's really *wrong* about it. Not fundamentally. To me, a fundamental 'something gone wrong' is when you find you're facing a crisis so profound everything else doesn't matter. Me being kicked out, for example. Nothing compares to that. Think about it. What the hell am I supposed to do? Accept it? Act as though nothing's the matter? ...All right, so I won't go there again." He swallowed another spoonful. "Or your wife leaves you. There's another one." He gulped more soup. "And that makes everybody at this table damned uncomfortable, so there you are. The fundamentals make us uncomfortable. So we end up talking about other things. Like me getting a job. Brings me back to where I was. It's the wrong answer, dammit! Here's—"

The waitress shot into the picture, replacing empty soupbowls with entrées, plates heaped with health-compromising mounds of metabolism-lowering foods. She paused when she got to Santa. "EhdrahOK?"

His eyes swam. Roxy intervened, "His soup is fine, he's just—eating slowly."

"Uh." She elbowed the soup aside and shoehorned a mountain of deep-fried chicken slathered in brown sauce and supplemented with wads of brown rice and a springroll. "Annoy your meeh," she murmured, and shuffled off.

"Yeesh." He searched for an entry point on the slopes.

"Why is it the wrong answer?" she persisted. "It's a job, something to do! Just because you haven't had a job outside NPI—"

"But I did have a job once, remember? Outside, I mean. Some damn consultant or other, he gets it in his head that I need to connect with the hardworking people, you know, the parents of the kids asking for toys outside the budget. 'Go to work at a real job!' he says. 'So you can understand what it takes to pay for one of your upscale toys!' Whoever he was. So I did.

"So they get me a job working for a major hardware store, right? The home improvement variety. Give me a green apron and throw me into a store the size of a small town in I think it was Des Moines. Americans have this thing about really big stores, stuff stacked from floor to ceilings that go thirty feet over your head. So they can come in and buy, I don't know, a water heater from Aisle Three and a set of floor tiles from Five and some insulation from the back and a pack of screws and some house plants. Because they need all that stuff." He attacked the chicken, scattering little rice flurries. "So here I am, working for OneStop Homeowner. I just want to be a sales guy, bury my head for a little while and forget I'm a CEO. Just a regular job, like the consultant said. Wrong. They tell me I'm an 'associate'. I remind them, so's the janitor. They chide me, they tell me I have the wrong attitude, I shouldn't speak about our cleaning professionals that way. I saw a couple of those 'cleaning professionals' out back, sound asleep, but never mind."

He took another bite. Ravi and Roxy exchanged glances. "...So, being an 'associate', I need to go to special 'Associate Development Training.' Off I go, somewhere across town, where this skinny suntanned woman starts bouncing around in front of us like it's some combo marketing and aerobics class. She gets all wound up about how the world has moved away from mere selling, you know? Manufacturers have moved past product quality and even mass customization. Now it's all about the consumer experience. Consumers should be the focus of everything we do, she says, and because that's the situation, they're not supposed to browse our stores, they're supposed to have an 'experience'."

Ravi chuckled between mouthfuls of General Tso's.

"I'm serious, Ravi, it's what she said. 'Never let the consumer alone for a minute,' she said. 'Be with them all the time. Orchestrate their entire experience.' I don't know, if I was a consumer and somebody was following me around all the time, orchestrating my experience, I'd be inclined to let 'em have it."

"That does sound kind of crazy," Roxy murmured. "Ravi, what *is* it?"

Ravi giggled uncontrollably. "I'm sorry," he said at last, catching his breath. "It's the music. I've never heard a Chinese version of 'Ode to Joy' before."

"Mmm," Santa grunted, mouth full. "So we all get back from the offsite, put our aprons on and get back to work. I'm standing there one day, I've had a mom with a screamer under one arm trying to get me to help her decide what kind of wallpaper should go in the little guy's bedroom. Then I get a bunch of Arabic folks all talking at once about kitchen cupboards, and all the while there's this really old guy wandering around in circles or something, he keeps coming through my section and asking where the bathroom is. I start thinking maybe Christmas is lost on these people, and then some guy comes up and asks What do I know about toilets? So I'm standing in front of this guy, trying to explain the difference between the Acme Saniflush, the WaterMiser, and the Pittsburgh PowerWhoosh, and all I can hear is this marketing lady saying Orchestrate his experience, and I'm thinking it's a goddamn toilet! Exactly what kind of experience am I supposed to be arranging for this guy? And do I really need the repeat sale?"

Now both Roxy and Ravi were giggling. Santa frowned, not seriously. "You guys are no help," he grumbled. "How can I vent if all you're going to do is laugh at me?"

"They've changed the music again," Ravi observed happily. "Hear it? 'You Can Trust Your Car To the Man Who Wears—'"

"Who the hell cares about the music?"

"I can't help it, my girlfriend was a music major."

"...You know, that's not the only dumb program we had at NPI."

"Oh, come on, Roxy, we never put on anything that stupid. Have we?"

"Not to us. But ask the average employee, you'd find out they were pretty entertained by what we dreamed up."

"Such as?"

"…Well, there's the Know Your Neighbor program, which got way out of hand because everyone gave it the wrong interpretation. And the Fuzzy Antler Awards."

"Hm. I suppose. But didn't consultants think those up, too?"

"We approved them."

"Fuzzy Antler Award," Ravi murmured into his dinner. "Wow, I want one of *those*."

Santa looked away for a moment. "I wonder what programs they've started now."

"…You could call."

He took a last bite, chewed absently. "What good would that do, Roxy? I'd just get Silvertongue again, and Silvertongue would give me whatever he wanted. A whole lot of nothing." He unholstered his cell phone and studied it. "They don't call. They're drifting. While I squat in this car town. The only way to know what's happening is to go back—which I can't do," he added hastily. "I *know* that. But I sure as hell don't want a job selling 'toilet experiences' all day long, either. I'll have to…"

"…What?" she said.

"Nothing." He reclipped the phone.

The waitress hurried to their table. "Aw duh? You wah bok?"

"No, no boxes," Roxy said.

"OK you wah disser or cookie?"

"No, no thanks," Santa said. "Just the check."

"OKtankyou." She scribbled a slip of paper and set it at his elbow.

"I can't understand this, either," he murmured, scanning it while reaching for his wallet. "There a bank nearby?"

"Down the street," Ravi said. "You want an ATM?"

"No, a bank." He plunked some money on the table, before standing.

Roxy stood too. "And you need a bank for—?"

"Certain things," he said. "A little extra cash, for one."

She appraised him. "Extra cash? What for?"

He headed for the cashier.

She sighed, shrugged her shoulders.

He paid the bill, nodding at the cashier's "Tangyoucumageh". They trailed him outside and into a rapid stride up Jefferson, along the downtown Detroit waterfront. "How far is this bank?" he asked.

"Couple of blocks," Ravi puffed.

"What do you need a bank for?"

"Money, Roxy, what else? Not ATM Chicklets. We'll need to pack today, too."

"*What*?"

"We're moving on, Roxy. Have to. I can sense it. I don't know whether it's because the press might turn up, or I haven't learned anything from this tin town, or —something else. But it's time. Ah, here we are."

Santa pushed through the glass Comerica Bank doors, heading straight for the branch manager's office. A couple of interesting conversations later, they were all heading back through the doors, leaving behind a befuddled manager and a couple of her underlings craning necks after them.

"That's a hell of a lot of money," Roxy said.

"That's what cash advance limits are for," he answered. "Before word gets out, we need to leave town."

"Yeah, for a lot of reasons," Ravi said. "You don't take that kind of money up Jefferson Avenue. Unless you have something interesting to buy. Or you're trying to get yourself killed."

"Why not? It's not like I've got a sign hanging from me advertising it. Stop rolling your eyes!" he growled. "I know what I'm doing and I don't have to explain—Will you look at that!" He stopped.

They almost smacked into him. "Look at what?" Roxy asked.

"It's perfect," he breathed.

They followed his eyes. "What, the car?" Ravi said at last. "You are serious?"

He had already stepped off the curb and was studying it from every angle, a squared- off station wagon originally bright red, but now with nameplates pried off and all four red doors replaced by green ones. "How old do you think this is?"

"Older than I am, I think," Ravi said. "These cars we see in India sometimes, but not usually so—remodeled." He circled it. "Yes I must say this is an American original."

Santa ran a hand along one door. "Hmm."

"Hey!" a voice shouted from across Jefferson. "Hey, y'all want to tell me what you're doing with my car?"

A skinny black man, not much more than a kid, really, advanced, arms waving. He wore black stovepipe Levis and a black T-shirt whose imprint lurked behind a faded green longsleeved shirt carelessly slipped over arms and drooping shoulders, flapping in the September breeze.

"Is this your car?" Santa asked.

"No, I *said* 'Get away from my car' because it's somebody else's. You always this brilliant, or is it just today?"

Santa smiled. "I'm Mr. Claussen." He held out his hand a moment, then dropped it. "And you are—"

"Name's Maur-*ice*. You in pickles or something?"

Roxy winced, but Santa's smile only deepened. "Very well, Mr. Morris, let's talk about your car."

"It's not Mr. *Morris*, it's Maurice. What about my car?"

Santa led Ravi and Maurice back onto the sidewalk. "Let me introduce my assistants, Roxy and Ravi. Don't bother, you two. Mr. Maurice does not, as a rule, shake hands."

"That's Mau—"

"Now, Mr. Maurice, I must tell you I'm interested in your car. How did it come to have such a unique paint job? The doors, for example."

"Maurice, no Mr.," Maurice muttered. "The doors, they were replaced. Part of what we call a 'drive by.' Interested how?"

"Well, to buy it."

Roxy's jaw dropped.

"But you cannot be serious!" Ravi protested.

"But I can. Does it run? Is it reliable?"

Maurice's eyes narrowed. "My car. You want to buy my car." He took a breath, and his eyes appeared to mist over. "My *first* car. The car I found my manhood in."

Roxy sighed loudly. "Like you're old enough to have a manhood to find."

"Like I was talking to *you*, Mama? And what exactly do you assist Pickles in, anyway?"

Santa's big hand encircled Maurice's arm. "I believe you were talking to me about the importance of this car, Mr. Maurice," he said in rich tones.

"That's—"

"And you were going to tell me how well this car runs, and how reliable it's been."

"Well I—"

"You wouldn't lie, now, Mr. Maurice? This is a good car, correct? One that you'd sell to someone in your family?"

Maurice disengaged and drew himself up like a spaghetti drying to its original shape. "This car has been in my family many years," he began.

"Or at least a few days," Ravi muttered.

Maurice glared at him before continuing, "It's a good car. My own mother drove this car. She took care of it. The doors—well. You can't help that, you know what I'm sayin'?

"I do." Santa looked hard at him. "You know, I can tell when someone's been bad or good, Maurice. And I know when I can trust someone. Why don't we go for a ride?"

Maurice stared back a moment, then shrugged. "OK, y'all get in."

"Seems like he's taking us for a ride, anyway," Ravi murmured to Roxy, as they folded themselves into the backseat.

When Maurice started the car, it sounded surprised to be put to work on such a restful day. The engine thrummed and throbbed, making the car bob nicely. When they lurched into the street, the car's body parts groaned and stretched, awakening. Ravi and Roxy glanced at each other. In the front, Santa's small talk was difficult to hear above the engine clatter.

They followed Jefferson into neighborhoods where the car seemed increasingly misplaced. At last, they pulled over, and Maurice restored suburban peace by killing the engine. "Like I was sayin', Mr. Pickles, I don't mind selling you this car, but it's what I use to get to work. So I don't know."

Santa got out, and the rest of them followed. They gathered on the unpocked sidewalk. "So it's no sale."

"I didn't say No Sale."

"So how much?"

"I couldn't let it go for less than—two thousand dollars."

"*Two thou—*"

"Hey, my own mother drove this car, Mama, so what's your problem?"

Santa pulled out a fat wad of bills, and Maurice's eyes widened. "I know this is difficult for you," Santa said, "So would two thousand five hundred do? Or perhaps three thousand."

Maurice's jaw dropped. "What the hell? Y'all Santa Claus or somethin'?"

Roxy gaped. Ravi tugged on Santa's sleeve. "'Scoose me, *'Santa'*, could we talk sir?" He shoved Santa well away from the openmouthed ones and began talking quickly and earnestly. "First of all, I don't care what neighborhood we are in, we don't wave around that kind of money, not in front of anybody, and especially somebody you don't know very well at all. And secondly, what do you think you're doing, you cannot be serious to buy an old beat-up car like that. Not for that kind of money. He is trying to take advantage of you. That car—I don't even know if that car would make it from here to the hotel."

"Hey!" Maurice said.

"Look, Ravi, I know what I'm doing," Santa growled softly. "You guys seem to think that because I'm not in NPI, I'm a little kid. There's a reason for this."

"But you cannot just give your money to somebody like this, it's not—"

"Hey!" Maurice said, a little louder.

"Whose money is it?"

"But still you cannot be serious!"

"Yo! *Krishna*!" Maurice yelled. "You want to stop interrupting my man Pickles? We got a car deal going."

Ravi turned, eyes flashing. "My name is not Krishna, and he is not a pickle!" He puffed himself up as large as he could. "My name is Ravinder Magadi Gopalakrishnan!" he declared, the r's rolling through the air.

"…Yeah like I said, Krishna. Let Mr. Pick- Mr. Claussen make up his own mind."

Santa's eyes had strayed across the broad expanse of Jefferson. "Actually, I have a better idea…" He started across the street, and the others had no choice but to follow.

"No way. No way!" Roxy exclaimed.

But Santa beelined for the car dealership, the sleek cat leaping over the words. He strode through heavy glass auto-open doors. The doors glided shut behind them, and they encountered the silent, refined world of a Jaguar showroom. The only other customer, a white-haired man, appraised them before stooping to peer at the nearest sticker.

"Now, Mr. Morris," Santa said, "Look around here and tell me what you like."

A tall, thin gentleman whose face had been filed from a broad forehead down to a narrow, pointed chin, appeared at their side, preening himself and arranging his dark suit. Santa turned. "Are you orchestrating my experience?"

The man held his hands up. "No no!" he said. "Please. Take your time." His eyes followed Maurice, who had wandered over to a low-slung deep blue XKR convertible. "My name is Michael, and I will be happy to take care of anything for you today, sir. Do you have any questions I could answer, or—?"

"He's the one to ask." Santa pointed at Maurice.

"I see." Michael ran a hand through thinning Grecian-formula'd hair. "And this—man's relationship to you is …?"

"He's my nephew."

"Oh, I *see*."

"He calls the shots," Santa continued. "Whatever he wants today. It's his birthday."

"Whatever he wants," Michael murmured. "You know, that's a seventy five thousand dollar car he's looking at." He glanced at Roxy, who'd gasped. "You sure that'll be all right?"

"It's going to be absolutely all right. Actually, it's going to be absolutely perfect," Santa replied. "I tell you what. Let's get started on the paperwork, while my nephew finds what he wants." He gestured towards the sales cubicles. "Ravi, Roxy, please stay with Maurice and help him in his selection. Thank you!" he said musically. "Now, Michael, let's continue."

In the short span of an hour, it was all over. They clustered in the back lot, waiting for the XKR to be brought around. Ravi kept a watchful eye on Maurice, who was dancing off to one side and rapping softly to himself.

"You know, Mr. Claussen," Michael ventured, "I've been in the business for a while. But it always amazes me when credit of that magnitude can be approved so easily."

"It pays to have clout in an organization."

"Who was that gentleman I was speaking to?"

"Silvertongue. He's very good at what he does. And he's a decent enough sort at heart. Though he may have forgotten."

"I'm sorry, forgotten?"

"Never mind, Michael, here's the car."

The XKR glided up, top down, and a tailored service attendant stepped out, keys in hand. "OK, who's the lucky one?" he asked.

"He is." Santa pointed to the rapping Maurice.

The service attendant glanced at Santa and then Maurice and Santa and Michael and Maurice and Ravi and Roxy and Michael and back to Maurice at last. "O-*kay*." He handed the keys to Maurice. "Michael," he murmured, as Maurice danced to the open door, "I think we've made that young man very happy, wouldn't you say?"

"My man, my man, my *man*," Maurice exclaimed. He slithered into the low-slung seat. "It be Christmas in September." He turned the key, and the engine growled. "Yo, Pickles! You one of the craziest white dudes I know, but thank you. Thank you, thank you, *thank* you!" He put the car in gear and started to slide past them. "Where's the street?"

Michael pointed.

"Just a minute, Mr. Maurice." Santa stepped off the curb.

"That's—"

"That's Mr. *Claussen.* One more question. Your old car. Does it have a title?"

"...Yeah, they call it a Volvo."

"That's not the kind of title I mean. Is there a title to the car?"

"...Uh."

"Well, never mind. Give me the keys. Now you go take this car, and you be sure you drive carefully. Do something nice with it. Take your mother for a spin. That should help her get over losing the other car."

"Yeah, I'm sure it will. Now step back, my man, Maurice is going for a ride!" Santa rejoined the others. Maurice gunned the engine. "Whoo, man!" he shouted. "Whoever said 'the truth shall set you free' ain't never sat behind the wheel of a XKR!" And he was off, zooming onto Jefferson.

"Well, this has been a different day," Michael said at length. "It was so generous of you to provide a year's worth of insurance for—ah, your nephew."

"Yes, let's hope he doesn't need it for at least a day or two." Santa held out his hand. "Perhaps we'll do business another time, Michael. You never know."

Michael shook all their hands, and they left the Jaguar world and crossed Jefferson to the elderly Volvo. Ravi took the keys and headed to the driver's seat. Roxy stalked to the front. They slammed the doors, and a couple of small parts pinged the street. "Let us hope those weren't important," Ravi said. He turned the key, and the engine surprised itself into life. Ravi checked in all directions before doing a careening U-turn.

"You want to tell me what the hell that was all about, Mr. Generosity?" Roxy fumed. She turned her head. After a moment, she turned back.

"What do you think?" Ravi asked, trying to glance at her while controlling this animal's balky gait.

"I think we're going to spend all our money feeding this stupid thing," she grumbled. "And dealing with his *Angst*, or his, his six-thousand-year-old half-elfin *Weltschmertz.* Damn him!" she muttered.

"Look at him back there, looking out the window, hatching something only he knows about. Living the ends of old plots for a company that gave him the boot."

"I cannot look at him, I am driving."

"Imagine it then, Ravi! While we chase after him and try to figure out what's going to happen next. I mean, I can understand the pain he's going through. He's forced out, and before that his wife of umpteen hundred years leaves him. All of that hurts, I know it. I know it. But *I* left things, too, Ravi. I left behind friends and family. I miss them, too. But he would have been all alone. Just him and his damned phone, connected to that slimeball, Silvertongue. So I stayed with him, supporting him. And now he's dragging us with him through all his troubles. He isn't listening!" She snapped at Ravi's cautionary gesture. "He's busy hatching! Dragging us through all this! And now, to top it off, he launches this hare-brained idea of trading a Jaguar for some beat up old monster, from some guy he doesn't even know! Why didn't he just buy the damn Jag for himself? And if this is how he treats people who stand by him, not even an explanation, well it's no wonder his wife left him!"

She turned around again. He was still facing the window, blue eyes searching. "Oh, I give up!" She whirled about, chest heaving.

After a moment, Ravi ventured, "You know, this is not a very pleasant drive, is it?" The car galumphed through a pothole like an angular, skittish horse. "We cannot give up on him now."

She turned back. "I know," she sighed. "He's everything Mats said he'd be."

"Mats?"

"An old friend. He warned me. But living through it is different."

After a few more twists, Ravi wheezed the car into the parking lot of their motor inn, a somewhat shabby low-slung affair cringing in the shadow of the Joe Louis Arena. Santa stirred at last. "All right. Let's freshen up one last time, pack our things, and meet in the lobby for checkout." The car door groaned as he thrust it open.

Roxy led the way inside, not looking back. "I'll meet you both in one hour," she said, and stormed up the stairs.

It was late afternoon by the time they and their bags hit the street. Roxy stood aside, arms folded, watching Santa and Ravi load the wagon. But it wasn't until the liftgate had been slammed down and they had opened the doors to get in that Santa said: "Roxy."

She glared over the roof of the car.

"I heard you," he said. "Every word. You can't yell at me any more than I yell at myself. So if it's an explanation you want, let me give it to you both very clearly. Those slimeballs, as you so rightly call them, have made very certain that I'm alone but not alone. Figure it out. They've given me all the money I need, funneled through this lovely credit card I used today. And every time I run that damn thing, they know exactly where I am and exactly what I'm doing. The problem is, they have the wall thrown up, so I have no idea what they're doing, except what I learn from the paper or the stupid radio. So they drift, but they keep a mooring line on me. And that mooring line fixes me in space and time. It isn't enough for them that the company cost me my marriage and they've tossed me aside, they need to keep control. They need to know where I am all the time. Why? Because they're still afraid of me.

"So what all this has been today, is my way of breaking free. Having fun, too. I took enough cash to give my Indian friend here the dry heaves, knowing they'd know I did it. I found this car, or it found me, and parleyed it into a Jag with my name on it, driven by an anonymous man. Because what we are now driving, my friends, is a car without a title, while those bastards think I've bought a Jag and pulled out a bunch of cash and checked out of this hotel on some devil-may-care holiday! They can trace that Jag anywhere they want! We are now, officially, on our own! And that is exactly what they do not want me to be!"

She watched him. "You still can't go back."

"Maybe now I can. They can't keep the routes shut down forever."

"But you shouldn't. And that much you know."

"Why?"

"We've been over and over this." She leveled a gaze at him until his eyes wavered.

He scanned the waterfront, biting his lip. "Maybe not," he said. "Maybe they need to go to a place I can't take them. Maybe I need to go there too. Whatever the hell that means." He left them behind and strode to the edge. "Maybe I just don't give a damn anymore whether they want to wreck it all, right?"—his voice rising, stride quickening, one hand reaching for his cell phone— "So maybe, I should, just, do, *this*!"

He hurled the phone out over the river, watched it sail through the slanted sun rays until it hit the surface with a tiny plop and disappeared under the green-blue waves. He turned around and stumped to the car, his head down. "Now we can go," he said quietly, and got in.

3.

The sky looked fickle, irritable, ready to congeal into high, hard storms. The sun rode somewhere behind those clouds, but already the weather was changing to the long, unbroken cold season. Saddler had seen this sky thousands of times. He knew better than to have the newest teams training against it. Only the more experienced ones bounced around up there, getting hard weather training. He hardly noticed them. His eyes scanned the north horizon. Beyond it lay the Near Zone. And much farther out, the Edge.

"How long have they been going out there?" a voice at his elbow asked.

He jumped. "Strapper, do you always sneak up?"

"I wasn't aware I was being quiet. So how long?"

Saddler didn't take his eyes off the sky. "More than two weeks by now. ...More than three, actually."

"Weather looks rough."

"It's changing. ...Maybe I should call it off."

"...Because?"

"C'mon, Strapper." He turned, scowling. "Look at the situation. Baylor's coming out here soon, hundreds of extra fliers are coming in, way more than we can handle. Demon's team has been out there day after day. They've found nothing. Nothing. No shred, no trace. And they're not likely to—"

Strapper surprised him with a hand on his arm. "Look. Let's talk about the real issue. None of us knows what we're doing, now that the Chief is gone. Oh, we can say we're still doing the same things. We can say we're still responsible for the same stuff, but we know it's not true. Change is coming. Just like that sky. Except we don't know when it'll get here." He looked away. "That's not true. It's already reached me. I don't know, the paperwork seems to have grown even more. Requisitions, herd delivery signoffs, quality forms, cost containment suggestions, notices about this new thing, that one." He looked up at the sky. "I shouldn't even be out here."

"Can't you burn all that stuff?"

"I wish."

"Why can't you? Have an office fire. What could they do? The stuff that's really important, they'd send a reminder. The rest—" he waved an arm "—Just don't blow the smoke my way."

Strapper laughed.

Crackling sounds. Saddler yanked his handheld from his belt and punched a button. "Yes?" he barked.

"Weather's starting to get interesting." Demon's calm voice filled the air. "Found him."

"What?"

"Found where he landed, anyway. Looks like it was a pretty rough shot. There's pieces of wagon wood all over the place, and when I look up … there's some of his flight suit stuck to a couple of fir branches. It's a pretty rocky spot. We're out past the Edge someplace."

"And—Tracer?"

"Not even here. Bounder had to land farther out, where it's flatter. He'll join me in a couple of minutes. We'll take up the search then."

"What do you mean, he's not even there?"

"What I said. I spotted some white stuff in the trees, swung around to make sure it wasn't snow, and when I saw what it was I landed. Found the wood, and then—hold on." The handheld sputtered to silence. Saddler tapped a foot, glancing at Strapper. A crackle. "There's reindeer hoofprints over here, where there's some softer ground. Looks like two sets, one big and one small. And then—Bounder's here with me, hang on. Bounder, over here! Hold it, there's some kind of—it looks like a burial mound or something, and there's antlers sticking out. It's fresh. Somebody buried a deer here."

"What about Tracer? You don't think—" Saddler's knuckles whitened.

"... No, I wouldn't think so. What do you think, Bounder?" They heard Bounder's muffled voice in the background before Demon continued, "Doesn't seem likely that he'd be buried here, but ... You know of anyone that lives up here?"

Strapper leaned toward the handheld. "This is Strapper. No, there's no known, no intelligent creature up there. Depending on where you are, you might be close to—Well. Nothing."

"Close to what, Strapper?" Demon asked quietly. "We're out past the Edge. I don't need a dance."

"...The Chief's Team is out that way. The original stable. But there are special routes to it. Classified routes. If you're out near the Edge, you could wander around forever and not find it. By design. So I was just figuring that the only thing out there would be his team, but they'd have to ... somehow get out and want to go after a crash-landed half-elf. Doesn't make a lot of sense. Besides, my people are up there every day at the stable. They'd know."

The handheld was silent a moment. "Well, he's gone," Demon said at last. "We could dig up the mound, but I'd rather not. He's not in there." A background shout. "What prints? ... *Where* do they go? ... OK, see if you can follow them. Get a sense of where they're headed. ...Saddler?"

"Here."

"OK, it goes something like this. He crash-landed, and at least one of the deer died. There are two sets of hoof prints, one large and one small, leading away. Bounder's trying to follow them right now. I'm thinking one deer from Tracer's team, and one other deer. So—Wait. There's bootprints next to the mound. He was on his feet. So then ... He must have walked or ridden out of here."

"Ridden." Saddler glanced at Strapper.

"Either one of the deer from his team, or the other one, the bigger one. Wait, here's Bounder."

"I followed the prints as far as I could, but they disappear in a rock field not far from here. There's two sets, big and little. No footprints."

A long pause. "Well, boss, looks like a dead end," Demon said. "We can't trace him in this country. Not when all we've got are hoof prints. But I said we'd find him."

"I know." Saddler frowned, watching the sky. A few bold teams negotiated the rough skies, and behind them, pinned against the churning gray, a black dot. He squinted. Was that some kind of weird bird?

"We could try to pick up the trail," Bounder offered. "It might take a while. There's no guarantee we won't lose it again."

"I hear you." Saddler kept watching the bird. Whatever it was, it was certainly big, and growing. "Strapper. Can they get from where they are to the stable, to Santa's stable?"

"Maybe." Strapper scratched a cheek. "I'd need to know exactly where they are, and then look at the maps, see if there's a way to do it."

"OK. You guys. Demon and Bounder, listen." The bird was getting even larger, and changing into an odd shape. "Strapper needs your compass points, because without… them…he's…going…I mean…"

Strapper stared at him. The radio slapped Saddler's hip. "Hey!" Bounder crackled. "What kind of instructions are those? You all right? Saddler? Hey, Saddler!"

Strapper's eyes followed Saddler's. "My God," he breathed.

The bird had huge and unbirdlike, changing before their eyes into a flying reindeer with a growth on its back. A second bird appeared in the distance.

"Saddler! What the hell! C'mon!"

Saddler raised the radio. "Stand by a minute. Just—stand by."

Now the growth changed too. "I don't believe it," Saddler said, allowing himself the faintest smile which, once it started, grew and grew as the shape grew and grew, until at last the old elf was grinning broadly, then shouting, then jumping, the handheld squawking "What—is—going—*on*—dammit!" like an electronic chicken. He ignored Strapper, who still stared, and dashed onto the landing field, jostling scads of other elves, all of them now converging on the shape become reindeer, a large reindeer, one of *the* reindeer, and astride its back, an unprecedented, impossible achievement, the JEDI half-elf, the accident waiting to happen, the keep-him-from-hurting-himself miracle.

Amid all the excited voices, Saddler remembered at last the squawking chicken at his side. "He's here, he's here!" he shouted into the handheld.

"What? Who?" Bounder snapped.

"Tracer! Come on home! He's back! He came in flying—! I don't believe it, bareback on a—on one of *them*, one of the Chief's deer!"

"You can't be serious!" Bounder exclaimed. "One of the Chief's?"

"I'm looking at it! Demon! Bring everybody in! He's here!"

"I hear you." Demon sounded surprised and happy. "I'll get the others turned around. Then I want to know everything. Everything, Saddler!"

"You will! Signing off!" Saddler slung the handheld onto his belt, and his eyes sought Tracer's. Another thump. A second, smaller deer had landed. A few elves ran off to tend to it, creating a small space near Tracer, into which Saddler moved.

"Hey! Kid!" he started, but his smile faded when their eyes connected.

Tracer jumped down, gripped Saddler's hand. "You and I need to talk."

Saddler stared at the Chief's deer. "How did you do it?"

A slight smile flicked one cheek. "Oh, there's a story," Tracer said. "A long one. It's in the cabin."

"The cabin."

"Yes. The cabin. And the rest of the team is at the stable. This is Vixen." He raised his voice. "Take care of Parsley, please! Thank you!"

Saddler struggled to make sense out of the sudden changes, Vixen in the compound, a new Tracer riding bareback, a story, a lot missing. "Where's the other one from your team?"

"Mystic? Dead. Killed in the crash."

"Yes. Demon thought so."

"Who's Demon?"

"Oh. Sorry. She headed up the search teams. We've been out every day, looking for you. She found the spot where you landed. I was just on the radio with her. How—how did you ride bareback? All the way from there. My God!"

Tracer surveyed the field. "Where's Strapper?"

"He's with me." Saddler looked around. "I don't see him right now, but he's probably somewhere on the field. Why?"

"I'm going to kill him."

"What? Why?"

"Well, not really. But I should." Tracer shook his head violently. Then he looked at Saddler as though seeing him for the first time. "Saddler, you have no idea what I've seen. No idea. Just a minute."

He spun around and strode back up to Vixen, excited elves falling back. He planted himself in front of her, took her long head in his hands, and spoke quietly and earnestly to her. She snorted, stamped a foot, and raised and lowered her head. Their eyes connected, and the compound was silent except for her breathing and his. Finally, he raised his head and turned around. "I need her taken care of. Special feed. It was a very long flight. Parsley as well. Take good care of them both."

A few senior elves stepped forward and carefully led Vixen away, with Parsley led by two others. Tracer rejoined Saddler.

"A long flight?" Saddler said. "For one of Santa's?"

"Strapper's responsible for this," Tracer growled, so fiercely that Saddler stepped back. "Him and his damned procedures, his you-can't-go-see-them policies. Dammit, Saddler, they were starving! Starving! Hoof problems, matted coats, stink! You can't believe it! If I hadn't lived it, *I* wouldn't believe it! What the *hell* is he thinking? What could he be thinking? Santa's team, and he's letting them rot! Where is he? If the Chief ever saw what it looked like up there, he'd ship Strapper to—!"

"All right! All right! Calm down!" Saddler shook his head. "They were *starving*?"

"They'd have died inside a week, my guess. Vixen managed to get out, for how long I don't know. She's the strongest. Even so, I was scared out of my mind asking her to fly here. Afraid it would kill her."

"My God. OK. Don't kill Strapper. Something must have gone wrong. Horribly, horribly wrong. Strapper's always taken perfect care of them. Perfect care. Not a bell unpolished, not a flake of paint chipped on the sleigh, not a crack in the leather. He prided himself on it. Even after the Chief stopped taking the team out. And now—Maybe it's because—No. He wouldn't. He couldn't."

"Maybe it's because what?" Tracer's eyes still flashed.

"C'mon, walk with me." Saddler tilted his head, calling over his shoulder, "I need to talk with Tracer and Strapper for a bit! Let me know as soon as the search teams return!" He lowered his voice. "I want to get you away from them. Especially that starvation talk. The mood they're in right now—"

"We can't tell them the truth?"

"It isn't that." Saddler studied the ground, and when he spoke again resignation shaped his voice. "You've been gone more than three weeks. Things have changed. The day you disappeared, we received word the Chief was no longer running things."

"What?"

"Kicked out."

"That's nuts!"

"That's NPI. That's business."

"They're crazy!"

"We know that. But we don't run it. They do. All of us up here, we feel like we're—well, purposeless. There's a lot of anger here. And sadness and disbelief, too. Things flash up in a heartbeat. Elves fighting. And elves never fight. Talk like yours could send them over the edge."

"And that's bad?"

"You don't think so?"

"Somebody has to stir it up. Those idiots down south, they can't just shovel change on folks, push everybody around."

"Maybe stirring up's good. But not at the expense of the deer. I keep coming back to that. The deer deserve our care, no matter what's going on down there."

"'The deer know.'" Tracer paused. "OK, so I don't kill him. But he has to tell me how it happened. What if they died, Saddler? What then? Business as usual?"

They had reached the administration building. Tracer pushed inside, shouting "Strapper? Strapper!" He stomped toward Strapper's office, Saddler in tow.

Strapper emerged from behind his paperwork, extending a lifeless hand.

Tracer slapped it away. "What the hell is wrong with you, Strapper? Do you know what condition the stable is in? Do you? How could you let it happen? Here I thought you didn't want me up there because it was restricted! So you kept visitors and JEDIs and other—*annoyances* away, but it was really because you were letting the team rot! Isn't that it? Isn't it?"

Strapper stumbled back, and Saddler jumped in. "Tracer! Enough! Strapper, take a minute. You know what he's talking about?"

Strapper sat down as though under the weight of all the papers on his desk. When he found his voice, it was a miserable little croak. "I—I wasn't letting them rot! I don't know what you mean. I had too much to do. Here." His eyes swam over the desk. "New paperwork, new requirements. New workload. So I assigned it to somebody else to do, to Gleamer. Gleamer was supposed to take care of the stable and report to me daily. But he hasn't reported, and I've, we've all been so busy with the extra teams coming in and the Chief leaving and—"

Tracer snatched up the phone. "Get Gleamer in here!"

Strapper stared at the receiver. "He's on the field," he said. "Let me get my admin. Saddler?"

Saddler leaned out the doorway. "Filer? Come in here, please."

A very small and narrow-eyed old elf slipped into the office. He glanced up at Tracer, then peered over half-rimmed glasses at Strapper.

"Filer, do you remember the order for Gleamer? The one about the stables." Strapper's voice was a bit stronger now.

"Yes. Just a moment." Filer slipped out and, moments later returned, a paper slip in his hand. "This would be the one."

"It was delivered, right?"

"I believe so."

Tracer's hands clenched and unclenched. "I want to talk to Gleamer, now!"

Saddler punched a button on his handheld. "This is Saddler. I'm in Strapper's office. Find Gleamer and get him here now. Have somebody fill in. Thanks." He reholstered. "He's on his way."

Strapper spoke up. "Tracer, I—What do you mean, I left the team to rot? I've been taking care of them! I have! It's just in the last few weeks—"

Tracer glared him into silence. They waited uncomfortably a moment longer, Saddler glancing sidelong at Tracer.

Stumping sounds. Saddler leaned out. "Come on in, Gleamer!"

Gleamer, a smallish elf with a huge mop of dark hair, entered the room. His eyes roved over the others before coming to rest on Strapper. "What's going on?"

"Gleamer, do you remember—Have you ever seen this work order before?"

Gleamer took the paper from Strapper's outstretched hand. "What kind of order is this?" he asked. Strapper's face collapsed.

"It's an IRFW, an Interdepartmental Request For Work," Filer piped up helpfully.

"Who uses *these*?"

"Technically, Gleamer, everybody does." Saddler sighed. "You're supposed to fill one out whenever you want somebody from another department to do something. So Stable Ops wanted you from Flight Ops to handle this." He scanned the form. "You're supposed to make a daily run to the main stable, and see Strapper about special clearance."

"I was?"

"Doesn't sound like you know too much about it," Saddler grunted. He placed the form in Strapper's trembling hand. "There's your answer. I never saw it either, and I should have, since you were borrowing him from me."

"My God," Strapper croaked, sitting down heavily. "That was three weeks ago. They could have—"

"They could have starved," Tracer snarled. "Because *you* keep them locked in the stalls. Vixen finally kicked her door open, and that's the only thing that saved them."

Strapper's face worked. Then he burst out, "It's this—damned *paperwork*! All of this!" He shoved a pile, and it toppled off his desk, tumbling to the floor at Tracer's feet. "More and more every day! Audits and reports and clearances and forms!" His voice trembled. "All of it piling up, I can't even begin to dig out of it! And I'm supposed to be responsible for *them*, too! I used to have somebody stationed, full time, taking care of things, cleaning the stable, making sure everything was polished and done up true! Then they said consolidate and cut costs. I don't remember how long ago. 'Nonessential efforts!' That's what they said! So I took it over, finding time, going out there every other day. But as for paint! And repairs! And then—Once every three days! My visits were down to once every three days! Then four! And then I try to delegate it, and it doesn't go through, and—Oh, what does it matter anymore? Why does it even matter? They're his team, and he's gone, and it's all falling apart! All falling apart!" His voice caught. He shoved another pile. "Why are we doing this to ourselves? Why?" He took out a handkerchief and wiped his nose. Gleamer and Filer looked away.

Tracer's face softened a bit. "Why, indeed," he said. He nudged the pile. "Strapper, it's over. The team's recovering now. I'm seeing to it. I need your help."

"What kind of help?"

"I need supplies. Feed, for starters, and medicine. And food. I'm in the cabin, and there's nothing there but soups and stews, which are fine, but I could use a change."

"I—I'll send someone—" Strapper's hands searched the papers.

"No. You'll send me," Tracer declared. Saddler stared at him. Was this the JEDI? "I'm getting them healthy, Strapper. I'm caring for them. You don't need to send anyone. You don't need one of your *forms*. Just get me a work wagon—" his mouth curled in a small smile "—a sturdy one this time, one that can take a big load. I'll take Vixen. Overland. It'll take a few days, but I left them with all the remaining feed."

"You'll need a map with the secured routes, at least!"

Tracer towered over him. "I have *Vixen*, Strapper. What sort of map do you think I really need?"

Saddler chuckled. "All right!" he said. "Things are under control! But you, kid, have some gaps to fill in for me—over a hot meal, if you don't mind!"

Tracer grinned suddenly. "Sure!" He studied Strapper, who was still trying to stop trembling, and he nodded. "Why don't we all go. You, too, Strapper. Get out of this dungeon for a while."

Strapper looked up, relieved.

Saddler's handheld crackled. "Hey! It's Bounder! We're on our way in!"

"Great! We're going to have supper with our miracle guy, here! You game?"

"Sure am!"

"How about the rest of you?" Saddler exclaimed, smiling as one by one they eagerly accepted. "Demon? You ready for supper? Demon? ...Demon!"

Eventually, the handheld crackled. "...Uh, boss?" It was Bounder. "...Um, Demon, well—"

"You don't have to tell me! She's broken radio contact, right?"

"Right. ...You want me to try and—"

"No. Just come on in." He sighed and switched off the handheld.

Tracer looked at him quizzically, a hint of the old awkwardness in his expression. "Aren't you worried about him? Who's Demon again?"

"Her. It's a she. At least, most of the time I think it's a she." Saddler frowned. "And no, I don't—I *can't* worry about her. It would be like worrying about the wind. C'mon, let's eat!"

4.

"Commissary."

Groomer rubbed his belly, belching softly into the phone as he scowled through his email. Behind him, tumbling across his scratched credenza, lay piles of briefs, opinions, discoveries, depositions, agreements, requests, rulings, filings, casework, contracts, statements. A rare email might cause him to reach back and blindly lift the exact document he needed. Not today.

"Groomer here. Half a dozen, the usual. No, wait. Make three of them specials. ...No. Special. From Sweden. ...Well, read the damn package labels! Figure it out!" He slapped down the receiver.

Silvertongue poked his head in the door. "You ready?"

Groomer grunted and nodded the smaller elf to a chair. He continued working his email. "I get more stupid stuff from my own department," he groused. "Every one of these guys wants to outdo me."

Silvertongue raised an eyebrow. "But you're the king bastard."

"Damn right I am." More clicks, and whole oceans of underling work disappeared. "Like I'd promote any of these idiots. Where's Oiler?"

"On his way. How's EI?"

"Any day now. The rabbit's already out. Our tests in Tinker's area show we can make this happen without too much trouble. I'm eyeball deep in the other work. The due diligence is just a formality, even though we're burning a few execs on it. This has so much money in it, Silvertongue. That's what drives it. Now it's figure out what shuts down and when. There's lots of personalities involved, and a lot of greed to manage."

"I understand. In all my discussions, everyone's ready to go. They can smell the bonuses. I've got statements I'll be dropping out there, one by one. They'll manage everything from the announcement to the merger itself. It's EI's facilities, mostly. And their greed."

"It's much more. Greed knows no boundaries. You'll have some local greed to manage, too, my good negotiator. Plus we get EI manufacturing locations and distribution outlets. They're all over the place! That's better than those stupid ranches the Chief set up."

"Ex-Chief."

"Doesn't matter. Nobody will take his title, after what happened to him. Ah, Oiler! Perfect timing! Knock that tray over, and you'll never darken this doorway again!"

Oiler had almost collided with the Commissary elf and her tray. She squeezed past him, the tray sliding under Silvertongue's nose and coming to rest in front of Groomer. She left noiselessly, and Oiler sat beside Silvertongue, wrinkling his nose. "You sure those things are all right? They smell different."

"They *are* different. Three of them, anyway. Specialty dogs. From Sweden."

Oiler glanced at Silvertongue, whose mouth curled upward. "You really are a bastard," Silvertongue said.

Groomer smiled, slicing one of the specialty dogs. "What's the latest from our friend and his paramour?"

Silvertongue's eyes hardened. He picked up a Groomer business card from its ebony tray and flipped it one-handed. "I approved a Jag for him."

"You what?" Oiler exclaimed.

"XKR. Top of the line, too. Seventy-five Gs. The Jaguar dealer was very polite."

"What the hell you giving him a Jag for? Aren't there limits to exec privileges? Especially ex-executives!"

Silvertongue's eyes never left Groomer as the fat elf bit down hard and a hunk of one specialty dog disappeared. "Oiler, figure it out," he said, his voice tightening. "He's much more visible in a Jag. We can trace that thing anywhere."

Groomer's eyes popped. "So where is he now? Still in Detroit?"

"Yes. That Jag's pretty visible, running up and down Jefferson. But he checked out of the Autorama. He took some extra cash out. Maybe he's going to an upscale hotel."

"Why's he in Detroit? With extra money and a Jag?" Groomer murmured. "A background check on Baylor? Has he checked in somewhere else?"

"Not yet."

"Hm. Want some? Has an interesting flavor." Groomer offered the remaining half to Silvertongue.

"No, thanks."

"We need to know when he checks in," Groomer said. "Maybe he's seeing the world."

"Would that be so bad?"

"Not really, Oiler. But we need to keep an eye on him." Groomer leaned forward. "How's your stuff going?"

Oiler shifted. "It's all worked out, ready to go. We're waiting for the right combination of events." He frowned. "Gardner pulled that damn audit on us."

"I know," Groomer said. "Sticking her nose where it doesn't belong. It'll get cut off soon. You managing the audit?"

"Slow-walking the results. They go to Crafter, but we're playing the game, rescheduling meetings, having production emergencies. Sooner or later, though—"

"Edythig I deedda do?"

"No, you gave it to me. Don't worry, I'll make it happen. …I will."

"Good." Groomer swallowed. "We need the union to focus on this, because that'll throw a big fat wrench into things. Then the audit won't matter. Hammer's been very hard to read here, but I think he'll raise the roof when this comes down. Baylor will be fighting on three fronts then. He'll be trying to consolidate his position, plus fending off Gardner and her self-righteous friends, and he'll have Hammer and the union coming down on him. When the dust clears, we'll have a spot on the Board. And if things get nasty enough—"

"A short tenure for our automotive friend?" Silvertongue suggested.

"Unless he's better than we think." Groomer set the knife on another specialty dog. "Then we'll finally be where we want to be. If not—" he sliced down, hard "—we'll figure out something else. Hell, if nothing else, we'll simply outlive him. But I'm not that patient, anymore." He took another huge, savage bite.

"I suppose none of us are, when we get this close," Silvertongue said. "So you haven't talked directly to Hammer."

"Dough way." Chili threatened to spatter everyone. "He bedieves id his guys. He'd dever foo aroud like dis." The eyes popped. "We have UEU contacts, but not at the top. Gardner's always had the best contacts. We're doing what we can."

"Hmm." Oiler frowned. "Would they consider Gardner? For the Board?"

"They would if it was the old NPI," Silvertongue said. "But we boxed her in on the incentives. And she's digging herself a pretty deep hole with her do-good attitude. You talk about a fight, Groomer. She had her meeting with Baylor."

"And?"

"According to Baylor's admin, it was pretty nasty."

"How so?"

"He's tearing down her employee-focused programs, Oiler. As expected. And she'll fight him all the way on that. Even though he'll win. Plus he's putting in ten-eighty-ten, no matter what. Which she hates."

"I thought we ditched ten-eighty-ten."

"We did, Oiler." Groomer rubbed a bean into his shirt. "So it's back?"

"What I hear. And mandatory."

"Meaning?" Oiler asked.

"Meaning the lower ten percent get fired, no matter what."

"Nice company," Groomer said. "A good start to the new regime."

"You think so?" Silvertongue raised an eyebrow. "What'll those ten percent do? Kiddie porn?"

Groomer snickered. "It's an option. Not our worry, anyway. Until we get what we want. Then we can get rid of it, along with

Baylor. If we find it's not working. But not before Baylor puts Gardner in that lower ten."

"With her record?"

"Performance doesn't mean shit, Oiler." Groomer sawed through another dog. "Not at that level. Performance in Baylor's world is tied to whether you agree with him. If you do, you're OK. If you don't, you're out. So much for diversity. And Gardner'll be out." He smiled. "Which is wonderful. Because she'll take her friends with her. Great news, Silvertongue."

"Thought you'd like it." Silvertongue brushed a crumb from his pantleg. "I understand they found that missing JEDI."

"Mm," Groomer grunted.

"He found the original cabin and stable. A real mess, too, what he found."

Groomer started. "He was *where*?"

"Santa's cabin. What's the big deal with that?"

"Well, nothing. Nothing." Groomer scratched his cheek. "It's just surprising. What kind of mess did he find?"

"The team was in pretty rough shape."

"Hmm. They ought to close that place down, now that the Chief's gone. Nobody's going out there anymore."

"Except the JEDI. He's maintaining the team," Oiler said.

"Maintaining the team? What the hell for?"

"Oh, what does it matter?" Silvertongue snapped. "So there's a JEDI out there taking care of things. Is that a crime? Does it mean anything? I don't think so." He leaned forward. "Tell me something, Groomer, tell me this. If that team out there refused to fly, if they came down with RFS. What would you do?"

Oiler scarcely breathed. Groomer looked at the last of the specialty dogs, picked up the knife, and licked the chili off it with his fat tongue. "I don't know, Silvertongue," he said. "What do you think I'd do?"

5.

Acres of Bronner's Christmas displays, and no road out. She floated down aisle after aisle, past groves of Christmas trees, green, white, silver, even pink and blue, past bushels of ornaments of every color, shape and vintage, past miles of light strands, twinklers, singing lights, midgets, nets, bubblers, icicles, white and red and green and blue and varied, past wreaths stacked like used tires, garlands like firehoses, cedar, white pine, red, jack, balsam, hemlock, holly, ivy, even oddball flora like cacti, past the garish, borderline obscene stuff, singing Christmas trees, sleeping santas, moronic-looking wide-eyed unsleeping bears playing Christmas carols endlessly on cue, ashtrays and even KrisKringle lava lamps, past confetti oceans of Christmas cards, the religious, the humorous, some with subjects and celebrations only remotely tied to the holiday, past religious displays, crèches, angels, baby Jesuses, Marys, Josephs, whole herds of stable cattle, throngs of wise men, gaggles of camels, about a billion Nubian goats, past tinsel, spun glass, fiber optic sprays, icicles, enough foil to wrap a city, then past santas, santas, santas, life-sized, ancient, modern, sunglassed, Slimfasted, portly, droll, serious, downright grim, jolly, and suddenly he was among them, stomping about, full-suited, New Orleansed, picking up likenesses of himself and hurling them everywhere, Julinesses crashing into Christkinds, Pere Noels skewering Babouschkas, Black Petes shattering Befanas, and he then raging through the store, tearing down displays, shotputting Christmas bulbs like little glass bombs, picking up toy trains and flinging them into tiny neighborhoods, snapping skeins of Christmas lights like bullwhips and sending sparking colored glass in all directions, and twirling in the midst of the mayhem he belted out HoHoHo after HoHoHo as though for once he meant it, and she, panicking, knowing he would be arrested and they would go to jail and the entire operation would be exposed and punctured and then deflated, dissipated—she stumbled toward his dance, feet crunching bits of bulbs and ornaments, slipping and falling

right into the glare of headlights. Roxy blinked, chasing bits of Bronner's. *Thank God none of that had happened.* She looked around groggily. He still slept in the back seat, and Ravi concentrated on the road. She yawned. What a visit it had been—the largest Christmas store in the world, in Frankenmuth, Michigan, and he treating it as the giant discount outlet it was, from his perspective.

They had arrived at Bronner's about an hour before the huge facility closed its doors to the public. She and the Chief had left a goggle-eyed Ravi wandering amid acres of Christmas displays, while they sought one of Santa's old partners, now a Bronner's purchasing manager. She couldn't remember his real name, but the sign on his office read "A.R. tenHoor."

"God, this place has grown," Santa grumbled, when they'd closed tenHoor's door.

"Your fault, Claus," tenHoor said. "You're suffering from a popularity explosion."

"Yeah, you're not helping it any with your 'International Santas' and 'Bagpipe Santas' and 'Celtic Santas' and the like," he groused.

"Items you approved," tenHoor reminded him. "Or somebody at NPI did." tenHoor had a face pointed like a flatiron, wavy gray hair meringued over a broad forehead, black doll's eyes behind overlarge glasses, and a neat, information-withholding corporate mouth. She found him difficult to look at, impossible to warm up to. "What brings you to Bronner's?"

Santa frowned. "You already know. I'm out. Temporarily." And though her blood had iced at that last word, still the conversation was mercifully short, a discussion of routes and possibilities. tenHoor spoke little, offered less, and as they left, his mincing "Good luck" playing in their ears, Santa muttered, "I don't even *know* why I bothered coming here. He's never been much help, and as for all *this* stuff, yeesh!" and they'd wandered the acreage, searching figurines, Christmas lights and endless nativities for a skinny Indian.

She yawned. A roadsign loomed: "Standish, 15 miles." She couldn't keep her eyes open. *I better not dream that silly dream again.* She smiled, drifting like snow, tiny trains puffing in the distance, lights and stars and santas dancing, dancing.

North of Standish, the rains moved in, cleaning the old Volvo's windshield. Ravi pointed the protesting machine up the two-lane road and into the northeastern lower peninsula. WJR, the Great Voice of the Great Lakes, fought loud static snaps for rights to the airwaves. Except for Bronner's, they had driven nonstop since Santa hurled the phone into the Detroit River. Day had yielded to murky dusk.

"How much 'Sports Rap' can you guys listen to?"

"Uh?" Santa awoke. "Where are we?"

"I wasn't listening," Ravi said. "I could change it."

"What's our other choices?" Santa asked.

"Let's see." Ravi twisted the dial, and they wandered through whistles, eerie wails, and snatches of music and conversation encompassing farm reports, country music, oldies, Dr. Laura, something in Spanish, daytime talk shows, born again shows, requests for money, top 100 hits, older oldies, Middle Eastern music, and what sounded like a baseball game.

"That was fun," Santa rumbled. "What about FM?"

"FM doesn't work," Ravi said, twiddling some more before finding a news station. "How about this?"

"Yeah, leave it."

The radio spewed stories about an apartment fire in Baltimore that killed five siblings, pre-election political jabs, a new oil slick off the coast of Scotland, the latest in a high-profile rape trial, accusations of police brutality in a couple of cities, an Internet fraud story that caused the stock of a teething dot-com to plummet, a dog that rescued three kids from drowning in a local pond, the latest Big Game winner, local construction problems, and the stock market.

Then: "In related financial news, North Pole Industries and Easter Industries have announced their intention to merge, a move expected to please Wall Street analysts. The deal requires shareholder approval, which is anticipated. Under the agreement, manufacturing facilities from both companies will be consolidated, and purchasing and systems operations will be combined. These moves are expected to trim operating costs from both organizations and contribute to improved profit margins. Jerome Baylor, NPI's new CEO, announced his intention to refocus the organization and streamline operations."

A Baylor sound bite filled the interior. "'We can't afford to be a company of entitlements anymore. Our markets and our shareholders demand superior performance. Our merged organizations must be lean and agile perform with speed and ruthlessness. Our own workforce needs to get this message.'"

The story continued. "Mr. Baylor's remarks were met with enthusiasm on Wall Street, where analysts said this is the kind of tough talk and—"

"Aw, shut the damn thing off!" Santa exclaimed. He stared gloomily out the window at fields studded with pine trees whisking by. "They've really done it now," he grumbled at last. "Merging with that damned rabbit! They're undoing it all, Roxy. All of it." He stared some more. "And it sounds like he's going to go through with his damned ten eighty ten, brooming out the elves he doesn't like. That little prick."

"Hey!"

"Sorry, Mom, bad language." He chuckled bitterly. "But it's a fair description."

Rain pounded the windshield. The road sliced through a darkening countryside under autumn's first touch, late-summer gold splashing the fields. Santa stretched as best he could. "Where are we, anyway? What was the name of that last town, Splat?"

"Spratt," Ravi sighed.

"Not much of a town," he rumbled. "Where are we going? This looks like a lot of fields and not much else. Hey!" He swiveled to keep in view an old, rust-colored building with antlers tacked over its entrance. "Did you see that building? It looked like an old reindeer stable! You don't suppose—"

"That's an Elks Lodge," Ravi interrupted firmly.

"What the hell is an Elks Lodge?"

"It's a place where a lot of fat old men get together and drink," Ravi clipped. "They need to get away from their wives, so they go there and shoot pool and get in pickups and drive like idiots down roads like this."

"OK, *OK*! Forget I asked!" He slapped Ravi's headrest. "Forgive me for thinking I saw something from my old life!"

"How do you know about these Elks clubs?" Roxy asked, tapping her foot.

"I don't want to talk about it."

"Girlfriend again?"

"Yes. Well, her dad. And her uncle. Uncles. Every old man she knew, really."

"The girlfriend." Santa sighed. "Ravi, when you and I get a chance, we should talk."

"What road are we on?" Roxy still tapped her foot.

"I thought I was taking the road up the coast when I left Bay City, but I made a turn somewhere after Standish. We've been going this way a while."

"A long while," Roxy said. "I need to find a bathroom."

"And I need to stretch out. This back seat's for the birds," Santa said. "What road was that?"

"I think it was number 32," Ravi said. "Roxy, did you see it?"

"Roxy, get the damn map out. Our Indian friend may be good at driving, but he's not much good at knowing where we're going."

Ravi slapped the wheel. "Listen you, Mr. CEO! I have been driving and driving and driving this heap of crap you call a car, trying to take us I don't even know where, just as long as we are a long ways out of town, and Ganesh please help me but I am tired of not knowing what we are doing, not knowing where we are going, just driving and driving and driving and then being accused, yes I say accused, sir, of getting us lost! And you something that you call yourself, an old half-elf in a young man's clothing, and you cannot drive, and she can't either, and so it's up to Ravi to take you from place to place, like I am in India and some kind of foot taxi! I should put you on an elephant if I had one, let you rattle around up there for a while! And—"

"Ravi, look out!" Roxy screamed.

It was all slow motion, the big white horned shape floating from the mists, Ravi veering the car toward the shoulder, side road a pale splash, old truck with rails rattling, trying to escape but moving about as effectively as a pig in a mud wallow, and the front of the Volvo caught the rear of the truck, hard, pushing it aside even as the Volvo hood clanged into an angular jumble, and still Santa scanned the jarring whirl for the vanished white deer. Thuds shook the Volvo's roof. Large things pummeled the car, five or ten seconds at most (though it felt as though whole thumping minutes passed), then silence, rain, twisted metal and strange brown shapes leaping and bouncing into the grass.

They each took body part roll call before asking each other if they were all right. The car's front end whistled and steamed like a two-ton teakettle. A sharp rap on the driver's window made them jump. A ruddy, round face peered through rain-speckled glass. "You all right? You all right?" the face was saying, muffled by the closed window.

Ravi struggled with the door before shoving it open with his left arm and leg. It groaned angrily and threatened to come off altogether if it wasn't left alone. He stood and peered down at the round thing facing him. "Geez, I'm sorry, Mister," the round thing said, "I tried to get out of the way, but there wasn't much chance in this rain."

More metal rasped from the passenger side. Santa groaned, stretching, and Roxy surveyed the front of the car. Ravi, shaken, tried to get his bearings. "I—I swerved to—There was this animal. I didn't really have any time—"

"It was a reindeer," Santa said in a peculiar voice. "A white one."

"I don't know about a white deer," the round-faced man said slowly. "But if it's a reindeer, it's one of Earl's. He's got a farm up the road."

"Oh," Ravi murmured, seeing brown lumps everywhere—on the road, in the ditch, on the dinged roof of the station wagon. "...Are those potatoes?"

"Yep. Potatoes for Posen." The man jerked a thumb up the road. An awkward silence followed, before he thrust out his hand. "I'm

Bob Towalksi. Got a potato farm up the road. And I run Bob's ACE Hardware here. You sure you're all right?"

Absently, Ravi shook Bob's hand. "Yes I—I've just never been in an accident before."

"What about your friend there?" Bob pointed at Santa, staring at the fields.

"I'm all right." He turned and offered his hand. "I'm Samuel Claussen." His eyes strayed to the car. "How bad is it?"

"You won't be going anywhere soon," Bob said. "Looks like the radiator took it. What kind of car is it?"

"It's a Volvo," Santa said.

Bob winced. "Might be hard to find parts, too. We'll have Tommy look at it."

Santa looked around. "Where's Roxy?" He cupped his hands to his mouth and boomed, "Roxy!" The sound met soggy darkness. "Roxy!" His voice rose a notch.

A shape emerged from behind a bush and headed toward them, becoming more distinct as it approached. She walked up to Bob and held out her hand. "Hi, I'm Roxy."

"Are you all right?" Santa said.

"I am *now*," she said. "Except for getting soaked. What do we do about the car?"

"Where were you all going?" Bob asked.

After a considerable pause, Roxy said, "Mackinaw City. We're going to Mackinaw City tonight, and the Upper Peninsula tomorrow."

"Mackinaw City? You didn't take I-75? You must have wanted the scenic route." Bob rubbed his wet cheek. "I tell you what. Best thing we can do is get you taken care of tonight. First, let's get you inside my truck, missy. Then your friends and I can get this thing out of the intersection." He tapped the Volvo.

"That sounds good to me," she said, heading for the truck.

It didn't take long for them to push the Volvo aside. They were busy stowing their belongings among the potatoes in the back of Bob's truck, when another truck pulled alongside, and a thin man jumped out of the cab. "Jesus, Bob, what happened?"

"Aw, one of Earl's deer got loose again," Bob said, arranging one of the bags. "Ran right in front of these people's car."

"They hit it?"

"Naw, they missed it and hit me."

"Hell." The other man spat into the darkness. "They need a ride to town?"

"Naw, they'll ride with me. Ravi, Sam, this is Ed Figurski. He's got a farm down the road, when he's not being school principal." They shook hands. "Ed," Bob continued, "can you see if there's any room at Ida's? Could be a problem with the Festival coming up. Have her get some hot food ready—I imagine these folks'll find out they're hungry. And see if Tommy's down at the Boxcar. We need this thing towed out of here, if he's still in any shape to be on the road. Or else he can get it in the morning."

"No problem. Let me get Tommy first. Meet you at Ida's?"

"Yeah."

Ed splashed to his truck and roared off. Bob finished securing the tarps over the potatoes and luggage. "Well, gentlemen," he said. "We're soaked, your car's not going anywhere, and it's pretty dark. We'll get you set for tonight, get something hot into you, find you a place to change clothes. Welcome to Posen."

"To Posen?" Ravi stared at the empty fields.

"Posen."

"What's Posen?"

"Home of the biggest potato festival in the world," Bob said proudly. "That's where this load is going. The town itself is up the road." He sloshed to the driver's door. "Let's get in."

"What about the rest of the potatoes?" Ravi asked.

"You want to wander around in the night picking potatoes out of a wet field, be my guest," Bob said. "I don't. C'mon, get in. Ida'll never forgive me if you guys catch cold."

The truck's ride was even bumpier than the Volvo's. Darkness mantled the land, and the rain changed to a drenching mist chilling to see even from inside the cab. Bob had to keep the defroster on high. Santa sat pressed against the passenger window. Beside him, Ravi peered ahead. Roxy sat next to Bob, one strong thigh pressed hard against his own. When he spoke, his voice cracked. "So, have you been through these parts before?"

At length, Ravi answered. "We have not, I'm afraid. How far are we from Mackinaw?"

"About an hour and a half. But you won't go anywhere tonight." He licked his lips, tried to move his leg. "I wonder if Earl knows one of his deer is missing," he said. "I don't know why he keeps those things, they're forever getting loose."

Santa stirred. "How many does he have?"

"Thirty or so. Seems like one or the other is always getting out. He calls them reindeer, but they look like dwarf elk to me." Another bump pushed her against him some more. "It's a wonder somebody hasn't gotten off—gotten a shot off at one of them before this."

"How far to Posen?" Roxy asked.

"A mile or two. We'll be stopping at Ida's. It's Ida's Hotel and Tavern. Ida Persson is her real name, but we just call her Ida. Showed up this year, from the UP we think, bought the old Tarnow place and fixed it up. She makes the best pasties you've ever tasted, UP or anywhere. She's got some rooms above the tavern, not much to look at from the outside, but clean and neat, and with good-sized beds. Or that's what I've been told. About the beds," he finished lamely, wiping a drop of sweat from his cheek.

"Well, we're grateful for everything you're doing," Roxy said.

"Yes, especially after we ran into your truck," Ravi added.

"My pleasure," Bob said. "And almost there. Here's Posen. Sorry you can't see more of it right now."

The fields had yielded to some small frame houses, black shapes huddled against the roadside. A field opened on their right, a low building in the distance. They passed more dark squares. Ahead on the road, a flashing red light beamed at them, Posen's main intersection.

The light was farther away than they judged. When they reached the intersection at last, Bob gunned the engine, and the truck labored into a right turn onto Posen's other major road. After only a short distance, he pulled the truck in front of a rather large two-story building that sported an RC Cola sign whose red-white-blue light spilled onto a smaller wooden sign underneath. IDA'S, this sign said, in simple, well-crafted letters.

Ida's door opened. Interior light should have splashed the street but didn't, because the door was clogged by the silhouette of a massive, squared-off creature with no appreciable neck to support a round head fringed by tight curls.

"What is that?" Ravi squinted. "A fuzzy bowling ball on a Coke machine?"

"Sshh," Santa cautioned.

They slid clear of the truck. The shadow freightered out to meet them, the eerie RC light revealing a large, friendly-featured woman, a sort of big-and-tall female Bob. "Let's have a look at our travelers!" she declared in a voice designed to summon cattle from distant fields. "I'm Ida. You figured that out. I hear you tried to launch some of Bob's potatoes." She looked them up and down. "Now, what hurts? I bet this knucklehead didn't even ask you."

"I did!" Bob hustled around the truck. "I asked them if they were all right."

"Not the same thing." She motioned them indoors. "People are too polite. You ask them if they're all right, they'll say Yes when they're not. You got to ask them what hurts if you want an answer." She steered them into the dining area.

"We are doing all right I think," Ravi said. "Except for being shaken up."

"Uh," she grunted, a tone reserved for lying children. "William! *Will*-yam! Get these people some coffee, and put some pasties on! Now, why don't you all get yourselves seated. If you don't hurt, you must be hungry."

"I'll go get your things from the truck." Bob hurried off.

They arranged themselves around the table. Still standing, Ravi extended his hand. "I'm Ravi. It's a long name, so I just go by Ravi. And this is San—This is Mr. Samuel Claussen. And Roxy. We've, um, we've come up from Detroit."

"*Dee*-troit! Escaped, you mean. I have a sister down there. Sit down, sit down! This is William."

A skinny, balding creature curled like an "f" edged toward them with a pot of coffee and a tray of cups. They took their seats. Ida's presented the traveler, or more likely the hungry local, with a choice of about a dozen tables of various sizes and vintages, vinyl red-and-white table covers hiding coltish legs. Liberally applied red mending tape created interesting patterns.

"Pasties?" Roxy asked. "What exactly is in a pasty?"

"Well," Ida boomed, as William poured the coffee and padded off, "there's meat and potatoes and spices I can't give away, 'cause it's a trade secret. And it's wrapped in a tasty shell, smothered with gravy, and—Honey, there ain't anything in the *world* like a good pasty!"

"Well—I'm not sure. I'm on a diet, actually."

"Listen, honey, that frame of yours could use some building up, believe me! We've got enough excitement here with the Festival starting up in a few days, and you could use the fuel."

Ravi sipped his coffee. "What's the festival?"

"You aren't from around here, or you'd know," Ida said. "The Posen Potato Festival. Puts this town on the map! In a few days, you'll see! We have all kinds of things going. There's potato sack races, carnival rides, potato beer, cookoffs, all-you-can-eat breakfasts, with potato pancakes, of course. And then there's potato carving, crop judging, potato spoon races. You name it, Ravi. If there's something that can be done with a potato, we've done it! And if not, we'll do it this year."

"I see. And people come to this festival?"

"Almost twenty thousand last year."

"My God," Roxy exclaimed. "They can't all stay *here*."

"No, sweetie, they don't. Lots of 'em are just everyday folk from around, farmers mostly. Then we get folks from farther off. They tend to stay in hotels not far from here, Mackinaw and Alpena and Rogers City. Or they camp. Not too many of 'em know about my place yet. I won't fill my rooms ahead of time. Except in an emergency. It's not the Holiday Inn, but the rooms are clean and cozy."

A heavily-burdened Bob paused at their table. "Take these things upstairs?" he puffed.

"If you would, Bob, thanks," she said. "We can sort out later, when we pick out rooms. Unless you need something?" Her eyes roved the table.

"I just need to use a bathroom," Ravi said, getting up.

"I think I could use something stronger than coffee," Santa said. "What's on tap?"

Ravi and Roxy exchanged dark glances. Bob stumped toward the stairs.

"Hm," Ida said, then boomed over her shoulder, "Will-*yam*! Sammy needs a beer!" Resting her substantial arms on the table, she let eyes blue like his fall on him again. "Now, Sammy," she said, and Roxy winced but Santa smiled. "You're evidently the one leading this expedition. What brings you to Posen?"

The eyes hardened ever so slightly over the smile. "Business," he said. "Business, and the opportunity to relax, too. And it wasn't Posen. I was heading to—heading to—"

"Mackinaw City," Roxy offered.

"Yes, Mackinaw City. In the toy business."

"The toy business? They got that up there? I thought they just had those forts, and ferry rides out to the Island."

"The toy business is everywhere, Ida, you can't stop it," he said. "Wherever there's a kid, or a grown person acting like a kid, there's a need for toys. I'm a broker. I ask the area businesses what they need, then work with companies to supply them."

"A middleman."

"You could say that."

William appeared with the pasties and Santa's beer. Ravi returned to his seat. Thumping sounds from the porch signaled Ed Figurski's arrival. "No Tommy tonight," he announced, making for the table.

"Too far gone?" Bob asked, creaking down the stairs.

"Too far gone." Ed scraped up a chair, eyeing the food. "He might stop by later. You don't have an extra one of those, do you?"

"Will-*yam*!"

The shoulders bowed a bit more.

Santa, Ravi and Roxy began eating hungrily, under Ida's approving eye. While they ate, the front door banged, and one by one the men of the town, farmers and small shop owners, Boxcar Bar men, drifted in. Little conversation puffs started up, the men watching the travelers from a respectful distance.

"Rain's lettin' up."

“Good weather tomorrow. Festival field might need some drying out.”

“Nah. Bob, you going to get that truck out of here any time soon?”

“I’m taking it up to the field. That’s where I was going before all this.”

“What happened?”

“One of Earl’s deer. Jumped in front of their car, and they collided with me.”

“They hit it?”

“Naw.”

“Too bad. Teach Earl a lesson. We could have had reindeer meat.”

“I don’t think those are reindeer. They’re some kind of small elk.”

“You think so? I think they’re elk, too.”

“Actually, reindeer are a form of elk.”

“Willis, you’re just too damn smart, ain’t you?”

“Tommy going to get that car?”

“Tomorrow.”

“Is he coming here?”

“He’d have to walk. You saw what he was like,” Ed said. Chuckles. “Reindeer. You’d think Earl’s got better things to do. Where could he get reindeer from?”

“I don’t know. Zoos, maybe.”

“You don’t get animals from zoos! You donate animals to zoos!”

“I hear there’s a reindeer husbandry group.”

“Not here!”

“No. But somewhere. I bet that’s where he got them, and just manages his herd now. He’s bringing some to the festival again, to give the kids rides.”

Santa looked up at this but didn’t say anything.

“That’ll be good.”

“…I wonder what reindeer would taste like? Wild, I imagine, like deer or elk.”

“Hey, here’s Santa,” Ida boomed. “Maybe we can ask him!”

The three travelers nearly choked on their pasties, until they realized that Ida referred to the front door, which had been filled by a solid, squared-off mass of flesh, a head of graying hair, black eyes, a salt-and-pepper bristle that partly obscured multiple chins, massive arms and legs, and a billowing gut which he rubbed with one hand. "Ida!" he roared. "Any pasties?"

"*Will*-yam! Half a dozen! Santa's here!"

"That's Santa?" Roxy said.

"Well, Stan. We all call him Santa, because he plays Santa every Christmas."

Floorboards groaned as Stan approached.

"This is going to be difficult," Roxy murmured to Ravi, watching Santa watch Santa pull up a chair.

"Room here, I imagine," Stan thundered. They cleared an acre for him. "I'm Stan," he continued. "They just call me Santa. I entertain the kids here at Christmas. Don't get up! I never do!" He laughed at his observation. They introduced themselves. "Pleased to know you. Ida makes the best pasties around." He stared at their food until Roxy put her fork down. "I heard you had trouble."

"Hey, Santa!" one of the others said. "What does reindeer taste like?"

"Kind of like lamb," Stan observed. "Best in a stew."

"Told you he'd know."

"*When* did you have reindeer?" Ida asked. "You sneak over to Earl's?"

"Years ago." Stan slapped a quivering flank. "You think all this is from pasties? This is a work of art. A, whatdoyoucallit, a long-term study."

"Longitudinal," Ravi murmured.

"What?" Stan squinted.

"Longitudinal study."

"It don't have nothing to do with geography! This was all put on over the years. There's Louisiana catfish in here, pastas, veal Oscar, beef Wellington, fifty-seven kinds of chicken—"

"I imagine there's whole chickens in there, Santa!" someone called out. "Couple of goats, too." General laughter.

"Oh, laugh all you want," Stan growled. "The narrow-minded have no idea what it's like to build a work of art over the years." He singled out Santa. "So. Car trouble."

"Crash, really." Santa said finished his pasty and signaled William for another beer. "White reindeer ran right in front of the car and disappeared."

"A *white* one?" Stan squinted. "I don't think Earl has any white deer."

The other men began pulling up chairs.

"Maybe it wasn't one of this Earl's," Ravi suggested.

"May be," one of the men said slowly. "But who else would have one?"

"No, it's got to be Earl's," Bob said. "But I didn't think it was white. You should have seen what it did to their car. Racked up the front end pretty bad. Radiator's shot."

"I thought they hit the truck."

William shuffled up with a huge tray of pasties for one Santa and a beer for the other.

"But the deer caused it. William, bring me a beer when you get a minute."

("Me, too! Me too!" chorused several men. The shoulders stooped even lower.)

The beer loosened them all up. They talked about the repairs, what Tommy needed to do, how it was a damn shame their car ended up in the ditch, whether Tommy had parts, maybe he'd have to send all the way down to Bay City for something, but he was a genius, Tommy was, could make repairs you'd swear couldn't be made with the stuff at hand, and was Vera going to bring her rhubarb pie to the contest, because if she was then the other ladies might just as well not try, and remember the time Wally decided he could bake just as well as anyone, and he made that chocolate cake but he didn't have enough regular flour so he used whole wheat and that cake made slices that toppled onto the plate like bricks, just like bricks, and you all will have to stay for the festival, so it's the best time to have a reindeer cut you off and send you in to Bob's truck, after all.

Through the ramble, Ravi and Roxy nursed their coffee. Santa downed a couple of more beers, quickly, his eyes never really moving off that plate, watching pasties disappear just as surely as their hopes of progress did, the Posen Potato Festival seeing to that, the whole town turning out for the events, Earl bringing in reindeer, and somewhere out in those fields beyond the last potato sack and the last squealing kid would be the deer, the one that had stopped them. He ordered another beer and drained that one too, before cutting through Ida and Bob and Ed and Stan and the rest, shutting down the conversation through the simple act of standing, a figure whose authority even now couldn't be hidden. "I'm sorry," he rumbled, watching another forkful of pasty in transit. "I can't stay any longer tonight. I understand we'll have work to do with the car tomorrow, or maybe after this festival. Thank you all for your hospitality. Stan—Santa—You remind me of someone I knew a long time ago."

"Izzat good or bad?" Stan mashed, mouth full.

"It's—well. It was a very long time ago. Nice meeting you all. I'll see you all again." He reached for his wallet.

Ida checked him. "Nothing doing," she said. "Pay up when you leave. I know exactly where you are, Sammy." She stood. "Let's sort out your rooms."

They goodnighted the group, Stan still hard at the remaining pasties, and headed upstairs, snips of conversation trailing them:

"He's a big one, too."

"Better not let the Pincher get a look at her."

"They'll be here a week, at least. At least."

"Them reindeer are nothing but trouble. We got to talk to Earl."

6.

The heat from the tea eased into Tracer's tired fingers. Polishing was hard work. He scanned the predawn sky, until a small sigh brought his gaze to the slender form sleeping lightly on the couch. *His* couch, he'd realized only when she appropriated it. The cabin was chilly this autumn morning, even though he'd banked the fire late last night. She had pulled the blanket over her shoulder, and just the slightest splash of red, close-cropped hair peeked out. He knew better than to think her vulnerable. Even now, she wore her black racing suit, just in case. Sometimes when he'd awakened during the night, emerging from a bedroom he never thought he'd occupy, he'd found the couch empty.

He watched the blanket rise and fall. How incredibly she had popped into his life. He had returned from the overland journey with Vixen and Parsley, pulling a cart laden with feed, medicines, and supplies. Cresting the last hill, his heart had jumped at the sight of the cabin he'd longed to come home to. Then he'd spied the sled, sleek and bold, parked in the yard. Smoke curling from the chimney added insult. He'd dashed down the slope, arms waving, only to be stopped a dozen paces from the door by a small figure leaning against the doorframe. "Hi. You're Tracer. I've heard good things about you. Demon." As he accepted her extended hand, its cool shock transformed his sharp outrage into unfocused anger.

"What are you doing here?"

"I was one of the search team. Saddler sent me out. We found where you'd buried the other one."

"I know *who* you are, but why did you come here?"

"...Because this is your private property?" Her sky-blue eyes stripped him.

"I—well."

"It isn't, you know. Nor mine." She smiled. "You've done a great job here."

"How can you tell?"

"I can see where they've been."

"But why—"

"I knew I should come here, after you'd been discovered. I knew they'd be all alone. That was dangerous."

"But this—The routes here are hidden! They're classified!"

"How did I find it?" A shrug. "I did, that's all. Is that Vixen up there? Who's the other one?"

"Yes, Vixen. That's Parsley."

"Let's get that cart unloaded. We can talk afterward."

And they did. With Demon, even talk was action. They talked while unloading the cart, while cleaning the stalls, while moving among a team happy to see him, while preparing and eating supper. It was late in the evening that first day when they made the connection—he with his voices during the fever, the footprints at the factory, she with her instinct.

"Somebody's snooping around here," she said. "I could feel it. That's why I didn't return with the others."

"What could they possibly want? I wondered the same thing when I was at the factory."

"Nothing good. Otherwise, how can you and I scare them off so easily, just by being here?"

"How'd they find their way here at all?"

"They were told."

"Strapper?"

"I doubt it."

"Then who?" He blurted, "The same ones who told you?" —and the fleeting look on her face made him go crimson.

"…I'll excuse that because of your age. And sense. Or lack." Then she smiled. "You have a passion about the deer and this place, don't you? …So do I. When I'm not up there, on the wind. You have the deer's eyes, you know," she continued. "Shot with gold, same as theirs. A wild streak I'll bet you didn't know you had." She turned from him, reading the skies.

Over the next several days, they'd fallen into a quirky partnership, sharing many duties. She took the lead retraining the team, while he set himself to maintaining the stable, restoring the sleigh, and numerous other repairs. Together, they visited the old factory, looking for more clues.

But in the evenings, while he dozed, a cup of hot tea at his elbow, she took to the skies, to points known only to her and her wild team—Windmere, Vaulter, Edge, and Hurricane.

His morning tea was cold now, and he drank the last of it. She stirred again. This time one lithe arm reached out, the blanket flew back, and she jumped to her feet, ramrod straight. She smoothed back her hair and looked through him to points outside.

"They're close by."

"Who?"

"Our snoopers."

"Snoopers! How do you know?"

She brushed past him to the door. "Get the Chief's team out of the stable. Then we'll go."

"Go?"

"On the sled!" she called over her shoulder. "Hurry! We need to catch them!"

His thoughts swirled before fixing on the team. He locked the cabin and dashed to the stable, leading the animals out to the field. The early morning sun sparked through the distant firs.

She was at the sled by the time he sprinted from the rise. Already her team was in place and as impatient as she was. She leapt into the sled, reached into its narrow nose, and tossed him a red helmet, a speed-stylized green reindeer leaping across each temple. "Here!" she clipped. "It fits."

"It does?"

She smiled. "Always thought I'd find you. Hurry!"

He strapped on the helmet, fitted the chinstrap, and wedged in beside her, realizing grimly that speed sleds were built for elfin speed, not half-elfin comfort. Watching what she did, he found the safety straps and strapped himself in.

"Visor!"

He found and flipped it down. The ruby glass red-tinged his world, images sharpened. "Do these helmets come with the sled?" he asked.

"Delivery helmets," she replied, making final checks.

"Delivery! Will we be—"

"Faster than delivery," she muttered, glancing skyward. "They've got quite a start. Hang on!" She snapped the reins.

They arced upward at an impossible speed. His body slammed the sled, cabin and stable shriveled, abandoned factory became a toy on a tiny stamp of land. Several hundred feet above the compound, she shrilled above the squealing wind, flicking the reins a special way. The sled halted, an improbable float high above this reckless world, the deer's hooves beating air slowly, so slowly.

The straps stretched as she stood, twisting about, eyes mirroring the bright morning sky, senses extended into the voids. She sat and flicked the reins again, and the team banked to the right and down, descending quickly but not overfast, until they bobbed above a band of trees on the compound's southern edge. "They're heading south," she said, pitching her voice above the cold wind. "Back to their base, or NPI. We need to come in low, get around them. Hold on tight."

She cried again, a different tone, and snapped the reins hard. The team responded, and the sled hurtled forward, slicing over treetops, tearing faster than delivery speed, darting and flicking past contours and upthrust firs, she handling sled and team as though one creature welded to the wind, and he merely a witnessing lump, images whipping and dissolving around him.

Another cry, and they swung hard over the trees and came to a dead hover just behind a jumble of boulders. "The Edge," she said, her voice level in the sudden quiet. "There they are."

He spied the other sled flashing among the shadows cast by the jumbled rocks. He could feel his heart pounding. How could they possibly catch them?

"Good fliers," she muttered. "Or incredibly stupid. If they don't play the wind right—" She cried softly, snapped the reins, and they shot into a dizzying ride, the sun flashing light dark light dark, boulders whizzing past, quick crosscurrents nipping at them, trying to trip them up.

He forced his eyes open, whistling rocks standing his armhairs, a single clip of stone on runner all it would take to fling them to shattering ruin. His peripheral vision blurred, and he fought to keep his head level when they cornered. He could barely see the dark blur dancing among the stones, slowly losing ground to Demon's relentless advance. They were parallel now, a hundred yards or so between them, two rockets hugging uneven ground that forced them up and down, flitting like bats in an unforgivingly tight space.

Then Demon cried again, and the team responded with still more speed.

Again his body slammed backward, recoiling from deadly forms targeting him alone. He lost the other sled, clenching his eyes, trying to return from the hysteric edge.

When they careened left, his eyes snapped open. They had cleared the rocks. The other sled had disappeared. They were riding a bit more slowly, hidden by a ridge that flanked their left.

She checked the team again, and in the silence he thought he could hear what she trained her senses on, the barest whistle of an approaching something on that cold wind. He glanced at her. Her eyes were shut, her lips moving soundlessly, until, after a few more seconds, she quietly said, "…And…Now!" She shot the team skyward, over the ridge and into the very face of the other sled, its driver forced to reel, the other team turning and tumbling toward earth, sled grounded and race over.

Demon landed her team, vaulted the sled and removed her helmet, motions smooth and deadly. Tracer followed with what grace he could muster. They approached the two elves, who still fought reins and balky team.

"So." Demon planted her feet widespread. "Nice flying."

One of the elves shoved the reins into the other's hands and took a quick step forward. "What the hell was that all about, you trying to kill us?" he exclaimed. "I should—"

"What?" Tracer asked, walking up. At least his height was imposing.

"Why are you here?" Demon asked. "Don't tell me training."

"Why should we tell you anything? Why are *you* out here?"

"I'm Tracer, and this is Demon. We're here under direct instruction from Strapper to take care of the Chief's team."

"Take care of them! What for? With the Chief gone—"

"They're animals." Demon's voice had a nasty edge. "They don't know why he's gone. You want them to starve?"

"Well, no but—"

"Maybe I should call Strapper." The second elf had quieted his team and now joined the first. He reached for his handheld. "We're within range now. See what he has to say about all this." The first elf made a restraining move.

Demon glared at the second one. "Why don't you? ...Then I will." She plucked the handheld from his grasp and punched the buttons. After a few long seconds, it crackled to life. "Strapper."

"Strapper, Demon."

"Demon! Where in—"

"I have Tracer here with me," she interrupted. "We're on the near side of the Edge. Why don't you talk to him?" Holding the mute button, she passed the device to Tracer.

"Hi, Strapper." Tracer talked as matter-of-factly as he could over the squawking protest. "We've got an interesting situation here. We chased a couple of elves on a speed sled away from the factory and the cabin, all the way to this side of the Edge." He glanced at the two elves, who shifted uncomfortably.

"Take your helmets off," Demon said very quietly. "Strapper's going to want to talk to you." They did as she asked, and suddenly, standing there with hair tousled, blinking in the sharpening light of the rising sun, they seemed very ordinary and harmless. She scowled at the first elf.

"No, we don't know why they're here," Tracer said. "We had a heck of a time catching them. You know who they are?"

The handheld was silent, only crackling every few seconds. "I have no idea why they would be up there," Strapper replied, a tone that surprised Tracer with its authority. "Get one of them."

Tracer wiggled the handheld. The second elf reluctantly reached for it. "Um—yes, Strapper," the second elf said. "This is—I'm Drafter. I was told to survey the cabin, the stables, and the area around it." The handheld remained silent. "It's a topology survey, land contours, locations of buildings, where there's water, and—and things like that." Silence still. "Uh, that's all, that's the only instructions I was given."

"Who's with you? Who's your flier?"

"Raven."

"Raven. When was he ungrounded?"

"Um." Drafter glanced at Raven, who was facing away. "I wouldn't know anything about that. I—"

"Of course you wouldn't. You could have been killed. Easily. Raven's banned from flying. He's too reckless. He kills his teams. He's lucky he's not dead already. Now. Who gave you the instructions? …Come on."

"Oiler."

"Oiler."

"Well, his area. I can't say Oiler himself. The instruction sheet had his letterhead and one of those, you know 's' things that substitute for signatures." Drafter's voice trembled a bit. Strapper's words about Raven were sinking in.

"So Oiler didn't sign it. But it had his name on it."

"Yes."

The handheld was silent again. "Do you know why you're doing this survey? What this survey is for?"

"The instructions just said do a survey."

The handheld appeared to go dead. Drafter was ready to disconnect, when Strapper's voice came on. "We have survey records here. Did he think the buildings had moved around?"

"Um—"

"Drafter. Listen to me. I don't know who the hell you are, or why somebody's decided Raven can fly again. Especially out there. On a speed sled, too. So I've made arrangements. Demon. Get on." She took the handheld. "I've dispatched a team to Near Zone, Training Point A. I want you to escort our friends to that point. We'll take them from there. I'll debrief. I'll get Saddler, and we'll three-way with Oiler. Once you hitch up with our team, I want you to fly Tracer back to the cabin and drop him off. Then, please. This time, come in. We need to talk about all this."

"Will do. Signing off." She tossed the handheld to Drafter and faced Raven. "Now I remember you. You heard it, hotdogger. Training Point A. Don't try anything. At all. This team—" she motioned toward her sled "—can chase you anywhere you decide to go. And they will, because I will. Do you get it?"

"I get it," Raven growled.

"All right. Tracer! Let's drop this baggage off."

After a tame flight to Training Point A, they met the pickup team, and the unfortunate surveyors had to content themselves with an escort back to the training compound and a likely series of uncomfortable explanations.

But as they prepared to leave, it hit Tracer. "Demon," he said. She continued working. "Demon. We're out here, now. We don't have maps or anything. How will we find our way back?"

She stopped, straightening, and for the first time, he noticed the sun trapped in the shine of her hair. She looked at him, the cool sky-blue of her eyes lightening. "I found my way there before, Tracer. Don't you think I can do it again?" She placed a small hand on his arm. "We'll go more slowly this time, I promise. And *you* have to promise something as well. Once I leave you there. Just be careful." She squeezed his arm. "Be careful. Do you understand? I—You'll be there all alone. I didn't search day and night for you to have something happen to you now. So." She withdrew her hand, and sky and wild, windy spaces seized her again. "We need to move," she said. "And quickly. Weather's changing. Get in."

7.

"It gets cold up here, doesn't it?" Ravi pulled his blue windbreaker close.

"Look at him," Roxy said. "See how he watches the children."

"I see it," he said. "He is perhaps thinking about it. The hurt is sinking in."

They stood at one end of the field in front of the Posen Vikings Consolidated High School. All around them, people swirled. Clusters of kids ran from ride to ride, ribbons of green tickets streaming from their hands. Behind the amusement area, various booths presented steaming samples of cooked potato fare.

Off to one side, large in the late morning light, he stood, black hair freshly slicked from a recent shower, big hands shoved into jean pockets, and eyes ever on the children, whose ceaseless laughter and squeals rang over the Potato Festival grounds.

"You're right. It *is* still sinking in, isn't it?"

"Yes. You see, a hurt like that is so deep, the injury is so profound, that what is felt at first is only the shock, you know. And it is only later that pain overtakes it."

She glanced at Ravi, a corner of her mouth turned upward. "Your medical training is showing," she said. "How are you feeling today?"

He sighed. "Groggy. I tried to keep up with him, but there is no way. I suppose it's because he's so much bigger. I don't think he's had more practice. After all, I did go to med school."

"How much later did you guys stay up?"

"Well, you went to bed around ten I think and we were there—until one."

"One?"

"I gave up then," Ravi said sadly. "William must have wondered, but he never said anything. He just kept bringing those beers." He winced. "That walk up the stairs afterwards, I must tell you. They added extra steps last night."

She chuckled. "Men. Or, well—" She glanced at all the people. "Yes, men. I think he came upstairs right after you. I woke up when I heard some thumping, and then his door. He must have slept pretty soundly. If he snores like that all the time, no wonder she left him."

"You could hear it?"

"You couldn't? …Oh, that's right, Ravi, you were in the same shape. I think they could hear it down at that local bar, the Boxcar? Or the next town over. I finally got to sleep by putting the pillow over my head."

"…I tried talking to him about her."

"Did you? Ravi, I can't talk to him anymore. Not without him turning it on me, or me getting—well, me getting unreasonably angry with him. How did you do?"

"I thought I could sound him out on it. Because we share—Because I've had at least something like it in my own life. So I started talking about women, and how sometimes no matter what you do, it just isn't going to work out. That was my experience, you know—not his. But it was at least a bit of common ground. He didn't seem interested. Not that it mattered. Not that much, anyway. So I decided, Hell with it, I have to go where he's going." He smiled tightly. "Sort of like driving, but this time it's conversation. So I started by saying his situation was different, but the end result was the same, and what happened?" He closed his eyes a moment, and when he opened them again he watched Santa watching the children. "Such a lonely creature," he murmured. "Such a lonely, lonely being. He's making himself lonelier by the day. First with the business, then with his wife, then…"

"…But what did he say?" she asked gently.

"Well of course he stared at his beer a while, picking up the bottle and turning it around and around. Then he said, 'You know,

Ravi, you're right. You don't know which way you're going to get slapped.' He talked about how he thought he'd been doing all right by her, she seemed to be happy. He knew the business was taking more and more out of him. But it was the only way he could survive. He talked about how he wasn't flying at Christmas because of all these year-end things to do. He was actually home when Christmas came around. He thought she'd be happy with that. Something was missing, though. She made the cocoa, had the cookies, all those things, but with him underfoot instead of coming home with the snows and the winds behind him, it was somehow all wrong. He thinks that was it, that things had slowly gone wrong, weren't fitting anymore. They didn't even argue. It was just a big surprise."

"So it hurt more."

"I don't think he even knows how much it hurts, yet. He's had the business pulled out from under him. And slowly now I think it sinks in there is nothing left except one person from work and some silly Indian kid driving him everywhere and drinking with him. Drinking a lot, lately. And a reindeer jumps in front of his car, just to remind him. He kept talking about it. 'The goddamn thing just jumped in front of us. Like I needed the reminder.' So he's here, but he's not. He's still trying to figure her out, and he's still trying to figure the business out. And he's even trying to figure out how to get back into it. He keeps talking about 'needing an idiot right now'. What does that mean?"

She smiled, watching Santa stroll to the far end of the field. "That's Dr. Id, his therapist. He calls him 'Idiot' when he's not around."

"That is another thing I find so disturbing. Why does he always say something like that about people? He's so cynical. He's always holding people at arm's length. When I think of Santa Claus, I don't think of this person. Not this way."

"Why indeed?" she murmured. "Ravi, when you spend six thousand years with the same folks, maybe that's what it is." She frowned. "No. It's recent. It all started when the business took him over. Politics, too. Media. Things that grew up around us over the past few hundred years. He holds everybody at arm's length now."

She observed the activity on the field a moment, then sighed. "Sometimes I've thought about what it would be like to be, you know, the partner in his life," she said softly. "More than I am at the moment. That's what the NPI bastards would like the world to believe," she continued bitterly. "But even when I look at who he is and all the things he's done—things that should make him *attractive* to me—I don't know. There's that wall. And there's his wife. Even if she told him it was completely over, it just wouldn't work. Not because of him. Because of me."

"How do you mean?"

"I'm not the person. Not for him. I'm not sure I know who I'm the person for. A half-elf, surely. But Ravi, when you're—when you're stared at all the time, by elves and half-elves and men, even your own gender, because of how you look, it would just be nice to be *seen*."

"*He* looks at you that way?"

"No," she said. "He never has. But he's never really *seen* me, either. Maybe it's because of the difference in our ages. I don't know. I suppose some day, when I'm least looking for it, somebody will, well, step out of the mists, swirl in on the winds and the snows, sweep me off my feet!"

"Do you know, Roxy, that is how I see it for you? Surely you know you are beautiful. But the chasers chase the surface. I did. Who knows, maybe I still would. But someone who sees beneath it all, he will be the one who 'swirls in on the winds,' as you say."

She laughed. "Until then, there's everybody else to manage."

He smiled. "Including Ravi?"

"I hope not!" They both laughed.

She shaded her eyes against the bright sun. "Uh-oh," she said, "I think he's found them."

"What, the reindeer? I see him over there. I wonder if they're from that guy, Earl."

"Who else? C'mon!"

They hurried across the field to where Santa stood. A ramshackle corral had been thrown together, temporary split-rail fencing enclosing a small space about a hundred feet on a side. In the center, a strange contraption like a large, rimless wheel spiked the earth, six short spokes radiating towards the perimeter. A thick rope drooped from each spoke, and attached to each rope but one was a reindeer. The deer plodded, antlered heads down, hooves clicking and deepening a rutted circular path. A couple of teenagers paced the animals, watching for problems. Perched atop the working backs, two children squealed with excitement, a third leaned forward, patting her animal's back, a fourth bounced mercilessly, and the last continuously flicked his reins, to no avail. The troupe passed so close to bystanders that eager children had to be restrained from reaching through the rails to touch them. A sixth deer stood in one corner, tied to the fence.

Santa stood to one side,was chatting with an older gentleman in a John Deere cap. Both of them watched the deer.

"What do you think he's thinking?" Ravi murmured.

"No idea."

"Ah, my friends," Santa boomed. "Roxy, Ravi, meet Earl. Earl owns these fine deer, and about two dozen more, is that right?"

"Yep. Couple of dozen back at the farm, plus these here."

"But no white one."

"No, no white one. Never heard of a white reindeer. Why do you ask?"

"Did you ever get that one reindeer back?" Ravi asked. "The one that jumped in front of our car."

"Yes. Sorry that happened. Truly am. Clayton got him."

"Clayton?"

Earl stared at Ravi like he was from out of town, then remembered that he was. "Most everybody knows Clayton. He's the local state trooper. When he's not on duty, he has a farm near mine. He found old Boris."

"Interesting name for a deer," Santa said. "But he wasn't white?"

"Nope. Just like these here."

"How do you come by your deer?" Santa asked.

"We have an association, the Reindeer Husbandry Group. We meet every so often. There's reindeer that are shipped down from the north, and we make arrangements and so forth."

"What's the matter with that one?" Santa gestured to the deer standing alone.

"Bob? Bob's got a hoof problem, just today. Started walking with a limp as soon as he hit the circle, so I decided to play it safe."

"I can see why he'd limp," Santa murmured. "Do you name all your reindeer?"

"Oh, you got to name the reindeer." Earl sounded genuinely surprised. "Otherwise, the children would be upset. I used to have standard names for them, Dasher, Dancer. But they said these weren't Santa's deer, I had no business calling them that. Children can get real particular. So I just give them regular names." He chuckled, a high-pitched cackle. "I usually name them after somebody they remind me of. I don't know if they'd be too happy if they found out."

"Who, the deer?"

"No, the people, of course!" Earl popped his hat off briefly, scratched his head, and put it back on. "Ride's over," he said. "Let me help my kids a minute." He jumped into the ring with the two teenagers.

"Walking in a circle," Santa muttered. "I wonder how they feel about that." He ambled toward Bob.

"Trouble," Ravi whispered, and started after him.

Roxy caught his sleeve. "Let him."

Santa stepped over the fence and laid a hand on Bob, all the while talking gently and earnestly to him. After a moment or two, the animal began to nod its head, pawing the earth and snorting. Santa knelt and ran one big hand over the affected hoof and leg.

"Hey, what are you doing over there?" Earl exclaimed, hurrying over.

Santa straightened, slowing Earl with a look. "Bob's leg is just fine, now," he said. "Walk him and see. But he doesn't want to be hitched to that circle. If you try that, he's afraid he'll just go lame again. You could walk him at that point and see that for yourself. But if you're the wise man I think you are, you'll just leave him alone."

"Who do you think you are, telling me what to do with Bob?"

"Earl," Santa said in a rich cocoa voice. "I know reindeer. I know reindeer, have known reindeer, a lot longer than you realize. And I know them far better than—well, than anyone else I know. I know you know it too. Bob will be fine."

He stepped over the fence, leaving Earl standing beside Bob. "That wasn't smart." He stumped off, with them in tow.

"Why?"

"I don't need to show off that way, Roxy," he retorted, threatening to run over people who jumped out of his way.

"So you told this old man you know something about reindeer, so what? Is that such a big deal?" He kept walking. "I don't understand why you keep stonewalling us, stonewalling me this way," she persisted. "You make a comment like this, and when we ask you what it means, you shut yourself up. Just like you're doing now!"

He stopped suddenly, and she bumped into him. "Face it," he growled, not even bothering to see who might be listening. "I'm thousands of years old under this mask. I used to mean things to people. Used to. But now I'm shoveled aside by my wife and my business. A business feeding people who see Christmas as a time to get through. A time to make fat guy jokes, red suit comments. Who cares about it, really? Who?"

Ravi looked about him. "These people do."

He wasn't listening; his eyes were on hers. "Go ahead, you old—*creature*," she hissed finally. "I'm not letting you hurt me anymore. God knows, I've tried to understand you. But if you insist upon being misunderstood, all I can say is, you'll get what you're looking for! So go ahead and claim you're the victim, go ahead and claim everything happens to you, go ahead and ignore your effect on everyone! How do you think it came to all this? Accident?" She spun on her heel and stamped off, he following and Ravi trailing helplessly.

"I know it isn't accident!" he puffed. "But how do you think it feels, *youngster*, to start with nothing at all, and to put everything in place—*everything*, only to watch it all crumble? Do you have any idea? Do you? No, you can't! So go ahead and spit at me, if you think it'll do you good. And you know what?" He spun her roughly about to face him, startling many people who gave way around them. "You know what?"

Her eyes still blazed.

"I hope it does do you good!" His voice began to lose volume, the anger draining out of it. "I hope you can—can stab and stab and stab at me with it, if it makes you feel better. If that's what it takes."

"I don't—want—to," she rasped.

"Look, you two," Ravi pleaded. "This is not doing us any good. There is a festival here. Can't we try and enjoy it?"

They stared at each other, strangers. "*You* enjoy it, Ravi," she said finally. "Take him and have fun. He needs it. I can't figure out what's right anymore." Her voice caught, but only just. "I can't. I'm going back to Ida's. I'll see you in the morning." She turned and left them standing in the field.

8.

Spinner stared at the papers massed on her desk before grabbing the top sheets, scanning, slapping them down. Turning to her PC, she sorted email, filtering, saving, responding, delegating.

After a few minutes, her fingers hovered over the keys, gaze locked somewhere behind the screen. She reached for the phone, winced, and returned to her email. When her desk clock chimed, she caught herself staring at the phone again.

She picked it up and dialed.

"Winnow."

"Hi, Winnow, it's Spinner. Do you have a couple of minutes?"

"Sure."

"Great, thanks." She cleared her throat. "This call might seem unusual, but I need to talk this over with somebody. About Halter."

"...Go on."

"Yes." A pause. "I know you and he have been—talking things over for a while. You know what he's up against, the quotas he's supposed to reach. Plus the work he's had to take on because of the casting furnace. And reinstating WonderFinish. ...So, I'm trying to have lunch with him a lot. Otherwise, he won't go. I'm watching what's happening, it's not good. You've seen him, right?"

"Yes."

"He doesn't eat. He orders stuff, and he just picks it over. I remind him, and he just glares at me. Like I'm one more person telling him what to do. What about you?"

"At lunch? The same. He just sits there. We talk about the usual stuff, and things seem to be all right. But he just pushes food around. I've learned not to talk about some stuff. Like this month's figures, or WonderFinish." She heard him take a breath. "And then this Drover thing."

"You heard."

"Who hasn't? My guys told me. Stuff gets around. And why Drover? Don't they go back a long ways?"

"I know," she said.

"What did Drover do wrong? Nothing, is what I heard."

"That's what I got from Drover. Saw him on break. I passed the coffee room the day it happened. He was alone. I could see something was wrong, so I sat with him. He didn't want to talk, but I kept trying, and he told me. He said all he did was move extra WonderFinish into the bay area, so it could be staged easier. When Halter saw it, he just blew up."

"I didn't think Halter ever did that."

"He doesn't. That's why Drover was so angry. Halter gave it to him right on the line, in front of all the guys. In all the years they've been together, that hasn't happened. Halter never criticizes somebody in front of others. Not even gently. It's a point of pride with him. He's coached me on it. For this to happen—"

"But what did he say?"

"Drover tried to tell me, but it was tough, he'd get so angry he'd stop. He said that without warning Halter started yelling at him, asking him under whose authority did he move the WonderFinish over there. Then he said even an idiot knows what a haz mat is, he expected more sense from his line super. Or words like that. And if there was any kind of accident with it, any kind at all, Drover would take the hit for being such a damn fool, handling it that way."

"Halter said all that?"

"More. He lit into Drover about production, said he was being too soft on the guys, they could produce more if they put their hearts in it. Then he grabbed one of the production sheets and asked who was putting the numbers down. When Drover said he needed to look on the sheet to be sure, Halter screamed at him. He said how could he trust somebody who knew so little about the operation he didn't know who was filling out what? How could he trust the information? How did he know they're telling the truth?"

"My God. He accused Drover of lying?"

"All but. I don't know if those were his exact words. I don't even think Drover knows for sure. It doesn't matter. He turned away when he told me, Winnow. Drover. You know him and I know him. Honest as can be. A tough union guy. Used to all kinds of shit. But nobody gets used to that, coming from somebody you trust, somebody who's tough when it matters, take you in his office and let you know what's wrong, but always be on your side publicly. That's what hurt."

"Spinner, this is amazing. Amazing. I can't believe—"

"Winnow, I had nothing to say to him. Drover. What could I say? He knew I sympathized. He knew I could hardly believe it. What could I say? Forget it? Halter was having a bad day? Things would get better? Don't worry, just get back on the line, it'll all blow over? How's he supposed to face the guys?"

The receiver was silent.

"It's the numbers, Winnow." Her voice barely topped a whisper. "The stupid, God-damned, shit numbers they're forcing on him. He doesn't understand it, you don't, nobody does. And on top of that, the audit that came through. All the paperwork that requires. Oiler was on his back nonstop!"

"But the audit might help."

"If it doesn't kill him first. Oiler on the phone with him all the time, get this report together, that one. How many elves are setting him up to fail, Winnow? Tell me that!"

"Spinner, you can't make a statement like that!"

"Why not? Who called the audit? Plus, he went to Crafter on his targets. Once, just before the audit. Crafter isn't close enough. He said lots of elves have challenges this year, and Halter's and Tinker's area have more because they're taking up slack. They're chosen because they're standouts. Management has faith they'll deliver." Her voice caught. "You know what kills folks around here, Winnow? Those words—'management has faith in you'. They mean them the best way, but what happens is they use those words on you, and you end up doing the impossible so you don't let them down.

"He'll die if he keeps this up, Winnow. We've got to figure something out. Look at him now, his color's all gone. He used to smile, his cheeks would get those deep dimples; now, Jesus, now, his face is set and his cheeks go down, and—Winnow, I haven't seen him smile in so long. He looks like he hasn't slept in weeks."

"He probably hasn't."

"He'll try to make a joke, when we're in his office. He'll say something that used to be funny, once, and he'll bring the corners of his mouth up and then down, fast. It's like watching a dog trying to remember how to do something. God, I can hardly stand it. He's dissolving, Winnow. His eyes are all hollow, every time I look at them I can see numbers. He used to be the dreamer, remember? What's he dream about now? What? Making the numbers? Yelling at his best guy?"

"Let me talk to him again," Winnow said at length. "I don't know what it'll do."

"Talk to him soon." The sweaty receiver almost slipped from her hand, and she hurried the next words. "Or Crafter. Maybe that's the wrong thing to do, you're his peer and it isn't your place to say something to the boss, but what else is there?"

"I don't know. Spinner, this whole Drover thing. Did it get to Hammer? What about Oiler, the EEC? I haven't heard anything, have you?"

"No, not yet. The whole UEU thing is getting ugly. When they started on this, this 'job enrichment' as the way to handle the furnace thing, they went right over the UEU. Those guys had to swallow hard and keep on going. Even with the new incentives. That's just promising extra feed after you work the deer to death. The line guys won't keep doing it if they see the crisis is over and there's still no letup. Then there'll be trouble. If not sooner. The lines aren't in good shape."

"I know. Neither are mine. And I've got it easier. I tell you, Spinner, if the lid blows off all this stuff and it gets to the EEC, who knows what will happen."

"Can Hammer call a strike?" she asked.

"He might. Or they could wildcat. The whole Chief thing sent them all reeling. There's a growing feeling that stuff should just be slapped together, no Chief, just produce, produce, produce. That's a hard thing for us to fight. And now with the merger, a lot of the guys are worried about their jobs."

"There's centuries on those lines!"

"I know. But the rumors are everywhere."

"And in the middle of all this, we're losing him," she murmured. "If we haven't lost him already. The dreams are gone, Winnow. The dreamer, too. Only the shell remains."

9.

Even the largest humans must feel small here. Gardner stood at the edge of the cathedral square, peering up at the tip of the south tower thrusting five hundred feet above the Rhine plain. *Köln. And the Dom. Mats can sure pick his spots.* She pulled her white windbreaker over her jeans, adjusted the blue baseball cap that nearly covered her hair. *At least most of the gray's on top.*

She glanced at her wristwatch. Early. She paced under the frowning towers, cathedral square hustle bombarding her, smelling German beer and German sausage and trying not to stare at some of the more unusually-decked young people strolling or rollerblading past. With half an hour to kill, she felt exposed under this high sky and its high towers, vulnerable in this packed place.

We can still move. Just an illusion? She caught her reflection in a shop window, adjusted the cap again. Router had managed the plane. And the special cell phone, bulky against her hip. "Use it if there's an emergency, and you need to get hold of me," he had said. "Or I'll call you. But only if I really need to."

Wasn't everything an emergency now? Spokes investigating some company he'd mentioned, a landholding venture with the three weasels all over it. She'd had her run-in with Baylor. Her own noose tightened. Crafter had reviewed the audit results and would reduce the production quotas for Doll Operations, starting next week—and that in defiance of Oiler's recommendations. She scowled. *What a nasty EEC. Oiler was furious. And Racer, well. No sense reliving that, the room crackling with heat. Battle lines are sharp these days. Too many of us are on the losing side.*

She sat on a bench and rubbed her legs. One bright spot—or was it a flame that would end up burning them? Mats had managed to get some of the more trustworthy suppliers to hold back on production. Shortages were beginning to collide with the incentives, making things pretty ugly. There'd even been a few exchanges, line elves bickering with their supers. But nothing like the Halter-Drover thing.

She checked her watch again. The second hand just dragged. *I need to get out of this noise. Maybe the Dom.* She hurried to the entrance, a small figure threading between knots of people crisscrossing the square.

Once inside, leaden silence blanketed her, centuries of accumulated faith. In the vestibule, a red-robed priest bobbed, a box inscribed "Für der Dom" hanging from his wattled neck. She fished in a pocket and dropped a coin into the box. *Oops, wrong pocket. Wonder what they'll think of a Santean?*

People strolled in groups of two and three through the cavernous, dimly-lit interior, their voices reduced to whispers capering across the stony spaces. Such statuary, so much gold, such detail in the tiled floors, carvings, treasures, stone! *I should come back when I can appreciate this.* She wandered through the emptiness, her thoughts ranging over the press of business, the crises that threatened to destroy them, the long span of years engaged in the only work she knew.

A hand touched her shoulder, and she almost cried out. "Sorry, so sorry," Mats whispered. "I thought I might find you here. I see we are both early."

She almost laughed out loud. "Let me catch my breath. Why did you think I'd be here?"

"Because this place draws everyone to it," he said. "You had a good flight?"

"Yes. You?"

"Yes. And I think no one knows we are here?"

"Router made sure. At least for me."

"Good. Now. Why don't we go on a little cruise up the river?"

"A cruise?"

"Yes. They have these little cruises they run, up and down the Rhine there. It would be better if we go there and—discuss things."

"All right." She followed him from the Dom, along its length and past the Roman Museum toward the river. They boarded one of the Abendfahren cruises and settled into chairs on the deck, their small table soon laden with glasses of light wine and a plate of cold fish, cheese, and small biscuits.

"So." He raised his glass. "I toast someone on the good side."

She smiled and raised hers.

"You are tired," he said. "It must be hard."

"It is."

"Are you still fighting?"

"I'm still breathing." She smiled grimly.

"That is good." He studied the river, evening shadows overtaking the Altstadt waterfront, the narrow buildings lighting up over the waves' gentle ripple. "We have been busy as well. We sent you some information, mostly in code, which I hope you could understand."

"Yes." She followed a smaller boat. "It gets worse, doesn't it?"

"Much worse. You must have picked on that."

"Picked up on it, yes. How's Kelli?"

"Recovering."

What?

"She is all right. The chance for physical danger, so far as we know, is over. That is, if they were going to try anything stupid. She is with a family in north Sweden, good friends of mine, two old half-elves and their adopted children. I don't think she knows about Gøran and Jenna, and of course the children will not say anything. Bill has seen her a couple of times. It was the emotional side that was so difficult, Gardner."

She nodded slowly. "Yes. The times don't let us grow leaders anymore, do they? We shove who we have into the fire, sprinkle some instant leadership powder on them and hope. It's certainly been that way with Kelli."

"As though you had freedom of the choosing. She has done very well. We are looking after her. The information she started collecting, the groundwork she laid with her work on the herds, well we are continuing all that, you know. And the picture is rapidly getting worse, Gardner. With our old friend out of the way, they have become much bolder. They are not as worried about reactions, you see."

He leaned forward. "Gardner, they smell the money. They smell the money in all this, and they follow their noses, not their eyes. They figure they can sell the whole action to any investor because of the money it brings them. And their noses will take them to places where they eat the business away from the inside, because they will say they are reinventing themselves. They will use business models from other organizations that seem to be successful, and these business models are only a few months old, but our friends think the models are mature and true. Because our friends don't know what they are supposed to do." He leaned back again.

"I understand." She frowned. "Greed and sprinting to the next quarter and the next analyst rating. Mats, we have to act. How much more traffic is there?"

"They are getting all the RFS from around the world. They are doing it quickly. Twenty thousand already have been processed. There is no better word for it, I'm afraid."

"Twenty thousand! That's more than five percent of the fliers! Or the ones that should be flying."

"Yes," Mats said sadly. "And processed means finished with. There are ten thousand more in transit. They are leaving the calves behind, because they don't know what to do with them, yet. But soon I fear those calves will be processed, too. If I were an orphan, I'd refuse to fly."

"My God." *The separations!*

"They will claim that calf meat is more tender, and—"

"Mats, stop it!"

"I am truly sorry, Gardner, but this is what we have been living with, you see. Bill has made contact with—I don't remember what you call them, a mold?"

"A mole. Go on."

"A mole, then. This mole has bravely leaked information to Bill, and Bill has prepared a report for you. It is here." He pulled a diskette from his shirt pocket and placed it on the table. "There are also images in there, the pictures that Bill and Kelli took at the processing plant."

Her mouth twisted. "The slaughterhouse, you mean." She slipped the diskette into her jacket pocket.

“Yes. I think we use the other term because, well don’t you know it is just very painful to say what you said.”

“We’ll use it when we go public,” she growled. “Now tell me about their visit. Tell me everything.”

Mats sighed. “It is not pretty. You should try to eat something, too.”

She picked up a wedge of cheese and bit into it, chewing rapidly. “Continue.”

“You will take more,” he said gently, “and some fish and wine, too. And we will sit for a moment. You will not stay strong, otherwise.”

She protested, but he remained shyly stubborn about it. She discovered her hunger in the midst of eating, and he joined her. Even afterwards, he insisted on waiting, deflecting her impatience. At length, he said, “Now we can begin.”

He leaned toward her. “It has been a few weeks since their visit. This is what they found. The plant is in Norbotten, north Sweden, just south of our old Sami friends. The roads are few. The area is remote. They fly the herds to Gothenburg, Malmö, and Stockholm, and they truck them from there. They hold the herds in the high valleys just west of the plant. The day’s allocation is driven down into pens that they keep on that west side. That part the mole told Bill. Bill and Kelli traveled overland and got into the plant using side entrance, avoiding all the security at the main gate. Inside, they saw many processing operations. Kelli saw where the carcasses are inspected, then where they are chopped into the various cuts of meat, and the other parts are sent away for the pet food processing.” He reached into his big jacket pocket. “I have some pictures of what they do there. It is not pretty, I’m afraid.”

He handed her several photographs, but at the last moment withheld a few. “As you can see here, the operations are quite clean and effective.”

She winced. “Where are they selling the—product?”

“Part of it is sold through Jokkmokk. The rest is being trucked elsewhere. We don’t yet know where they are going. But some even goes to NPI.”

She turned picture after picture over in her hand, staring at the images, transporting herself there. "How did they ever take all of these?"

"It was not easy," Mats said. "They were in danger of being found out, of course. But it was also so hard for them to see it and do nothing. Kelli especially. She had a bad experience there. It got to be too much for her, and—well. She stumbled outside the plant and finally took these, which were the last things she saw before Bill carried her out of there."

He hesitated a moment, then gave her the last few photographs. Her eyes widened as she took in pictures of frontloaders loading tiny heads and antlers into the waiting dumpsters. "So that's how they want it to end." She turned the photographs over. "It's a good thing the pictures are too small to see the eyes."

"Yes. But she did, unfortunately. And so did he. Can you imagine it, Gardner?" Mats's voice sank to a hoarse whisper. "That youngster was all alone in there, seeing things you and I would never imagine an elf would see. And yet, there are other elves doing the work there. Such things are unbelievable." He leaned back and passed a hand through his hair. Then he smiled slightly. "She is pulling through this, though. Her new family will help her there. And Bill has been to see her. At least twice."

She glanced at him. "Professional interest?"

The smile grew. "That, too."

She allowed herself a small smile. "I see. If it should get serious?"

"I don't think we have to worry about that. It is a pretty long shoot."

"Perhaps. But if it should, she'll need counseling. You know what it's like—seeing somebody you love grow old and pass away in front of you."

He nodded, and she knew he remembered his own mother's struggle.

She looked out over the deepening shadows on the water.

"So, my friend, where do we go from here?" he asked at last. "We have critical evidence, and only a little time. I can talk to the news people."

If only I could pull the answers out of the waves. "It's not yours alone to do, Mats. Even if you have more freedom. They'll just dismiss what you say and shut you out of the business. We have to do it together. But there's more we need to pull together. We have to shape it very carefully, so the shareholders will get the whole story. Even then, it'll depend on whether they look up from their portfolios long enough. It is, as you say, a pretty long shoot."

She felt him watching her. Then he turned and sighed, watching the waters. "All too true, I am afraid."

Her hip vibrated. *Dear God.* She reached around and unhooked her cell. "Mats." Her voice trembled. "This isn't good." She put the phone to her ear. "Yes?" She kept her eyes on Mats as she received the information, Mats, whose honest and deep-lined face held her firm as she got the news, asking an occasional single-word question, Mats who she knew could see that in this single phone call everything was changing.

She flipped down the phone and reclipped it, her face set in hard, decisive lines. "Mats, we have to get back. Immediately. You must come with me. There's been a terrible, terrible accident."

10.

"How long do you think this fine little bar has been here, Ravi?" Santa asked. "Couple of hundred years?"

"Not so long as that."

Singly and in twos and threes, the Boxcar Bar regulars banged open the squeaky front door, clumping across the old floor under dimmed lights. A velour hanging of a whitetail buck springing from a gold and white winter forest dominated one wall. Another wall displayed all kinds of things—sepia prints of the Bar over the years, photos from recent Potato Festivals, somebody's best ice fishing day, a yellowed *Detroit Free Press* story on the Festival, a Michigan State University green-and-white Spartan beanie, some framed papers that probably legalized the place, and a pair of velvet stag paintings that challenged each other across all the stuff in the middle. The regulars, men in their fifties with a couple of rookies thrown in, took their seats at the dark, lacquered bar or at various tables guarded by all those deer. They left Santa and Ravi alone under a blinking red Bud sign near the front window.

Bits of conversation poked the silence.

"Pretty good Festival this year."

"Yeah. The weather held off, so the parade was a big hit."

"Think anybody figured out the Queen?"

"Naw. Nobody got close enough to the float to be sure."

"Some of the guys in the crowd stared at her pretty good."

"Yeah. Wouldn't they be surprised if they only knew?" General chuckles.

"How did Ronnie get to be Potato Queen? Whose idea was that?"

"Poteet's. Sort of. There was a big fight between the moms of the two finalists, Jennifer and Serena. One of them accused the other of manipulating the vote, and the other one trashing the first one's name in town. It got pretty ugly, I heard."

"I heard that, too. That's when I heard Poteet decided neither one of them should compete. That went over real big." More laughter.

"Makes you wonder whether Poteet will run it next year. He isn't even Polish, and that hasn't set square with a lot of people."

"He's part Polish. On his mother's side."

"Part ain't enough for some. You know how it is. Anyway, once Poteet kicked the girls out, nobody wanted to step forward. So Ronnie did it."

"Boy, somebody could accuse them of taking advantage of a slow youngster."

"Youngster! He's twenty-eight."

"Yeah, but what do they fix him at? Six or seven? Sweet guy, but there just ain't much up there. He can't use sharp stuff, he'll hurt himself, sure. He can't drive. He's the elf at Christmas for Santa, and the little helper for the Easter Bunny, and then he does odd jobs at the ACE for Bob, and that's about it."

"Makes a good Queen, though. Smiling and waving and all."

"Well, I think it's a shame they did it. Should have left it with no Queen at all. That would have made a statement."

"I think they were thinking of the younger kids, the ones who worked so hard on the Queen's float."

"Hm. Maybe."

The conversation faded, mixing with the undefined hum of the place.

"I wonder if this is all there is to do here." Santa hefted a beer bottle and peered at the label. "Sit around drinking and talking about the Festival coming up or the Festival going down. ...This potato beer is pretty strange stuff. And the name: "Posen Poison." Wonder who thought that up?" He took another long pull on the bottle.

"You should go more slowly," Ravi cautioned. "You don't know how strong that stuff is."

"Skip the lecture," he grumbled. "What do you think her problem was today?"

Ravi hesitated. "It has been very difficult for her, too. Surely you must see that."

"Of course I do!" he snapped. "She's been terrific! I don't know what I would have done without her. But lately, she's so angry all the time."

"She has two people to take care of," Ravi said finally. "You as well as her. There is no one to take care of her."

"Hmm. Maybe," he muttered. He signaled the lone waitress, a harried woman who kept her short blond hair in an easy-care style and whose blue eyes told anyone who thought he had ideas to just watch it. She nodded slightly and hustled toward the bar.

Ravi took a breath and plunged ahead. "Besides, it is very difficult to watch someone you—someone you care for go up and down. The way you have. I know that feeling, because it happened to me, too. You want to help. You want to help the other person feel better. But you get nowhere. Or you think you get somewhere, and you don't. It can be so frustrating."

"I can imagine." His eyes strayed.

"No you cannot!" Ravi said sharply. "You cannot, because you haven't done it!"

"Listen, little man, you've known me for a few weeks. A few weeks only." He leaned close. "You alone in this place know who I am. So you alone know how long I've been on this earth. So you alone here should realize that you *don't* know me well enough to say I haven't done it."

Ravi bit his lip. "But you haven't. It would show if you had."

Santa sighed, leaning away as the waitress wordlessly thunked down the Poisons. "Maybe *you* should take care of her, wise little man."

Ravi shook his head. "There you go pushing away again. Solving the problem by—"

But Santa was staring at the range of backsides arrayed at the bar. "I don't believe—It's not possible," he murmured.

"What now?"

"It—*is*," Santa said quietly, standing now. "Down at the end of the bar, by himself, on the left there. It's—by God, it's the rabbit!"

"What? What rabbit?" Ravi swiveled and took a good look at the backside of the one Santa had pointed out, and every other backside as well, just in case he was missing something. "'Scoose me, Santa," he hissed, "but that is not a rabbit, that is a man. There are nothing but men in here, excepting the waitress. You cannot be seeing a rabbit, and that is all."

Santa kept nodding. "Oh, it's the rabbit. What the hell is he doing here?" He flagged the waitress. "Could you do me a favor and tell that man—" pointing "—that I'd like to talk to him? Thanks."

Moments later, she tapped the shoulder of a man wearing a dark red windbreaker and a small captain's cap. The man turned slowly. His eyes met Santa's, and he smiled. Ravi's eyes bugged.

The windbreakered man stepped lightly through the crowded bar until he stood, beer in hand, staring silently at Santa.

"Rabbit!" Santa exclaimed at last. "Let me shake your—well, your hand! What the hell are you doing here?"

"Don't use that name!" the rabbit hissed. "I don't use yours. It's Mr. Hopper."

"Hopper!" Santa roared with laughter, causing several heads to turn. They sat down. "Who the hell thought that up?"

"Will you keep your voice down?" The rabbit hunched toward them. "The stupid Board, who else? Or one of their damn consultants. Probably the same one that named you after a pickle company. He's laughing somewhere, collecting his hundred grand."

"If only a hundred," Santa nodded. "Don't tell me. You've been kicked out?"

"Sure have. I know all about you. It was all over the news. So we finally have something in common." The rabbit glanced at Ravi, who had finally closed his mouth. "Who's this guy?"

"This is Ravi. He's traveling with me. He was going to be one of the santas." Ravi and the rabbit shook hands, and Ravi peered at his before curling it around his beer again. "That's before I discovered diversity trouble and shut things down. Back when I was making decisions like that, instead of what beer to drink. Roxy's traveling with me, too."

"Roxy! What's your wife say about it?"

"She left me, rabbit. I thought you knew that."

"*Left* you? Whoo! That makes it even better. You and—"

"Rabbit, no."

"But—"

"*No*. N-O. Geez, does everybody think that's what's going on?"

"Well, look at her! Just look at her! I know I have! You know, if you're not interested—"

"Rabbit, don't even go there! That's what gets you in trouble in the first place!"

"But you have to admit…"

Ravi tried. "How did you end up in the same town as Mr. Claussen, here?"

"Relatives."

"You got relatives here, too?" Santa exclaimed. "Is nowhere safe? You got relatives everywhere!"

"I know." The rabbit sighed. "Years ago. A former Potato Queen. And before that, one of the Klompen dancers in Holland. And there was a coed at Ball State, because I just couldn't resist the name. And—"

"I don't want to hear about all this!" Santa waved a big hand. "You know, they have *regular* rabbits for that kind of thing! Don't ever make that part of your training requirements. They'd be falling all over each other to be recruited! Lowering the gene pool, too." He drained his beer and signaled the waitress again. "Hopper, they're merging us."

"I know. I fought like hell. It's probably what got me kicked out."

"No offense, but I didn't like you very much. It was business, not personal. I think it was all that candy. Thought you had it in with the dentists. Or the tooth fairy."

"Tooth fairy!" The rabbit snorted. "There's a stupid operation. Hasn't made a profit in centuries. Not even a good takeover target." He took a long drink as well. "I felt the same way about you. Any and every toy, game, you name it was going into that sack of yours.

Greedy little toymaker, that's what I thought. That's why I fought it. Our cultures were so different."

"That's how I felt, too. I couldn't see taking over your operation and making you into an extension of NPI."

"You think that's what would have happened?"

"Well, face facts. We're bigger. It's likely, over time, that it would."

"Or there'd be a blend."

"Either way," Santa said. "But I didn't want it to happen. I used to tell my folks I hated you. But that's not it, not really. It's—well, I just knew it wouldn't work. And it isn't because I thought you don't know how to run your business. You do. Or did. But yours is a different business. More than that, it's a different, a different—*brand.*"

"I'll go with that." The rabbit gulped again, watching Santa out of the corner of one eye. He thumped the bottle down, then leaned forward. "Do you ever find you hate them?" he asked softly.

"Who, humans?"

"Who else?" He belched softly. "Think about it. Somehow, over all this time, our existence got all tangled up with theirs. At first it was easy. Remember? A few families here and there, all within a day's distance. Then word got around. And it just mushroomed after that. Production demands, schedules, inventories, raw goods, exploding workforce, PR, on and on. First it was all expansion, then it was sheer keeping up. And now, sheesh! You don't have a minute to yourself. It gets easy to hate them. Running into department stores and scarfing up Easter baskets, and now there's the Internet, my God! Where will it stop?"

"Good question. Look at all the junk I have to put up with at Christmas. I just saw a load of that crap down at Bronner's. Santas everywhere, some of 'em not even trained in our program, plus all kinds of figurines, cards, weird ornaments, you name it!"

"And if your operation's like mine, you don't make half the crap that's out there! I was in a store this year." The rabbit lowered his voice. "One of these big American department stores, has one of everything. You should have seen all the Easter garbage. They got bunnies in every color and size you can imagine. When's the last time you saw a purple rabbit, huh? Or a green one? Not to mention the baby chicks, and the chocolate this and that, plus those little green peanuts that nobody on the planet eats! And my God, the commercial where the rabbit lays the egg! You brave enough to eat what comes out the back end of a rabbit? Huh?"

Ravi giggled into his beer. "I'd be a coward, to be sure."

"Stupid egg hunts, too," the rabbit continued. "Plus I gotta screen for health in my department store program. *You* just have to look for fat guys who can wear red suits! My guys have to put this bigass outfit on and sweat to death in it!"

"Hadn't thought of that," Santa said.

"Don't have any reindeer, any flying anything. Run my fool ass off all over town, delivering these stupid baskets. Could never get the numbers you did, all the rah-rah programs you have." He took another long drink. "So yeah, I hate 'em."

"I don't know." Santa took a swig himself. "I can see why in your case. But for me, 'hate' is too strong. If I really hated them all, I wouldn't miss it so much."

"Yeah, maybe you're right," the rabbit said at last. "Maybe despite all of it I love running all over the place. But what do you miss?"

"All of it. As crazy as it sounds. And there are days, yes. Days when you want to pitch it all over the fence, let somebody else handle it. Especially when you're out on a storm somewhere, wondering if the team can find their way, the sleigh will stay in one piece. And why? For more and more people who'll open their presents in five minutes flat? We weren't given a choice about doing it, though, we just do it. But when they kick you out, you don't have a choice, either. You'd give anything to get back in. Go figure. I should hate them now, I really should."

"But you don't."

He took a smaller sip. "No. There's no hate. Not even now. We're tied to them, rabbit. As contrary and aggravating as they can be. We don't have a choice. It's the children. It's not their fault, whatever the adults are up to. Kids have no defenses. When a kid looks at you, rabbit, well, you know. Right there, you know what you have to do. Children.

"And in the middle of everything, when it's taken away by a, well some adults on a Board somewhere, we spend all our time thinking about how to turn it around."

The rabbit picked at his Poison label. "You're right. You know what else? You could have taken me over easily. I thought you wanted to. Now I see it was just another line from that dumb Board of mine. I should have called you directly. We could have sorted the whole mess out, and I might have stayed where I was."

"Might have. But look what happened to me, rabbit. It wasn't just the merger, it was all kinds of things. Guys like you and me are liabilities. Our familiarity is a curse. They have this need, this obligation, to move the brands away from anything to do with tradition. New business is all about reinvention, replacing new with new. You and me, we're dinosaurs."

"But we *have* changed. Plenty," the rabbit protested. "You more than me, I think. We've gone into factories, gone online, diversified, gone global. Name it. What more do they want?"

"They don't know. And the funny thing is, rabbit, it used to be 'we'. Remember? 'We' called the shots. 'They' didn't. Now it's something worse—the 'them' isn't even the Board, it's investment banks, arbitrageurs, people who pile money on money and make money off speculation. Nothing matters except billionaire deals everywhere! We'll probably be part of a leveraged buyout one of these days. Sheesh." Santa flagged the waitress again. "Anyway, not much of this is interesting to my good man Ravi, here. Ravi has the good fortune, or misfortune, of driving Roxy and me all over this state. Then some blasted reindeer jumped in front of our car and ran it into a potato truck. You should have seen the car, rabbit. A red and green beauty. About thirty years old, I think. Doors falling off, the whole bit. What did you call it, Ravi?" Santa clumsily imitated Ravi's Indian accent. 'A real piece of crap'. I traded a Jag for it down in Detroit."

"You traded a—" the rabbit lowered his voice. "You traded a Jag for some piece of crap car that your friend here wrecked?"

"It wasn't my fault!" Ravi said. "The reindeer jumped right in front of the car."

The waitress returned with three more Poisons. "This should be more than enough, my good woman," Santa declared, pressing a twenty into her hand. "Bring us another round in a few minutes, if you would." After the waitress left, shaking her head, he continued, "A Goddamn white one, too, I say, though nobody will believe me. Not even Earl, who keeps them on a farm I'm going to visit one day. Soon. I got the car because I—well, I don't remember all the details, but I got it for a good reason. And now it's wrecked for good. So we decided, so I decided, to see the Festival, fun things like potato races and some transvestite Potato Queen."

"Where are you staying?" the rabbit asked. "You're not staying at Ida's, are you?"

"Yes, we are," Ravi said. "What's wrong with Ida's?"

"Nothing, really. It's just that you could stay in one of the bigger towns. Where the accommodations might be better. Which way are you heading?"

"We're taking the old Bridge route," Santa said. "One of our guys down at Bronner's thinks it's still open."

The rabbit shook his head. "I'm not so sure. They busted up a lot of things when they put in the Interstate."

Ravi scowled. "All this talk about bridges and old routes and things," he grumbled. "I suppose I will have to drive you to the North Pole, too!"

Santa belched softly. "Ravi, you're too God-damned serious right now. And you're falling behind. Finish the one you have there, so you can keep pace. …There, that's better! …Now, rabbit, we never had a chance to talk business like we should have, like you said. So let's start."

For the next couple of hours the rabbit and Santa all but ignored Ravi. He got up several times to pee, mainly to give himself something to do. The place seemed to draw in on itself, lights brightening and sounds picking up. No one was in a hurry to leave, now that the Festival was over.

Loud thumping, and the front door banged.

"Hey, it's Santa! C'mon in! Hey, Santa!" several of the men shouted.

"Oh, no," Santa groaned. "Not this fat jackass again."

Ravi looked up, bleary-eyed, from the Poison label he was studying, having tried repeatedly to count the eyes in the potato drawing. Stan filled the doorway, looking like he'd spent time in another Boxcar, even though this Boxcar was the only bar in town. He swayed a moment like an oak in a strong breeze, his stained unsnapped windbreaker revealing a belly peekabooing from a straining flannel shirt. Behind him teetered a weird dark-haired sapling. "Been sampling some of Tommy's special brew," he sloshed. "Need to compare it to this year's Poison. Right, Tommy?"

The sapling nodded.

Stan's gaze bobbled around the bar until it settled on the empty chairs at Santa's table. "Hey, it's my friends! Sammy and Hopper!" He bumped toward them like a barge in a narrow canal.

"Oh, geez," Santa groaned, head down. "You know him, too?"

"Doesn't everybody?" The rabbit managed a wan smile, then struggled to his feet, the chair scraping behind him. Santa and Ravi awkwardly followed suit.

The five of them stood there blinking at each other for a few seconds before Santa said, "Aw, what the hell, why don't we all siddown? I'll buy this round. Hey, my good lady!" he boomed at the waitress, "How 'bout a double round of Posen—Posen—Poison for all of us?"

The waitress leaned toward bartender before heading toward the beer chest.

The group crashed into their seats.

"So, Stanley," Santa said, "How are you tonight? You seem to have been having fun doing—whatever."

"It was a great Festival," Stan rumbled. "Lossa great recipes."

"Yes, you seem to be wearing most've 'm on your shirt," Ravi mumbled.

Stan flagged the waitress and ordered a double plate of kielbasa and pierogies. "So, did you enjoy yourselves?" he boomed. "You appear to be enjoying yourselves now."

"It was pretty good," the rabbit said. "But I've been to them before, so I can compare them."

"How 'bout our friend Sammy here? See any more reindeer?"

"Only the ones 'at Earl has." Santa picked up his bottle and thumped it down. "Why's he wanna go chaining up perfeckly good reindeer for? Having kids ride 'em and all. Can't he see how sad they are? They should—they should be flying."

Ravi sat up in alarm before he forgot why and reslumped.

"Whaddaya mean, flying?" Stan said slowly.

"You know, Santa," Tommy piped up. "Jus' like you're supposed to."

"Oh. Oh, yeah."

"Yeah." Santa leaned forward. "Surely the Sanna Claus of this town would know he's 'posed to fly the damn things." He tipped the bottle, and some of the potato beer ran down his chin. "'Sides, he ain't the real Sanna, I am," he mumbled.

"Whaddaya mean, you're Sanna?" Stan tried to lean forward but couldn't.

"What I said, I think," Santa said, sounding surprised. "Or what I think I said. Whadid I say?"

"Misser Claussen means," the rabbit said, "that he's played Santa before, in other places, so he's an expert at what it means to be Santa. Right, Misser Claussen?"

"Right. Right? No, I'm th' real Sanna—*Santa* Claus." Santa squinted at him. "And yer a rabbit, remember?"

"Wha th' hell is this, 'Harvey'?" Stan rumbled. He thwabbed at his chest with a fat hand, and bits of potato pancake broke free and tumbled like rocks peeling off a cliff-face. "*I'mmmm* th' Sanna 'roun here. Have been for years. An' I'm noddabout to give it up to summ-summ-summ…"

The waitress slammed a large steaming plate in front of Stan. Bar conversation quieted briefly. She glared at them all. Stan struggled to find his butt before saying, "Jes' put it on my tab, dear, 'n' I'll get it in th' mornin'."

"OK, OK, forget I said it," Santa grumbled. "Les' talk about sumpin' else. Ravi? Ravi! You're always good for a story right about now! Tell us sumpin' 'bout Krishna. Or sumpin' 'bout—sumpin' 'bout—I dunno, *you* figger it out!"

But Ravi had given up at last and snored quietly in place.

Santa swiveled back and focused on Stan, who was forklifting a load of kielbasa and kraut into his face. "My God, it's Groomer," he murmured.

"Whad're you rabblid od aboud?" Stan thrashed.

Tommy got up and lurched unsteadily toward the men's room.

"Evil lil shidduvan elf that works for me," Santa groused. He thumped a fist on the table so hard that glasses rattled and men throughout the bar looked up, though Ravi snored on. "An' I'm not about to sit here in a town with a trans—trans—with a guy playin' a Queen, watchin' some fake Sanna shovel food in his face, no more!"

"Hey, don't talk about Ronnie that way!" someone yelled.

Stan rocked back and forth in an angry attempt to stand. "You callin' me a fake?"

Santa proceeded to tell Stan where he could put his kielbasa, a prospect appalling to everyone in the place, sober or not. "…if you c'n *find* it," he finished, before Stan threw the plate of food in his face.

The waitress and bartender had witnessed this kind of thing plenty of times before. They just cleared the furniture, and they and Posen's finest let the big guys go at it for a while, Mr. Hopper weaving unsteadily among them, unable to do much to stop it, and the quiet Indian kid safely asleep in the corner. Stan couldn't get his arms too far clear of his fat body even when sober, and Santa could only aim well enough to land a few open-handed swings that impacted like a tennis racket hitting a bedsheet. They slapped and swung at each other for a while, until the bartender signaled a few of the regulars who enjoyed getting a free beer this way, and they all waded in and unceremoniously tossed Santa, Stan and Hopper through the front door and into the dust of the parking lane in front of the bar. They left Ravi snoring harmlessly.

Outside, flopping in the dust, Stan turned his head to see where his tormentor lay. He gaped, and a little drool slid from his slack mouth down a fat fold toward his neck. He watched his enemy try to get to his feet, helped by Mr. Hopper. In the process of helping, the captain's hat had come off. Mr. Hopper seemed to have grown a large set of furry white ears. Then he was all fur, appearing to change into something not possible, not even in Posen. Stan blinked, but the white-furred creature continued to help a flailing Mr. Claussen struggle to his feet and lurch away into the shadows.

"It *is* 'Harvey'," Stan mumbled. "I'm inna Goddam movie. I'm not drinkin' that stuff never again. Not if this happens. I'm inna movie. A Goddam movie." He rolled onto his back and began snoring.

11.

He'd pushed her away again, and she'd stalked to the factory floor. He simply wanted to be left alone. Was that so hard to understand? But it wasn't Spinner. It was the voices, the numbers that tormented him, relentless, demanding of him a performance he knew he couldn't match. Where would it end?

On his desk lay the latest order, an indefinite extension of accelerated production, this time to recover from unspecified "anomalies" arising partly from the casting furnace repair but now ominously tied to more subtle performance indicators. This was a carte-blanche approval to continue the ridiculous pace until elf and machine fell apart. And he could do nothing. All because he'd tried to stand up to them.

He lifted the order gently, then crumpled it into a tight ball. He squeezed the ball until the ache in his fingers forced him to loosen them. His fingernails left red crescents in his palm. He threw the order on the floor. He stepped on it, once, twice, breathing heavily. Then he picked it up and with careful and deliberate motions he smoothed it and stared at it some more.

He sat down and started his word-processing program. While it churned to life, he switched to email, staring at dozens of new messages he'd received over the last several hours. He began to delete them, regardless of topic or importance. He deleted message after message, until the word processor finished loading.

He switched to it, typed the date in the right-hand corner of the screen, then typed Crafter's name on the left. He hesitated, then cc'd

Oiler. He typed the one-word subject and began, "For reasons that will become clear below, I can no longer… "

He stood up and circled the machine. He gazed dully at his bookshelf, took a deep breath and sat down again. This time the words flowed out, his fingers first tapping, then pounding the keys. He would indict them all and dismiss them. Paragraph after paragraph assembled themselves on the white page, and he paused only occasionally to save his work. He quoted statistics, events, statements, anecdotes, industry facts, studies, comparisons to other companies, comparisons to other lines within NPI, personal observations, meeting minutes, on and on and on and on, the paragraphs building with a cold logic that outdid even Silvertongue's icy skill, the words leaping and flashing across the screen, with scarcely a backspace or correction of thought or fact.

When he was finished, he saved and printed his work, and when he had proofed it he seemed to forget about it as though it were a dead thing. He placed it on the keyboard and stood again, observing the piles on his desk. He glanced at the dead thing again, and then, attracted by a small glaring beam, he looked up and spied the picture, his favorite picture, he and Drover standing, the doll line elves behind them. He was presenting Drover with an award for top-quality production, and Drover was beaming, the two of them so happy. Tears started in his eyes, and he angrily brushed them aside, shaking his head and stamping his foot. He bowed his head, and when he looked up again the picture too had become a dead thing.

He returned to his desk and picked up a sheaf of papers, prioritized into A, B, and C piles. He didn't know which pile he had lifted. Clutching the pile, he reached under his desk and yanked out his personal shredder. He began to shred. He shredded the stuff in his hand first. He reached for more papers and shredded them too. He was only marginally aware that what was going into the shredder's mouth were reports, instructions, memos, letters, minutes, threats, production counts, statistics, numbers, numbers, numbers.

When the shredder was full it made a choking sound. He reached into a drawer and pulled out a new plastic bag. He unhooked the shredder top and set it aside. Paper entrails jammed the underside, and he sliced the back of his right hand pulling them free. He stuffed them into the full bag, bright red drops mingling with the shreds. He tied off the bag and tossed it aside. He shook open the new bag, blood droplets flying, shoved it into the shredder container, snapped the top back on and grabbed another sheaf of paper.

He was still shredding when the alarm went off.

12.

Router sat at his desk, sipping coffee. Through the glass windows of his second-floor office, he could see a couple of truckloads of supplies hit the enclosed dock. He'd lobbied long and hard for what elves like Racer had felt was unreasonable comfort, funding the brightly-lit, hangar-like structure, but it had been a Godsend when weather was bad and shipments still had to move. He liked to think his innovations made a difference, but he was enough of a pragmatist to give credit to the elves who worked the area and who were constantly making improvements.

Several of them were busy unloading those two trucks. Router could see them milling about the trucks with more than the usual activity, first checking the schedule, then examining the trucks. One of them was making a face.

He stood. This was getting interesting. He could see the dock supervisor trot over to inspect the shipments, snatch the receiving schedule, and head toward the service telephone on the pole by the dock.

Router picked up on the first ring. "I saw. What is it?"

"Hard to say, except that it—well, it stinks pretty bad," the supervisor squawked. "You know, if I didn't know any better, I'd say it smells like—"

"Yes?"

"Well, it smells like reindeer crap."

"You're kidding." Router tried not to chuckle. "Reindeer crap?"

"Reindeer crap, boss. Don't ask me why."

"Who's the shipment for?" Router watched an elf bring the supervisor a paper.

"We didn't find any—Oh, wait. Here it is." A pause. Router could see the supervisor scanning the paper, turning it over as though to find answers on the back. "It's for Silvertongue, from somebody named Fernandez, of the Argentine government."

"The Argentines?" This was getting good. "What else does it say?"

"Hang on. Oh, here it is. It says, 'Mr. Jorge Fernandez, on behalf of and with the agreement of the Government of the Republic of Argentina, respectfully ships to Mr. Silvertongue of North Pole Industries forty-eight thousand pounds, or twenty-four tonnes, of premier Argentine reindeer manure, fresh from Rancho NPI outside of Gobernador Mayer. Based upon prior conversations, which, though interesting, have not yielded specific recommendations, Mr. Fernandez is offering to Mr. Silvertongue free of charge, and with all shipments prepaid, these excellent manures, knowing that Mr. Silvertongue's wide experience will allow him to find a ready use for them.'" He dropped the paper to his side. "What the hell does all that mean, boss?"

By this time, Router was laughing outright. "It means," he said when he could catch his breath, "that one of Silvertongue's negotiations has hit a rather fragrant impasse. 'These excellent manures!' I love it!" He laughed again. "All you need to do, sir, is get 'Meester Seelvertongue' on the phone and advise him to take immediate action to dispose of 'these excellent manures!'"

"Will do!"

Router hung up and watched the supervisor place the call. He could just imagine Silvertongue's reaction.

He strolled to the coffeemaker and stretched out one hand. But before he touched the cup, a loud buzz echoed across the docks. He hurried to the window and checked the Andon display suspended above the trucks. One of the panels flashed yellow, a general and rather serious alarm. He squinted. Doll Operations, Halter's area. He bit his lip. General alarms were rare. Something must be up. Gardner.

His hand hovered over the phone. Not yet. Best to call Halter or Spinner, find out what was going on. He picked up the receiver.

The ground shook. Seconds later, a low rumble forced him to steady himself against the desk. The startled dock elves latched to whatever they could find. The Andon board went red, and an all-hands alarm whooped.

Work ceased on the dock. Router tried Halter's number, then Spinner's, and then the ops floor. There was no answer on the first two, and the third gave a peculiar, unnatural busy signal. He slammed the phone down and dashed from his office.

He was joined on the way to Doll Ops by other elves, emergency officers like himself. He could see dense smoke pluming from the top of the central factory building, and the acrid smell of something that shouldn't be burning assaulted his nostrils. He hustled around a corner of the old redbricked building and sped to the main entrance, where a number of elves darted about. Sirens wailed in the distance as ambulances and fire engines scrambled.

He caught sight of Spinner near the entrance and shouted her name. She held up a megaphone and waved him through the crowd.

"What the hell is going on?" he shouted.

"Hard to say! We've got explosions, wrecked machinery, a real mess. Situation is not in control now, not in control!"

"Halter! Where is he?"

"I spoke to him a minute ago. He's directing the main evac. The explosion is on the traditional line, Drover's area. Probably that damned WonderFinish!" She waved her arms. "There's Winnow! I have to talk to him!"

She dashed away, and Router sprinted to his assigned area in straw dolls, making sure things were locked down, elves filing out as orderly as possible. The air pulsed when another rumble shook the next area over. He tried not to read the line elves' faces, focusing instead on bodies and names, making sure everyone was safe.

When he had them all gathered outside and the operation secured, he left their area super in charge and ran to the front of the building. Other elves were already assembling there, filing their reports. Ambulances, lights flashing, pulled as close as they dared. In the bullseye, clutching her clipsheet, Sprinter checked names, her face strained and eyes flashing.

Two of the ambulances screeched away, sirens blaring. At least two down. He hustled up beside Winnow to give his report. Smoke still poured through the structure, and the firefighters were struggling to control the blazes.

"We've got everybody out, except Drover!" Spinner shouted. "He's in there somewhere! The zone is way too hot to send anybody in!"

"When will the firefighters be able to move in?" Winnow asked.

"Not for a while. Winnow, we may have lost him!"

"I know! We can't tell them yet. They'll try to go in after him. We'll have to get Halter! Have you seen him?"

"I haven't, not since we started!" She gestured with the megaphone. "He directed the main evac!" She spied Router. "Router! Have you seen him!"

"No!" he shouted, and he saw fear jump up in her eyes.

"My God, where is he?" she screamed.

"Spinner! Take it easy!" Winnow exclaimed. "He's probably—Oh, no. No, no!"

They followed his stare to the security cubbyhole by the factory entrance, where emergency air pack suits hung for quick deployment. One peg was empty.

Their eyes met and they knew. Spinner dashed forward, and Winnow caught her, hard. "We can't help him! Not now!" His gaze drifted toward the building, where an arcing electrical explosion sent sparks flying. "If he's in there, he's—" He shook his head. "He's—" He shut his eyes, clasping Spinner.

Router numbly scanned ruined building, smoke, sparks, milling elves, Winnow and Spinner. He spied a utility telephone and knew what he had to do. Striding to the phone, his eyes streaming from smoke and shock, he placed the call to Gardner.

13.

The minute they told him Drover was trapped, he turned the evacuation over to the nearest line super. His injured hand still stung from when he'd thrown on the air pack.

They didn't warn you how noisy the suit was, or how clumsy you feel barging around with it on, or how you could hardly see. The suit had a light on its forehead, like a miner's helmet, and he switched it on, white light stabbing through curling black smoke and flaring up twisted metal shapes that had once been the pride of his professional life, the traditional Doll Operations line.

He stumbled forward, cursing his clumsiness, and pitched onto his hands, the air pack heavy on his back. Suddenly, thousands of little eyeballs glared up at him in the lantern light. His mind flashed to Tracer, so long ago, and he actually laughed out loud as he picked himself up, remembering the squawking Winnow and the start of their friendship.

He looked about him. Smoke everywhere. Even the air pack couldn't totally filter out the smells of burning oil and ozone. The few emergency lights that still functioned threw bluish white beams over the chaos.

He picked his way over the mass of eyeballs. *C'mon, Drover, you son of a bitch, where the hell are you?*

Pieces of the line had been blasted apart. *WonderFinish.* He inched past station after station, feeling his way through the black smoke. Doll parts lay everywhere, heads, arms, torsos, fragments, many melted and charred. *I'll pull Oiler apart when I find him.*

He stopped again, searching the wreckage. Nothing. Sudden holes, gaps in the line, presented hiding places that hadn't existed before now. Smoke curled across the machines. He could feel heat pushing through the suit.

His breathing came hard, choppy. The flames had been reduced in this area. The Cardox system had flooded the area with liquid carbon dioxide, expanding as it warmed and sucking all free oxygen out of the area. He shuddered. If Drover had been caught in one of those waves, it would suck the oxygen right through his skin.

He cast wildly about, then realized he had to control his head movements if the lantern was to be useful. He spied what was left of the orange WonderFinish barrels. Some of them had been blasted, shards of metal lying all about. That's where the accident had started. Intact barrels teetered behind the first ones. The blast had rolled forward, catching the line and whoever was at the finish station.

He crept toward the barrels. His heart pounded. Any second, they could blow. An outthrust metal shard threatened to tear the suit, and he stumbled away just in time. Between noxious fumes and the Cardox threat, any tear could be fatal.

Drover, Drover! His hand throbbed. Steps to a catwalk opened at his feet. He had reached the stairs to the overhead inspection walkway that spanned the finish end of the line. The stairs pitched eerily in the gloom. He scanned their twisted length from bottom to top, and the lantern beam caught something on the top landing. He peered again. A foot. Drover at last.

He clambered onto the walkway, and the entire structure howled. He set his teeth and crawled, trying not to think of what a sudden spark from metal to cement floor might do with all that WonderFinish about. He pulled himself forward with his left hand.

He reached Drover and looked down. The supervisor's body sprawled on the catwalk. Small flames danced far below, light flickering through the metal grid. Drover was still breathing. Halter sighed and grunted, "Come on, you old son of a gun, we've got to get you out of here!"

He braced himself and started to slip his good arm under Drover's body. The far end of the catwalk groaned, and he felt it suddenly give way, a loud wrenching sound. Instantly, they pitched forward at an impossible angle, sliding and tumbling, landing in a heap on the far side, scattering doll parts. Drover's body slammed on top of him.

He looked up at the catwalk's weird incline. "That's one way," he grunted, almost laughing. He hunched his shoulders and lifted Drover onto his back, Drover's cheek resting against the suit visor. He staggered along the far side of the line until he reached the concrete shelter of an op station, designed to withstand just about anything. They couldn't stay there because of the fumes. *Damn it, why didn't I bring a pack with me?*

He slid Drover gently to the floor in this comparatively calm space and staggered forward to catch his breath. The worst was over. He'd managed to get Drover out of the most dangerous area. He peered one more time up the line.

With a final, shuddering crash, the catwalk gave way completely and the wall of barrels crumbled. But suddenly, impossibly, they were all bathed in a beautiful yellow flash, and he watched helplessly as the yellow flash boiled forward and

the sky was beautiful and cold, high and blue, and he sailed above the treetops, reindeer dancing around him, sparks flashing from their hides, the bells ringing and ringing. He saw his mother speeding towards him, laughing and flying on a wild reindeer, but he himself danced among the very heavens without any aid at all. The cold wind lashed his bare face, and he saw himself clad in the green leggings and tunic of ancient childhood. He called to his mother, who seemed to be disappearing even as he followed her into the brilliant sun: "Look at me, Mommy! Look at me! I can fly! I can fly! I can fly!"

14.

Under a sky just blushing pink, a truck rumbled up Posen's Main Street, carrying a load of lumber to Bob Towalski's ACE Hardware Store. Today was cleanup day. Residents would pitch in and clear the Viking High School field of debris, stray banners, empty cans, streamers, and the like. The town prepared to settle into its quieter existence.

The truck's wheels spat a piece of paper, Ida's recipe for down-home potato pancakes. The recipe drifted up and to the side of the road, floating lazily above a small concrete patch into which an old-style post lamp had been anchored beside a green historical plaque. The recipe drifted toward a bench beside the pole. On the bench lay a large, dark-haired sleeper. Traces of old drool still clung to one cheek. Remnants of potato beer had seeped into the front of his shirt, mingling with sauerkraut shreds.

The recipe landed on the sleeper's face, tickling his nose and teasing him into a brief, bleary wakefulness. He raised himself painfully on one elbow.

"Ravi?" he croaked. "Roxy?"

He squinted in the early morning sunshine, shivering as the cold wind attacked him. He shut his eyes tight and passed one hand over them as though trying to drive out intense, pounding pain. He groaned upright, his head bobbing wearily against his chest.

Eventually, he opened his eyes and coughed. He peered at the plaque next to the light pole. Carefully, very carefully, he moved his lips to sound out the words:

> "The first utility pole set by Presque Isle Electric Cooperative was erected near this site on September 22, 1937. Established in 1935, the Rural Electrification Administration (RFA) was a New Deal program designed to help cooperatives provide low-cost power to rural areas. On December 22, 1937, Presque Isle Electric Cooperative energized its first seventy miles of line from Norway Dam in Alpena to Mottke Township in Presque Isle County, bringing electricity to eighty-two families."

He stared at the plaque a while longer, alternately nodding or shaking or bobbing his head. Then he gave up, lay back down, and started snoring gently again. Across the field behind him, in the distance, a couple of cattle mooed in wonder as they always did at the dawning of a new day.

MAGIC

IV

1.

The rescue teams found Drover first, almost as soon as they'd been cleared to enter the still-smoking structure. He lay tucked behind the remnants of Operator Station B, Assembly Area A. The blast had blown off the top of the station, and fragments of cream-colored brick lay strewn all along the line. He looked as though he'd been placed there, his body curled protectively, a small heap of bricks partially covering him. By some miracle he was still breathing, even though it had been several hours since the last and largest explosion had blown out the back half of the building, scattering glass, bricks, bits of metal and thousands of doll parts across the manufacturing complex.

They hurried him to the area hospital and brought his family to him, and doctors and family were still debating where to airlift him when he died.

They didn't find Halter until the following day, and even then only by lucky chance. One of the emergency electricians, working some distance from the blast site, sounded the alarm when he found a sliced rubber boot sticking out from under some rubble. When they cleared everything away and saw the condition of his body and the remains of the air pack, they agreed it was a blessing he'd been killed by the blast itself.

In a press release, the first of many that NPI needed to provide, Baylor announced personal sadness at what had happened and promised a full investigation. From cafeterias and gathering spaces, meeting rooms and training facilities, elves and half-elves from line and office watched the broadcast, murmured among themselves and returned to work.

Doll Operations remained closed indefinitely. Crews were already hard at work setting up emergency power, so that portions of production could be restored as quickly as possible. Huge temporary lights were brought in first, their high sodium glare sharpening the jagged wreckage, in the tortured midst of which the investigators stooped and studied. They turned orange barrel shards in latex-clad hands, hoping for clues. Others gently questioned the elves who had been working in the area, but the workers' shocked memories often produced fragmented and inconsistent answers. And the two elves in the finishing area, closest to the accident, remained in critical condition.

Dr. Id dispatched counseling teams to provide round-the-clock assistance to anyone requesting it. One the principal worries was Spinner, who spent the next few days in seclusion, only occasionally talking to Winnow.

The day after Halter's body was discovered, and the day after NPI's first press release, Hammer broke his long silence, issuing a statement at UEU headquarters, situated across the complex from the shell. A small, round figure, he stood before a cluster of half-elf reporters he'd personally selected and whose confidentiality he'd personally approved over NPI officer objections. He stood between the press cameras and the ruins, yellow caution tape behind him twisting in the cold breeze. In clear and simple terms he began, speaking first of misguided policies, fatigue in the ranks, critical mistakes, running too fast. He combined the gloom he saw in the rank and file with the strained expressions on office workers, joined union and salaried in the deaths of the two elves, described survivors, lives permanently changed, and thousands and thousands of eyes, questioning. He declared a loss of balance, a collision of Christmas and business, an emphasis on ebusiness at the expense of real workers sweating in real casting heat, setting steel on real lines, assembling real toys. He raised the questioning eyes to the level of NPI's leaders, and beyond, pitting those eyes against the shadows of the Street, the trading pressure pushing a shortsighted merger with a company whose production strategies were so at odds with NPI.

"And why?" he said. "Just to look good. Just to show Wall Street we're growing. If the other guy does it, that doesn't make it good for us. Thousands of my brothers and sisters on the line are asking, 'Will I lose my job over this?' What do I tell them?"

He pointed a finger at the cameras. "And to our directors, who ask me to consider the value of our stock, I say that I have a stock portfolio, too. And when I see *my* share of *my* trust being abused this way, then I have to question whether those leaders are using my money wisely. That's all. I'll take your questions."

Hands shot up and voices outbid each other. Hammer thoughtfully answered each question. A reporter shouted, "Will there be a general strike, this close to Christmas?"

He surveyed the group for a long minute, frowning. "Neither I nor anyone else in this organization has full control over what those workers may decide to do." He excused himself and strode through them to his office.

The next day, bells tolled throughout the compound, and all work ceased. They buried Halter and Drover side by side in the old cemetery, where so few elves and half-elves lay, victims of accident or rare disease over the centuries. Prior to burial, they held a brief and simple double ceremony in a natural shelter formed by firs and shrubs that blocked the cold wind. Gardner and Mats stood together, faces set and grim. Router spoke softly with Spokes, shaking his head. Oiler, haggard and hollow-eyed, trembled beside a downcast Silvertongue. Groomer, still puffing, stood behind Racer, whom he had wheeled to one side of the gathering. Spinner sobbed softly and constantly against Winnow's arm. Crafter and Wheeler stood near, but not too near, Baylor and several Board members.

Elves from Drover's line made up the first rank behind these officers, ready to bear the caskets. Behind this first rank stood the hundreds of line workers, office staff, IT analysts, marketing strategists, finishers, painters, sales managers, buyers, paralegals, metalworkers, electricians, personnel planners, PR supervisors, millwrights, elves and half-elves of all positions and functions. Hammer gave the eulogy, not looking at the Board, but instead allowing his eyes to rest briefly on elf and half-elf, reminiscing.

Following the eulogy and the burial, the Board met and issued a public statement of consolation, after approving a production plan to shift resources to unaffected lines and to increase the pace to take up the slack. They publicly vowed to continue the investigation until root cause could be established and explained, and they privately authorized Groomer to seal Halter's office and to review all contents in anticipation of a wrongful death suit. They reassured investors that the accident, while tragic, would pose no material risk toward meeting production and profit targets, and at the same time they quietly evaluated a stock buyback tactic to prop up the share price and to ease key market traders' overextended positions. They reaffirmed their public commitment to the spirit and meaning of Christmas that they emphasized had always been part of NPI's culture, and they secretly contemplated extending the highly profitable reindeer processing beyond the RFS culls. They recommitted to focusing on the basic strengths of the organization, reiterating that their workforce was clearly their most important asset, and they paused to give a quick nod to a plan binding NPI and EI more tightly together and realizing a future workforce reduction of twenty percent.

Very late that same day, Baylor summoned Gardner and directed her to do everything she could to contain Hammer. He snapped, "I expect you to do whatever is necessary to avoid this incident touching off a general strike. If that strike should happen, I'll hold you personally accountable"; to which she icily replied "I refuse to be held accountable for an event caused by the policies of this Board. And its leadership." She turned and stalked from his office, knowing he glared after her.

Darkness fell, the wind picked up, and the first true snow of the season blew into the area. The snow sifted over the graves and blunted their sharp edges.

2.

"Santa! *Santa!* C'mon, Santa, wake *up!*"

A small hand prodded the sleeper's shoulder. Then a bold finger poked the sleeper's cheek.

"Whoizzit?"

"I'm Mary Alison, and you had better wake *up*, Santa!" The finger jabbed on each of the last three words.

One of the sleeper's eyelids popped open, and a blue eye stared out. The sleeper's big hand reached up to explore cheeks, chin and hair. Then both eyes opened and wandered about for a few seconds, until they discovered Mary Alison, all three feet-something, her lower lip stuck out and her round cheeks framed by short straight blonde hair, standing in front of him in a dark green coat that reached to her knees.

Her finger traced his jaw. "What did you do with your beard? Did you shave it off? Are you using that greasy formula stuff on your hair, like Grampa?"

The sleeper heaved into a slump. "Get outta here, kid," he mumbled, shaking his head ponderously and then wishing he hadn't. "I'm not Santa Claus."

"But you *are!*" Mary Alison declared. "You just cut off your beard and used the greasy formula on your hair."

"Grecian."

"What?"

"Grecian Formula." He sighed, staring at the historical marker. "That's what they call it. I think. I don't use that stuff." He brought her almost into focus. She stood, arms crossed, watching him. "Look, I told you I'm—not him."

She sighed as loudly and adultly as she could. "I can tell when you're lying, Mr. Claus," she stated. "You can't just cut off your beard. Are you playing hide and seek?" She climbed onto the bench and sat beside him.

He watched her guardedly. "No, I'm—" he began. Then, more softly, he continued, "Not really." He rubbed his chin again, then rubbed his nose. "So. Mary Alison, is it? How did you realize I'm Santa Claus? Now, I'm not admitting it!" He held up a warning finger. "But if I was Santa Claus, how would you know that? After all, I'm sleeping here on a bench in the middle of town, and I hardly look like the real thing."

"Santa. First of all, kids just know things. Grownups never seem to understand that. So when I saw you on the bench, I knew it was you. I know your hair is dark and your beard is gone. And it's not even close to Christmas. But that doesn't matter. I'll let you in on a secret."

She made a motion for him to bend down, which he did, and she whispered in his ear.

He roared with laughter. "The way I snore! How does that give it away?"

"You whistle, Santa! If you had your beard, that's what you'd whistle into. And just before, you rubbed your nose. That's what you do. Plus it's in your eyes. Anyone can see that."

"What's in my eyes?"

"The twinkle! It's there now! There was only the snore at first, but now I've got all the rest!"

He laughed again. "All right, Miss Mary Alison. If I'm Santa Claus, what—what do you want for Christmas?"

"*Now* we're getting somewhere," she said with deep satisfaction. "First of all, I've been good."

He smiled a kind of smile he hadn't used in a long time. "I can tell."

"I know you can. So it's no good lying." She swung her small legs back and forth. Spreading the short fingers of her left hand, she counted on them with her right. "I want the Marvelous Mazie doll—

the deluxe model, of course. *And* I want a model horse, and the Big Book of Magical Stories. The second edition." She tilted her head and looked at him. "Are you going to remember all this? You still look a little sleepy."

His smile widened. "I'll remember. I'm magical that way. Is there anything else?"

"Well... There *is* the big doll house in the department store in Rogers City. *But* Mommy says I can't have that until I'm older and less likely to break things. So I don't know if—"

"Mary *Alison!* There you are!" Footsteps snapped through the air.

"*Uh*-oh." Mary Alison hopped off the bench. "Mom's calling! But Santa." She looked him up and down, hands on her hips. "This will never do," she said. "You need your beard and hair back."

A young bluejeaned and sweatered woman, not very tall and with blonde hair arranged in short waves about an angry face, grabbed the youngster's hand. "Mary, you come with me right now!" She glanced darkly at the stranger on the bench.

"Good morning," he said quietly.

"Good morning," she dismissed, pulling Mary around the bench and down the sidewalk, their voices fading.

"How many times have I told you not to talk to strangers?"

"But Mommy, he's not a stranger, he's Santa Claus!"

"Did he say he was Santa Claus? Did he? Did he try anything?"

"Oh, Mommy, no, he was sleeping! I had to wake him up and tell him he was Santa Claus. *He* said he wasn't, but I know better!"

"Oooh! Your imagination! Young lady, one of these days it'll get you into trouble!"

The voices disappeared. Wind whistled in Santa's ears. Cows mooed in a distant field. He ran a hand through his hair and scanned the fields, not seeing anything. He blinked once, twice, several times. Then he shut his eyes tight.

A hand on his shoulder jolted him. "About time I found you." Ida. "Out all night. They had to carry your little Indian back."

She stepped around the bench and towered over him, her square bulk blocking just about everything else. "Aren't you the great fighter."

"I—I don't remember that," he mumbled.

"Just as well. Hopefully, Santa won't remember it, either. Don't look so surprised! I came out looking for you when it was clear you hadn't come back. People are already talking." She held out a big hand. "Now, get up. I found you, all right, but sure as shootin' you're walking back to my place on your own."

"All right, all right," he grumbled, waving off her hand. He struggled off the bench and had to work at first to keep up with her not-very-rapid pace.

They walked in silence, two large figures ambling down Main, until eventually she spoke again. "Ed Figurski found Santa staggering around the rail yards back of the bar. He was going on and on about some giant rabbit, Santa was, said he'd seen it outside the bar, just like the Harvey thing. Said he was going to stop drinking and join Weight Watchers. Hah!" Her laugh rang out across the empty intersection as they turned the corner and headed toward her place. "Can you imagine! Santa on Weight Watchers!"

"Please don't call him that."

"Why do you care? Anyway, Bob took him home, to sleep things off."

They reached Ida's place and stumped through the front door. The place was empty, except for William polishing the bar. Santa headed for the stairs to his room.

"Not so fast!" Ida declared. "Will-*yam*! Tea! Chamomile. Sammy, follow me." She led the way through a smaller, "Employees Only" door just left of the stairway. After a short walk down a narrow hallway she opened a door at the far end, and they both stepped through it and onto a fair-sized screened porch, whose cement floor supported an odd collection of patio furniture.

Ida motioned him to a dark green plastic chair next to a vinyl white table, while she plunked herself heavily onto the other chair, a dark blue plastic one threatening to collapse under the shock. "This is my back porch," she said. "Some of the people around here know about it. Santa's been back here. And Tommy. Others, too. I figured I'd have somebody out here the day after the Festival. And here you are."

He looked at her a moment, then turned his gaze on the view from her porch. The ground sloped away over a long, wide yard informally bounded by a line of scrub bushes and small trees, blended into a meadow, then a cornfield in the near distance, then another field beyond that where some cows stood or wandered at will, then a dark band of forest and finally the horizon. Late morning sunlight burned the chill off the land. He watched a hawk circle the middle field, tiny black figure against brilliant blue.

A distant moo floated to them. He stirred at the sound and cleared his throat. "Lovely view," he said. "You must come back here often."

"When I get a minute. Ah, here's William."

The slight man stooped, dropping off a small tray with a pot and two mugs.

Ida poured the tea. "Chamomile. Best antidote for that potato beer. I hate that stuff. It's one thing I wish they never did with potatoes."

He sipped his tea, feeling its hot mint go to work. "How long has the Festival been going on?"

"Long enough. Usually there's somebody, or several somebodies, who take the Festival right into the bar. Last night wasn't unusual. Except for people from out of town." She studied him a moment. "Where'd the chip on your shoulder come from?"

"…I'd rather not talk about that."

"You don't get tea, and you don't get this view, if you don't talk." She leaned forward. "So."

"…So. So why do you think I have a chip on my shoulder?"

"Not hard to figure. You come into town, never crack a smile. People talk to you, and you act like you don't have time." She leaned back, wincing briefly as she sipped her tea. "You sure have your lady upset with you."

"She's not my lady."

"Oh, you don't think so. But she is."

"She can't be." He looked away.

"Because you're married to somebody else."

He nodded.

"Who hasn't been around."

He nodded again.

"...All right, so she's not your lady," she said softly. "But she's clearly trying to take care of you, Sammy, and I'm afraid you're not making it easy on her. As a matter of fact, you're making it damn hard. On her, and on that little Indian guy, too." She leaned forward again. "Drink your tea, it'll loosen you up."

"Why should I talk to you?"

"Listen, Mr. Chip-on-his-shoulder. Are you planning on living in Posen?"

"No."

"Staying for any length of time?"

"Only until I can get my car fixed."

Her big laugh rang out over the fields. "You think Tommy's going to get that car fixed anytime soon? Might as well hitch a ride on one of Earl's deer!" She took another sip. "But you will be moving on, right?"

"One way or another."

"OK. So, Sammy. What do you think I'm going to do with your story? Tell others? What'll that do?" She took a bigger sip of her tea. "I see a lot of people come through the doors of this place. Not all of them are happy. Sometimes I bring 'em back here. And sometimes they tell me stuff they probably wish they hadn't. At least not until they realize that what they say goes nowhere. And you know why it goes nowhere? Because if it did, who'd come to Ida's place anymore?

"So that makes me a lot like you. I have a business. Part of that business is based on trust. My customers trust me not to spill the beans. And just because you're some Big Important Person from out of town, you think that makes you different?"

"After I leave, you could say whatever you want."

She scowled at him. "You don't get it, do you? People around here know I can keep their secrets. It's part of my business. They know I won't blab. So why would I blab on an out-of-towner? Even an oh-so-important one? Besides," she continued, pouring more tea for both of them, "it ain't me. That's all there is to it. People around here can see me for who I am. Only the clever ones from out of town can't."

Pushing herself up with an effort, she thumped to one corner of the porch, where an old box lay half-shadowed. She rummaged in it a few minutes before straightening up. "People are always leaving things behind," she grumbled, walking back to the table with a brightly-colored metal thing. She set it on the floor in front of them. "Now, Mr. Toymaker, what is that?"

"A top."

"One you made?"

"...Maybe."

"No matter." With considerable effort, she reached down and pumped the top, spinning it until the patterns on the outside blurred. "You know," she said, as the top spun around and bumped blindly against their legs, "you fast-trackers from big business remind me of spinning tops. You're moving so fast and spinning around each other so fast, you have no idea who you're talking to. Everybody just spinning, bumping into things. And everybody looks the same. One of you can be traded for another. You don't care. You're ice cold." They watched the top slow down, the blurry patterns resolving into colors and then finally into brightly-painted images before the top made its final turn and came to a full stop. "Not so out here." She picked up the top and held it. "Out here, people take time. We don't spin like that. So we can see each other's colors. We can appreciate each other's style.

"And we can accept somebody like Ronnie, somebody you had the foolishness to say something about in that bar last night. Ronnie's got more problems than the average person, and when he was in high school, others didn't let him forget it. So I'm told. I've never had Ronnie out here. I've had his tormenters, though."

She turned the top slowly, looking at the images. "You all forget how to do that, down there in *Dee*troit and Chicago and New York and all them places. You all forget to take the time." She handed him the top. "So. Do I get to hear what colors *you* are, Mr. Fast Mover? Who *are* you, Sammy? What's wrong?"

His eyes never left the top. He turned it around and around in his big hands, feeling the cold metal, seeing the craftwork. He watched the images change as he turned it, images that started as carousel horses but eventually changed to reindeer, images in a motion all their own. He talked. He talked business first, and deals, and growth patterns, and challenges, and customers, and labor force issues. He talked people and his years of experience. He talked changes, and frustrations, and mounting pressures, and a sense of losing focus. He talked of things spinning out of control, of speed, of constant reinvention. He talked words that grew into grafted and artificial things, satisficing and technobabble and ebusiness and the like. And through it all, as though the very references were an anchor, he talked of those who stayed with him, of Gardner and Spokes, Crafter and Halter, Roxy and Mats and the rest, and especially his wife, she who had stayed with him so long but at last had been forced to leave by a business that increasingly demanded not only his time but his warmth too, finding no place for her.

Lastly, he spoke about a little girl, a blond Mary Alison, who'd had the childish brashness to presume he was Santa Claus and then prove it to him.

When he was through, the teapot was empty, though his cup remained half-full of cold tea. He set the top on the table and leaned back.

"You haven't told me everything," she said.

"I told what I could."

"I got no doubt about that. But you've kept your secrets too, Sammy. Who you really are. Where you work. Those people you work with. You told me some. Enough, I imagine. By your look, you're wondering if you told too much." She let her eyes range over the fields. "Maybe. Trust is always harder than betrayal. Trust builds, betrayal tears down. Always easier to tear things down." Then she frowned. "No. Not always."

"What do you mean?"

"You've been trying to tear things down with Roxy. It hasn't worked. And you tried hard, you know it. Business," she grunted. "You make it sound like it does things to you. Maybe. Sometimes. But business didn't push your wife away. You did that. Business didn't even push you out. You did that yourself. This talk about markets, and the forces you went on about. What are markets? People. Who's in your business? People. Sometimes they're dumb, sometimes they're so far ahead of you. Just like in there." She jerked a big thumb toward the door.

She got up and picked up the tea tray. “I’ll leave you out here to think things over. I haven’t got answers for you. You do.” She pushed through the door. “Come in when you need anything, like lunch,” she said, and he was suddenly alone.

He chewed a thumb, surveying the fields. He scowled at some inner thought, then brought his hands together sharply, as though to hit something. He stood, a sudden motion, and paced the porch several times before stopping at the table and hefting the top. He held it close, seeing reindeer riding the wind, snow all about, a fierce storm, a tiny red figure in its midst, the team now hurled about, losing control, falling and falling.

He shut his eyes and tucked the top under one arm before hurrying through the door.

Only a few of the men were in Ida’s dining room, and they scarcely looked up from their meal when he strode past them and up the stairs to his room.

He emerged, an hour or so later, and it was just as well that the men had departed. Only William remained, behind the bar as always, while Ida sat on a barstool, going through receipts. When William saw him standing at the head of the stairs, he put down the glass he’d been polishing and glided over to Ida.

She turned and stared, but only for a moment. “So,” she said at last. “So it *is* you. I thought it might be. Now I’ve seen it all, even magic, here in Posen. Your lady will be happy to see you’re on your way back. The Indian kid, too. But if you go to see Earl, you’d better get rid of that beard.”

3.

"*Coun*sel, this is a mess. A real mess."

Groomer scowled through an email. "I'm going to strangle Oiler." He looked up. "Why are you smiling?"

"Because a mess is good," Racer wheezed. "In some ways. Look at the situation. You have an accident that regrettably went a little farther than you wanted it to—"

"A little? Two elves are dead, two critical, the union's up in arms, we've got a factory out of service indefinitely! The merger will go right into the ditch!"

"Oh, the merger will survive. There's too much money at stake for it not to. You've described chaos, Counsel. That's nothing more than the state of your shirts. Why do you think chaos is bad? Does it look like things are out of control?"

"Do you have any doubt?"

"Doubts? Plenty. But not about our control. Take what you've just described. Two elves are dead. Regrettable. Puts pressure on Baylor to defend production policies in public. But look at what's been sacrificed. Doll Operations was old, and its leadership was backward. Dreaming. Dreams are perfectly all right, Counsel. But only the right dreams."

"We can't go back to production the way it was!"

"Not now. Perhaps not even soon. But you'll see. We'll bravely respond to the crisis, and soon it'll be over. We'll be stronger. And we'll rebuild Doll Operations to be more responsive to where the business is going. And your other worry, the union. So the elves call a strike. What of it? Remember, Counsel, our goal is to get one of ourselves on the Board. This is our opportunity."

"Not Hammer."

"Of course not. He's much too loyal to his people. But that's our advantage. Hammer knows there needs to be a union presence on the Board. He's the logical choice, and he knows that, too. But he's practical enough, Counsel, to realize that if someone rose to the top through some popular means—" Racer coughed softly "—that's the elf who should get the nod."

"So it's Hammer, or it's some elf Hammer approves." Groomer frowned. "I don't see how—"

"You're not following, Counsel, and you're not making connections," Racer interrupted gently. "I thought you were better than that. Think about the situation. Chaos is our opportunity. We simply make sure that the voice those Union elves listen to is someone we've selected."

"And that would be—?"

"Oh, I have someone in mind, Counsel. I may even tell you ahead of time. But not yet. It'll be someone with Raven's qualities, masked under an earnest and forthright appearance. It's unfortunate about Raven, isn't it?"

"That damned flier, that—Demon, is it? I should—"

"Patience, Counsel. I have this continuing need to teach you that. We have bigger fish than a high-minded flier. We have Gardner. Mats is back."

"I know."

"I know you know. How did he get here, and why is he meeting with Gardner?"

"Router must have been involved."

"And still is. We need a strategy that neutralizes all three. Something in herd management, possibly. Link them to illegal RFS profits, perhaps, then leak it. Bridle could be frightened into doing the book adjustments." Racer rubbed a wrinkled cheek. "Of course, all that will take time," he continued. "Possibly too much time. We also need a few statements to cover ourselves. We'll use Silvertongue."

"I thought you didn't want to use him."

"Of course I don't! The fool can't even manage a problem with reindeer shit! But until we find someone else, we'll have to use him."

"And then?"

"Let's talk about disposals. I think you'll agree Silvertongue has shown he doesn't have what we need in an officer. We'll move him elsewhere. Public Relations, most likely. Something juicy enough to keep him hungry. Of which there'll be a promise, nothing more." His voice grew harsher. "Oiler is dead. Everyone can see his hand behind this. What a monumental bungle!"

"So he'll go where?" Groomer belched softly and rubbed his huge belly, putting down the insurrection within.

"I don't give a damn where he goes! So long as he's out of the way! Let's just hope it isn't necessary to kill him to get him there! Now, Halter. Have you sealed his office?"

"Yes."

"What did you find?"

"Not much." The rumbling insisted. Groomer rubbed harder. "We checked his PC and found a resignation letter, with lots of incriminating statements. Backed up with facts, too. Pretty well written, I have to admit. Unsent, according to the mail logs. Naturally, we electronically shredded the file. It could easily have been a problem."

"Was there a printed copy?"

"We couldn't find one. He'd been doing all kinds of shredding up there, he might have shredded it."

"I don't like that you didn't find anything. You're sure?"

"We looked everywhere. There was some blood in the office, too. He must have cut himself on something. It's possible he never printed the note. He may have written it just to get it out of his system."

"He always was more of a dreamer, wasn't he? Still, it's a tiny loose end. Well, it can't be helped. What about our ex-Chief?"

"Still in Detroit, apparently."

"Apparently?"

"He withdrew a large sum of money. And he bought a Jag."

"I'm aware of the Jaguar. Didn't he buy it with the cash?"

"No, on account. Silvertongue approved it, figuring it would keep him visible."

"A good thought. You've lost him, haven't you?"

"We've contacted a detective agency in the area."

"So you *have* lost him."

"Temporarily. That Jag won't be too hard to find."

"If he's driving it. Is that your belly?"

"Sorry."

"*Try* to control yourself, Counsel," Racer sighed. He shut his eyes for a moment. "Maybe he and his girlfriend have gone on a trip. We can point the press that way."

"Silvertongue won't."

"Bah! He's too principled! All the more reason to replace him. We don't need him for it, anyway. But in case our ex-chief gets homesick, keep the airspace shut tight. Remove Router if he challenges it. So there's no way our ex can get back. And we keep our friend Mats here, where we can keep a close eye on him. We'll have to watch over the ex-team. Pity they've been made well again."

"That's the JEDI's doing."

"You needn't remind me. That interference can't go on much longer. It gets in the way of our survey. Something must be done, both to him and the team."

"He'll never leave that team. His suspicions are up."

"Accident, then. With a more deliberate outcome this time. We don't have the same restraints we put on Oiler. Our JEDI has a reputation for being clumsy, hasn't he?"

"So I've heard."

"Then I'll leave the details to you. Use Raven. He won't have a problem this time: I know him too well. When it's done, and things get back to where they belong, we expand the RFS, step up production, bring in the profits, please the investors. And get ourselves on the Board. And from there—Well. I've run ahead too far. Too far. One thing at a time, Counsel! One thing at a time. But see that they're all executed perfectly. Flawless execution. That's our watchword." He swiveled his chair and creaked out of the office.

Groomer stared at the empty doorway, then jotted down Racer's instructions. As one hand scribbled, the other picked up the phone and tucked the receiver against a flabby cheek. When the Commissary voice answered, he ordered three regulars and three specials and returned to work.

He was emailing by the time the Commissary elf ducked inside and set down the tray. The knife clattered to one side, and she leaned over his desk to pick it up. She scanned the desk, but Groomer's eyes never left the dogs. She retrieved the knife, put it on the tray, and darted out.

He rubbed his hands happily. "At long last!" he chortled, picking up the knife and stabbing the first one. He ate rapidly, regular or special, gulping it down almost without chewing. He popped his eyes a couple of times, belched more loudly than usual, and let his eyes sweep the tray.

They lit upon one of the specials this time, and he picked up the knife and expertly sliced it in half. He raised the nearer half to his mouth and stuffed it in, savoring the juices and the wild taste. He returned to his email and opened a joke message from one of his underlings, the punchline hitting his eyes and forcing a laugh just as he started to swallow. The eyes popped. He tried to swallow again, and the eyes popped again. It wouldn't move, this chunk of RFS something-or-other that had lodged somewhere in the narrow pipes hidden under folds of skin. He reached for his throat, making horrible gurgling sounds, then thrust his head back and forward sharply enough to do injury. His legs thrashed uselessly, bashing the cubbyhole under his desk. He flailed his stumpy arms, scattering briefs, notes, opinions everywhere, sweeping aside the list he'd made of the Racer items, knocking his phone to the floor, sending his business cards flying, launching his keyboard to dangle uselessly off the desk. His cheeks billowed and his eyes widened. He arched his back and sent the tray of dogs flying, chili and ketchup and bread and meat landing wherever they would, his face turning purple as the chair spun around and his legs, unable to bear his weight, refused now his desperate attempt to stand, the chair spinning and spinning and then tipping over with a crash that brought elves from all around flying into his office, and they unable to do anything but to gape for a moment and then be overcome as his immense bowels, loosened by his final extremity, voided themselves, the stench sickening and overpowering them and sending them scurrying out to call for emergency support, for others more able to deal with the blackened face and the soiled room and the horrid stink and the papers, papers, papers everywhere.

Abruptly, the room fell silent, except for the ticking of a small clock. Frenzied sounds intruded from outside and slicing through them, quiet footsteps. The Commissary elf, handkerchief over her mouth, tiptoed into the desecrated office, gaze darting rapidly over the scattered papers. In a moment, she found what she'd been seeking, its freshly-penned scrawl partially obscured by other papers. She plucked it from the mess and scurried from the room.

4.

Red. Vermilion, almost. That was the gold's work, the shine from its thickest lines haloing the crimson field. Turn your head, let sharper periphery do the work, and the lines resolved into – what? Golden deer? Or evergreens. No, that was the bold forest splash beneath, a hunter's green arrow slicing upward into that red, red of apples, apples of cheeks, nose and suit, red of berries, of holly, surely, green of pine and hemlock and yew, ancient trees and aged symbols, fused through effortless art, hands from some previous age dipping the brush and tracing magic onto wood and, satisfied at last, preserving all under a brilliant smooth sheen.

The lacquer remained a mystery. The book spoke only of its application, not its composition. But its strength defied all decay. The cabin might disintegrate, the stable collapse, and the team wander the wild corners of the earth, but the lacquer would protect the sleigh, and the sleigh would stand, though its runners fuse to the iron land; and the red and green of original Christmas would challenge forever the stark and sterile whiteness of the snow.

Long fingers moved chamois over these smooth surfaces. Then they paused, finding a nook, and attempted to work the cloth into the angle. But the fingers were simply too tired. Everything had been polished and repolished, shined and shined until no more gleam could be teased from it. Still the half-elf wasn't satisfied. But aching fingers forced concession. He dropped the cloth into its protective sack and straightened, easing at last his long-suffering back.

No matter how many times Tracer worked its surface, the sleigh continued to surprise him with a new detail, interpretation of a design, filigrees that chided him, because he couldn't see what they had to say. He sighed, letting his gaze run over contours now so familiar.

These past few days, the sleigh had occupied most of his time. Thankfully, the protective wrap had saved that magnificent finish; rework would have been impossible in this weather. Still, the runners had to be canted and adjusted, and the leaf and coil springs oiled. There were endless nuts, bolts and wooden joints on the thing.

Polishing the runners had been the worst. Something had caused the metal to pit, and when he'd hitched two deer for a trial pull to the clearing, even he could see that the empty sleigh resisted the snow. The deer weren't too thrilled about it, either. So he tipped it on its side, working the runners first with a special polishing file and then with successively finer finishing cloths.

He reflected on tasks accomplished so far. He'd fixed the cabin door and worked the leather harnesses. He'd made a nameplate for Parsley, attaching it above her stall door, and another for Mystic. This he'd set above the empty stall. He chuckled, comparing his amateur brasswork to the team's plates.

Then he'd set about polishing and tuning the bells. That had been difficult, getting the tuning just right. The book provided musical guidelines, but his fingers still remembered the hours he'd spent working some dented bells on an old harness he'd found in one of the unused stalls. Practice bells. He'd removed the bells from the harness and worked them one by one, crimping the hard metal with special tools, learning over countless hours just how much pressure would force a quarter tone here, a half tone there. These bells had to be reattached to the harness and the whole contraption slapped against the tuning bench, to ensure that every bell harmonized, individual pings resolving into the signature of each deer. He'd made plenty of mistakes on the practice set before starting on the team's.

Prancer's had been the hardest. His bells required the finest tuning, and they had to be reattached to the harness with equal care, preserving a signature song that trailed into a dwindling rise, a question-mark. That had taken a couple of long days to get right. And of course, after he'd slapped the harness on the bench, listened for what the book described, and made final bench adjustments, there was still the field test—leaving the bells on a fencerail, until they and the harness reached outside temperature. He'd strike them again at that point, trusting his awakening ear to his instinct and newfound music sense. The team test followed, attaching the harnesses to the deer and seeing how the bells sounded in unison. And now, the flight test. The book spelled it out, no exceptions.

He draped the cloth over one side of the sleigh. The chill wind funneled into his ears, and he drew the hood of his parka close. The air carried a deep chill these days. Sweeping winds drove snow everywhere, and while no huge storms had roared through, what snow fell accumulated steadily. Even today, snow devils swirled about the rise, twinkling above the grazing team.

He frowned at the sky. Angry gray clouds hurried across the dark blue, capable of hurling stinging streams of snow, if they could but pause. "Demon sky," he muttered, watching the clouds shift and splinter.

She hadn't returned. Some days, busy outside, he thought he heard her high and distant cry, but only iron sky met his searching gaze. And sometimes at the end of a long day, when he sat at the desk, a cup of cooling tea at one elbow and the Journal and book near the other, he'd catch himself glancing at the green couch. He'd gone back to sleeping on it.

She would decide how and when she returned. *Just like the wind. Just like Saddler said.* He smiled. He could see her, small and taut, playfully distracting him. If something involving the deer challenged him, he'd catch himself asking her advice. The isolation did it, of course.

What were they all doing back there? He'd seen no sign of anyone, surveyors or others, since Demon had dropped him off that wild day weeks ago. The snoopers wouldn't be back, or if they were, they'd be very circumspect.

He still looked all ways whenever he left cabin or workshop.

He'd expected a weekly visit from someone in Saddler's area, but that hadn't materialized, either. *Something's probably dreadfully wrong. When will I find out? I can't get news from NPI. Nothing to switch on, no phone, nothing. But how often would I do it? Once a week? Twice? Daily? Ever?* He sighed, heading for the rise.

He watched the team for a few minutes, smiling when one sailed across the field, effortlessly performing the flight he'd once doubted they'd ever manage again.

Parsley grazed a little apart from the others, and he crunched over the snow to her. He spoke softly, running a hand along her back, and her ears flicked to and fro.

"Well, young lady, we've come a very long way together." He looked up again. "Seems like the sky can't decide whether to storm. Gets much worse, I'll have to get you all indoors. I'd rather not. I've got a lot planned today. I want to hitch up the whole team for the bell test. It's what the book says to do. Which means I take the sleigh up." The hand paused. "Whoever thought it would get to this," he murmured, "where a JEDI kid ends up doing it? It's unbelievable. Where have they all gone?"

He chased the clouds. "Demon would read this sky way better. I wonder if she's out there." His fingers tapped Parsley's twitching back. "Good thing I insisted on all that extra feed. Something must have happened. Once I finish the sleigh, I'll take Vixen down and find out what's going on. After my last visit, you'd think…" He sighed.

"And the dreams, Parsley. Nothing I can put my finger on. Just this feeling when I wake up, my heart's racing and I don't know why. I know I dreamed something, but I don't know what it is. Except it's dark. There's shadows that retreat when I wake up. But not very far. Not very far. Especially if it's the middle of the night." He stopped tapping and started rubbing again. "You have that deer wisdom, young lady. What are these dreams for?"

She grunted and continued grazing, moving slowly forward under his arm.

"I get this feeling, Parsley, every day I'm here I'm less safe than the day before. It's stupid, really. Probably because I'm alone. I keep looking for those snoopers, but I don't think they're coming back. Not for a while, anyway. That's another thing. If I leave with Vixen to go back down there, will they show up while I'm away and—. I feel like I'm being watched, someone's waiting for a chance to strike."

He shook his head sharply and then smiled. “Now I’m really losing it,” he said. “Must be this place. Being up here all alone, you just—. Maybe what I need is lunch, soup and bread or something, get me going. After that, I can hitch the team for the trial. That’s it, Parsley. I need to be *doing* something, so I don’t get carried away!”

Returning to the warmth of the cabin, he took off the parka and hung it on a peg beside the front door. *How familiar this all feels!*

He shivered and glanced at the fireplace. The fire had gone quite low. He walked over to the log rack, picked up a couple of logs, then put one back. *No sense building it too high just for lunch.* He poked the remaining log into place.

He crossed to the pantry, started to get himself a can of soup, then decided in favor of a bigger can of meat stew. *I need something that's going to stick to me longer today.*

He prepared the stew and sat down at the desk, eating it quickly and without ceremony. As he ate, he idly turned the pages of the book, his eyes drifting over now-familiar topics.

He washed the stew mug and the pan and paused a moment, grateful for warm soapy water. *What'll I do when the sleigh is done? Wait? Why does it feel like—* He felt his neck hairs stand, and he spun and peered about the cabin’s interior.

He turned back, let the water run down the drain, and rinsed off his hands. *This is not going to do at all! Tracer, you've got the weirdest sixth sense. Weird because it's wrong. I better see Saddler soon, before I go nuts. Tomorrow. Tomorrow I can go, if today works out. I better get moving.*

He strode to the cabin door and slipped into the parka. A large brass key on a small keyring dangled from a lower peg. *Better take no chances.* He double-checked the fireplace, then snatched up the key and stepped outside, locking the door behind him.

No sign of anything. *Give it a rest.* He stopped and studied the clouds. The temperature had dropped some, and the clouds had started to fuse. *I better get at it quickly. I don't want to crack up in a storm.*

He headed for the stable to get the harnesses. He slung them over his arm and headed toward the rise. All the bells jingled, music high and complex, with each step.

The team stood bunched next to the sleigh. *Odd how they know things.* Only Parsley remained aloof, content to graze even as the winds picked up.

He worked quickly now, strapping on their harnesses. The gathering clouds kept him from stopping and reflecting. It was the second time he'd outfitted the whole team this way, the first using the sleigh. He set the traces and hitched the team in the ancient order.

He paused only as he prepared to climb into the sleigh. "Forgive me," he murmured. "But it has to be done."

He settled into the large seat and checked things over one last time. The red and green lacquered surfaces gleamed in the cold afternoon light, gold trim glowing. He inspected the brass guides along the front rail, making sure the leather traces didn't catch when they moved forward and back. The bells jingled softly. He tried to concentrate, though his heart thudded and his hands trembled.

He took a very deep breath, held it, and exhaled slowly. Another. *Now for it.* He flipped his snow goggles down, braced himself, cleared his throat, and gave the cry.

The team responded. Slowly, the sleigh began to slide over the snowy surface, swishing runners mingling with the increasing voice of the wind. Now faster and faster they glided along the field, until with an easy and almost imperceptible motion the ground melted away and they banked into a lazy turn, rising over the fir trees at the clearing's edge.

The compound fell away. Smoke curled from the toy cabin's chimney, and Parsley's tiny antlers tilted toward the sky, hidden ears catching the sound of those ringing bells. "Yes!" he shouted. "Whooiee!!" The wind whirled his happy cry around his ears. He had managed to get them right. He knew by the way those magnificent bells combined and recombined, their voices joining the wind and melting into the heavens through which they flew. His heart pounded. Everything—fir trees, sleepy factory, cabin, stable, snowfields—was etched into permanence by the sleigh flying above them.

He let the team make two passes over the compound before he guided them down to the rise. The sleigh slid to a halt. He leaned back. He had brought it all to completion, from a sick, starving team and a dusty old sleigh and an abandoned cabin and a neglected stable, to this point. He looked over the traces and the team, polished bells depending so naturally from the backs of these magnificent, healthy and wise creatures, the leather of the harnesses supple and smooth, the sleigh polished, shining and ready. They had flown twice over the field and now stood motionless, as though they'd done nothing at all.

"I'm not even Tracer anymore," he said, watching their ears flick. "I'm this—stuff, whatever it all is—the magic of this place and, and all of you. ...But for what purpose?" He gazed over the compound, his eyes resting on cabin, stable, rise. He watched Parsley graze, an act as natural and timeless as the place he'd come to know so well. His chest rose and fell. *For nothing, probably. For a memory. For a dream. For—Oh, I don't know anymore. I should go in and get a cup of tea going, think about it all, the whole crazy story. Demon. Saddler. Everything I got wrong. Maybe I got this feeling wrong, too.*

He noted the clouds' angry, darkening reassembly. *Best get us all indoors. That storm won't hold off much longer.* He prepared to jump out, but his legs buckled, and his tall body smacked the moving sleigh, reins taut from his useless pull, the eight deer intent and working, ignoring his shouts. He managed his seat just as team pulled the sleigh aloft. Nothing he shouted and nothing he did made the slightest impression on them.

"Not again!" he wailed, hurling the traces down. The compound spun away, and as they circled it he glimpsed a dark shape hugging the ground, black and sleek like a bullet, gliding in and out of the trees toward the stable. *Speed sled. Not Demon's, it's the wrong color. Somebody else, a snooper. My God, Parsley!*

He could still see her, a tiny deer looking up. "Parsley!" he shouted. "Get out of there, girl! Fly, fly!" He was too far away. She didn't move. The bullet sped closer.

The team twisted into so steep a dive he could barely hang on. The wind roared past his ears and blasted the parka hood off his head as they stooped towards the field. Instinctively he understood. They leveled off and skimmed the edge of the rise, hidden from the approaching sled, and he leaned out and yelled as loudly as he could when she flashed past, "Parsley! Come on, girl! Fly!"

She flew at last, a surprised leap into the heavens. He could scarcely keep track of her, a small form bobbing in midair, so swiftly did the team spin the sleigh, rocketing upward at delivery speed. She followed them for only a few seconds before veering away. Desperately, his eyes followed her tiny figure and then the speck until first it and then the compound vanished from sight, and when that happened his eyes continued to follow where both speck and compound had been, before they shut tight, and he gripped the sides of the sleigh, safe but helpless, as the team took him skyward, skyward.

5.

"Kelli!" Mr. Folkeson's voice boomed up the stairs. "Someone is here to see you!"

Kelli put down the book she'd been reading, smiling at *Pappa's* quaint reference to "someone," even though Bill had visited several times these past few weeks. She continued to report herd movements, tracking things as best she could in this far-flung location. And she'd insisted on her laptop, over Bill's and *Pappa's* objections. She had to keep working. Even now, she made new and disturbing connections. Bill needed to know, quickly.

She looked at her watch. Seven-thirty. His last two visits had been evening ones. Their conversations, while usually about work, now included discussions about life at NPI, snow, skiing, music, books, movies. They had migrated there so naturally, a simple question resulting in first one sentence and then a longer answer, and she had been surprised not so much at the many things they had in common but that she wasn't surprised by it.

She greeted him in the parlor, and they strolled to *Pappa's* study. "I've got some new information to show you," she said, switching on her laptop.

"I've got some, too. How are you doing?"

"I'm all right."

"I still worry about you going through these numbers."

"You don't have to," she said, smiling. "It's my part in this crazy battle we're all in. And besides—" she stretched as the laptop booted up "—it feels so—*safe* here. With the children and all. Such a slow, calm pace!" The study's books suggested contemplation and rest. A small TV hunkered on a thick corner shelf. "I could almost forget the business." The screen flashed. "Except for what they're doing to it."

"Yes, what they're doing to it," he repeated. "And to good folks like you."

She blushed. "Here's the latest report," she said. "It's got a twist."

"Yes," he said, and she felt his eyes return to the screen. "What twist?"

"The herd mix. All this time, the RFS herds have been culled and shipped by plane and truck up here. Then the shipment numbers started taking off. So there's either a whole lot of new RFS deer, not accounted for in my projections, or they're bringing in fliers."

"They're still shipping them, right?"

"Right. I'm not sure why."

"Because they know we're watching for anything unusual, and the flights would tip their hand." Bill chewed his thumb. "What's the overall tally?"

"Looks to be around—" she frowned "—twenty-seven thousand."

"Going up like a rocket. Well. That rocket may crash soon. There's something on CNN tonight."

She wrinkled her nose. "The Board? More on the accident?"

"No. A wildcat."

She whistled. "So that's your news. Hammer's fighting back."

"I'm not sure. Mats thinks some of the elves are doing this on their own, and the UEU's looking the other way."

"Wow! So that's making headlines?"

"All over. Couldn't happen at a worse time for the Board. Production timetables are screwed up like you wouldn't believe, and the investors are getting itchy. Stock's dropping like a stone. Even a buyback rumor can't stop it."

"So the Board's squirming a little?"

"A lot. The Halter-Drover tragedy puts a spotlight on everything. The big shots can't keep a lid on it the way they want to. Not anymore. The disaster saw to that. Plus Hammer's first news conference."

“I thought they shut him up.”

“They want to, but they can’t. They couldn’t when they thought it would cause a strike. Now they can’t because they need him to get those elves back on the lines.” He paused. “They’re putting the squeeze on Gardner, though. They’re setting her up to take the fall for the strike.”

“Gardner! How do they figure that?”

“According to them it’s her job to keep Hammer under control.”

“But you just said this strike has nothing to do with Hammer!”

“Doesn’t matter. The real thing is, they want her out. She’s too strong for them. They’re afraid of her. Best way is to use the strike against her.” He lowered his voice. “Besides, who knows what Hammer really told those line elves to do. So the Board will use the strike to take some sweeping actions. All in the name of correcting things. They’ve already started with Router.”

“Router! What?”

“Moved him aside. Put somebody in his place. Somebody who’ll make sure the airspace stays closed.” He sighed. “And that leaves Mats up there.”

“Mats is still there?”

“He’s stuck there. It’s getting ugly. But—” He crossed the room and switched on the TV. “Tonight will be very interesting.” CNN’s rapid chatter filled the study. “It’s on in a couple of minutes.” He poked his head out the door. Hey, Gøran! Want to see the conference?”

He sat beside her. Heavy footsteps sounded in the hall, and *Pappa* peered in. “So, who will we see tonight?” he asked.

“Well, Hammer for sure. Some guest appearances, too. Come in, we won’t bite! Wait, wait, here it is.”

A “Special Report” splash lit the TV. “CNN now switches you live to North Pole Industries, the beleaguered giant toymaker, where a special news conference has been called by the head of the powerful United Toyworkers’ Union, John Hammer. With him tonight is the Executive Vice President of Employee Resources, Jennifer Gardner, and Mats Larsson, CIO of Sverige, the Scandinavian supply giant.” The splash screen disappeared, and Kelli gasped at the image, first of

Hammer and Gardner, then of Mats, and behind them a blown-out factory.

"Look, they've played the angles beautifully," Bill murmured. "You can't see the size differences."

"We have good folks on those cameras," *Pappa* agreed. "Not a Board member in sight, too. Only the Union could manage that."

She caught herself holding her breath. Hammer made a brief statement explaining such an unusual conference in defiance of the Board. But it was Gardner who delivered the heart of the argument, Gardner whose black eyes flashed when she described in clear and incisive tones the story that had unfolded at NPI these past months. Kelli watched, mind spinning over a complex landscape of events. Where had it all started? Prior to her seeing Gardner, probably, in those awful moments when she'd tried to concentrate on her work, knowing that something was being hatched by Silvertongue and the rest, Oiler and Groomer especially. The image of Groomer, toadlike and obscene, swam up.

Gardner's words rolled on, outlining drastic actions taken on the tame reindeer herds NPI maintained for petting zoos and rides worldwide. Now images lit the screen, and she shuddered, seeing picture after picture she and Bill had taken. She shut her eyes tightly, drawing comfort from the large hand that placed itself over hers, warm human flesh holding her, and she accepting the comfort, twining her hand with his. Still the words flowed. Gardner was fighting the fight of her life, in cold and logical and powerful terms explaining the CEO ouster, the merger, production squeezes, hidden deals with food giants, secret meetings and agendas. Still she felt that warm hand.

Now Mats spoke again, explaining numbers she had provided, and her heart jumped. It had all been worthwhile, from Gothenburg and boredom to the ride here, the factory and the horror and beyond. She'd had an important part to play. The hand acknowledged this, squeezing hers gently.

Finally, it was Hammer's turn. Reading from a few crumpled pages, he drew a powerful portrait of Halter. He spoke of the strike, how the workers had unilaterally decided it was time to show solidarity and to walk, throwing production schedules off and jeopardizing the Christmas timetables. He added that since the workers had made that choice, knowing the consequences, the Union respected their decision.

Gardner wrapped it up with additional surprises: the exposure of a hidden real estate group, and the sudden death of Groomer. Kelli trembled with amazement. All of it was out at last. How much there was.

And then it was over, except for a few trailing questions. She was suddenly aware of the warm hand again. Did *Pappa* see it? She pulled her hand free.

Bill cleared his throat. “Well, there’s a conference the Board will wish never happened,” he said, turning off the TV.

“What do you think will happen to them?”

“I don’t know, Gøran. Hammer, the union and the workers seem pretty tight, so I don’t think he’s in any danger. They can’t touch Mats directly, other than issue some pretty powerful denials and try to throw some mud our way, but I think we’ll be able to withstand it. Unless they cut us off. We’ll have to wait and see. This was a pretty desperate move.”

“Yes, a ‘long shoot’, as Mats would say. Why do they do it now?”

Bill sighed. “I don’t know. They may have felt time was running out. They may have felt something was planned against them, they had to strike first. They could have seen Router’s removal as a sign.”

“What about Gardner?” Kelli asked.

Bill shook his head. “Gøran, what do you think?”

There was quite a silence as *Pappa* pondered the question. “It is over for her, I think,” he said, his big voice sad. “They will use her honesty to do her in. Well of course she knows it, too. But you’re right about the squeeze. She had to come out now. Still, it may work, but… I don’t think so. I think they are too smart at this. I think she played into them. I think she knew it. But it was the only way she could have played.”

“Yes,” Bill said grimly. “The only way. And now we see where it goes from here.”

6.

No matter what Roxy did, the wind tore her hair from under her furred parka hood and whipped it about her face. Several ends caught underneath her snow goggles, and she yanked them loose yet again. *This is insane.* She slouched even lower in her seat and glared at his big back hunched before her. Perhaps he used magic to thread the gales. *He'd better use something. I'm a jet traveler, not somebody who can –*

Storm winds pummeled them, and their fragile craft—a work wagon, jury-rigged and put to the test—bounced and creaked. She glanced at Ravi, who like her tried to find some security in the wagon's bottom, one hand clutching the side. His lips moved constantly.

"What are you saying?" she shouted above the storm.

"I'm praying to Ganesh!"

"What good will that do?"

"I don't know! I'm praying to him to get me on the ground again, where I will build him a temple for rescuing me from some tom-fool creature who thinks he can fly reindeer from Posen to the North Pole!" The craft bounced again. "Oh, Ganesh, who is—" Ravi's voice trailed to a low babble.

She gripped the rail. Images flitted past, life on the ground in Posen, Ida and Earl and Bob and that obscene what-was-his-name, that Santa thing. *I'd pray to Ganesh, or whoever he is, if he could get me back there!* Her mind raced. She had been so angry with him for his idiotic, hostile behavior. Then had come that awful night, when he and the Santa slob had brawled drunkenly in public. But the next day, when she answered the soft knock on her door and took in the full beard, the blue blue eyes, the ruddy face, she'd nearly broken down. "It's time," was all he'd said: "It's high time."

They'd talked through it all, an often-angry exchange. "You're too close to me, Roxy," he'd finally said. "You think I've got it all figured out. I don't. But now I've got enough to go on." And every step and motion thereafter had purpose. There was no hesitation, no backtrack, from changing back to his younger self, to going to Bob's ACE for heavy-duty outerwear and goggles, to locating a hidden pasture, to working a generous deal with Earl for four reindeer, to taking the deer to the pasture and training them quickly, an incredible exchange resulting in their astounded leaps into the air.

Even Ida, who slapped a *Detroit Free Press* in front of them earlier today, with a "You better read this," knew he'd moved on. The business pages showed it all—the press conference, the exposure, the accident, the strike—and he had read it twice, nodding as though none of it surprised him. Only when she'd pointed out a second article, a police report of an arrest involving a black man and a Jaguar, did his eyes widen momentarily. He gave a brief nod, an acknowledgment, a filing away.

No detail escaped him now. Anger drove him, rage at what they dared do to the herds and the culture. Somehow he contained his feelings behind a steely mask.

That very night, in the hidden pasture, with his magnificent beard and hair displayed, he'd hitched the team to a big farm wagon, pulled her and Ravi aboard, and leapt into the night. It was the craziest thing she had ever done, to stay with him, and as for Ravi…!

Her hair whipped loose again, and she tucked it back, peering over the side of the wagon at snow tearing past them. She had no idea how high they were, or how fast they were truly going. References to Ganesh continued to bubble from Ravi's side of the wagon. She straightened a bit and shouted, "Are you going delivery speed?"

"What?"

"Delivery speed! Are you—"

"Not with this team! They're too inexperienced! As it is, I'm pushing them now!"

"What happens if you push too hard?"

"I won't!"

"But the storm!"

"I know!"

"How do you know where you're going?"

"I told you! There's an old route this way! They may have closed the airspace and kept me from getting back, but this way might still be open! Even if I don't have my team! So there's a chance!"

"How much chance?"

"Some! What's Ravi doing?"

"He's praying to Ganesh!"

"…That's a very good idea!"

She grimaced. *It had to be this way. How else would he have lived? Us as well. He'd have dwindled to nothing.* "God knows what would have happened to me," she gasped. "I guess Ravi could have gone back to med school, passing out."

"What are you mumbling over there?"

"Nothing!"

"That was a lot of nothing words! Are you praying, too?"

"Why don't you teach me?"

"All right! But remember, Santa is riding the mouse right now!"

"What do you mean? What mouse?"

"The mouse is his desire, according to Ganesha! He has to ride the mouse of his desire and keep it under control, otherwise it takes him for a ride!"

"I don't understand!"

The wagon bounced, hard, and Ravi nearly lost his grip. "There is no time to understand," he wailed, "there is only time to pray!"

Huddled in the back of the wagon, they recited the words, Ravi desperately, Roxy clumsily, their murmurings ripped away by the wind. The wagon threatened to disintegrate under them. Still the big half-elf stayed bent to his purpose, teasing the old route out of the blackness, pushing the makeshift team to their limits.

When they reached the line in the prayer about "protector of all that is precious in this world untouched," they pitched forward, slamming into Santa's legs. The wagon tilted into a steep dive. She clung to Ravi, fighting back a scream, shutting her eyes tight against the roaring, cold wind blasting Ravi's "Ganesha! Ganesha!" into the void, and would it be this instant or the next that they met the ground and disintegrated?

At the last moment, the wagon pulled up, and they slapped the earth, she losing her grip on Ravi, and then she was flying, sailing clear, sounds of splintering wood and terrified beast-cries assailing her ears, before landing on her back in a huge drift of snow, its softness cushioning the shock, Ravi plunging face first beside her.

She lay gasping, cold air stinging her lungs. The snowdrift sucked the heat from her body. Snow whirled and lashed. She struggled to sit up, then shook Ravi hard. He was so still! "Ravi!" she screamed.

He stirred, flailing the snow. Finally, he worked himself free and heaved onto one side, facing her. "Where are we?" he groaned.

She looked wildly about. Through the storm winds, the darkness, and the driving snow, she could barely make out a big shape moving among beast-shapes. "I don't know!" she cried. "I hope he does!"

"Where is the wagon? My ankle, ow ow ow!" Ravi's hands shot down and clutched his right ankle. His face twisted with pain.

"My God!" She stumbled to her feet, fighting a wind that tried to push her flat. "Ravi, how bad is it?"

"It hurts! I think it must be broken!"

"Oh, God! How will I—" She peered toward Santa, still struggling with the team. "Ravi, don't move, don't try to get up! I don't see the wagon! I have—we have to get you into shelter, make some shelter somehow! Stay there!"

She stumbled off. How small her words sounded, tiny cries against that wind, and behind the wind, the Ganesh-prayer, its "invested with the knowledge of the universe" resounding. There was no wagon, only some sticks she crunched on her way to Santa.

She reached him at last. "Ravi's hurt!" she shouted. "What happened?" She stared in horror at the team, all four deer sprawled out on the snow, gulping and gasping.

"I must have pushed them too hard!" he cried. "I thought I was doing all right, but I don't know. I was thinking about it all and trying to get back too fast! Roxy, I—"

"The wagon's gone!"

"I know! Where's Ravi now? How bad is he?"

"It's his ankle! I don't know how bad! We have to get him out of there, he's in a snowdrift! He'll freeze if we can't find some shelter!"

They both peered into a storm that seemed to intensify by the minute. Santa pointed. "There's some rocks over there," he panted, "not too far off! We should be able to get Ravi there. Then if we bunch the team around us, we have a chance of staying warm enough to ride this thing out!"

"And then what?"

"Let's just ride the storm out now! Let's hope we can last that long!"

Her heart jumped. She staggered back to Ravi, her mind reeling. His mortality and hers had never been in question. Even during that wild ride, her faith in his timelessness had carried her. But under this screeching wind, this starless darkness! They might not make it. They might be drifted over, vanishing from the world under clouds of white snow, and the story of Christmas with him in the center would simply cease to be. *No! I'm too young, too young! This can't happen!*

She forced her legs to churn. She and Santa lifted Ravi and half-carried him through the howling darkness, propping him against the rocks Santa had found. These provided hardly any shelter. Ravi wouldn't last long if this was all they could find. She could feel the cold drawing the warmth out of her, even as they worked to pull the team over to where Ravi lay mumbling about Ganesh, wisps of sound surfacing only when the wind slackened.

Once they had gathered the team, they huddled with Ravi, trying desperately to keep him warm. She shivered uncontrollably, as the snow whirled about them all. The flakes sparkled and danced before her, and she could discern faces, bright and brief, some smiling, others grim, Bridle and Silvertongue, Gardner and Halter, Crafter, others, filing into the Chief's office, the room bright white, and then Dr. Id, a pair of grinning lips, from the lips a question: "Yes, Roxy? You need to elaborate? Why didn't you order the ice sleigh?" and her numb answer, mouth moving soundlessly, and behind Id the New Orleans santas thumping and bellowing.

She shook her head and looked around drowsily. Santa slouched in the snow, relaxing at last, his breath smooth and even. Presently, he began talking, his voice strong at first. He rambled from topic to topic, from today's ride to how things had changed over the centuries, to Mrs. Claus, and then to the team. "I've ignored them, Roxy," he mumbled. "The greatest creatures of the world. I used to fly and call their names. Remember, Mom, how I used to do that? Oh, you're not Mom, you're not Mrs. Claus, you're the youngster, you're Roxy. I remember now. I used to call them like this:

On Dasher!
On Dancer!
On –

—somebody. I—there's eight of them, I recall."

From her other side, Ravi continued to murmur prayers to Ganesh, and she began to see the elephant-boy:

"*—son of Parvati, recreated by*
Shiva, blessed by Brahma,
cherished by Vishnu, your
elephant head a gift from Indra
God of the three worlds,
bringer of rain; rich too with the
multiple of rain; rich too with the
multiple benedictions bestowed
upon you at your birth by
Surya, Chandra, Vayu and Agni.
Beloved of the gods, you are—"

She settled back and closed her eyes, waiting to hear more, but Ravi had stopped. He sighed. "I hear the bells," he murmured. "Mother, I hear the bells, the festival is beginning. Can I watch when they bring Ganesha down the lane?"

She struggled to one elbow. "Ravi, what are you saying? You're not in India, you're—somewhere else. And I—" She cocked her head. She could hear the bells, too. *Maybe we're all in India.* "I hear the bells. Santa, do you hear Ganesh's bells, the festival bells? Can you hear them? Santa?"

She pushed her way to the bearded figure, rubbing his face until his eyes opened at last. "Do you hear them? The bells!"

"Prancer," he slurred.

"What?"

"Prancer. I hear Prancer."

"What? No, the bells! They're on the wind, somewhere. Ravi says—"

"You can hear the question mark. That's Prancer."

She shook her head, and it seemed at that moment that the wind died just slightly. She could hear them now, tinkling sounds carried across great distances, tiny voices teasing her out of the deadly sleep. "Prancer? Prancer?" She shook him, hard, then leaned over and shook Ravi as well, willing them to alertness. "Listen, listen!" she cried to Santa. "Is it Prancer?"

The blue eyes shut a moment before opening again. "And Vixen. I can hear her low voice. And Dasher—" his legs began thrashing, and she helped him struggle to his feet. "And Donder and—and—"

They leaned into the dwindling wind, ears straining. The tiny sound flickered, then held. The skies opened, and the glimmer of a high full moon cast fitful light across the wide white landscape.

Staring hard into that high darkness, Roxy's watering eyes found and focused on a shimmer, a waver, a smudge. It faded in and out of her vision at first. Snow from the dying storm scrimmed it. As it grew, so did the jingling, rising and falling. A wave of dizziness overtook her, and she flung her hand out to steady herself, grasping Santa's arm. He trembled so much her own arm shook.

"What is it?" she whispered, straightening. The smudge became a collection of moving parts. "Could it be…?"

The shape beside her had already begun laughing. "It is, it is, it *is*! It's them! *On*, Dasher! *On*, Dancer!"

But then his voice cracked and ceased. Still they came on, the bells unmistakable, hooves churning the snow, the legs high-stepping, antlered heads tossed back, on and on, closer and closer. Now she could see the tiny puffs of steam from their breaths, and at last she could make out the small figure in the sleigh. *Who's done this?*

The ground trembled. The terrible storm faded with each step the prancing shapes took. She didn't dare blink, lest they disappear into dreamstuff. But the bells, those magnificent, perfectly tuned harness bells, held her fast.

Now she could hear the runners swishing over the snow. The stormwinds died to nothing, and the chill seemed to vanish from the air. The clouds parted completely, and the moon fired the field, white on white. The team crossed the white blaze and stopped at last, magnificent, disciplined, eight hot breaths steaming over antlered heads, eyes watching, waiting. The bellsongs died to silence. In that moment, the entire universe around her, the universe of Christmas and elves and half-elves and people and Ganesh and other gods, of centuries of year-upon-year struggles, doubts and visions—this universe now paused, seeming to her to breathe lightly, as eight deer waited the bidding of their ancient master.

The rider stirred and jumped down, landing shin-deep in the snow. He struggled forward and stood before them, and she could read in his face the same purpose and discipline as the team. He pulled off his goggles, and she gazed deeply into dark eyes that had yet to rest on her but instead had widened, the mind behind them a mass of conflicting thoughts and emotions. "My God," he said at last, etching with those words the music of his voice into her heart. "It *is* you. How could they have known? And you're all the way out here? …I—I'm Tracer. I'm a—I was a JEDI. I've been taking care of them, bringing them back to health. I—Now I know why."

Santa said nothing, and as she reached toward him, he suddenly stumbled forward and embraced Tracer, sending Tracer's snow goggles flying to her feet. She picked them up, carefully shaking snow sparkles from them. Santa released Tracer, and she presented the goggles to him.

His eyes changed, their color deep and dark, almost black, yet shot with gold. He caught his breath. "I'm Roxy," she said. "I'm his—I've been with him all this time."

"Roxy. Yes. From back there. I—well. I'm privileged to meet you." He extended his gloved hand, and as she placed the goggles in it he covered her hand briefly with his free one.

Santa pushed through the snow to the team and now walked among them, talking softly, his voice wavering and singsong, words impossible to catch. They watched him a moment before she tugged

Tracer's arm. "There's—we have to help Ravi! He's hurt his ankle! He's in the snow, over there!" She pointed.

Tracer hurried to the body lying propped against the rocks. Passing the other reindeer, he brushed the backs of two of them, and they parted to let him through. "Who's Ravi?" he called over his shoulder.

"Someone we met! A santa candidate!"

"Ravi!" Tracer shouted, stooping over him. He bent still lower. "What's he muttering? I can't make it out."

"It might be Hindi!" she said.

"He's in and out of it! Hang on!" Tracer grabbed a handful of snow and rubbed it hard against the Indian's face.

Ravi spluttered. "What son of a backward donkey—" He stared at Tracer. "Who the hell are you, Mr. Snow-Rubber? What the hell are you doing?"

"Saving you," Tracer said loudly, slapping Ravi's face. "Bringing you back from India, I think."

"Ow! You can stop with the slapping of my face, too, Mr. Yeti from the snow fields!"

"Actually, I'm a JEDI."

"Then I will call you JEDI-Yeti." Ravi scowled at him. "So you can cut it out now and help me up. Ow!"

"That's your ankle, remember? And that's a very good sign."

"Good? It hurts like hell!"

"Exactly! Roxy, help me lift your good-natured friend to his feet, so we can get him to the sleigh."

"Mr. JEDI-Yeti has a sleigh, too," Ravi grumbled. They lifted him free of the snow. He continued griping as they staggered forward. "How convenient! I suppose it has a Jaguar in the back seat! And the next thing you'll be telling me, Mr. JEDI-Yeti, is that there—Ganesha be praised! Is this real?"

"This is as real as it gets, Ravi," Tracer grunted. "Roxy, climb in the sleigh. You can help pull him in."

She climbed aboard, and he prepared to hoist Ravi up, then stopped. No, wait!" He looked over the deer. "Let's go to my old friend Vixen."

He hobbled over to Vixen, pulling the protesting Ravi with him. She could see him talking earnestly to the big animal but couldn't hear what he was saying. She saw Ravi's eyes widen again when the big reindeer nuzzled his ankle. Vixen worked it over a couple of times, and if a reindeer could look puzzled, this one did.

Tracer dragged Ravi back, shaking his head. "And what was that all about, Mr. JEDI-Yeti?" the Indian grumbled.

"I don't understand why it didn't work," Tracer puzzled. "Maybe because he's not a half-elf like me. Oh, well. Roxy, get ready!"

She pulled Ravi aboard, settling him into the back and tucking around him some blankets she found under the seat. Impulsively, she kissed him lightly on the cheek before clambering out.

Tracer was watching Santa move among the team, the big hands reaching out shyly to touch the waiting animals, the voice still low and quavering. "Look at him," he said. "How long has it been?"

"...He's had to come a very long way."

"So have they. I wonder. The difference may just be that they knew the way, and he didn't. They had to find him."

She studied his profile, reading his eyes as they watched the deer. "And where did you come from, savior? What long road did you travel?"

He smiled. "Savior! All I did was take care of them and go along for the ride."

"...There's more than that."

He nodded. "There's a lot more. Maybe I'll have time to tell you, if he flies us back. But if he doesn't fly them, I will." He turned toward her. "Let's see if we can get your team hitched to this one. You work with deer before?"

Heat assailed her neck. "Well, just this last week, I guess, I—No, not really."

Warm gold flashed in his eyes again. "I haven't really done it that long, myself. Don't worry! They teach you as much as you teach them. More, usually."

They brought the other four reindeer and managed an arrangement that nested the smaller team behind Dasher and Dancer and between Prancer and Comet on the left and Vixen and Cupid on the right. The four looked quite small between the others. While they worked, Santa never stopped talking to his team.

Roxy took a seat in the rear of the sleigh. Tracer stepped forward and placed a hand on Santa's shoulder. "We need to go," he said quietly. "Your friend is hurt. And—well, you know the situation at NPI."

He nodded. "What can you tell me about the accident? And the strike? Who died? The newspaper story didn't say."

"Accident? Strike? Who—I've been at your stable, the cabin! I didn't know!"

"They're killing the deer, too. You didn't know that?"

Unmistakable shock registered in Tracer's face, and he took a step back, instinctively resting a protective arm on the nearest deer. His mouth worked, and anger darkened his face. He snapped his snow goggles on. "Let's go," he said. "Now."

They climbed into the sleigh. Tracer took the reins and hesitated only a moment before placing them in Santa's hand. "I brought them this far," he said. "It's your turn."

Santa stared at the reins. "I can't," he whispered at last.

Tracer studied him for a long moment. "Why not?"

"...I just can't." His free hand brushed his cheek.

"You can. Whatever you think you've done, they're here. They've forgiven it. All along." He curled Santa's hand tightly about the reins. "Try."

Santa took a deep, shuddering breath, then began. "On—" His voice wavered uncontrollably. He bowed his head.

When she felt her voice could be steady, she called out, "What was the name of that little girl?"

"...Who?"

"The one you saw just before Ida found you."

He lifted his head. "Mary Alison."

"So," she said. "For Mary Alison?"

"For Mary Alison."

"And for the rest of them?"

"And for the rest of them."

"Who all believe in you?"

"Who all—believe in me." The reins trembled.

Tracer tightened his grip. "I'll help," he said. In a barely audible voice, he continued: "On Dasher…"

"On, Dasher."

The big antlered head at the front of the team jerked up as though responding to the crack of a lash high in the air. Hooves pounded the snow, and steam billowed upward.

"You see?" Tracer said softly, loosening his grip ever so slightly. "Now. On Dancer…"

"On, Dancer."

Another head lifted.

"On Prancer…" Tracer let go of Santa's hand.

"On, Prancer!"

"On Vixen…" Tracer moved to the rear of the sleigh and sat beside Roxy.

"On, Vixen!" Santa sat down. The sleigh began to glide over the snow.

"On Comet…" Tracer whispered. She felt his strength next to her.

"On, Comet!" The sleigh picked up speed. She held his arm fast.

"On, Cupid!" Santa continued, his voice ringing through the night now. "On, Donder, and on, Blitzen!"

And then they were aloft.

"Ganesh be praised," Ravi murmured drowsily, warm under the blankets.

She gazed at the moon, its big bright circle above Tracer's shoulder wavering and dissolving as gentle tears washed it away, tears that ran down her cheeks, cooled by the passing wind. On and on she wept, silently and peacefully, feeling his strong arms cradling her, as the sleigh sailed northward through the heavens.

7.

Long-stemmed roses spread like a scarlet-tipped hand above the scalloped clear lip of their vase, green stems interrupted by deep cuts in the crystal. One petal floated down and rested, edges curled, scarlet against the snowy tablecloth. Light from a crystal chandelier scattered into leaf-patterns on the cloth.

An older elf darted into the room, arms laden with dark green dinner plates. Briskly, she arranged them on the table. From a cherrywood broadfront behind her, she pulled out crystal glassware and set the pieces on the table edge nearest her.

A much younger elf walked into the dining room and waved her dust cloth. "Need any help there, Henna?"

"No, Jewel, it's all right," Henna said. "I've been doing this so many years, it's down to a routine."

"Well, let's hope it continues." Jewel buffed dark-framed artwork on the wall, summery landscapes that smiled over the table. "I just don't know. Have you seen her?"

"Yes."

"How is she?"

"Oh, you know. It would take a lot to bring her down."

"Well, I know *I* wouldn't be in any shape at all, if it happened to *me*." Jewel dusted furiously.

"She isn't out of the company yet."

"It's just a matter of time." Jewel stopped and faced Henna, the hand with the polishing cloth set on her hip. "How can you be so unconcerned? I mean, she only brings me in for special nights like tonight. I doubt I'll be coming here any more. But you! You've been in her life for years and years!"

Henna smiled, arranging the glassware. "Don't make me feel older than I am."

"Oh, you know what I mean! What'll happen if—"

"Nothing will happen to Henna."

Jewel colored and whirled about. Gardner stood in the doorway, smiling. Her black hair with its silver highlights sparkled in the light. She held a glass of water in one hand, cupping it with the other. A string of white pearls and a small silver pin shaped like a leaping reindeer adorned her simple navy dress. "Henna will stay with me, Jewel. I'm not them."

"I didn't say that!"

"I know." She sipped her water. "I'll have more dinner parties, too. That's if I go. It's not like I'll be begging on the streets."

"What'll you do?"

"There's always something, Jewel. Probably work for Mats, in Sverige."

"But it wouldn't be the same!"

"No." She sighed, very lightly. "No, it wouldn't. But it would be work, and it would be connected to—Well, to whatever is left of Christmas." She took another sip. "Come to think of it, maybe I wouldn't work at all for a while. Henna."

"Yes?"

"We've got many years between us. More than any of those humans on the Board. You never know."

Henna pulled the silverware from the broadfront drawer and continued setting the table. "But could you just do nothing, do you think? Could you last?"

"Good question. It's one we've never asked ourselves. If Christmas is gone, what happens to elves? Do we just grow old suddenly, and die? Become part of the earth again? Maybe that wouldn't be such a bad thing."

Henna made a sharp tsking sound, and Jewel said, "That's not even like you!"

"No, it isn't, is it?" She smiled wanly. "Must be the water. Henna, that looks wonderful as always. You two are simply the best." She wrinkled her nose. "Is Flaxen setting fire to my kitchen?"

"You know she doesn't do that!"

"I know, Henna. Between your cooking and hers, that kitchen got pretty small today. Ah! There's the door! I'll bet it's Router, first as usual!" She handed her glass to Jewel.

One by one, Gardner's guests arrived, Router, then Spinner with Winnow, then Spokes, Crafter, Hammer, and last of all Mats, ducking as he entered. They gathered in the parlor, where cold meats, smoked fish and cheeses greeted them. Jewel and Henna glided among them, replenishing glasses. The parlor grew suddenly small, warm and comfortable with laughter and easy, though tired smiles.

By the time dinner was served, they had left much tension behind, and they conversed like the old friends and colleagues they were. They toasted their friendship, toasted, too, the efforts that had brought them this far, knowing that careers and Christmas hung in the balance. The food was, of course, perfectly prepared and impeccably presented, with enough portions and courses to satisfy even Mats's half-elfin appetite. They could read in each others' eyes the battles of many years, centuries of stuff that had happened, major events that had loomed like mountains and then become boulders and then rocks and then grains of sand, as the years rolled on and the important things of the here and now dwindled to become the specks of distant centuries.

When dessert, coffee and tea had been served, Gardner leaned back, brushed aside a stray lock, and said, "Well, all of you. Not to bring up an appallingly boring topic, but we probably should talk about where we're heading."

Tight chuckles. Mats rested his big elbows on the table. "Well, of course it is this. They will deny it all. They will invite an investigation that will turn up nothing of consequence. They will throw some dirt on us as well. While this is happening, they will try to stop the strike, quietly and in the background. They will be talking about negotiation but privately they will be threatening. And Gardner, they will demand that you do it."

"If they don't fire me tomorrow."

"If they don't fire you, true. If they haven't fired you already."

"I know. Maybe that's why this feels so easy. I feel like I've been fighting so long. Quietly at first, then more and more." She sipped her coffee. "I don't know, Hammer, should I threaten you if you don't get those elves back on the lines? What'll I threaten you with?"

"You could accelerate the merger and throw half of us out of work," Hammer said. "Like we want to be in the egg business, anyway."

She chuckled. "I wonder if they know we're having dinner?"

"Without Groomer and his little intelligence network?" Crafter sipped his water. "I doubt it. A lot of ugly little knowledge died with him."

"Oh, he was a piece of work," Spokes growled. "And what a mess at the end!"

"Please." Gardner frowned. "I don't want his name used here. But it *has* made their situation more problematic. Too bad for them."

A cell phone buzzed. Router put a quick hand to his pocket.

She gave him a hard but not unkind look. "I thought we were going to try to stay undisturbed tonight." Router raised an eyebrow and excused himself, the phone to his ear. "There's one they can't control," she continued, "even if they reassign him to Argentina. They'll learn. Spokes, what's happening with that real estate probe?"

"I've got some folks chasing it. Looks like it was a deal between Groomer and his two buddies, so with all of them out of the picture, it probably died."

Hammer leaned forward. "The real thing," he said, "is that the folks on the line are just sick of the whole damn mess. That's why they walked. What happened to Halter and Drover just tipped the scales."

Spinner blinked and looked away, and Winnow placed his hand on her wrist. "I hope you stay out for a long time, Hammer," he said. "Let those greedy bastards know—"

"They'll stay out. It would take a hell of a lot to bring them in now. Another week or so, and that'll be it."

"Hammer's right," Crafter said. "In another week, no matter what we do, there won't be enough time to get ready for Christmas, not even if we go full bore."

"What's more worrisome," Hammer murmured, "is whether they'll resort to violence."

"Elves?"

"It could happen, Gardner. These business models, they've got fear and anger built right into them, who knows? I meant it at the press conference. I said I don't know what they'll do. I still mean it."

Spinner lifted her head. "Isn't there a way we could stop it?" she asked. "All this speed, everything whirling round, it's—for us to throw Christmas over! How can we even do it? All the children! I don't think—Halter wouldn't want this."

"I know," Winnow said. "None of us can believe it. But you get to the point where going into work is like going into some burned out shell. The lines are there, the offices are there, but everything's dead inside. And outside, when you're walking past the workers, you're looking at each other, and you see in their eyes, they're saying, Can I trust you? Are you selling me out? Even your lifelong friends look at you like that."

"I don't think even Halter could change things," Crafter said, "if he were still alive."

"Not the way he was at the end," Spinner muttered. "Couldn't you all see it?" She glared at Crafter. "First the numbers, then the stepup, and then that audit! He looked so hunted all the time. Couldn't you have done something?"

Gardner bowed her head. Eventually, Mats said, "It's always easier afterwards to see what could have been done. It's not as easy in the midst of things."

Gardner looked up when Router returned. "Not good," he said, sitting down. "That was Traffic. I told them to keep tabs on the RFS thing, in case it got out of hand. Rumors have taken over reality out there, especially at the ranches." He paused. "They're saying RFS is much worse. But what they also told me is that—and this is unconfirmed right now, unconfirmed—the Argentines are, they have some kind of deal going with poorer countries, where they're culling the herds and…"

"Go ahead," Gardner said, her voice steely. "Dinner's over. Are they killing them?"

"It's rumor."

"And selling the meat on the black market to the poor nations. Flyers and nonflyers alike?"

Router held up his hands.

"The damned fools! We have to stop them."

"How?" Router said. "First we have to find out if it's going on, and then, thanks to Silvertongue, they'll probably only deal with him or Baylor. Baylor doesn't care, and Silvertongue's not assigned to it any more. So they'll just deny it and drag their feet as long as they can."

"That's no answer," she declared. "We have to get to them. We have to stop them before others get the idea. How good are your Traffic connections?"

"Good as ever. They just moved me. They can't break the ties that easily."

"I figured. Who's there?"

"A skeleton shift. Traffic's a mess, now there's a strike. We've got folks figuring out where to put inbound stuff. Plus calling suppliers and suspending orders."

"Use them. Get them going on this. I don't care if it all falls off the docks. These are the herds! Without them, we don't do anything at all! I'll call the Argentines myself. They'll listen. They have to. Bargaining's over."

"You still need Silvertongue," Router said.

"That creep? I can't trust him."

"You might have to. And since the accident, and the shipment, he seems—well—"

"He may *seem* to have changed," she said. "Is this the time for him to prove it?"

In the sharp silence, Mats intervened. "Router is right. We may have no choice. He has all the knowing up here." He pointed to a temple. "I will be involved, too. We can send some people down right away."

"All right. But I'm in the room when he makes that call. Mats, you too. Or we conference with them. I'm not having it any other way. Router. Get any elves you can. Don't use the cell. We're going in. Get into an office, use a regular—"

A beeping sound interrupted her. Hammer unslung his text pager and read it. He placed it in front of him and stared at its tiny green screen. "There's a fire. In the main factory area. We *think*—we don't know—the elves over there may have started it."

"My God, it's all crashing down," Winnow murmured.

"Not yet," Gardner said. "My office. We'll use it as a base. Hammer, you probably have to go to the area directly. Crafter?"

"No. I can work things out with you."

"All right. The rest of you. We're all in it now." She stood and looked them over. "You know, this would make a great operating council. I wonder if we'll ever get the chance. Let's get our stuff and move."

They dispersed from the table, Gardner explaining the situation to Henna and asking only that they clean up. "Then Jewel and Flaxen should stay here. I don't want you leaving the house until we have more information. I'll call when I get a chance." She joined the others at the door. "I'll call you, I promise!"

They could see smoke and orange flickers long before they reached the factory complex. Angry shouts flew about the wind, along with clangs and sirens. Fire trucks whizzed past them, showering them with dirt, but it scarcely slowed them down. The sleek, modern recycling building blocked their view, but as they dashed around it and the full scene opened to them, they paused. "Dear God," Gardner breathed.

"My factory!" Winnow shouted, and he would have sprinted into the mob had not Mats grabbed him and held him kicking like an angry child.

"You cannot!" Mats exclaimed. "They will tear you to bits!"

Elves milled and shoved each other. One group had planted itself before the smoking Train Factory entrance, many with arms locked, others brandishing pliers, hammers, catspaws, shovels, heavy dowelling—anything that could act as a weapon. The other group, equally equipped, writhed like a snake looking for a strike point. Barely thirty feet of sidewalk, the walkway to the factory, separated them. Some elves had climbed several walkway lightpoles. Tools strewed the area between the groups. “Get out of the way!” one of attacking elves shouted. “We’re taking over!”

“Hammer!” Gardner exclaimed. “Crafter, Router! Come on!” And before anyone could stop her she plunged between the factions. She and the others formed a dense knot facing the bristling gangs.

The action created only the barest sliver of silence, and Hammer used it, facing the band attacking the factory. “What’s going on?” he shouted. “Are you bent on destroying yourselves? What are you doing?”

“Ask them why!” the same elf shouted back. “Production increases, more and more work, and no end in sight! Am I right?” The mob behind him roared.

“They want to destroy the place!” one of the defenders yelled. “They’re not interested in anything else! Just fires and wrecking things!”

“You’re the ones doing the wrecking!” the first elf screamed. “Staying on *their* good sides! Can’t you see it! They’ll work us like mules and then get rid of us! What’ll happen when they bring those scabs in here?”

Gardner held up her arms. “This solves nothing!” The firm authority in her voice commanded a brief silence. “If we destroy it all, where will we go? Our only chance is to work together! We—”

“Hey, it’s the ten-eighty-ten lady!” someone shouted, and that set them all off again, hoots and catcalls, until Router picked up a shovel and swung it against a nearby lightpole, hard, the clang bouncing off factory walls, the light wavering.

He tossed the shovel aside and shouted, “Whoever thinks that is the biggest damn fool I’ve run across! Who didn’t see the news conference! If you did, who’s so stupid as to think she hasn’t been trying to stop it all, the programs, the production stepups, the—the deer slaughter!” Angry mutterings met this last statement. Router pursued it. “That’s right! You think *anyone* here would approve killing a single magical deer? Get your heads on!”

“But they don’t listen!” the first elf yelled. “She can’t stop it, you can’t, you’re all part of what’s pulling this place down!” More shouts. Someone hurled a crowbar at the factory, crashing it through the plate glass above the entrance. Slivers showered down on the defenders, and the attackers prepared to move.

Gardner broke from the others and strode straight into the attacking group, singling out the spokesperson and yanking him into the clear area. "So!" she shouted, and again the complex fell silent. "So you have all the answers! Look around! Look at them! I said look at them! And remind yourself that elves will not, will *not* get out of this alive! Is that what you want? You think that'll stop the killing? Or hitting the next factory for increases? Or finding another merger? Or changing it from ten to twenty? What, you think I can do it alone? You think I don't know what it means to work on those lines? How we depend on all of you? Do—"

"Don't listen to her!" someone yelled, and someone else snarled, "Yeah, they're just trying to save their own skins!"

Glaring at her, the elf broke free, turned and caught a catspaw somebody tossed him. He spun back, advancing, arm upraised.

She didn't flinch, cold fire in her eyes. "If you think it will work," she leveled, "then do it." And waited.

But Mats couldn't, wading in and plucking the elf off the pavement, roaring, the groups streaming toward each other, colliding, shouts and screams, glass breaking and clangs echoing across the grounds, so that they couldn't hear the dark cars pulling up, black-suited half-elves or possibly humans boiling out, truncheons ready, wading into the mob and swinging. And behind them, an elf in a wheelchair and a man in a suit waited and watched, a small smile on the lips of the elf.

The truncheons did their work, both sides melting before the heavy swings. Scores of elves had fallen in the confusion, struck by who knows what, wielded by who knew. Gardner sank to her knees, dress torn, pearls scattered, alone in the midst of the chaos, face turned to the sky but eyes closed.

Then one of the truncheon goons did something unheard of in all their centuries of production, firing a single shot into the air. The report ricocheted off the buildings and capered in the high spaces of the complex.

They froze. Into the absolute silence dropped the creaking of a wheelchair.

When he reached Gardner, Racer paused. "So," he wheezed. "We meet." He looked beyond her. "Is this your army?" He coughed. "The best you could do?"

She opened her eyes and stood. "You are all that is slimy in this world."

"Me?" He raised his eyebrows and next, his voice. "How am I slimy? All I did was create a business model. It would have worked, had it not been for you and all your interference! I gave them incentives over your objections!" (Mutterings from the crowd at this.) "As for the deer, well, how you and your big boyfriend could lie like that" (she gasped) "in front of so many news cameras, I simply do not know. Photographs! Those can be fabricated!"

He turned his wheelchair to face the crowd. Baylor stepped up behind him and placed a hand on each handle. "So!" Racer surveyed them mildly. "Do we look so evil? Regrettable, that we had to use some force here. But look what you would have done otherwise. Where would Christmas be then? Have we forgotten the children?"

"Killer."

The word slipped through his speech like a dirk. She pushed through the elves and stood beside Gardner. "It's all I can do not to spit on you. WonderFinish was your idea. And Halter paid the price—" her voice barely wavering "—and Drover. You killed them. You killed what we're about. You—and you." She glared at Baylor.

Baylor returned her gaze. "I regret what happened to Halter and Drover," he said. "In all sincerity I do. But we have to move on. You can die one of two ways. You can kill off old ways and join the modern world, whether you agree with all of it or not. Or you can die by degrees. We thought—I thought it would cause less pain, over time, to make the adjustment now."

"Adjustment!" Spinner cried. "Elves die, and you call it an adjustment! Oh, which of you is the more evil! I—"

Gardner laid a hand on her arm. "Don't," she said quietly. "Listen."

"I don't want to listen! I've heard everything I need to hear!"

"I don't mean that. I mean listen." Her face tilted upward. "Pray you hear it."

A breeze lifted the NPI flag and snapped it over the rubble. Now everyone had faces upturned, ears straining, as darting in and out between the flaps of the flag they heard, or thought they heard at first, a tinkling on the wind. Silence. Then the breeze swung their way, and on it, unmistakably this time, jingling. They peered into the blackness, some shading their eyes as though they expected sunlight, some smiling, many openmouthed. The jingling grew, question mark and low voice blending among other bells of such perfect pitch and harmony, fused to the wind, that there could be no mistaking. Weapons became tools again and clanked to the cement. Elves who'd been fighting helped each other up. The truncheon goons seeped out of the crowd and phalanxed behind Baylor.

Mats saw it first, a darker shape against the darkness. "Old friend," he murmured, smiling. "You said not to be surprised if you show up."

The crowd flattened itself against the factory walls that separated them from Racer, Baylor and Baylor's guard. Spinner rejoined Winnow. Only Gardner remained, straight and slender in her dress like a blue wand fixed to the clearing they'd made. On his sleigh came, bellsongs growing.

The big craft circled the compound and as it did, the crowd opened into a murmur, then a soft roar, and finally a cheer, the sleigh now making its final approach, twelve deer and their magic leader whistling from the sky and landing with hardly a scrape on the walkway. When it stopped, he faced Gardner, read all in her eyes and on her cheeks. He nodded, took her hand briefly before giving it to Roxy and jumping down.

The roaring ceased. Heavy clumps rang across the clearing.

Baylor glowered at him. "You can't just land here like that!"

"I just did." He pulled off his gloves, glaring down at Racer. "Hell of a flight," he said. "Shutting down the airspace and cutting me off like that. Good thing I had my team." He glanced at Baylor's guard. "What the hell is this, 'Men In Black?'"

Racer's eyes drifted to Roxy and then Tracer, who had joined Santa, snapping off snow goggles and staring at them, dark eyes flashing with gold lights. Behind Tracer, Gardner and the others had assembled. "The JEDI," he murmured.

"Yes, Racer, the JEDI," Santa said. "You should explain how you knew."

"You have no authority here!" Baylor snapped.

"Tell it to them." Santa gestured toward the elves. "I suppose legally I don't, at the moment. But think about it, you little reptile. Ask your investors." He spoke quietly at first, but his deep voice nonetheless reached every ear. "In no time flat you screwed up production, liquidated our core business, tried to get a stupid merger going, had a huge accident, killed a couple of your workforce, and created this!" He waved an arm. "Now you're trying to figure out how to keep them from burning the damn place down! I just flew over this compound," he roared, "and I can't *believe* what a shambles I saw! And you're going to contain this with a few flimsy press releases? What the hell are you thinking?" He scowled at Racer. "And why," he growled, "are you working with this *liar* here?"

Tracer stepped forward. "Who authorized killing the deer?" A murmur shot through the crowd.

"In good time, Tracer." Santa restrained him. "Let's go back to what can be done and what can't. Authority. Baylor. How do you propose to dig yourself out of this monumental mess? Keeper of the share price!" His voice dripped with disdain. "Buy back stock? Issue a statement? Sweep everything under the rug? Kill more deer to improve cash flow? Force the elves back and assume quality will be OK? Open up the airspace, stop choking suppliers? What do you think?" He swept his arms, spinning around, embracing the whole place. "You think Christmas is a quarterly return on investment?" he boomed. "Is that what you think goes on here?"

"You put the structure in place," Baylor hissed. "I didn't force my way in."

"You're right," Santa said. "I did this. It was wrong. Or maybe it was right, but the players were wrong."

"You need a Board! You can't function properly in modern business without one. Who'll handle your investors?"

"Who's handling them now?" Santa shouted. "You? At the rate we're going, this place will be a leveraged buyout in a month! Is that what you intended? So you can declare the fundamentals are good and look for a white-knight bailout? And you can get your golden parachutes and move on? It ain't gonna happen!"

The elves flowed past the sleigh, encircling Ravi still huddled in the back, sluicing around him toward the Chief.

"Baylor, you're through," Santa said. "Any of your precious shareholders can tell you that. Performance stinks so bad around here, it's a wonder they can't smell it in the southlands. Your big fund managers will want a change."

"Back to you, I suppose."

"Back to me." They glared at each other.

Racer stirred. "Yes, it's the only way," he wheezed, looking over his shoulder at Baylor. "I warned you, didn't I? I told you the elves would never go for their Chief being removed." Baylor gaped at him. "As for your other policies, no matter what I said—"

"Racer, shut up. Nothing comes out of your mouth that isn't a lie," Santa growled.

"Lie?" Racer's mouth twisted. "Your not going to believe Gardner and her—"

Hammer strode up. "Chief," he said, and got no farther before Santa embraced him. "Chief." He pulled away and reached inside his jacket. "Before you entertain them any longer, read this." He pulled out a crumpled sheet. "Did they tell you Groomer's dead?"

"Dead? How?"

"Choked to death. One of his hotdogs." Hammer glared at Racer and raised his voice. "They did an autopsy, and they analyzed the hotdogs. Reindeer meat."

Santa's chest rose and fell.

"Before he died, he wrote this down," Hammer continued. He unfolded the sheet.

"Let me see it." Santa snatched it from Hammer and read rapidly, his face darkening. Then he crumpled it. "So! Surveying. A plot to stage an accident at my cabin. My cabin! RFS book adjustments. On and on! What do you know about all this, my good CEO?"

Baylor's eyes widened. "Book adjustments! Accident! What—?"

Racer shifted uncomfortably.

"I thought not. Our little elf-spider has spun one too many webs."

Racer sniffed at the paper, as though it contained spoiled remnants of Groomer's food. "Marks on a paper. Doodles! What do they prove? Nothing! Our *Coun*sel always did have a good imagination. Do you really think I—"

Several shouts. Elves pointed skyward. Another dark shape flitted there like a bat, briefly, before whisking down and landing silently next to the sleigh, parting the crowd like a knife. One helmeted figure dragged the other from the speed sled and hustled it toward Santa and Racer. The first one yanked the helmet off the second, whose arms were bound tightly, before undoing its own. A blaze of red hair lit the night.

"Demon!" Tracer exclaimed. "What's this?" Roxy moved a step closer to him.

"Take this—slimebag and do something with him," Demon snapped. Her eyes met Tracer's. "Deerkeeper. You're safe, I see." She regarded Roxy a long moment, then shifted back to him. "Meet Raven, again. Found him out by the cabin."

"The speed sled," Tracer breathed. "Parsley! Did he—"

"She's safe," Demon said. "I saw her flying the skyfields, so I know she returned to the stable after I corralled this one." She slapped Raven's back. "Why don't you tell everyone what you told me. Remember? Why you were nosing around up there?"

Santa appraised the silent elf. "Raven. What? The truth. I'll know otherwise."

Raven's chest rose and fell. "I was to stage an accident."

"What kind?" The blue eyes didn't waver.

"It was up to me. So I decided, a fire." He stared at Tracer. "If I set fire to the stable with some of the deer inside, you'd do everything you could to rescue them. Then in the midst of it all—"

"Who put you up to it?" Santa said, very quietly.

Raven pointed.

"I thought so. Demon, get him out of here. Now, Racer," Santa continued. "You want to explain how this works *for* NPI? You haven't exactly been forthcoming."

"Kill him!" one of the elves shouted, and another began shouting, "Deerkiller! Deerkiller! Deerkiller!" –the crowd picking up the chant and advancing.

But Santa held his arms aloft and shouted, "That—is—enough! Now!" And he laid a finger against his nose.

All light vanished. The chant broke into a confused gabble, then ceased. A long, long moment passed. The breeze died. Utter stillness reigned.

Into the black, a light blazed—but it was only the glow from the tip of one finger, so bright in that dark space. The finger moved upward, outlining a timeless, magical face, ruddy cheeks and deep blue eyes, white eyebrows, massed curls, flowing beard. The mouth moved, and the voice spoke. "Now I'm supposed to go up the chimney and disappear. But I won't.

"This is how it all started, really. A single light—call it a beacon—coming to me and resting inside me, untold years ago. It began while I tended those wonderful beasts over there. How I came to be, elf crossed with human, really doesn't matter. Only that I was. And am. Creatures like me, and Tracer, and my wife, are lucky and unlucky at the same time. We're lucky enough to have elf-stuff in us, unlucky enough to have a side that can forget, if we're not careful. And then Christmas will go out. Like this."

The compound pitched into total darkness. They heard high keening voices on the wind, harsh laughs and howls. "It can be like this," he said. "Or—" the light flared up again "—we can keep the flame going, light our way through the darkness. We start with each other—" he reached out, touched Roxy, then Tracer and Hammer, and all were bathed in a gentle light. Roxy hesitated. "Go ahead," he urged. She touched Gardner, and the light flowed between them like water. "You see?" He shook his head. "What I'd forgotten. What we'd all forgotten. And as for all of you..."

He held his finger above his head, and light arced from it to the crowd, where gasps and amazed laughter erupted. "How easy it can be, if we stop and think. No, not think. Not just think. Be. Silence ourselves. This—frantic world we've created. We can only survive if we become more frantic than the next guy. Idiotic model. We run our world based on fears and inflate ordinary problems. They become these gigantic dragons we feel so important slaying. They don't matter."

Tracer circled and touched Baylor and his guard. Truncheons clattered to the pavement, but no light appeared. "It doesn't always work," Santa said. "But it tells you something here. Too bad in the unmagic world, you can't see who's what so easily. And there are some for whom this touch is, well, deadly. Racer. Shall I try?" He towered over him. "Or do we just recognize you for what you are?"

Racer said nothing.

"All across NPI now," Santa said, "there's darkness." His eyes never left Racer. "A darkness we created. But everywhere, elves are touching each other. Each light grows stronger when they do. There are elves who remain dark. Whether we ever get them back remains to be seen. That's your legacy, Racer, you and your type. I hope you're proud. Now. Baylor. Choose."

"Choose what?" Baylor's voice croaked from the darkness.

"You're still CEO. Choose to keep going your way, which in my humble six-thousand-year opinion is suicide. Or choose me. What'll it be?"

Harsh breathing. "All right," Baylor said at last. "I'll give it up. But I want a package."

Tracer snorted. "Your life's your package."

Santa nodded. "I'd agree with that. The little folks, the ones you broom aside when you make your deals. What package do they get? But I wouldn't worry in your case. Or any Board member. Wall Street has great tolerance for high-profile failure. You'll find a way to raise money, and you'll all be off and running again." He put his finger down, and the compound lights flared.

Hammer handed Santa his cell phone. "I've got company broadcast on speed-dial. Thought you might want to get a message to everyone."

Santa put the phone to his ear. "Hi, it's—" He smiled. "Well, thank you! It's good to be back! OK, so a message for everyone. Tell them this. Tell them the Board's dissolved, Racer will be replaced, we'll get production back up and running, I'll be straightening things out with the suppliers and the investors, the airspace will be opened up, we'll be making the flight plans as usual, and that I—that I—No. Wait." He took a deep, ragged breath. "Just tell them the Chief's come home."

8.

Somehow Gardner's office still felt the same. Just a few days ago she had left it for a dinner party among friends. So much had changed! She brushed that renegade wisp from her forehead again. So many things to do, so many actions to take! Day and night they'd worked, willingly, starting with the Argentines the moment he'd handed the phone to Hammer. Even the unflappable Henna had gasped when told the news via phone and instructed to pull out the food for some very special late-night guests.

Her mind ranged over many topics. *We're not done by any means. There's deals, conversations, all kinds of bruised relations here and outside, our new course, legal, on and on. And going over it all again. He's been as much the whirlwind as I have.* She remembered catching him elbow-deep in papers, assignments, sticky notes, everything sprawled over her office floor, the whiteboard covered with strategies, actions, reassignments. They'd looked at each other and laughed, conspirators, setting up the new business almost from scratch. Right then and there she'd had to resist the temptation to reach out and muss those magnificent white curls. She knew he would have laughed, too.

She smiled, staring at the scribbles. A soft knock. "Come in." She glanced at the door, expecting Router or Mats, perhaps Spokes.

For an instant only, she paused before whisking around her desk, arms outstretched. "Kelli," she whispered.

They embraced a long moment, before Gardner pulled back. "You are well?"

"I'm pretty good," Kelli said, smiling. "Want your laptop back?"

Gardner laughed. "Hardly!"

"Good, 'cause I'm not letting it go!"

Gardner took her arm, and they strolled from her office. "You *are* coming to the meeting, aren't you?"

"You know I am. An EEC. And you know why."

"Yes I do, I approved it! Director of Herd Operations. It sounds good. You'll make a good partner to Router. He's got Oiler's old job."

"No more WonderFinish."

"No more WonderFinish." They walked toward the main conference room.

"So, who else is getting new assignments?"

"Well, Santa will make the announcements, so I won't steal his thunder. But at the meeting we'll see his new Indian friend, and Mats, Hammer, plus Router, Wheeler and Crafter. Roxy of course, and Tracer. Demon may show up. Winnow and Spinner. …I'm probably forgetting somebody."

"And Bill?"

Gardner smiled sidelong at her. "He and Anders will audio. He'll be quite challenged in his new position."

"Which is…?"

"He didn't tell you?"

She laughed. "He did. COO of Sverige Feed Supply, with Anders taking Mats's place. I just wanted to confirm it."

"Wise elf! Ah, here we are!"

They entered the conference room and took their seats. Except for the Chief and Roxy, the others were already there. Ravi's cast stuck out prominently under the table.

Spinner fussed with the conference phone. "Mats, what's the number for Sverige?"

In a couple of minutes, Bill's voice crackled. "Anders is here with me. Everybody there?" he asked.

"Everybody except the Chief and—"

The room filled with spontaneous applause. Santa and Roxy had arrived and stood at the conference table head. After no small amount of time, Santa motioned for quiet, and everyone sat down.

He surveyed the room, blue eyes twinkling the old twinkle. *How I've missed that!* Gardner caught Roxy's eye—had she been watching Tracer?—and Roxy tried vainly not to smile. No one made a sound, and at last the conference phone buzzed. "Hey, are we still connected?"

The room erupted into laughter. "Bill, you pass the test!" Mats called out.

Santa cleared his throat. "The reason why there was such a long pause, Bill," he began, "was because …well. We've been through a lot. All of us. And I don't know how to thank all of you, except to put you all to work!"

More laughter. "How long have we all been together?" he asked. "Even the younger folks—except, of course, for Bill and Anders there in Sweden."

"*And* Ravi," Roxy reminded him.

"*And* Ravi, of course. But we've been through so much with Ravi, I feel as though I've known him a lot longer. And what we've all been through these past few months—has there been anything like it in all our history? I don't think so.

"Now we've got a big job. Our biggest. It's been a few days since we threw out the Board, days we couldn't afford to lose. But we lost ground, despite all our hard work. Let's get the worst business over with first. Router, Mats?"

Router began. "RFS operations have been stopped. That's a relief, but it's creating headaches with our new partners."

"Ex-partners," Santa broke in. "I'm already making sure of that. And legal has stepped up to fill the rather large void Groomer left. There'll be some short-term financial hell, but make no mistake, this program's *over*. Have you talked to Sweden?"

"Yes," Router said. "We approached the Swedish government about the operations there and our intentions. Bill?"

"Sweden agreed we can dismantle. Your legal department has been very swift with this one. And it took a nicely-timed phone call to cinch it."

Gardner waited. Many of them looked approvingly at their Chief. *This'll surprise them.* "Not me. Silvertongue."

"Exactly," the conference phone squawked. "After his call, we got the green light. So Anders and I are working with Gøran—who says 'Hi' to you, Kelli, by the way, and the children miss you—" (Kelli blushed, and Gardner squeezed her arm) "—and we'll begin the dismantling operations as soon as all the signatures are in. We're already working with the local firms to truck the remaining herds back south, where they can be put on cargo flights to the Central Stables."

"Great! Hmm," Santa rumbled, "Strapper and Saddler will have their hands full. Let's talk assignments and announcements. Here's how things are working out. We'll get charts going when we have time, but for now, we'll just have to remember it all. Somehow. Let's start with our most difficult ones. Silvertongue. He managed to be of real use in Sweden. Plus he brought the Argentines back to their senses, with help from Gardner and Mats. So. There'll be a new operation. A green one, which will help our corporate citizenship. He'll head it up, and he'll even have a chance to name it. I think a first shipment's already in, courtesy of the Argentines."

Router burst out laughing.

Gardner leaned forward. "Laugh all you want, Router," she said, "but you'll need a special area on the docks. I suspect there'll be a lot of that stuff coming in. Unless we locate the operation elsewhere."

"Why not in Sweden?" Mats asked. "Convert the factory."

She smiled at him, remembering Köln. "We could do that."

"We could." Santa toyed with his moustache. "Although it spoils my other assignment a little. Racer. I was going to put him in charge of dismantling the operation, bit by bit. A one-elf show. The way I saw it, it would take him about a thousand years to pull all that equipment down by himself. If he didn't fall in a grinder or something. But maybe that's too harsh, even for a spider like him. Gardner, you and Mats are right. Locate all three of 'em there. Have Racer dismantle the old operation, Silvertongue make the deals with the ranches and the countries, reopen talks with the Swedes to get it going. And Oiler—Oiler can shovel. Or whatever else. We can keep an eye on all of them there, and it'll be nice to have the tonnage figures referring to fertilizer. That reminds me. Roxy, have Id set up something special to handle the elves who were part of those operations. I'm sure most of them didn't realize what they were getting into until it was far too late."

And from there, he moved on to finances and production, outlining in that old forceful style the things they'd hashed through in the wee hours. She bit her lip. They would build it back. It would work again. Of that neither she nor he had any doubts.

His voice rolled on. "Spokes, get a plan together on the financials, give the Wall Street kids something they can live with. Let's let e-business simmer down before we jump back in. New York's learning you have to have profits, not just revenues. Remind—who was it, presenting all that e-stuff a while back?"

"Sprinter."

"Sprinter. Bit player. Remind him of the profit side of things. And clean up some of the stuff they've been doing down there. Just because we *can* sell something doesn't mean we should. Now, Crafter, Hammer. Let's talk the real stuff. Where are we?"

"Everyone's back, working full tilt," Hammer said. I've asked the union reps to make sure the guys look the other way if salaried folks help out. You know what one of them said? He said, 'You have to ask? It's a given.' So we'll see our way through this, all of us, together. Something, I might add, that Halter would have been proud of."

"Yes." The white curls trembled. Gardner remembered that first meeting, when he'd had to come to grips with it all, and both she and Roxy were needed, simply to listen. "That hurts. And Drover. And all the injured elves at the end. Good thing none of them were hurt seriously, especially by those goons. Router, we sent them packing?"

"First available flight."

"Good. The price of all of this was far too high. Hammer, you and Crafter put something together, a legacy, a memoriam, something—something to remind us all, so we never let this happen again. For both of them. And—and for their families, and—"

After a considerable pause, she took it up for him. "...Let's go on. Crafter. Production. How do things look?"

Crafter stirred. "We'll make it. Scaled back some, and Doll Ops will be hardest hit, but there should be enough. Winnow and Spinner are working out a plan to adjust schedules between them. It'll be tight, but then—" he smiled "—it always is, this time of year, isn't it?"

Chuckles drifted through the room. "Yes," she said. "Some things at least feel normal." She looked his way and raised an eyebrow. "Announcements?" She bit her lip again to keep from grinning outright at his smile.

"Announcements. Let's start with our long-time friend, Mats. I've asked him to assume COO, now that Racer has other challenges. And he'll have a seat on the Board."

He continued, his remarks punctuated by applause and congratulatory shouts. Gardner's pulse quickened. He released the names into the room, and images glided past, veterans and newcomers, work of centuries, struggles of the moment, and the fight to save it all. Spinner, heading Doll Operations. Kelli, Director of Herd Operations. Router, replacing Oiler as Logistics chief. Ravi, Santa Diversity.

And Demon. "Demon will have a strategic assignment as training specialist, working closely with Strapper and Saddler. When they can find her. I'd give you a title for it, Demon, but I know better." He and Demon traded knowing glances. "Someday I'd like to know how you found the old place," he chuckled.

"And while we're talking flights and schedules, let's figure out the santa situation and the flight teams. Who wants to start?"

"I've got a plan for bringing in new santas," Ravi said. "If we crash train enough diversity guys, we'll get there. They'll be green, but that's the best we can do."

"It'll make for an interesting Christmas," he rumbled. "News reports all over the place. Keep 'em clear of any weather balloons, that's all I ask."

Laughs around the table. Still grinning, Ravi said, "Of course, if this doesn't work out, we can always do agency."

Santa roared with laughter. "At least I'll know about it this time!"

"We're working out flight schedules now," Router said. "There are still routes to choose from." He rubbed his chin. "What about you?" he asked. "And Tracer?"

Gardner leaned forward, caught him studying Demon.

"Tracer has work to do at my place," Santa said. "Which I'll talk about momentarily. He could take out a team, when the time comes. But as for me…" He looked around the table, his eyes soft. "You know, with everything else, I hadn't given it a thought. There's much to do. But why not? Why not. Get me a route, maybe a Scandinavian one. No. Wait. I'll make one special trip this year. It's a little town called Posen. In the United States, in Michigan. I have to visit a little girl there. With her very special list. I'll need my suit, which of course fits very well."

He glanced sidelong at Roxy, who smiled. "Will you be making your phone call there?" she asked.

"To Mr. Hopper?" He grinned. "Yes. We have to unglue the merger. Plus, we need seats on each other's Boards, to stop this from happening again. And there's one more thing, Roxy, which you and Ravi know about. I need him to take care of a special situation in Detroit, involving a Jaguar and a new relative of mine."

Gardner blinked. *No mention of this!*

Ravi and Roxy burst out laughing.

"I'll explain one day," Santa chuckled. "Maybe. So." He held up a big hand. "We've talked RFS, and Argentina, and herd operations, and flights, and production, and EI. That leaves one more thing."

Gardner's eyes met his. *Uh-oh.* "Gardner," he said, "you've known about every assignment made today, because you had to approve them all. More than that, you know exactly why we took every action. Except for two. Me, and you."

She felt someone, it must have been Kelli, take her arm.

"Everyone here knows the Chief is back. Well. Yes… and no. We've set things in motion and have things back on track. But as for me…" He looked at the ceiling a moment, taking a deep breath. "I've learned some things while I was away. It's hard to put it all into words, other than to say I've been a spinning top for too long. Too long. It's time for me to step aside."

Gasps flew about the table. She put her free hand to her mouth.

He held up a hand. "Not totally! I'm not retiring to a beach in the Bahamas, like a fat old millionaire. But away from direct involvement. It's what got me off track. Sure, there's operations, logistics, deals, strategies, all that stuff. There have to be. But I need to *connect* with something far deeper. If I don't, I— Well, you saw. That's what a little girl taught me without knowing it. That's what a bunch of folks in a small town taught me, too. And a big tavern-keeping woman. Tracer knows what it means to connect."

Her heart pounded. Where was he going? She was aware of looks flying about the room. The lights sharpened, and it all felt suddenly so bright, so bright, with rich, clear words ringing off closing-in walls. She stared at him, large mouth moving under magnificent curly beard.

"What I learned is how many presents I'd been given without realizing it. Or thanking the givers. All of you here Your time, your efforts, your courage. For the people. For the children. For a little girl.

"So I'm going home. I'm going back to the cabin and the stable, where my team and I will live and work. We'll find Christmas in small towns everywhere, and cities and farms, and neighborhoods. Where the children are. Where I am, with them. Tracer will go with me, back up there, to oversee the stables he loves so well. We'll bring the old factory back to life. Make it a creator of hand-made toys, the 'old world' way. We'll work out the details as we go. Bring some of the craft elves up with us. And Roxy will, in time, join us, when—"

Gardner jumped when Roxy slammed her fist. "I'm joining you *now*," she declared. "I'll live in one of those factory homes. Tracer can restore it. If you think for a minute I traveled thousands of miles and listened to all your—well, all your *crap* for so long, only to be told to stay here while you *connect* with something, well—"

Santa and Roxy stared at each other. The room fairly crackled in the sudden silence. Then a corner of his mouth turned up ever so slightly. "Why, Roxy," he said mildly with artificial inflections, "someone's got to run my office. Who did you think it would be?"

The room resounded with more laughter. Santa faced the others and bellowed, "Tracer! *You* may have liked things up there the way they were, no email, no radio, no phone. That needs to change. I'll have to have an *office* there. Roxy will run it. Keep me from getting into trouble. I hope so. And we need to change our plans. Get this *troublemaker* up there as quick as you can, before she creates problems. Get her one of the houses. And if that isn't enough to keep her going, well, there's the factory. She can try her hand at production control. Whip those crafters into shape. When she's not listening to my *crap*, that is!"

Then those twinkling eyes fastened on Gardner. Kelli's grip tightened on her arm, and the next words seemed to float over vast distances.

"—because somebody has to run the doggone place down here, I turn the CEO position over to Gardner—" shouts and applause "—so you'll have to find somebody in ER to take your place!"

And he was bounding up and over and she was standing and he was smothering her in a big bear hug, roaring and—was it the others, cheering? *Kelli? Is that your hand?* "Congratulations!" he shouted above the general din. "And boy, are you ever in for it!"

The roaring resolved into applause, then conversation, then her own trembling, her own breathing, her own heartbeat. He released her, grinning broadly. And she, feeling every bit as small as ever she had felt in her long life, grinned back.

Kelli kissed her cheek and then was pulled into a bear hug from the new COO. In the midst of it all, Router walked up to Gardner and extended his hand. "Congratulations, Chief," he said.

"Oh, no! Not me." *Will I ever catch my breath?* She tilted her head. "He's the Chief. And he knows it! Even though he'll be way up there, he'll be all around us!"

"Especially after I get my office set up," Santa said, as Roxy strolled up. "Here comes my real boss. ...But I mean it. This is yours, Gardner. You deserve it more than anyone. Call when you need to. But not too often!" He cupped his hands over his mouth. "Hey, Tracer!" he shouted. "Get over here!"

"Hang on!"

Tracer broke off his conversation with Ravi, paused a moment to say something to Demon, her small hands in his, before joining them.

"Well." Santa clapped a big hand around Tracer's shoulders. "There aren't enough words for what this one's done!"

"No, I was just—"

"Don't say anything!" Santa declared. "Just this." He stepped back from Gardner and Router, with Roxy beside him. He spoke quietly, rapidly. "These routes, these flights. We're going to need help this year. But the team you brought back, I—They're yours if you want them this year. Pick any route you want and take them."

"Your team?"

"My team." He nodded.

Tracer faced him, his mouth working. He blinked rapidly a couple of times. Then he grabbed Santa's hand. "It's beyond any dream I could imagine," he whispered. "But they're yours. I always knew I'd give them back to you. I'll find a team, and a route. You have a special appointment. Remember? You have to take them. Just—" He turned away a moment, turned back. "Just always—Take the time with them. You know all their special wants, the things each of them likes best. I mean—I don't have to tell you—" Roxy slipped an arm in his.

Santa held his hand a long moment, looking deep into those deer eyes. "Roxy," he said finally, "our friend understands Christmas better than anyone else in this room."

He released Tracer's hand, and Tracer stepped back, struggling, Roxy's arm twined in his. Gardner's own eyes shone. *The long road home.* She smiled and took a step toward them both. *The long road home. But here we are at last.*

9.

It snowed every day now. Every day, Saddler and Strapper oversaw operations so numerous they taxed to the limit the deer under their guidance. The factory deer were most willing and most challenging. For them, the magic of flight had to be restored gently, but still with an eye on the pressing deadline. Teams of all skills speckled the skies, and by some miracle the accident rate didn't climb. Tracer's return had helped, but he was due to leave soon for the cabin.

He stood beside Saddler, scanning takeoffs and landings through his field glasses. "I don't see her anywhere," he said.

Saddler grunted. "And that surprises you?"

"Well, no." He let the glasses dangle around his neck. "But I was kind of hoping…"

"Don't get your hopes up too high with that one," Saddler said. "I've never once seen her meet a timetable other than her own." He eyed Tracer. "If it's thanking her you want to do, or something else like that, you don't have to. She's not that kind."

"I know it."

"Well," Saddler said at last. "I've got other things I need to take care of. Hope you find her." He strode across the field to one of the teams, leaving Tracer alone.

He brought the glasses up again, smiling. *Like trying to find the wind. Or chasing a dream.*

He put the glasses down and rubbed his eyes. And then he knew he'd sighted her, a dancing speck in the corner of his left eye. His heart jumped, and he began walking. Oblivious of the other teams, he walked with bowed head across the field.

When he looked up, she had already unhitched one team and was busy hitching another. He took his place across from her, the deer separating them. His hands worked by habit when his voice wouldn't, helping with the fittings.

She glanced up. "Hello, Deerkeeper."

They worked silently for a while. "You went away for so long."

"When?"

"Before. When I went back to the cabin. I finished the sleigh and the training, and I wondered where you went."

"Did you think I'd drop by for a visit?"

"Well, I—"

"Deerkeeper." She stopped working and rested her arms on the rump of the nearest deer. "I was back at the compound a while. We all had a lot to do."

"You were at the compound all that time?"

"Other elves have learned never to ask me."

"I'm not fully an elf."

She laughed. "Not yet. But what is it? Did you miss me?"

"Yes. I did."

"Don't," she said, and it seemed to him as though her eyes went elsewhere for the briefest moment before regaining their steel. "You might as well miss the wind. That's how they all describe me, isn't it?" She followed the track of a team taking off somewhere behind him. "So don't miss me, Deerkeeper. Besides, there's someone who'll take care of you much better than I would." She looked him over. "I've seen how she looks at you. She's very beautiful, you know."

"I know." He smiled awkwardly. "But so are you." He moved around the deer to stand beside her.

She laughed gently. "Me? Perhaps. And so are deer, and clouds, and stormy skies! All beautiful. All with parts that are untamable. As of course you know, you of the unplanned sleigh ride through the heavens!"

They both laughed softly at that. Her eyes turned skyward again. "But that's the stuff I'm made of, Deerkeeper. Snow, and wind, and the high heavens. There'd be some dark, nasty night, when you might want to—want someone to be with, and I'd be up and out, riding the night skies."

"You're more elfin than most," he said. "You and your ghost team."

"So I've been told," she said. "Who knows? Someday I might cease to be of this earth altogether and become nothing more than a cry on the wind."

He reached out and touched her arm. "You feel pretty solid to me."

"Now. Today. But tomorrow? The time may come when we all disappear, all elves, when the people turn inward and lose sight of everything around them."

The deer moved under her arm. "Until then, though, there's plenty of work to do." She looked up, her eyes searching deep into his, and he could see the very vastness of wild heaven in hers. "Go to her, Deerkeeper. Maybe in a different world, a different time, different points in our lives, this would have worked. But I knew, because—I just knew. You'll be good to each other. And I'll be watching over you. Both of you. Always."

His voice trembled. "You call me Deerkeeper," he said. "No one else has—no one else will ever call me that. So let me give you a name, too, something only you and I will know. Let me call you Windrider."

She smiled, her eyes bright. "I like that," she said. "Very much. It suits me. Me and my ghost team."

She drew away from him and returned her attention to the deer, making her final preparations before leaping lightly into the work wagon. "When you're situated up there, I'll visit. Soon. You'll have to keep your place in order all the time, because you never know when I might stop by." She leaned over and kissed him lightly on the cheek. "And if ever she doesn't take care of you, she'll have to answer to me!"

She slapped the reins and called to the team, and they moved off. "Good-bye, Deerkeeper!" she called over her shoulder. "Good-bye for now!"

He stood in the middle of the training field, as teams all around him took off and landed. His face upturned, the falling snow melting on his cheeks, he watched her team dwindle to a speck and vanish into the restless skies, her cries fading until they blended into the swirling winds. And though his eyes saw nothing more and his ears heard nothing more, still he watched and still he listened.

SPRING

1.

On a cool, crisp and bright Scandinavian morning, under a deep blue spring sky, a chief executive officer and her chief operating officer met for morning coffee. The waters of the Rosenlunds Canal gleamed in the gathering light. They studied the ripples from their vantage point in a little corner café.

Gardner sipped her coffee and leaned back, sighing. "Gothenburg in spring. It's always so beautiful. I'm glad we could use Sverige as an excuse to get here."

"Yes," Mats agreed. "Almost a morning like this can make you forget about the rest of it, all the things going on back there. Actually, it's a wonder we found a place open right after the Feast of Valborg, the 'welcome to spring'. Our youngsters are all at home sleeping it off, I can assure you."

"The first of May." She shook her head. "Amazing, don't you think? The warmer weather, the flowers! It's this time of year when Christmas seems so far away. We're through with all our post-holiday things, and in June we'll start thinking about fall rampup. But May! May is vacation time."

Mats nodded. "A time to reflect," he said. "On all that changed, and all that stayed the same."

"You're right. You know, Mats, a lot more stayed the same than I thought. We got production worked out so we met our quotas. We actually started rebuilding things. And we managed to restructure the delivery assignments. Everything went off as it should."

"Not a child without a Christmas, then?"

"Not a child without a Christmas."

"An impressive debut."

"I couldn't have done it without you and all the rest, Mats!"

"Who had the idea of using elves as santas this year?"

"Ravi."

"A stroke of genius, you know. As simple and as obvious as it seemed to be. Do you think you'll be able to keep them in the factories next year?"

She smiled. "Hard to say. They certainly enjoyed themselves. How is Sverige, now that you're not there? Have you talked to Anders?"

"He is a good man. It was a challenge, but he did all right. And of course, Bill has stepped neatly into his boots as COO. He finds plenty of reason to visit NPI, you know."

"I know. Visiting our Director of Herd Operations."

"Did you talk to her about it?"

"I did, Mats. They both feel young, and that makes it so difficult. So one day I had lunch with her, and I started to spell it out to her, about how hard it will become to watch the one you love grow old and weaken before your eyes, and you can do nothing about it. And of course your children will see it, too."

A sadness came over his face. "What did she say?"

"She stopped me in the middle of my little lecture. She said they had talked long about it. She'd been through so much with him, this choice was simply natural, even with what the future would bring."

"She says that now."

"Mats." She laid a hand on his arm. "Of course she says it now. This is how it always is. It was the same in your family. And Gøran's, with his adopted children. Did it matter in your case?"

He shook his head.

"It doesn't make it easy," she murmured, rubbing his arm, "but it's their choice."

They sat silent a moment, watching the morning sun light buildings along the canal. Mats cleared his throat. "I have worked with you some months now but never asked you. How has it been without having him around?"

She studied the waters. "Different," she said at last. "Not bad, just—something to get used to. At first we were so busy, right through Christmas, it hardly mattered where anybody was. But then, in the winter months, when things began settling down a little, that's when we could feel it. Like a hole. Maybe I feel it especially. There's no one to turn to, at least not officially. I guess that's expected when you're CEO. But other than looking at your shareholder ratings, how else do you know how effective you are?"

"Look around. Your workforce is happy, your operations are coming under control, your suppler relations are improving, and your reindeer are flying. Those things should tell you."

"But it's so hard to know!"

"It feels that way. But you have done the job. Trust Mats on that. We have all come through this with flinging colors."

She smiled. "I never wanted the job, you know."

"Which is why you do so well," he said. "Those who want the job so badly, they're the ones who get themselves and their companies into trouble."

"Well, Mats, we survived it." She took another sip, and her face grew serious. "This time. This year. Those business models haven't gone away. Neither has Wall Street. It'll all come back again, like waves crashing ever higher. Will we be strong enough next time not to let it get to the same point? I just don't know. Now I understand what he'd been complaining about all this time. And look at the price we paid. How many reindeer did we lose?"

Mats shut his eyes, thinking. "About twenty-seven thousand. Plus some few hundreds more."

"Twenty-seven thousand deer. And elves in therapy today, trying to get over it. Plus the disaffected ones. And Halter and Drover killed. And the Chief leaving. The price was too high, Mats."

"I agree the price was high. But we had no choice, you and I, others like us as well, except to fight this way. As for the business models…" He sighed. "We can only hope they will change in time, they will go back to something a little less ridiculous. But I don't know. Usually something like that doesn't happen until there's a crisis that makes it happen. Forceful personalities can help. And the

Chief, he is doing what he wants and needs to do. ...You saw his speech."

"I did. To a bunch of CEO's, too, his old peers. I like what he said about shareholder value. Remember? About NPI's shareholders being children. Anyone's child, anywhere in the world."

"Yes. But then he said the important thing, Gardner. He looked them all in the eye, those old men, and he told them that when you really think about it, really think about your important businesses, children are the only shareholders who should matter. They put the cameras on the crowd then, and I saw a lot of uncomfortable faces. It will take time for that to sink in. But if he reached even a few of them, that will make a difference. They'll stop thinking about the next quarter maybe and think about the next decade."

"I hope so. But I don't know. Business is so—*compelling* these days." Her eyes softened. "I don't see him very much, now."

"No. He has gone away, just as he said he would."

"He tells me he's fixing up the cabin and taking care of his team. He's got the office installed, but I hear so little from there. And he's planted flowers and bulbs all around the grounds. I told him those flowers would die in the winter, unless he used magic on them. He said the flowers would live or die according to their wishes, not his, that they would bloom and live if his heart was right. They tell me he's planted all her favorites."

"Who tells you?"

"Tracer and Roxy. They're in a couple of the factory cabins, a little ways from his. It's lovely to see them together. They're so good for each other, you know. And if only..." Her voice trailed off.

He nodded his head, watching the waters. "He has planted all her flowers," he said. "He is going back to who he was, and he is waiting."

"Mats, do you think she'll ever come back?"

"Well that is of course the big question," he said. "She waited a very long time for him to come around. So he may have to wait as well. But in the end... In the end, I think she will come back to him. If he doesn't go back to what he was becoming. Then she would stay away. She would never return."

The waitress came by with more coffee. “I hope you’re right, Mats,” Gardner said. “About her coming back. It will break him if she doesn’t, I’m afraid.”

“He is strong. He will wait. And wait. And if I know his thinking these many years, he has already made up his mind to plant those flowers and to live there, and to accept whatever will happen. But it will be a sad thing if she doesn’t return. Still, I am a believer in the happy ending.”

Her eyes twinkled. “You don’t make a good Swede, Mats.”

“That is a bad stereo thing, and you know it! A CEO, making a statement like that! And speaking of happy endings—” he leaned forward “—you seem to see a lot of your Director of Logistics! Eh?”

She colored. “That is business, Mats! Router and I have a lot to discuss!”

“Well.” His eyes danced. “He is very good for you, and you for him, if an old half-Swede can make a statement. See that you both continue to have plenty of business to attend to, my friend!”

She laughed then, and so did he. They sipped their coffee, looking out over the blue waters, and up and down the canal and all along its buildings and the buildings of Gothenburg and all the lands round about, the long level rays of the rising Scandinavian sun reached in and warmed their world with promises of spring.

2.

The squeaky front door banged open and shut with the same frequency tonight as it had on just about every weekend night so far this spring. Heavy-booted men, Boxcar regulars, stumped from fields and shops, garages and feed stores to line up on the stools, toss back a non-potato beer or two, and discuss the Posen spring. Bob Towalski sat at one end, his Deere cap pushed back on his head, next to Ed Figurski, with a couple of other guys next to him, then Tommy, and finally (making a rare appearance) Earl.

They talked, often looking straight ahead, as if what they had to say was strictly between them and their bartender (who wasn't always in front of them, and who wasn't always listening even when he was). Their talk ranged over the important things, from springtime planting, to the best new fertilizers, to problems with the Viking school boiler, to who had to go and see the doctor all the way in Alpena, to downstate politics and those bastards from Lansing, to taxes and broken promises, to weather predictions for this season, to the good job Ronnie had done as the Easter Bunny this year.

One of them said, "Didn't seem much like Christmas this year without him."

"What'd he want to lose all that weight for? He must've dropped a hundred pounds in two months!"

"What a sight that was, too! He ended up looking like one of them sharpy dogs."

"That's shar-*pei*. Tommy, you're pretty close to him. What got him on this weight-loss kick?"

Tommy guzzled before answering. "I think it started with that big fight right after the Festival last year. Remember? With that big guy and the little Indian kid."

"Yeah, who was that? The pickle guy or something."

"Naw, he wasn't into pickles. He just had that name."

"Vlasek?"

"Naw, Claussen! Bob, if that's your short-term memory, I don't want to be buyin' no nails from you!"

Chuckles. Then Tommy. "I'm pretty sure that's when it started. 'Cause right after that, he started babbling about that giant rabbit he saw."

"Yeah, that was something," Bob said. "I don't want to go back over that again."

"Anyway, right after that he started buying that SlimFast. Wouldn't drink no beer or nothin'. You couldn't get him in this place anymore. He just sat in the living room of that little house of his, watching TV."

"Just like Jack Kerouac."

"*What*? Figurski, who the hell is Jack Ker- whatever you said?"

"He was a writer. Wrote a famous book, called *On the Road.* Anyway, legend says he dropped out of sight after that, watched TV every day until he died."

"Figurski, nobody here knows who your friend was, so why even bring it up?"

"Maybe he saw a rabbit, too."

"Will you guys shut up?" Tommy said. "So then Stan just started losing weight. And you're right, it must have been a hundred pounds or so."

"All his old friends."

"What?"

"Remember? Said he could name every pound. This one's a veal cutlet, that one's a pierogi."

"Oh, puh-lease."

"And then he decided he wasn't the real Santa anymore," Tommy continued, "so he refused to do it for Christmas. Ronnie had to do it for him."

"Not that Ronnie didn't do a good job, but it just didn't feel the same. Why'd he think he wasn't the real Santa anymore? It didn't have anything to do with that pickle guy, did it?"

"Maybe. The pickle guy bought some of my reindeer."

"Earl. If I bought some of your reindeer, took 'em out on my back lot, shot 'em and ate 'em, would that make me Santa Claus? Would it?"

"Well, no." Earl frowned. "And don't be talkin' about my deer that way. But there was something about that guy."

"I agree. Couldn't put your finger on it."

"You're right. I don't think he was into pickles at *all.*"

"He wasn't! Bob, I'm not even going to buy a pack of *gum* from you!"

More guffaws. "So what was he into, anyway?"

"I think it was toys."

"Oh, this is too good. Man says he's into toys, buys reindeer, and then disappears."

"Well, he did!" Earl protested.

"He didn't disappear, he probably just took 'em up north somewhere and let 'em loose, so he could take a few shots at 'em."

"You know, not everybody's got a one-track hunting mind the way you do."

"Well, Mary Alison thought he was Santa," Earl continued.

"OK. A seven-year-old. You believe everything a seven-year-old says?"

"Well, no, but—Well, she had a pretty good Christmas, from what I hear."

A burst of loud laughter. "And that proves it!"

"Well, she did!"

"What I heard, too," Bob said. "She got everything she wanted, including that big doll house she'd had her eye on, the one in Rogers City. They must've had another one in the back, 'cause that one's still on display, too. And you know Lydia can't afford no doll house."

"Did the little girl say she *saw* Santa Claus, too?"

"Naw, she said she didn't have to see him to know he'd been there. Lydia told me it was the doggonedest thing, 'cause she sure didn't get no doll house or any of that other stuff, but there it was."

"Lydia told you all this?"

"Yeah, when she came in to buy new locks. She changed all the locks on her house after that."

"So she told you all that. You makin' a play for her or somethin', Bob?"

"Oh, for crying out loud! Man can't even have a conversation with a single mom without it getting blown all to hell!"

"Bartender, hit me with another."

"I gotta pee."

"Oh, like we all needed to know *that.*"

The conversation lulled a bit before Bob began again. "Hey, I hear Ida's leaving us."

"What I heard, too. She's packing up after this year's Festival."

"Well, it won't be the same without her, that's for sure."

"You know, she's been here just over a year, is all."

"Funny, isn't it, how it seems like she's always been here."

"I know. Seems like she has long memories on all of us, too. You could sit down with her, and it's as if she knew all about the things that you'd been through that day, and the month and year before, too."

"I'd agree with that."

"Me, too. But it didn't sound like her going was a permanent thing. The way I heard it, she's going to do another Festival and then winter over in the south, with her sister in *Dee*-troit or something."

"That's where that weird story came from!"

"There's a lot of weird stories that come out of *Dee*-troit. Which one was this?"

"Don't you remember? It was in the paper last week. About that black kid they arrested for having a Jaguar. They accused him of stealing it, so they threw him in the county lockup and impounded the car. They were going to bring the whole thing to trial, but all of a sudden this—this what-do-you-call-him, this 'mysterious benefactor' bails the kid out and restores the Jaguar and buys a house for him and his mom, too. Never did find out who that was, the story says. Only that the 'benefactor' said the car belonged to him, but that the kid could have it."

"Now *that's* Christmas! Tommy, see if you can steal us a Jaguar apiece, so we can all get bailed out like that!"

"Wonder if she'll take William with her."

"Who?"

"Ida, Bob. Try to follow the conversation here."

"Why wouldn't she? Boy, he's the weirdest guy I've ever seen! Never says a word. All bent over, too. I bet he gets his clothes off the 'curly and narrow' rack!"

"I heard they got a waterbed. Lasted all of about a week before they gave it up."

Laughter. "I can just imagine," Ed declared. "He's layin' there in bed, and she comes galloping in, takes a flying leap, and launches him right through the window."

Loud guffaws. "I can't believe they'd get a waterbed," Bob said at last, wiping his eyes. "Sounds like some of the old 'Ida legend' to me!"

"She's certainly ripe for those kinds of stories," a new voice said. " 'Legend' has a nice ring to it, too."

Bob peered all the way down the bar past Earl. "Hopper! When did you get here? I didn't even know you'd shown up!"

"Been here for a while."

"You have not!" Earl protested.

"What's in your beer, Earl?"

"Yeah, cut him off!"

"Where the hell you been, Hopper? Haven't seen you since January! Looks like you lost some weight, too!"

"I had business. Detroit and other places. So Ida had a waterbed," Hopper continued. "Or didn't. Some think one thing and some think another. Sounds like legend to me."

"Aw, don't talk nonsense! You heard she's leaving?"

"Was sitting right here when you brought it up."

"But I—"

"Earl, shut up! She's heading to *Dee*-troit after the Festival this year, is was what we were saying."

"See I didn't hear that," Ed puzzled. "I thought she said she was heading north."

"*That'd* be like Ida. Everyone else goes south, and she heads north for the winter."

"Yeah," Ed continued. "She said something about following the old route home."

"What old route, Old 27?"

"Maybe she's got relatives up in Mackinaw City or something. Why the hell would she do Old 27? Just take 65 up to 23, through Cheboygan."

"It's her route, not ours."

"She selling the place?"

"No," Hopper said. "But she'll be leaving right now, not later, for a couple months. She needs to visit some people, set some things up. Then she'll be back to see the harvest through. I think she really likes the Festival here. Good business opportunity. I might go north with her, too. I've got some business up that way. Besides, I got relatives in Mackinaw City I haven't seen in a while. Former Miss Bridge."

"A relative?"

"Distant." Hopper finished his beer and threw a few bills on the table. "That should buy a round for all of you," he said, standing up. "I gotta run. I'll tell Ida you were thinking of her." He paused at the door. "But I won't say anything about the waterbed legend. At least not until we're over a couple of county lines." The door banged shut.

"So long, Hopper!" one of the men called after he was out of earshot. "*Hop* in any time!"

"That was so bad, it made my nose bleed."

"So, who'll be Potato Queen this year?"

"Can't be Ronnie again. Rules. No two years in a row."

"They'll figure it out, somehow. They always do."

3.

As soon as she stepped outside her cabin, Roxy knew this day would be the warmest so far. The late morning sun washed over the browns and grays of the old factory, sleepy no longer. Dozens of elves bustled about the place, cleaning windows, restoring machinery, upgrading electrical systems. All these activities took place under the watchful eyes of Tracer and Strapper—Strapper who, like so many other elves, had decided against a late-May vacation, preferring instead to get the old place back in order.

She strolled down her front walk, between colorful rows of daffodils, crocuses and other early spring flowers. Tracer had planted these, telling her that Santa wasn't the only one who could do it.

She smiled, walking by the factory. Several elves working the grounds stopped and waved, and she waved back. How different the pace was up here—so purposeful, measured, matched to the pulse of this world. Her relationship with Tracer had deepened in the same measured way. At first, they relied on each other's skills to make the most of their new lives—his, how to take care of the deer, and hers, how to take care of the Chief. Through their work, they began also to talk through their experiences and to heal the wounds they had both suffered.

She passed his cottage. He wasn't inside. She knew where he'd be this time of day, so she followed the familiar path between his cottage and the next. An arctic hare, its fur already brown for summer, paused on the path before bounding aside. She climbed the small hill behind his cottage.

He stood in the clearing, face uplifted. She walked up and took his arm. "Lovely morning," she said.

He turned to her and put his arms around her waist. "Now it is."

"God, that's schmaltzy!"

"I learned it from the deer."

"I see. 'The deer know.' I didn't know they filled their heads with that kind of stuff!" She disengaged and scanned the skies herself. "So," she said. "Do you think she'll come and visit today?"

He smiled. "She might. Looks like it's a pretty dull day up there."

"I should be jealous, but I'm not."

"You might as well be jealous of the wind. She's where she wants to be. So am I."

"But still."

"Still what?"

Her eyes never left the sky. "There's a part of you that will always be up there, isn't there? With her."

A moment passed before he answered. "Do you remember the old saying? About Christmas being 'in the sky and in the deer.' Demon is as close to what Christmas means in this world as anyone I've known. So because she's in the sky and in the deer, and so am I, then yes, part of me is with her." He sighed lightly. "But I did have to learn that the heart sometimes asks for what it's not meant to have."

"So you'll settle for me," she challenged gently.

"Settle?" He laughed in amazement. "Settle? Roxy, you can't mean that. This is where I want to be now. And you—" He took both her hands in his. "Your strength, how you give to everyone in your life. And you watch over them. The way you watched over Santa. And me. Sometimes I wonder if you're real, or if I'll wake up suddenly and find out this was all a dream. A wonderful, wonderful dream."

Her eyes softened, seeing the earnestness in his. Those gold-lit eyes saw her, truly, all the way to her heart. Willingly she let them in. And though a part of him would be wild, more elfin than human, riding those untamable Demon winds, it was that very wildness that made him whole. "I understand," she said. "And I *am* real."

She took his arm in hers and faced the sky again. "I think she will come today, after all," she said. "And you're right, I'd like to see her, too. What is it about these wild things, anyway, that makes us love them so?"

"Ask the deer. Maybe we should ask them why they love us so much." His eyes remained restless. "Something's in the air today, though. Can you feel it?"

"Yes," she said. "Or I think I do. I've begun to feel that deep magic you've described. I don't think I feel it the way you do, yet."

"Something's happening," he said. "I don't know what." He followed the path of a large bird sailing across the sky. "Hmm. Anyway, want to come with me? I'm going to update Santa on the factory."

They strolled down the hill, passing the factory on their way to the rise. "It's come a long way from how we found it," Roxy said, watching the activity. "You've done great work, Tracer."

"Most of it's Strapper. You can't keep him away from the place. I know he feels like he needs to make up for what happened, but boy! What a bundle of energy!" He was silent a moment. "I had to bring him to see the team. He wouldn't go on his own. Was ashamed to. So I took him to them, and—well, you know the team. They don't know how *not* to forgive. They were genuinely pleased to see him. Of course, he was pretty emotional about the whole thing. And why not? It was a very close call. They came so close to dying, and taking all the magic with them."

"You think the magic comes from them?"

"It comes from somewhere."

"What about Santa?"

"I don't think even *he* knows. Not fully. Or he's forgotten. Though I doubt that. Probably—" Tracer paused, concentrating "—probably it came to him with the deer, or it began to work on him, slowly, over those years and even centuries, I imagine, before anyone realized what he was about. Before even *he* knew what he was supposed to do."

"Mm," she said. "And now we have the business down there, and all the santas and reindeer and all that crazy stuff. And up here we have a factory we're restoring the old way, and elves, and reindeer, and flowers. A simple life. Where do you see it all going?"

"Hard to say," he said finally. "This is a grand experiment we're undertaking. Just like the first one was. I mean, can you imagine? Can you just imagine? That first time, a handful of elves, a couple of reindeer hitched to an old sleigh, a bag of crude toys, and a wife worried sick about him! What was it like? What did he think he was doing? He must have thought he was crazy. The same way I thought I was crazy, doing all that work. Why did I do it? Because I couldn't stop. Because the magic doesn't let you stop. It compels you."

"But will it continue?" she asked. "...Can it? Look at what happened! Look at what it took for us to get things back!"

"You're right. It took a lot. And we lost—we were terribly hurt along the way. I don't know." He stopped walking and scanned the skies again. "You know, Demon said she might someday fade away until she's nothing more than a cry on the wind. That's what could happen. It might all disappear." He brought his eyes earthward. "Christmas might be overtaken by other things, I don't know, the Internet, e-business. Maybe her cry will be replaced, or confused with the squeal of electrons carrying commerce back and forth. Who knows?"

She put a warm hand to his cheek. "And if it should," she said softly, "if it should all go away, we'll still be here. We'll live out our lives, and grow old, and pass away. Gently. I have to believe that somehow we'll be allowed a special dignity that way."

He smiled, the gold highlights in his eyes shining. "And in spring, and with a factory, and with toys, and Santa returned, and with all those children out there—I think it's a long ways away." He started walking again. "Now c'mon, there's plenty to do!"

They reached the rise, and there was the team, busily grazing. They moved among the deer, caressing and speaking softly to each one. Tracer spent an extra minute or two with Parsley. They prepared to descend to the cabin.

She stopped him. "Look," she said softly, pointing. "The old gardener."

"Like he's been doing it all his life," he murmured.

They watched the portly, bearded form, busy among the flowers. They thought they could hear him humming to himself—or was it the buzz of bumblebees, floating through the warm, sleepy air? All of it seemed to fade—commerce, noise, decisions, media, intrigue, politics, anger and fear—replaced by a simple creature doing simple things. Every motion was relaxed and sure, a snip here, an arrangement there, the flowers nodding and the leaves trembling under a blue blue sky that masked the universe beyond.

A deer snorted, startling them. Tracer followed the sound. "Vixen," he said. "What is it? What do you see?"

Vixen had lifted her head, her gaze carried out over the small clearing to the left of the cabin. From that clearing began the narrow wagon lane that wound on and on and eventually connected this place to the Central Stables, and to NPI, and to the wide world beyond. They could see only a small part of the path before it twisted into a narrow band of firs.

"Listen!" she whispered.

"I hear it!" he breathed.

They held their breaths, better to hear the quiet thud of hooves approaching, the creak of wagon wheels, the small music of harness bells. Still the portly form puttered among the flowers. Perhaps he was distracted by the bees, or by his own humming. Or perhaps the cabin itself blocked the sound.

She took Tracer's arm and squeezed it when the wagon emerged from the firs, two reindeer at its head, and a white-haired, friendly-featured creature seated in the box next to a strangely rabbit-like man.

The wagon approached, and now the half-elf in the garden heard the sounds at last. He straightened, and they couldn't be certain whether it was stiffness or amazement that slowed his motions, the wagon now rounding the corner of the cabin and emerging in full view, the friendly-featured magical companion stepping off and walking through a garden she was surprised and happy to see, walking amid the bursting blooms until she reached the portly figure now kneeling again. She stretched out a small, soft hand, to stroke the glistening cheek and to murmur words of forgiveness and reconciliation that Tracer and Roxy could only imagine, seeing it all through the shimmer of their eyes. In the warm sunshine, the white-bearded form knelt, his face upturned to meet the ageless caress, while all about him the timeless flowers of spring bloomed and the bees hummed their ancient, resonant song.

4.

Snow swirled from the starless void, surrounding them all as they made the last preparations in the clearing. Voices on the wind spoke of a night like so many others he'd faced, filled with terrors and strange unknown things that only he had the strength to dispel, his voice a strong cry over the other voices on the wind, his big hands holding the reins and pushing the magical team onward through hostile heavens. They for their part had prepared feverishly for this night, working fingers beyond the aching point, sewing colorful clothes for dolls, weaving brightly-colored blankets to ward off a hard winter's chills, stitching together winter garments from bolts of brilliant cloth. She had spun and spun and spun this year, miles and miles of threads, yarns, skein upon skein, to be fashioned by her work team into these wonderful things.

Others now hustled through the yard, puffs of steam escaping their small mouths, heaving packages into the sleigh. Always it amazed her that everything fit, as though the sleigh interior yawned into a mysterious world capable of storing all those gifts.

They hitched the deer to the sleigh, eight of them this year. Two more had to be added because of the increasing number of toys and articles, as more and more of the strange people to the south began to point northward and whisper of the jovial creature who rode the heavens on the appointed night, spreading joy throughout the hard lands.

The deer stood patiently, oblivious to the harsh winds whirling about their antlers. Saddler and Strapper jingled the bells one last time to make sure the songs were in order. She marveled at the new sounds she heard. With the addition of Donder and Blitzen the music of the team had changed yet again.

Now all was ready. The huge reindeer tossed their heads, and a few of them stamped the snowy earth. The winds whistled. They all drew back and waited. This was the moment that thrilled her the most, the moment before the door to the cabin boomed open. Then he would stand there, framed by the light, magnificent, red-suited, a gold-and-green exquisite sack his wife had fashioned clutched in one large hand. He would look them over, his cheeks apple-red, and without words his eyes would thank them all for yet another year of dedicated work.

She could feel her heart pounding. What was keeping him this year? A last sip of the magical cocoa, to ward off the night-creatures? What? She watched Saddler approach the door, hesitate, then knock, knock, knock, saying, "Are you coming? Are you ready?"

"...Spinner?" The knocking continued.

Her mind wheeled from the ancient days through the years, from the dark and cold voids to the present, to the here and now, to the bright lights of an office, her office, a distance unimaginable yet real, covered in an instant, her eyes roving the walls, searching, focusing at last on a picture of two elves, one presenting an award to another, the Doll Operations elves beaming behind them.

"Spinner?" Kelli asked. "You joining Gardner and me for lunch?"

"Kelli, oh!" She shook her head, seeing beams of light scattering everywhere. "...Hi. ...I was just dreaming. Come on in."

About the Author

Michigan native David Soubly has worked in the corporate world for many years. When not writing fiction, he enjoys recording piano improvisations, working out, and tinkering with personal computers. "Santa" is his first novel, but not his first story about the grand old guy. He lives in Plymouth, Michigan with his wife, son, some fish, and a dog and cat whose relationship can best be described as neurotically symbiotic.

He is busy on his second novel.

Printed in the United States
1436200003B/34-153

9 781591 134343